193

1/16

3

THE NIGHTMARE STACKS

THE
NIGHTMARE
STACKS

CHARLES STROSS

www.orbitbooks.net

ORBIT

First published in Great Britain in 2016 by Orbit

1 3 5 7 9 10 8 6 4 2

Copyright © 2016 by Charles Stross

A CIP catalogue record for this book
is available from the British Library.

ISBN 978-0-356-50534-3

Printed and bound in Great Britain by
Clays Ltd, St Ives plc

Papers used by Orbit are from well-managed forests
and other responsible sources.

MIX
Paper from
responsible sources
FSC
www.fsc.org FSC® C104740

Orbit
An imprint of
Little, Brown Book Group
Carmelite House
50 Victoria Embankment
London EC4Y 0DZ

An Hachette UK Company
www.hachette.co.uk

www.orbitbooks.net

In memory of Terry Pratchett,
who showed us all how it's done

Treason doth never prosper: what's the reason? Why, if it prosper, none dare call it treason.

—John Harington (16th century)

No one would have believed in the last years of the nineteenth century that this world was being watched keenly and closely by intelligences greater than man's and yet as mortal as his own; that as men busied themselves about their various concerns they were scrutinised and studied, perhaps almost as narrowly as a man with a microscope might scrutinise the transient creatures that swarm and multiply in a drop of water. With infinite complacency men went to and fro over this globe about their little affairs . . . No one gave a thought to the older worlds of space as sources of human danger . . . Yet across the gulf of space, minds that are to our minds as ours are to those of the beasts that perish, intellects vast and cool and unsympathetic, regarded this earth with envious eyes, and slowly and surely drew their plans against us.

—H. G. Wells, *The War of the Worlds*

PART 1

RELOCATION PLANS

1: OH I DO LIKE TO BE BESIDE THE SEASIDE

A vampire is haunting Whitby; it's traditional.

It's an hour after dusk on a Saturday evening four weeks before the spring gothic festival. Alex the Vampire strolls along the sea front, his hands thrust deep into the pockets of his tweed jacket. There's a chill breeze blowing onshore, and he has the pavement to himself as he walks, eyes downcast and chin tucked into his chest, lost in thought.

What profound insight does the creature of the night contemplate as he paces along the North Promenade beside the beach, opposite a row of moonlit houses? What ancient wisdom, what hideous secrets haunt the conscience of the undying?

Let's take a look inside his head:

Alex is fretting about his Form P.764 Employee Travel and Subsistence Claim, which he will have to fill out once he returns to his cramped room in a local bed and breakfast. The form looms as large and sinister in his mind's eye as a vision of his own lichen-stained gravestone. Nevertheless, it provides a welcome distraction from the eldritch undead horror that is his Student Loan Company statement.* And that, in turn, pales into insignificance compared to the worst dread of all: how he is going to explain everything that has happened in the past few months to his parents. Or at least those bits that aren't classified government secrets.

---

* The SLC seem remarkably unwilling to countenance the possibility that in moving from his last job in software development at a Merchant Bank to a career in the Civil Service he might have taken a 70 percent pay cut, and their demands are becoming increasingly unreasonable and threatening.

(Alex hasn't been a vampire for very long, and he isn't very good at it yet. But at least he's still alive—if that's the right word for his condition—unlike several other members of his brood.)

The tides are coming in, along with the clouds. The wind is chilly on his skin, so Alex turns and begins to retrace his path towards the steps up to the high street, striding past the Pavilion and the whalebone arch, past shuttered cafes and the museum. He walks towards the cliffside, wondering if he's made a mistake. He's not sure, if he's honest with himself, that coming to Whitby was the right thing to do. He's supposed to be in Leeds, where he'll be working for the next few weeks. Someone in Travel had booked him a seat on a Friday afternoon train, the better to enable him to make it to the office at nine o'clock sharp on Monday. They obviously hadn't got the memo about flexitime hours and Persons of Hemophagy.

Spending the weekend in Whitby was entirely his own idea. He's never visited the small coastal village before: indeed, he only knows about it for two reasons. Whitby is famous from the novel *Dracula* (as the harbor where the ghost ship *Demeter* comes aground) and, more recently, it plays host to a number of goth festivals—themselves attracted to the village because of its famous fang-infested foreshore. Why Whitby, if not because of the obvious cliché? (For Alex is not a goth.) Well, Whitby has one other advantage. It's not close enough to his home city that there's any risk of him running into his parents or younger sister by accident.

Whitby is Alex's excuse for not being in Leeds while he's not working, and not being in Leeds is his excuse for not visiting his family, and not visiting his family makes it a whole lot easier not to tell them about the V-word, which is an awkwardness he's been grappling with in ever-increasing discomfort for months now.

The season for goths and their steampunk siblings may not have arrived, but Whitby isn't entirely devoid of the flagrantly ahistorical. There's a group of drama students staying in one of the B&B's on the high street, and as he's passing it the front door bursts open. Alex suddenly finds himself adrift in a sea of Mina Harkers and Abraham Van Helsings, with a trio of diaphanously clad Brides of Dracula eddying around him. They giggle and laugh at some private joke as they swish past, bringing a flush to Alex's cheeks. (He has a bad case of wandering male gaze, a side effect of his monastic upbringing. He is mature enough to find this mortifying, but not sufficiently strong-willed to suppress it in the presence of so much well-displayed cleavage.)

"I say!" Alex skids to a stop just in time to avoid colliding with a fellow in white tie and tails, a red satin-lined opera cape draped across his shoulders. "I say, old man!" The fellow doffs his top hat with white gloves that glimmer theatrically in the darkness. Obnoxiously dedicated to staying in character, he exudes a passive-aggressive politeness and assured self-confidence that suggests it is Alex, and not he, who is an intruder from the wrong century. Alex fights hard not to take an instant dislike to him as he continues: "I don't think I've seen you before. Who are you supposed to be?"

Alex does a double-take. He's not wearing a costume, but in the darkness his tweed jacket and open-necked white shirt (with a scarf worn cravat-style against the late March chill) could be mistaken for a period costume. An imp of the mildly perverse whispers in his ear: "Quincey Morris," he tells the amateur Dracula, feeling slightly smug about knowing his Stoker (although in truth he just skimmed the Wikipedia plot synopsis on the train over).

"Capital!" chortles the fellow: "And I am Sir Arthur Holmwood, so I suppose that makes us rivals in love for the hand of the delectable Lucy"—a twitch of his chiseled chin indicates a robustly athletic student doing her best to portray a consumptive Victorian beauty—"at least until the fiend snatches her away, ha ha!"

"Ah, right."

"Come! There's no time to lose! We received a report by telegraph," he adds confidingly, "that the fiend has been sighted up by the graveyard! We'd better head straight there—"

"Is Jeremy always this much of a ham?" the first Bride of Dracula (verdigris hair and a copper nose-ring, shivering in a strapless, pin-striped bustle dress) whispers in the direction of the second (straight-haired blonde: also shivering, in crimson corset and yards of tulle). It's not meant to carry, but Alex can't help overhearing.

"Not usually, but he was hitting the Red Bull and vodka pretty hard," Bride Two observes *sotto voce*. She grimaces and adjusts her plastic fangs. "He uthually mellowth out oneth he getth hith groove on."

"Follow me!" declares the bumptious Arthur Holmwood, gesturing theatrically as he strides up the cliff-side path.

"Are you coming?" Bride One asks Alex brightly.

"I suppose—" Alex checks his priorities and rapidly realizes that the alternative is a torrid date with his Form P.764. "Yes, of course."

"Then would you lend me your jacket? I'm freezing!"

As they sashay towards the cliff Alex confesses, even as he hands her his outer layer, "I'm not a LARPer: I hope you don't mind."

"Nah, that's cool. Tonight's the dress rehearsal." The green-haired girl pulls his tweed jacket on over her bare shoulders. Alex remembers he's supposed to extend his elbow, and feels a rare spasm of gratitude to his sister Sarah for having hijacked the living room telly for one too many Regency costume dramas in years gone by. She takes a firm grip on his arm: "I'm Cassie! Who are you?"

"Alex." Alex feels himself carried along, out of control, as if he has indeed been abducted by the Count's alien and seductive brides. He's not totally unsocialized, but he's the product of a single-sex schooling followed by graduate and postgraduate studies in a field with institutional gender bias. When you subject a statistically significant sample size of otherworldly male nerds to this treatment what you end up with is a certain proportion of twenty-four-year-old virgins. Also, all the female vampires he knows in real life (that's both of them) terrify him. He therefore takes a moment to remember that most people would deal with the current situation by making friendly conversation rather than wigging out or freezing. "You're rehearsing a performance of *Dracula*? For the festival?" he manages eventually.

"YesYes! It's a strolling play." Cassie leans close as they pick their way up the steepening incline. "Me, Veronica, and Louise are the Brides." Her hand is warm, but behind the burbly front she sounds slightly distant, as if she's translating every sentence from a foreign language before she speaks. "There's a confrontation in the park, a fight scene in the graveyard, then we pursue the Count to the ruins of the Abbey for the big climax! It's the whole vampire thing, very dra-

matic, very sexy . . . What brings you to town?" Alex spots her studying him sidelong, and his guts clench as he realizes she's close enough
to see that he isn't in steampunk drag or here for the goth weekend
experience: he's just woefully unfashionable.

"I'm"—Alex's brain freezes as he remembers the fearful oath the
smiling man in the blue uniform made him swear as he signed the
Official Secrets Act, using a calligraphy pen loaded with his own
blood—"a mathematician. I work for the government." *Nerd out,
fool,* his socially adept superego swears despairingly.

"That's funny." Cassie stares at him: "You're too short to be Alan
Turing!" She means Benedict Cumberbatch, in the movie. "You mean
for GCHQ, right? The, the spooks?" Again, that subtle pause in her
speech, as if she's reading from an internal script.

"Not GCHQ," Alex says hastily, mortified. "No, it's much more
boring than that—" Which is what he *has* to say to the smoking hot
girl on his arm, because if he tells her the truth his new superiors will
be *extremely disappointed* with him. (The *geas* attached to the oath
of office forces most Laundry employees to act in accordance with
their perception of the organization's best interests. As a vampire Alex
is partially immune to such compulsions, but he is disinclined to explore the consequences of disobedience, for various reasons.) "No,
really. I'm just here for the weekend, getting away from Leeds because
that's where work sent me." A thought strikes him. "Do you *really*
think I look like Alan Turing?"

They've reached the top of the hill and are nearly at the park as he
asks, and Cassie releases his arm. "Hey, Ronnie, they're already here!
We're late!" Veronica mumbles something inaudible around her choppers. Cassie turns back to him: "I'm really sorry but we're on in sixty
seconds and I've got to get in character and I don't have time—" She
slides out of his jacket and hands it to him, and while he's fumbling
it on she opens a tiny clutch and pulls out a pair of plastic fangs.
"Thorry about thith, thtick around for the afterparty?"

"Oh *yes*—" says Alex. Cassie nods, but she's already turning away
from him. She and the other two Brides of Dracula raise their arms
and proceed to writhe languorously—for Jeremy is not the only ham
here—towards a small clump of mostly black-clad onlookers in the

middle of the park's neatly manicured lawn. He watches Cassie's enchanting back recede, and manages to stare, moon-struck, for all of thirty seconds before his phone begins to play the *Ritt der Walküren*.

What the— Alex pulls out his phone and sees a most unwelcome caller ID. It's the head office. "Hello, Alex speaking, I mean, uh, Dr. Schwartz here. Who is this?"

There is a brief pause. "Please hold." Another voice comes on the line: male, older, weary. "Dr. Schwartz, this is the DM speaking."

Oh hell, what does the DM want with me? Alex has heard of the semi-legendary, reclusive Dungeon Master. He was covered in one of the Friday miscellanea sessions last month. These are briefings someone in External Assets has arranged to bring the surviving members of the vampire Scrum up to speed on their new co-workers. Alex racks his brain desperately, trying to remember what it is that the DM does for the Laundry. (Something to do with directing teams of agents in the field in realtime. *Or was it running the world's weirdest Turing-complete variant* Dungeons & Dragons *campaign using a rule set isomorphic with first-order transdimensional summoning algebra—* Alex squelches the thought before it trails off into the mists of memory. "What can I do for you?" he asks.

"According to the Duty Officer you're in Whitby. Are you in Whitby, Dr. Schwartz? If so, what are you doing there?"

"I was just"—*chatting up the Brides of Dracula* seems like the wrong thing to say, not to mention being an over-optimistic interpretation of the situation, so he settles for—"taking an evening stroll. What can I do for you?"

"Whitby." The DM pronounces the name of the seaside village in a doom-laden tone that Alex feels demands a more ominous payload: something like *The Third Reich*, or *Mordor*. "You just *happen* to be taking an evening stroll in Whitby. Tell me, have you noticed anything out of the ordinary on your perambulations?"

Across the park the Brides of Dracula are running for their lives, pursued in circles by a squad of fearless vampire hunters brandishing stakes that look suspiciously like out-of-season cricket stumps. "No, why?"

"Did you see anything along the sea front?"

Behind him, the audience claps appreciatively: one out. "I mostly saw the sea. What were you expecting, mermaids?"

A pause. "Quite possibly: I'm led to believe that a BLUE HADES with a class three glamour can pass for a mermaid, yes. But that's not quite what I was asking about."

"Well I didn't see anything." Alex hunches his shoulders instinctively. "Well, apart from the usual: an out-of-season tourist sea front and a troupe of actors rehearsing an outdoor performance of *Dracula* for the goth festival."

"Did you even read your briefing pack?" The DM's tone is waspish.

"What briefing pack?" Alex is perplexed.

"What—please hold." The phone goes silent for perhaps half a minute. Alex makes his way along the side of the park, watching a Van Helsing rescue a sleepwalking Mina Murray from the clutches of an undead Lucy Westenra. There is no sign of Cassie while he waits for the DM to resume the call. Finally, a tinny throat-clearing sound emerges from the speaker. "Dr. Schwartz, please accept my apologies. I'm monitoring an operational scenario in your vicinity and naturally assumed from your presence in the grid that you were part of it."

An operation? Alex shakes his head. "I was sent to Leeds for next week. I'm working regular office hours, so I'm sightseeing right now."

"Why are you not *in* Leeds?" the DM demands, as if Alex's delinquency (on his time off) is something he finds personally offensive.

"Have you ever seen Leeds on a Saturday night?" It may not be the real reason for his absence, but it's a perfectly serviceable excuse. The nightlife in the city center is raucous, even when there isn't a big match on.

"Well then." The DM seems to come to some sort of conclusion. "Would you like to make yourself useful, Dr. Schwartz? The field team is short-handed—there's a stomach bug going round—and I have a little job for you . . ."

Two hours later, Alex is bitterly regretting the helpful impulse that made him agree to the DM's request. Knowing that he's officially on the clock for overtime at pay and a half is absolutely no consolation for being cold, increasingly hungry, and not getting to hang out at a theatrical troupe's after-party with Cassie. (Who he gloomily realizes he will never see again, having failed to exchange phone numbers or Facebook handles on the walk up from the sea front.) Facing off with a Form P.764 on his lonesome looked like a bad enough way to spend a Saturday night, but what the DM wanted is even worse.

"Whitby is part of a pilot scheme for our next-generation extensions to a camera network called SCORPION STARE," the DM explained. "There are networked high-definition CCTV cameras on most of the approach roads and along the sea front, disguised as one of the traffic-monitoring services. The field service team is out there now, testing a live update to the target acquisition and tracking firmware, but they're short-handed. I don't suppose you can grow bat-wings or fangs, Dr. Schwartz? Or some other distinctive characteristic?"

Alex bit his tongue. "I'm told I look like Alan Turing, only shorter. Will that do?"

"It needs to be something associated with a high thaum field. If you could solve a four-element Vohlman tensor in your head, that might suffice—"

Alex shuddered. He could do that but it might awaken his V-parasites, which would make him *hungry*. "I can stick my teeth out," he offered. His canines have developed an unfortunate tendency to grow, rodent-like, since he acquired his V-parasite infection: like the other PHANGs, he needs regular (and painful) sessions with a security-cleared dentist. "Will that be enough for you to work with?"

The DM fell silent for a bit. Then, "In light of the peculiar restrictions imposed by your condition, it will have to suffice." He spoke in such tones of withering condescension that Alex felt his self-esteem shrinking to the size of a walnut. *No bat-wings, no opera cape, no sexy undead brides—I'm not a* real *vampire! I don't even have proper fangs! It's not fair.* "Go ahead. If the new firmware revision can't get a lock on you when you're only semi-active it's not fit for purpose anyway. I'll email you a walking route shortly."

Two hours later Alex is shuffling alongside High Stakesby Road. He is shivering with cold, increasingly tired, foot-sore, and full of regrets. There is open countryside on one side and a soulless suburban housing estate on the other. A random spattering of rain falls as a white Ford Transit van (similar to ones used by the Police hereabouts) drives up alongside him.

It is nearly eleven o'clock. Alex is acutely aware that he is alone in the middle of a badly lit nowhere, and something about the curb-crawling van fills him with a numinous sense of dread. But before he can reach for his warrant card or his smartphone the passenger door window winds down and someone calls, "Are you Alex Schwartz?"

His heart skips a beat, then settles down: "What if I am?" He turns and looks at the man leaning across the van's front seat. Something about him is naggingly familiar: shaven on top with a bushy mustache and a black beret and thick-rimmed glasses—*he looks like that guy from* MythBusters: "Who are you?"

A hand comes out of the window, and unfolds a familiar-looking ID card. "The DM said we're done for the night so we should give you a lift home. Is that okay?"

Alex peers at the warrant card. His recent affliction gives him the ability to read fine print at a distance, even at night under street lighting. The card tells him that the white van man works for Tech Ops Support and is known by the code name *Pinky*. The rain is falling harder. "A lift back to my B&B would be great, thanks."

"Okay, hop in." The sliding door behind the driver's seat groans open to reveal an LED-lit rat king's lair, all cables and electronics racks. Another TOS rodent hunkers down on the bench seat, wearing a pair of bulky goggles with a pen torch strapped to either stem as if he's auditioning for a stage role with an Orbital tribute act. Both boffins are in their late thirties or early forties, and surprisingly buff for backroom types. "Hi, glad to meet you!" He shuffles over to make room for Alex. "He's Pinky, I'm Brains. Together we—"

"Try to take over the world!" choruses the driver. "Ba-da-boom. Where are you staying, Alex?"

Oh Jesus, just throw me to the clowns already. Alex shakes his head, and gives them directions. "Just what are we doing here anyway?" he asks. "The DM said something about some kind of network called SCORPION something?"

"We're testing the latest threat-recognition upgrades to SCOR-

PION STARE," Brains explains as he slams the side-door shut. "Networked basilisk guns," he adds as an afterthought. "Throw the switch to set them to automatic and any thaum-emitting target in view that doesn't code as friendly will experience the warmth of fractional carbon-to-silicon transmutation from the inside out."

"You're kidding me!" A hot, dizzy flush runs up and down Alex's spine. "Tell me you're kidding me?"

"If it's any consolation we were only testing the threat-recognition firmware." Pinky grinds the gears into third and careens towards the high street, windscreen wipers thudding monotonously. "The basilisk firmware isn't loaded, we just needed to know the grid could lock on and identify a low-emission target reliably. Turns out it was around 98 percent accurate in identifying *you* as a threat—but we got a 0.3 percent false positive rate. Awkward, that."

"But, but, basilisk guns!" Alex tries not to gibber. It's hard: he *wants* to gibber. He's seen a basilisk gun in action. He's seen what happens to a centuries-old vampire elder who gets hit by one. They sparkle momentarily before they explode. It's the thaumaturgic equivalent of a claymore mine, and his current reference point for arse-puckering terror. "*Automatic* basilisk guns. Are you people out of your *minds?*"

"Nope." Brains sounds psychotically chilled to Alex's rattled nerves. "We've actually had them out there since the late nineties as part of the MAGINOT BLUE STARS program, but they've needed a human operator in the loop until now. Which is a bit of a drawback, when the target case they're designed for includes horrors that can crash your neural wetware if you catch a glimpse of them. So the firmware's mostly never been loaded. As we're getting into CASE NIGHTMARE GREEN territory these days, needs must. We won't fire up SCORPION STARE in a major city unless the alternative is mass fatalities on a scale matching a strategic nuclear attack—in which case a few thousand deaths from friendly fire are the least of our worries—but we need it available, see?"

"But—but—Whitby!"

"Where better to test it?" Pinky asks rhetorically. "In a couple of weekends there'll be a whole lot of decoys on the streets here. Plan is to inject a few Residual Human Resources—nobody will notice a couple of zombies at a goth festival—and give the threat recognizer a real workout. If we can get the false positives down to 0.1 percent then it should be ready to deploy during a major incursion. At which point, hello London! Hello Liverpool! Hello Glasgow! Hey Brains, show him what you've been logging: it's pretty cool. I love the smell of muons and gamma radiation in the morning . . ."

For the next five minutes, Brains terrorizes Alex with grainy nighttime CCTV footage. Here's Alex walking along the sea front, up a hill, through a graveyard. There's a targeting grid centered on his thorax, TARGET LOCK flashing in the bottom right of the screen. And there are some false positives, too. Such as a view of his own back, climbing the cliffside path with Cassie wearing his jacket, the green wireframe of a lock-on caging her head.

The van finally turns into the narrow street leading to Alex's B&B, for which he is grateful. Visions of strolling Brides of Dracula burning like ghastly human candles up and down the length of the promenade haunt him. In his dim-lit nest of rack-mounted instruments, there is something insectile and menacing about Brains—something that sends shivers up and down Alex's spine. And Pinky's glib Armageddon rap is not a source of amusement either. What they're discussing so lightly is a thing of horror. Shocked, Alex bites his tongue as he tumbles out onto the pavement beside his lodgings. He fumbles for the door key as the chilly rain falls and wishes he hadn't answered the phone. Suddenly the irritatingly tedious prospect of a family visit seems almost comforting.

But what is he going to tell them about the new job?

DEAR DIARY:

```
main = putStrLn "Hello, World!"
```

That's the Haskell version. In human, that would be:

Hello, World!

I am Dr. Alex Schwartz, PhD, aged twenty-four and three quarters, and this is my secret diary. I'm not normally into self-disclosure or Facebook and so on, but apparently we're supposed to keep diaries when we work for the Laundry—who knew? It's secret because my whole new job is secret, by which I mean government NATSEN/UK EYES ONLY secret, not Diary of Adrian Mole secret. Not that its secrecy means that nobody is ever going to read it: I fully expect men in blue uniforms with no sense of humor whatsoever to snoop on it regularly, because apparently that's the way things work around here. Or if not men in blue uniforms, it'll be motherly middle-aged ladies wearing twinsets and pearls with absolutely no sense of humor. People with a security clearance for OPERA CAPE and the existence of PHANG syndrome who don't trust me, anyway.[*]

(So I want you to know that I copied the stolen files into a USB memory stick and duct-taped it to the outside of one of the window frames at Canary Wharf, but I've forgotten exactly which one. (Oh, and the Semtex is in the bottom of the fridge behind the body parts.))

I didn't ask for this to happen to me. Until eight months ago I was happily ignorant of the existence of the Laundry. After I finished my PhD at University College Oxford I was headhunted by a banker called Oscar Menendez who was setting up a skunk works team of quantitative analysts inside a very secretive merchant bank. We were working on a better way of visualizing statistical market trends—as part of our efforts to build a better high-frequency trading system—when I accidentally stumbled across one of what I later learned are called the "dark theorems." Which installed itself in my brain and summoned up a swarm of microscopic extradimensional symbionts—the V-parasites—that confer certain powers on me, as long as I keep them well-fed.

Living with V-parasites is a bit like living with HIV: as long as

---

[*] That's Photogolic Hemophagic Atypical Neuroectodermal Gangrene, aka Vampirism. The G is, strictly speaking, misleading, but some acronyms are too good not to use.

you keep up with the treatments and avoid certain activities, you'll live a long, if somewhat restricted, life.* The treatments aren't any fun, either—even less so once you start thinking about the implications.

Luckily the Laundry doesn't pay me to think about the implications. They pay me† to think about higher mathematics and the multiverse we apparently live in, where there's a higher-dimensional space in which mathematics is a structure and *things* in other universes listen when we solve theorems—*things* our ancestors called demons. Magic, it turns out, is serious and quantifiable and getting stronger and more powerful as we move into a scalar field where this shit gets real.

It's an age of miracles and wonders. Some people are in the news headlines this year because they've acquired superpowers and can fly, or turn everyone in the Albert Hall into zombies, or something. Me? I just came down with the magical equivalent of AIDS. Side effects include immunity to the usual consequences of trying to solve dark theorems in your head—excuse me, cast magical spells—namely something called K syndrome that progresses a lot like mad cow disease. On the other hand, I now have a tendency to burst into flames in daylight. And I have to feed the V-parasites regularly by drinking enough human blood to set up a contagion link with the nervous system of the donor, who rapidly dies of V-parasite-induced dementia, which is extremely ugly. But if I don't keep them well-fed they'll chow down on my gray matter instead.

There's a reason everyone thinks vampires are sociopaths: it's because only a sociopath could comprehend what they've become and still be able to live with themselves. But Her Majesty's Government has a use for a cadre of tame PHANGs and, *as long as I do my job*

---

* Risky activities include going out in daylight, going to parties with a black light show, or spilling a bag of rice on the kitchen floor.

† Really, really badly by merchant banking standards. Not that I had time to get used to banking pay and bonuses before I came down with PHANG: just to the 100-hour overtime culture and the workplace bullying.

satisfactorily, once a week there will be an ampoule of fresh blood drawn from a donor* waiting in my in-tray.

I don't think I'm a murderer.

(I might be deluding myself, though.)

Anyway: after I rediscovered the V syndrome theorem and accidentally infected myself, like an idiot I went and exposed everyone else in the Scrum to the same disease. Which some of them mistook for an opportunity to act like bandits, mostly because they failed to ask themselves why exactly nobody knew about this thing already. Two months later half of us were murdered (shock, horror) by a vampire hunter. It turns out that the first law of vampire club is *vampires don't exist*, and if a vampire *does* allow their existence to come to light the other PHANGs will do their best to kill them, lest the government notices and institutes mandatory naked noonday identity parades.

Well, part of the government *has* noticed and, as noted previously, they have a use for us survivors. The part that noticed us is known as the Laundry; it started out as part of the Special Operations Executive during the Second World War, and today it's the occult equivalent of MI5 or GCHQ. You probably have some idea of the uses a secret agency might have for agents who have super-strength and unnatural powers of persuasion?† Well, you'd be wrong: because I'm not James Bond, I'm a twenty-four-year-old virgin with a maths PhD and AIDS. Anyway, so far the job seems to consist entirely of Human Resources interviews, training courses, form-filling, and, oh, a 73.21 percent pay cut. All in return for that weekly keep-you-going ampoule in the in-tray. Ha ha fuck you no it's not very funny, is it. Not very funny at all.

(I'm not bitter or anything.)

Anyway, this is my work diary. It's pretty boring right now be-

---

* The donors are terminally ill patients who are in hospice care and dying. I'm shortening their lives by hours or days, they're lengthening mine by weeks or months. It's not a calculus I'm terribly happy about, but it beats the alternative.

† Bursting into flames in daylight, not so much.

cause my work is pretty boring, and if you're sitting here reading my diary that means *your* work is pretty boring. Maybe I'll try and liven it up by telling you all about my family, or coming up with some more lies about the Nazi gold, the stolen secret files, or the IRA Semtex. Except I'm not very good at lying.

Go on, fuck off. It's not as if anything interesting ever happens to me, is it?

It's a cold, damp Monday and Alex is ready for work.

It's still early enough in the year that he can be out and about at five in the afternoon without fear of immediate photocombustion, as long as he covers up and slathers himself in heavy-duty sunblock. So he loiters behind the snack kiosk in the entrance to the city railway station, the collar of his coat turned up and his hat pulled down like a spy movie cliché. He's already drawn a couple of curious glances from the transport police, but they're too busy to check on him. Meanwhile, the kiosk provides some cover from the homeward-bound throng of commuters as they stumble through the echoing concourse, eyes downturned, attention focussed on their phones.

The 17:12 from King's Cross is showing on the Arrivals board. Alex figures this means his co-worker and nominal mentor will be with him as soon as he puzzles out the maze of escalators and overhead walkways from Platform 10 to the ticket gates. Alex shifts from foot to foot resentfully. He knows in an abstract kind of way that Pete has a wife and a young baby, and was in any case needed in the New Annex for a morning committee meeting (something about a scary American televangelist), which is why he couldn't come up at the weekend. Still, Pete is effectively forcing Alex to wait in public, and he feels horribly exposed. He's always been a little bit agoraphobic, and PHANG syndrome gives him every reason to dread public spaces—it's not that accidents don't also happen to normal people, but he can't help morbidly rehearsing the possible fatal outcomes. *Leg broken by a hit-and-run driver, he ends up on a hospital ward, screaming and sizzling as the dawn light breaks through the window.* He can distract himself for a while if he starts counting the passers-by, but the counting thing is obsessive, and that doesn't end well in a busy railway station at rush hour. So by the time Pete finally arrives, Alex is a bundle of raw nerve endings.

"Wotcher, cock! Ow's yer whippet?"

Alex directs a withering glare over his shoulder. "Je ne comprends pas. Parlez-vous Yorkshire?"

"Sorry, I thought that was how they spoke up here?" Pete grins, an expression that takes a decade off his face. Wearing jeans and a biker's jacket with hands thrust deep in his pockets, he's not exactly anyone's picture of a spook—or a Man of the Cloth for that matter.

"We're not scousers. Listen, you're late. We *could* get a bus but it's tipping down and the nearest stop is a ten-minute walk away and anyway it isn't dark yet. Can you sign for a taxi?"

"Um." Pete thinks about it. "There are two of us, so yes, as long as they give receipts and you countersign the claim."

The taxi rank is outside the front of the station, snaking around a weird circular sixties concrete building with a broad awning. (Originally the Transport Police offices, today it's a bicycle shop.) Alex scuttles for cover from the elements, Pete following close behind with his wheelie bag. They join the queue, and a couple of minutes later they're in the back of a Toyota creeping around the traffic-choked Inner Loop towards the bottom of Woodhouse Lane. Destination: Lawnswood Cemetery, out in the blasted wilderness beyond the northern arc of the Leeds ring road.

"Have you visited the local office yet?" Pete asks.

"Not yet." Alex shrugs. "I've been holed up in my hotel room today, to be honest. Night shift suits me best for now."

"Awkward." Pete leans against the other side of the taxi's back seat. "Are you okay here? I mean, living out of a suitcase—"

Alex cuts him off: "I'm fine. The sooner we look the site over and report back the sooner we can kill this stupid idea and go back to London."

"Kill—" Pete raises an eyebrow. "You mean you don't want to move to Leeds?" Alex can't tell if he's being sarcastic. "Bright lights, big city, affordable housing?"

"Listen." Alex tries not to spit: "I *grew up* in Leeds. I spent eighteen years here before I escaped. Trust me, it's a *stupid* idea."

"But it's going to—" Pete glances at the front seat, realizes that they're in the presence of ears that do not possess a security clearance, and changes the subject. "Is the weather always like this?"

"It could be worse. They could be looking at relocating to Manchester, where the locals are evolving webbed fingers and gill slits. But if you're used to the southeast, everything hereabouts looks kind of gray and squishy."

"Leaky roofs. Hmm . . ."

DEAR DIARY:

I've been part of the Laundry for nearly six months now, and I still don't have a clue what I'm meant to be doing, but I'm told this is entirely normal and I'll figure it out sooner or later if I live long enough.

(I can't make my mind up whether that last qualifier is entirely serious.)

I spent the first week with no clear idea that the Laundry even existed, mind you. It was all Mhari's idea. She used to be in Human Resources and she basically conscripted us under irregular circumstances which were later shoveled under the rug. (Probably because if they hadn't been, some *very* embarrassing questions would have been asked.) It was for the best, I suppose, but it meant that from the very first month I was dumped in at the deep end with no idea what was going on, except for an endless string of interviews in dingy government offices, forms to fill in (don't get me started on the Official Secrets Act, As Amended), and interminable committee meetings. It was like all the worst aspects of being back in university crossed with *The Office* by way of *Nathan Barley*.

Then I nearly died.

Lots of other people *did* die, so I suppose I got off lightly. But it's a hell of a reality check when you spend just three days in hospital recovering from third-degree burns to your face and hands, the bone-deep kind that should leave you scarred for life. Fortunately for me, as long as my condition is well-managed, I heal like a Hollywood movie hero. Unfortunately for me, my ability to heal like that makes me useful for an organization that needs . . . well.

To make matters worse, at about the same time all this was happening they sprang a mentor on me.

My mentor is the Reverend Peter Russell, MA, D. Theol. He's fifteen years older than I am and he's a vicar, although he rides a motorbike and has long hair and a beard and does aikido. Pete's primary qualification for mentoring me is that he's been in the organization fully three months longer than I have, and has lots of experience in helping disturbed young men come to terms with the vagaries of life. He's the modern, intelligent, progressive, the-Bible-is-just-a-metaphor type of clergyman, and he's a nice guy, even though he grumbles about having to neglect his pastoral duties in the name of national security. He seems to spend most of his office time reading sermons, checking some *really strange* Bible concordances, and frowning furiously. (NB: I don't know many vicars, so for all I know they're all like this, but I'm just saying: he's not what I expected.)

I asked what he's doing here. It turns out he got sucked into the Laundry last year because Mr. Howard knew him socially and needed an expert on Biblical apocalypses in a screaming hurry, in order to stop said apocalypses from coming true. I'd feel sorry for him, but even knowing about the tentacle monsters from beyond spacetime hasn't shaken his faith or made him bitter or anything. Never mind Gödel's theorem or Kolmogorov–Chaitin complexity, let alone the Turing Principles on which the whole field of computational magic is based.

For the past six months we—me and the other PHANGs—have been fumbling our way through a series of one-week intensive orientation courses and stacks of briefing papers, making it up as we go along, with the occasional nudge in the right direction from our managers. There is a screaming rush on pretty much all the time because the Laundry is taking on new staff, gearing up for something unpleasantly big, and we're a little bit short on managers and experienced senior people because a number of them ended up being taken away in body bags after a couple of asshole elder vampires used me and the Scrum as pawns in a lethal chess game.* Mr. Howard once told me he was here for two whole years before anyone even sent him for training in out-of-office operations. Pete and I don't have the luxury of that much time.

Anyway, this week they've sent us both up to Leeds as part of the task force preparing the way to move our main emergency command center out of London.

Apparently the Laundry used to occupy a ramshackle government building in Westminster.† That building, Dansey House, was closed for complete renovation under a public-private partnership about six years ago, while everyone moved to a variety of temporary (and not very secure) satellite offices. It was due to reopen three years ago but there were, apparently, "problems" relating to thaumaturgic contamination of the ground it was built on—problems too big for remediation. It turned out to be the necromantic equivalent of a toxic waste site—and that was before we discovered the hard way that an elder vampire had single-handedly infiltrated the department. He'd spent literally decades installing a *geas*—a procedure or spell that induces a compulsive cognitive bias in whoever it is applied to—on Dansey House, with the effect that people who work there *don't believe in vampires*, even if their office-mate sleeps in a coffin under the desk and leaves bloodstained cups in the break room sink.

In the absence of evidence that this was the *only* compulsion woven into the brickwork of Dansey House, Mahogany Row came

---

* Note to readers: holy water does not work on PHANGs, even the newbie incisors-aren't-growing-yet variety. Crucifixes don't work. I *like* garlic bread (we still have to eat). We aren't *actually* undead, unlike the Residual Human Resources on the night shift: we're just *socially* undead.

† When it was started during the war, it occupied the building above a Chinese laundry in Soho, hence the name. Technically we're Q-Division, SOE, but SOE was officially wound up/ absorbed by MI5 in late 1945 when we were spun off. Yes, there is a history of inter-service rivalry.

to the decision to sell the site for redevelopment and move elsewhere. Which then left them with a big headache: where to relocate to. The New Annex, where I was initially assigned, was ruled out. It turns out that the New Annex isn't proof against pissed-off vampire elders. Also, it's too small. Apparently we're facing some sort of nightmarish conjunction—due to a combination of circumstances we're in a period when computational magic gets easier to do, and the effects are amplified—so the organization needs room to grow. And, London property prices being what they are, a decision was made to move most of us out of the big smoke.

Leeds is a big metropolitan zone in the geographical middle of England, sitting at the intersection of a bunch of major transport routes. I suppose it was inevitable that it'd be one of the top options, along with Manchester, Newcastle, or possibly Cheltenham (because of the strong GCHQ presence). I come from Leeds. Which is why, even though I'm a wet-behind-the-ears probationer who's up to his ears with training courses, they saw fit to shove me on the train up here with Pete to look around various outlying facilities before we get the grand tour of the proposed new headquarters building in the city center, Quarry House, and go to town on its perimeter wards.

Please God, why couldn't it be Manchester instead?

The taxi takes almost a quarter of an hour to slither out of the city center and onto the Otley Road. But they get there in the end, and while Pete adds the receipt to his battered paper organizer Alex climbs out and looks around. The car has parked beside a rather forbidding hedge, on the other side of a dual carriageway from a row of poplars. Beyond the trees he can just make out the lights of the police station. There are few houses hereabouts, but a driveway leads out of sight beyond the hedge. And it is, predictably, raining even harder.

"We're not going to have much luck getting a taxi home from here, are we?" Pete says as the cab pulls away.

"Nope. There are buses, but they'll only be running every twenty minutes at this time of evening." Alex doesn't explain that he has this part of the Leeds bus timetable memorized cold. He turns and heads up the gravel drive, avoiding the worst of the pothole puddles. They come to a chain-link gate and an unfriendly sign: DEPARTMENT OF WORK AND PENSIONS—THIS PROPERTY IS MAINTAINED BY TELEREAL TRINIUM—KEEP OUT—G4S SECURITY. The padlock that holds the gate shut is grimy with rust stains, but a prickling in Alex's fingers tells him that the site is heavily warded. Only authorized visitors will be able to get in. "Did you bring the key?"

"Sure." Pete fiddles with the padlock, and they step through the gate. The drive dog-legs behind another hedge before it passes out of view of the road. Black poles surmounted by the hooded eyes of CCTV cameras stare at them, and Alex suppresses a shudder of dread. Beyond the second hedgerow they come to a low building with narrow frosted-glass windows set high under its eaves, like a public toilet or a cricket pavilion. There are more signs: KEEP OUT, ENTRY FORBIDDEN, THIS SITE IS ALARMED. "Do you ever get the feeling that we're not welcome?" Pete asks.

"Hello, ma'am, we're from the Jehovah's Witnesses, do you have a few minutes to talk about our Lord and Savior?"

Pete winces as he produces a key and tries it in the door lock. It doesn't fit. He fumbles with the keyring in the chilly rain, trying various others until he finally gets a result. The door creaks open to reveal a bare concrete-floored lobby surrounding a circular stairwell, descending into darkness. "Get the lights, will you? I know you can see in this but I can't—"

Alex flicks the switch and a bare bulb flickers on above them, illuminating the staircase down to the tunnel that leads to the entrance of the former Leeds War Room Region 2 bunker.

Peeling paint, the smells of stagnant water, wet concrete and mold, cobwebs: these are Alex's first impressions of the 1950s cold war installation. It skulks on the edge of the city, bookended by a police station and one of the city's larger crematoria, as if to underline the brooding horror of its purpose. Perhaps the rising damp and other signs of neglect are a good thing. Better by far if it could be left to decay on the scrapheap of history. But the Laundry has plans for it.

Pete parks his suitcase at the top, then starts down the staircase, boots clattering on the treads. The skeleton of a motorized winch squats rusting on a rail that spans the top of the stairwell, unused since the last time anyone needed to move furniture in and out of this horribly expensive hole in the ground. "Remind me again who thought this was a good idea?"

"Don't be silly, Alex, it's perfectly safe: it's maintained by our cuddly friends Mr. Telereal and Mrs. Trinium, it says so right on the rusting sign by the front door. If we slip and break our necks or get ourselves electrocuted in the waterlogged subbasement, squatters are *sure* to find our bodies within a few months—aha!" At the bottom of the stairwell they find another lobby. An arch-roofed corridor, ceiling festooned with ominously fat cables, slopes down into the ground. The fluorescent tubes flicker, their ballast circuits dying, but about a third of them are still working and it's enough to see that, although the paint is peeling and the tunnel smells musty, the floor is clear. "The way in is down here, according to the map." Pete refers to a thick sheaf of photocopies that he clutches in one hand. "There's supposed to be a caretaker in residence, but I don't see any sign of—"

Alex's nostrils flare. "We have company."

"Jolly good: you go first." Pete nudges him forward.

"Bastard," Alex says without any real rancor; "I want danger money."

"If the caretaker shoots you I'll sign off on your hazard pay."

The corridor curves as it descends. Just as the entrance stairwell disappears from view behind them, they come to a wide vestibule. A huge steel blast door, painted so many times that it appears to have developed map contours, is very pointedly wedged open with a pry bar jammed under its lower lip and wooden chocks rammed into its hinged edge. Beyond the door a different corridor veers off at right angles, its walls painted institutional cream. They've clearly been renewed not less than a decade ago. (The tunnel beyond the blast door comes to a dead end punctuated by heavy steel grilles into which a steady breeze blows, evidence of well-maintained air conditioning fans.)

"Oi! Who are you—"

Alex was aware of the caretaker's presence almost from the bottom of the stairwell. His stertorous breathing is almost as loud as the distant traffic noise. But he waits until the man shuffles into view before reaching into his pocket and pulling out his warrant card. "Ministry of Defense, Alex Schwartz and Peter Russell. We're on your approved visitors list for this week."

The caretaker is about sixty, the heavy burden of his years slowly crumpling him into an envelope of wheezing lassitude wrapped around a bloated core of abdominal discomfort. He wears a security guard's uniform, but Alex can't help noticing that he's tucked his feet into a pair of rubber waders with a fake wool lining. His breath smells . . . *bad*: or maybe it's not his breath. His exhalations merely smell of cheap stale cigarettes. But something else, some miasma he carries with him like a shroud, makes the things in the back of Alex's head stir and chitter in the darkness. Alex clamps down, but Pete is oblivious as the caretaker makes a show of examining the warrant card. "We're here to conduct a site visit and check the works list." Pete brandishes his stash of photocopies, which Alex now sees includes blueprints and floorplans for the ancient radar control bunker turned regional emergency center, along with what is probably a surveyor's report listing what will need to be done in order to restore it to operational capability—if not for a nuclear war, then for another equally grim purpose. "If it's in order, I'll be back tomorrow with another inspection team. You're living in the Regional Commissioner's rooms, aren't you? Can you give us the tour of the accessible areas? We'd particularly like to see the broadcast suite, the telephone switchroom, the generator and supply rooms, and the air conditioning units."

"Aye, I can do that, but I was 'aving me tea? Can tha be waiting five minutes?"

"Did someone say tea?" Pete brightens. Alex doesn't have the heart to translate the word into London-speak: tea means supper up here.

"Nay, but I can be making tha'a cuppa. Come along now." The

caretaker turns and shuffles wearily back into the depths of the secret nuclear bunker, a hermit retreating into his cave. Pete glances at Alex, who shrugs before turning to follow their host. It's not as if he's got anything better to do this evening . . .

2: INTERLUDE: ADVERSARY

DEAR DIARY:

A lot of stuff has happened in the month since I wrote about visiting Leeds, and I'm not sure I understand it all.

(Of course, that probably puts me ahead of the game: it turns out that most people understand *nothing*.)

The short version: my working life stopped being boring almost immediately after the visit to the bunker. In fact, everything got unpleasantly exciting! Although not all at once, of course. You know the urban legend about how if you put a frog in a saucepan of cold water and bring it slowly to a boil, the frog won't notice the heat until it dies? I was that frog. Mind you, at first I thought it was my personal life that was getting exciting, and pleasantly so at that. I had no idea about the huge events taking place in the background and what they would mean for me. Or for *us*.

The long version . . .

Because of the whole stored-institutional-knowledge thing I'm supposed to make this a complete account of what happened this April. To fill in the gaps between what actually happened to me, and what was happening elsewhere, a lot of this is going to consist of a fictionalized account of documented events. (Don't worry, I have expense claims and memos to work from.) I'm also trying to pull together reconstructions based on interviews with an uncommonly well-informed source, random bits of guesswork, and of course my own workplace confessional.

Oh, and Cassie, if by any remote chance you ever read this? I'm very, very sorry . . .

Some time before Alex had his fateful cliffside encounter in Whitby, then visited the moribund bunker housing the Leeds War Room, an audience was held in another underground bunker that would ultimately have a huge impact on his life.

The bunker lay beneath a plateau in the foothills of a mountain range at the western end of a large landmass. Bleached slabs of white limestone pavement poked through holes in the plateau's surface like the bones of a mummified continent showing through its desiccated skin. Constellations similar to those of Earth wheeled across its skies every night, but the darkness was not relieved by sunlight reflected from a giant moon. Instead, the plateau was illuminated by the sickly radiance of a planetary ring, a cyclopean arch of green-gray rubble circling the waist of the world. From time to time the flicker of meteors lit up the southern horizon, for planetary rings are seldom stable. The debris belt created by the shattering of the moon had already bombarded the equatorial latitudes, leaving a pockmarked belt of sullen, glowing craters around the world. Autarchies had been shattered, hermit kingdoms destroyed. Almost a billion had died in war, plague, starvation, and madness. But worse was yet to come, as what passed for civilization on this world guttered and faded beneath the penumbra of a darkness deeper than eternal night.

The few surviving warriors of the Host of Air and Darkness hibernated in caves beneath the plateau on the murdered continent. They had been there a long time. The once-natural network of limestone vaults and water-worn grottos had been extended to provide an underground fortress for the western defenders of an empire. Since the war, it had been pressed into service as a deep survival bunker. Dispersal bays near the surface, close beneath overground blast doors, were occupied by the hibernating bodies of the Host's aviation group. Shafts spiraling down into deeper bedrock housed the stasis cocoons of armored cavalry; deeper still, access corridors drilled by civil engineering magi riddled the plateau, leading to slave barracks and supply depots.

The members of the Host were not exactly human, but neither were they entirely alien. Picture, if you will, a human primatologist's eyes widening in excited recognition as they see the twitching ears and elegant features, then utter the fateful words: *"Another species of gracile hominid, only with hypertrophied pinnae—"* before horrified recognition sets in (followed by a swift and gruesome death). The word they use to denote their own kind in the High Tongue might best be translated as People. But in form and in mind the People were no closer to a contemporary human being than to a Neanderthal.

Most of the sleepers lay in an envenomated coma, wrapped in cocoons spun by purple-bodied spiders the size of fists. They hung in rows beside the huge gauzy cauls of their war-steeds. Here and there among them festered a browning chrysalis, its occupant deceased. The rotting husks of hominid skeletons, mummified lips drawn back from silently screaming jaws, were a mute testimony to the desperation of this gambit: hibernation was far from foolproof, especially on the scale of an army group fleeing across a gulf of centuries. The Host had already lost many of its number. Before much longer the survivors would be forced to awaken for the last time, to eat and recover their strength, lest their sleep deepen into eternal death.

This desperate flight into the unknowable future had been forced upon the All-Highest by the total logistical collapse of the Morningstar Empire. It had started when the acolytes of one or another of the Dead Gods had performed a ritual that shattered the moon, opened the way to the realm of demons, and plunged the entire world into chaos. Famine, war, and nightmarish alien intrusions had spiraled out of control in every nation, wrecking the intricate hierarchies upon which civilization depended, leaving only chaos and death behind. Only a few far-flung military outposts had survived around the world, untouched by virtue of their remote locations and deep defenses. And this base was now the last surviving remnant of the Morningstar Empire.

When the full scale of the disaster had first become apparent, All-

Highest resolved to wait out the collapse of civilization, to carry intact into the future the last surviving army on the continent. But the collapse had been deeper and more catastrophic than anyone imagined—not merely the wreckage of empire but the actual looming extinction of the People as a species beckoned. Death and madness from beyond the stars claimed everybody who still lived on the surface of the world. The skeleton staff who stood watch down the years waited for some indication the sleeping Host might safely emerge to recolonize the surface: but as the years stretched into decades, and decades into centuries, conditions on the roof of the world became worse and the warehouses beneath the bone caves slowly but inexorably emptied. Now they held barely enough food, *mana*, and materiel to support the Host through a single week-long schwerpunkt maneuver. All-Highest, his headquarters staff, and his magi might live like rats in a cellar for another decade or two while they searched for a way out past the rampaging nightmares that stalked the hellscape above: but the end-game was becoming clear.

The Host was originally a perimeter force, surrounded by the savages of the outlying archipelago. Its task was to guard the empire's sparsely populated western coastline against invasion by the enemies who dwelt beyond the chilly ocean. All-Highest had originally been no more than a slave-general, bound by the iron will of his queen, the undisputed ruler of the Morningstar Empire. It was not a choice command, far from the seat of power in the lush lowlands of the drained inland sea far to the southeast. But the empire had fallen, the queen and her heirs crushed in the capital by the fall of a kilometer-long meteor early in the Necromancers' War. Of all the far-flung war camps, only this chilly northern outpost had survived unscathed—nearly fifty-five degrees north of the equator, far beyond the zone of bombardment.

When the imperial court and army high command died together in the meteor strike, the intricate network of magical bindings that held the empire together had propagated down the chain of oaths of fealty, until it landed like a dying god's battle hammer on the brow of the highest ranked survivor in the hierarchy. The slave-general was driven half-insane when the royal *geasa* wrapped themselves around his mind, bringing to his will the power to command and release an entire empire: but he survived the fall and its aftermath, and now all that was left belonged to him.

The general's quarters were built within a natural limestone cavern, the roof of which was decorated with the dangling ossified fangs of stalactites. In shape it resembled a castle in the antique mode, built from pink marble imported from the southeastern uplands; in truth it had been forged as a single structure from heat-metamorphosed limestone, assembled by war-magisters at the command of one or other of a previous general's military architects. Flying buttresses supported its decorative, steeply pitched roof; crenelated battlements adorned with the fossilized bodies of name-stripped felons gathered a bone-pallid patina of limestone beneath the constant drizzle of underground rain. The fruiting bodies of bioluminescent fungi lay in shelves and smears of color around the walls of the grotto, and a meandering underground stream wrapped around the palace in its horseshoe wandering. The hiss and rumble of underground falls could be heard, very faintly, from the stream bed as it flowed out of the chamber beneath a scaly pelt of living rock.

While small and austere by the standards of a God-Emperor, the palace is pleasing to the eye and is furnished with all the conveniences that a commander might require during years or decades under siege. There are carpets of sweet-smelling purple grass, furniture carved from exotic hardwood timbers from other continents, walls hung with tapestries and paintings of limpid beauty that depict scenes of leisure and comfort forever lost to the devastation of war. Within the principal audience room at the center of the chateau there is a throne of white bone, intricately carved from the mortal remains of the honorable regimental dead. (Felons may be left to fossilize by rooftop happenstance, but it is a sign of recognition to be incorporated after death into a seat of authority.) Around the throne are arrayed the All-Highest's counselors, children, and concubines: variously standing, sitting, or abasing themselves as their respective ranks dictate.

In their midst All-Highest broods upon his charnel throne, listening as a brazen golem merges the reports of the scouts who go about the overworld into a stentorian rumble of intelligence. Words cascade through All-Highest's mind in a wash and tumble of power as he grapples with the vexatious question of what to do, and contemplates the wisdom of a course of action that has been proposed by Most Honorable Second Wife, Highest Liege of Airborne Strike Command.

Second Wife is young, hungry, and fearsomely ambitious: she displaced formerly Honorable First Wife (Highest Liege of Armored Cavalry) in his affections six months previously, shortly after his decision to abandon the plan to sleep past the end of the world. First Wife did not react swiftly or favorably to the change in circumstances: Second Wife stole her true name, and now First Wife's mortal husk dangles from a machicolation beneath the roof of the high tower, calcifying slowly, as an adornment to Second Wife's ambition. All-Highest is not stupid. He has bound his new spouse to fealty and enjoined her against interfering with his other children or taking certain actions to his or their detriment. She will have to prove her mettle before he will allow her to give him an heir. But at this moment, as she follows the report from the overworld with her own proposal, he can taste the sharpness of her mind, like an overeager knife:

> We cannot go south, for the cosmic bombardment will render all our efforts futile for years to come. We cannot go east, for Fimbulwinter comes and the Dead Gods' tentacles scrape bare the valleys for tribute. We cannot go west, for beyond the ocean Hy-Brasil has succumbed to the flowery death. North is inadvisable. This leaves one direction, and one direction only, Oh Husband and All-Highest, and I have consulted the Oracle and they agree that it holds to the highest probability of the Host's survival.
>
> The ghost roads are still available to us. It is just a matter of choosing which to open . . .

3: THE GATHERING STORM

DEAR DIARY:

I have a bad record of letting Pete talk me into sticking my nose into dusty, mildewed sheds. It's getting to be a habit. First there was the MAGIC CIRCLE OF SAFETY public information campaign posters, which we found amidst huge quantities of junk stored in a warehouse on the outskirts of Watford. (The less said about that, the better: a vampire elder was using it to hold his personal stash, some of which was still alive and twitching.) Then we were sent on a couple of training courses in the secure document storage tunnels under Dansey House. And now we've drawn this fool's errand.

I'm a mathematician with an interest in higher-dimensional topological deformations, and a recent career track that includes designing visualization systems for directed exploration of stochastic market movements with application to the Black–Scholes model—a weaponized banker, in other words. I have *zero* training or understanding of architecture, facilities management, structural engineering, or logistics. So I'm somewhat puzzled that Management have shoved me out here with Pete (who, as a vicar, is just as unqualified as I am) to tramp around various decaying crown estate assets in West Yorkshire and pronounce on their fitness for refurbishment for various missions that I am not yet cleared to know about.

I suppose it *could* be that, as unqualified but not unintelligent laypersons, Pete and I are both deemed to be free from the pre-existing prejudices and unreasoning enthusiasms of our expert facilities management people. So we're not automatically going to deliver the message that Facilities think Management want to hear, as opposed to the truth, whatever that may be. On the other hand, maybe the organization is just so short-staffed that sending untrained amateurs into the field is the best they can do, because everyone who actually knows what's going on is running around naked with their hair on fire shrieking about the end of days. I'd rather not think about that possibility, because in this time of cuts it's all too plausible—even without the looming prospect of CASE NIGHTMARE GREEN, whatever that is.

Does CASE NIGHTMARE GREEN loom? I'm not sure: I haven't officially been briefed on it yet. However, every time anybody who knows anything mentions the code name they twitch nervously and look over their shoulders like it's the end of the world. This does not make me happy, because these are people who work with zombies, demons, and Civil Service Documentation Standards on a routine basis.

Anyway, back to the present. Yesterday evening Pete and I went down the rabbit hole out at Lawnswood. We waited patiently while Bert Finney finished eating his sandwiches. Then he collected his keys and torch, and gave us a tour of Leeds War Room Region 2, also known as The Bunker.

Shorter version of the report I am about to spend the rest of the evening writing up: the bunker is a dump, a trash-heap, a shit-hole. A damp-infested slum. It probably *can* be restored to functional use, but not at any reasonable cost.

Slightly longer version: while the bunker is structurally sound—it has walls made of prestressed concrete two meters thick—internally it's a mess. There's a pile of broken furniture in the canteen. Virtually none of the fittings elsewhere in the bunker are usable: it has largely been stripped. The cable ducting in the Operational Control Room is rusted, the telephone switchroom contains a Strowger mainframe unit that predates the discovery of fire, the subbasement storage area for dry goods is flooded to a depth of nearly a meter with raw sewage from a leaky toilet outflow, the air conditioning filter packs have crumbled or moldered away, and the caretaker has installed a cat flap in the Secretary of State's apartment so that his pet can sleep there when it's not fighting a desperate rearguard action against the rats. This is *before* we mention the early 1990s when the sleeping quarters were used to host illegal raves, and the period during the late 1990s when the canteen was a heroin shooting gallery. There is lead in the roof and the 1940s era smoke detectors contain Americium capsules so intensely radioactive you could make a dirty bomb with them, making it a toxic waste site as well.

Given several million pounds and a multiyear timetable I think the bunker could probably be renovated to a high standard: but my understanding is that we need a new national headquarters building, not an emergency hole-in-the-ground for when the air raid sirens go off. The only conceivable use I can see for it is if CASE NIGHTMARE GREEN turns out to be an alien invasion, in which case we're totally fucked.

What are we doing here? Can somebody explain that to me? *Please?*

Tuesday afternoon is overcast and cloudy. Silently cursing the jobsworth who scheduled him for a pre-dusk meeting with his new local supervisor, Alex approaches the discolored aluminum entryphone at the back of the Arndale Centre in Headingley with a deep sinking feeling. *Is this it?* he thinks disbelievingly. He's at the right address, and the cracked plastic face-plate next to the fourth doorbell holds a card lettered with CAPITAL LAUNDRY SERVICES in hungover handwriting. But the card has slipped down, one corner is stained a suspicious shade of brown, and the door opens off the car park of a tiny, ancient suburban shopping mall. Alex raises a gloved hand and holds the remote entry keyfob he's been given against the plate as he pushes the button. The lock buzzes, and he steps inside.

Facilities have leased a number of private sector offices and storage facilities around the outskirts of the city, for temporary use by the London-based staff commuting to Regional Government Continuity Centre (North)—as Leeds is designated in the stilted language of internal Laundry memoranda. These offices are supposedly only temporary, and will vanish like the morning dew as soon as the Laundry manages to kick the Department of Work and Pensions out of their Kremlinesque palace on Quarry Hill, but Alex knows instinctively that the rival ministry is going to fight viciously to hang on to its status-symbol headquarters building.

Meanwhile, the temporary Arndale Centre office makes the New Annex look like a five-star luxury hotel. Take an early 1970s British copy of an early 1960s American shopping mall—small, dingy, and with parking spaces sized for 1950s runabouts. Cycle it through four or five recessions and a couple of renovations—a real American mall would have been bulldozed and rebuilt three times already by now—then, as the most recent recession bites, turn the old stock rooms into cramped offices aimed at neckbeard-wearing, flat-white-swilling hipster wannabes who can't cut it in London but oh so desperately want to be cool. Allow the offices to fester for three or four years while the hipster startups go bust, then rent them out as payday loan call centers and, finally, as overflow offices for the surviving rump of Her Majesty's Civil Service—the bits that can't be outsourced, and desperately need short-term lets.

It's all a bit of a come-down to Alex, who until recently studied in the Hogwartsesque ambiance of Oxford University, then toiled in a blue-chip investment bank's opulent London headquarters. He grits his teeth and trudges up the scuffed concrete steps. They're dimly lit by flickering fluorescent tubes. The lack of natural daylight is welcome in view of his peculiar condition, but it's not exactly a luxurious affordance: quite the opposite, in fact.

There is a front desk at the top of the stairs in front of the rat's warren of windowless cubbyholes that pass for offices here. The security guard seated there startles as Alex opens the fire door, and reaches for a hidden button as he speaks. "Sir, you can't wear that—"

Alex raises the visor on his full-face motorcycle helmet. "Give me a sec," he says irritably, fumbling with the chin strap. He rode here on a rattly old Honda moped with L-plates, which he's left leaning against a concrete pillar in the rooftop car park. He bought it yesterday for the princely sum of five hundred pounds. It'll probably fail its next MOT test, but it's a great excuse for wearing a helmet between hotel and office. He pulls the offending item off. "Alex Schwartz, from the New Annex. I'm supposed to report to Mrs. Knight? I'm hot-desking here for the next two weeks . . ."

Juggling helmet in arm, he worms a hand inside his jacket and pulls out his warrant card. The security jobsworth relaxes slightly, then frowns. "Sir? My list says you were supposed to be here for a meeting at nine?"

Alex glances at the clock on the wall. It's a quarter to three in the afternoon. "So? I'm just very, very early."

"Sir, it says here, nine a.m. . . ."

"Hang on." Alex wishes for a moment that he had three hands: with some difficulty, he pulls out his phone. "Nope, that's wrong, should be nine p.m. I don't work mornings. Or daylight hours, for that matter. Is she still in?"

"I don't think she's gone home yet, sir." The security man looks distinctly perturbed. He thrusts a clipboard at Alex, who for the first time notices a pair of CCTV cameras mounted on a frame behind the guard's shoulder. He suppresses a shudder. The guard continues: "Would you mind signing in, please?"

Mrs. Knight has not gone home, and she's still in her office when Alex knocks on the flimsy plywood door. "Yes?"

"Alex Schwartz." He pushes the door open. "I'm here for a meeting; there's been a screw-up over the time, I only work nights."

"Oh, gracious." She pushes her hair back—Alex is just about experienced enough to recognize a hastily suppressed eye-roll—and waves him into her visitor's seat. (It's armless, foam hangs out of one front seat corner, and a suspicious water stain decorates the back.) "Let me see—no, it says nine a.m. in the calendar." She bats the ball brutally back into his half of the court, crosses her arms, and waits.

"Well, the calendar's wrong." Mrs. Knight reminds Alex of a particularly uncooperative type of university administrator he's met before, a kind he's never really been able to get a handle on, so he buys time by glancing around. Over the past few months he's gotten used to the make-do-and-mend ambiance of the New Annex, but even so, this is a distinct step down. "Have you been briefed on OPERA

CAPE?" he asks. She nods, almost imperceptibly. "I'm one of them," he says briskly. *Deal with it.* "So I work nights. Someone obviously cocked up the meeting slot, that's all."

To her credit, Mrs. Knight doesn't blanch, recoil, or reach for a crucifix. Alex finds this interesting, and starts to pay more attention. She's in her late forties or early fifties, with tightly permed graying hair. She wears her office suit like a uniform. Ex-military, he guesses, or otherwise accustomed to disciplined austerity. She's clearly made of stern stuff. Her office fixtures and fittings are beyond shabby, but everything is clean and tidy. "You're part of Facilities, aren't you?" he asks. "That's what this is about, isn't it?"

"Oh Lord, they didn't brief you either, did they?" *Now* the eye-roll comes out to play in earnest. "You're the second today—do you know a Dr. Russell? He was through here earlier, I think Jack is still sorting out his desk—"

"He's a vicar, not a doctor," Alex says absent-mindedly. "Yes, Pete's my official mentor. Is he still—"

"Well then," she interrupts, standing up, "let's go find him, grab a meeting room, and hear what you think of the bunker."

The Arndale office has a conference room. To Alex's eye it looks like it was once a store cupboard, or maybe a stock room. Now it's filled by an outsized boardroom table so large that there is only room for chairs along two edges. A row of mildewed lever arch files slowly collapses on a sagging chipboard shelf on the wall above the far side of the table: Alex makes out the runic inscription *ACCOUNTS PAY-ABLE 88-89* on the spine of one of the binders. Mrs. Knight parks him at the end farthest from the door with a mug of institutional coffee that is almost exactly the same shade of beige as the carpet, then goes in search of Pete. She doesn't take long to find him: they're back almost before Alex has time to zone out.

"The bunker," Mrs. Knight begins expectantly. "What did you make of it?"

Alex cuts to the chase. "Why hasn't it been condemned? The basement's flooded, it's about thirty years overdue for maintenance, and it's in the middle of nowhere."

"Dr. Schwartz, the Civil Service doesn't simply *abandon* everything it can no longer think of a use for." She smiles at him, experimentally, and the temperature in the room drops a few degrees. "If it did, your kind would get short shrift, wouldn't they?" Pete raises a hand as Alex bristles, but she pushes on regardless: "We don't abandon people—like you—or *things*. The bunker has been underutilized for twenty-three years, but it has certain advantages. Besides being blast-proof, it's fireproof and has daylight-proof accommodation, doesn't it? It's just off the ring road, on a major artery running right into the city center. One might even speculate that with a little modernization to bring it up to scratch it'd make excellent accommodation for photophobic employees?" Her smile is as bright as the dawn.

"But—" Alex feels unaccountably panicky. The bunker is terrifyingly close to a certain suburban estate near Adel that Alex is desperately trying to avoid—the one where his old bedroom lurks in wait—but there's got to be more to it than that, hasn't there?

"Calm down, Alex." Pete lays a palm on Alex's forearm. Alex can feel himself twitching, the end of his biro rattling on the desktop as if he's auditioning for a hair metal band's spontaneous combustion spot. Pete frowns apologetically at Mrs. Knight: "That wasn't decaf, was it?"

"Why? Is it important—"

"Oh dear." Pete winces. "Alex, it's my fault: I didn't spell it out properly." Pete's tone is soothing. To their interlocutor, he continues: "Alex doesn't do caffeine, these days: it makes him a little too intense."

It's mortifying: in the months since contracting PHANG syndrome, Alex has discovered that he's become sensitive to caffeine. He's not just mildly sensitive: a cup of milky tea has the same effect on him as a double shot of espresso on a normal person. (A regular filter coffee ought to come with a twelve-month sentence for possession with intent to supply.) He tries to nod, but the effort of doing so while keeping his teeth from clattering defeats him. Mrs. Knight looks at him dubiously, then back at Pete. "All right, then . . . can you present your colleague's findings while he gets over it?"

"Certainly." Pete opens the folder he's carrying: it contains a printout of Alex's 5 a.m. email report. "I've looked at the basic bill of works to put the bunker in order and we're looking at two to three million just to make it structurally safe, drain the subbasement, identify the source of ingress and block and damp-proof it, safe disposal of the medium-level radioactive waste, install a new sprinkler system, and bring the power supply up to modern spec. New mains interconnect, new diesel backup generator, that kind of thing. Then there's the air filtration system—cost unknown, cold war nuclear-proof air filters aren't an off-the-shelf product—and the entire telephone and network system to rip out and replace. I'd be surprised if it was less than another million and a half on top. Double everything if it's done by our wonderful private sector partners, then add the cost of refurnishing and restocking the installation to house forty staff on 24x7 rotation and crisis manning with two hundred bodies for six weeks . . . and that's before we add the special extras our department requires. Bindings and wards and suchlike. Is it really worth it? I mean, there are warehouse units out near Elland Road we could customize more easily at a tenth the price."

Mrs. Knight sighs. Then, to Alex's surprise, she leans back in her chair, peers shortsightedly at the ceiling, and announces, "You're right. Although it's a bad idea to admit it. In fact it's a potentially career-limiting move to say that. You could embarrass whoever was involved when the bad decisions were made in the first place, twenty or more years ago."

"Do go on," Pete encourages her.

"No." She sits up again and smiles alarmingly. "I saw you palm that card, Doctor."

"I'm not a doctor—"

"So *he* says." She nods at Alex. "Rule number one, gentlemen, is that you are *out in the hinterlands* now. To the jobsbodies who keep the public works going and run the spreadsheets and authorize the payments, *this* is a technical service department and *you* are the eggheads from Research and Development in London. So you need respect, or they'll ignore you, which is why Jez Wilson"—who is Alex's line manager—"tipped me the wink to take you in hand and explain the facts of life to you. You are both doctors—doctor of divinity isn't it, *Doctor* Russell?—because otherwise you're just two trainees out on a provincial junket, getting underfoot and messing things up.

"Whereas, in fact, your brief is to report on the bunker. Not on *whether* it's suitable for the proposed use, but on *how* to make it suitable. Considering alternatives is not on the table."

Alex can no longer contain himself. "Wh-why not?"

"Because policy. Or, if you mean *why policy*, because ley lines. You're dead right about the warehouse units on the southwest, or all the other sites—but we need the bunker as well because it's in exactly the right place to make best use of the local ley lines. Leeds grew up as a major transport intersection during the industrial revolution. It's on a canal, a river, a couple of major railway lines, and at the intersection of three major motorways, but there's an older significance to its location, since it was just a medieval village—"

Ley lines. Alex zones out because *of course* it would have to be all about the geometry, wouldn't it? Not the trivial geometry of megadeath architecture, of planting a concrete bunker with walls over a meter thick right at the intersection of the ring road and a main road to the city center, just beyond the 5psi overpressure contour of a quarter megaton air burst directly above Vicar Lane . . . no: Alex is flashing back to the higher-dimensional occult geometry that winds a nightmarish golden braid through alien continua, where undead alien minds gibber and howl at the darkness. At the projections of higher-dimensional paths into our own curved four-dimensional spacetime that give rise to ley lines along which distance is distorted—paths created by the activities of computational thinkers, be they machines (British Telecom had terrible problems with clock drift in their 1960s microwave tower network due to spontaneous line formation) or concentrations of villagers praying to beings with webbed fingers and dubious dietary preferences.

"Alex?" Pete elbows him discreetly.

"What? Oh, yes. Ley lines. Of course." Mrs. Knight sends him a cool stare while he struggles to focus through the caffeine buzz. "I take it the bunker is particularly convenient for the, uh, proposed national headquarters?" There, he's said it: admitted the horrifying possibility that the Laundry is serious about upping stakes from London and transplanting most of its infrastructure to Leeds. It sticks in his throat, but what's a boy from Bramhope to do?

"You could say that." Mrs. Knight's stare loses its acuity by increments. "We're two and a half kilometers out, here in Headingley. The bunker is another one point five. But if it's refurbished and we can create a new endpoint anchor in the center of town—I gather R&D has some people looking into amending the construction plans for the Merrion Centre replacement project to distort the local geomantic contour map—we can bring it down to a virtual two hundred meters from the back of Quarry House! You ought to be able to dash that far without catching fire even in bright daylight."

"And—" Alex blinks. "Right. A nuke-proof regional continuity of government bunker that's just two hundred meters from the new HQ building via ley line, with access to the national ley line network, I can see why that would be . . . interesting." Assuming the newly energized track doesn't attract eaters and class two or higher agencies to feed on the fleeing personnel, it'd be quite an advantage. "Doesn't Quarry House also have a bunker?"

"Of course it does." Mrs. Knight opens her own folder and pulls out a sheaf of dog-eared papers. "But firstly, it's in the city center, and secondly, it's smaller, and third, no on-site geomantic nexus. It's right in the bullseye of the target zone for any major incursion, Dr. Schwartz, and if by some mischance anything *does* hit Leeds, getting stuff in and out of NOH will be nearly impossible—"

"NOH?" asks Pete.

"National Operational Headquarters. That's what the overall project's called." She pulls out another file. "The project to take the fourth largest metropolitan district in the nation and turn it into a fortified coordinating center for repelling alien invasions when the stars come right, *without being obvious* about it." Is that a nervous tic, a twitch, or a sniff of sly amusement? Alex wonders. "So you see, Dr. Schwartz, it's not about *whether* we refurbish the bunker—it's about *how*. And when. And how best to use it to reinforce NOH's peripheral defenses.

"Now. Shall we go over your preliminary report together? I have some questions I'd like you to consider . . ."

* * *

Alex does not work all night at the Arndale office: for one thing, almost everyone else goes home by 7 p.m., and for another thing, there's nothing to do there. After their meeting Doris Knight tells him that the next day someone from Internal Resources will assign him a desk, then politely suggests he go home—which in his case means returning to his hotel room. So Alex is out in the city center by 8:30 p.m., wondering moodily whether to try one of the newer Chinese restaurants, when his phone vibrates with the urgent SOS pattern he's assigned to family members, relatives, and other unwelcome intrusions from the so-called real world.

"Oh hell," Alex mutters aloud, perturbing a dog-walker as he fumbles the big Samsung out of his jacket pocket and clamps it to the side of his head. "Hello?"

"Alex? Alex, is that you?"

He recognizes his mother's slightly querulous tone instantly, and although he knows he ought to be glad to hear her voice his heart sinks and in consequence he feels a stab of guilt. He can guess why she's calling and he really doesn't want to have to think about it.

"Yes, Mum, it's me. What is it?"

His mother is fifty-three, with curly brown hair (or so he believes: she's been dyeing it for some years now), slightly saggy-cheeked, with eyelids that droop at the corners. She wears face powder that smells of lilac (not the choking chemical warfare fragrance of a seventy-year-old, but it's still an olfactory assault on his senses), and she is still married to Eric, her childhood sweetheart and Alex's father. She works full-time as a VAT audit clerk for HMRC, in the regional tax headquarters. Her specialty is takeaway food joints. If he could talk to her about his new job he would be surprised by how much their working environments have in common, but this is all irrelevant because Alex is suffering the tachycardia, sweaty palms, and overwhelming deer-caught-in-headlights freezing panic that comes on when he realizes she's about to put The Question to him again.

"Are you in Leeds yet? When are you coming to dinner?"

Alex is in the habit of phoning his parents every week, usually on

Friday evening around seven o'clock, before they sit down to dinner. It's a long-standing ritual that got started when he first went away to university: if he doesn't call them, they get anxious. Since working for the Laundry he's been given a back story to explain any anomalies in his habits, and so far it's just about held together—despite some unfortunate problems he's trying to get fixed. But last Friday, seven o'clock found Alex scrunched into a south-facing window seat in second class on an East Coast Main Line train barreling past Peterborough on the way north. Phone signal dropouts and an unwise moment led him to let his guard down and admit what he should, at all costs, have kept to himself: that he was coming home (even if only briefly, because of work). Visiting Leeds is not in and of itself catastrophic. But it gives Mum an excuse to ask The Question once more, and his stomach gives a sickening lurch as he realizes she's going to do it again.

"I don't know, Mum, I'm working evenings and into the early hours and commuting back to London at weekends, so I'm not sure—"

"But how about staying up here the week after next? Sarah is going to be home from college by then and she's dying to see you! Perhaps you can come over for dinner on Saturday? It'll be just like old times!"

Sarah is Alex's kid sister. She's four years younger than him, all elbows and knees and frizzy hair the color of a dead mouse. He remembers her for freckles and dental braces, but he understands she's twenty now (how did *that* happen?) and in her second year at Nottingham, studying Management and Accounting. She probably thinks she's a grown-up. Worse, she probably has a boyfriend who thinks she's a grown-up, and who she will in due course bring home to introduce to the parents over dinner, at which point The Question becomes an unavoidable, fiery source of mortification and embarrassment—

"I can make that Saturday," he hears his traitor mouth admit as his attention splits to drive his feet in a wide berth around a pavement pizza. "But honestly, if it's too much bother you don't need to—"

"Nonsense, I was going to cook anyway! Sarah's going to bring Mack." This is the first time he's heard a male name attached to his younger sibling and he almost walks into a lamppost in surprise, even though it's entirely in line with his earlier speculation. "Are you bringing, anyone?" He almost misses the brief pause. "We're dying to meet her, your mystery girlfriend!"

This is The Question, and Alex's stomach lurches queasily. He's about to recklessly say *I met this girl called Cassie*, but then he suddenly realizes that they *didn't* meet. He didn't even get her phone number. His social life is as bereft of feminine company as ever. "I'll have to see if she's free," he says flatly. "Call you back later?"

"All right! Saturday at seven! Love you, dear!" And Mum ends the call, leaving him twitching on the hook, its viciously barbed point cramping his guts.

Here's the thing: Alex's parents are, well, *parents*. Subtype: well-meaning, very ordinary folks. They live in a nice semi out towards Adel, in a classic sixties suburban development (subtype: British, which means self-conscious, cramped, and embarrassed by the trappings of prosperity). Mum, Dad, son, daughter. Two cars and a one-car garage. They're living the dream, for Marks & Spencer values of the dream, working really hard at being sober-sided middle-class professionals. Dad (never Eric to Alex) is a chartered accountant, Mum (never Samantha) is a tax officer, and Sarah is going to follow in Dad's footsteps because Alex, the eldest son, insisted on taking his uncanny mental acuity with mathematics to a higher level—but their initial misgivings subsided when he completed his doctoral thesis, replaced by genuine pride when he got a *real* job in the City.

Alex is the eldest child and only son, and Mum and Dad have certain expectations involving the eventual patter of tiny feet. They waited patiently through his schooling and first degree: he was awfully *busy* studying, they agreed. And they waited some more during his PhD. But now he has a *real* job, and a high-status, high-paying one at that, by their lights, so why isn't he dating an elegantly dressed Jessica from Gilts, and dropping pink-eared hints about engagement rings?

About eight months ago Mum popped The Question and, in a second of weakness, Alex didn't so much deny being single, let alone pull an imaginary girlfriend out of his hat, as evade The Question and allow his mother to draw her own conclusions. It wasn't that he *wanted* to mislead his parents as that he was deathly tired of the ritualized ordeal. But he now realizes he should have nipped her misconception in the bud immediately. Mum has somehow convinced herself that Alex is hiding a girlfriend from her, which can only mean something unspeakable. Or worse: he's hiding a boyfriend, which will force her to confront her own easy assumption that she's not prejudiced.

In truth, Alex *is* hiding something, but it's not what she thinks. Alex doesn't work for the bank anymore. (He's on indefinite unpaid leave, which is much the same thing.) Alex's salary has dropped by over 70 percent and there are no juicy bonuses depending on his year-end review. He's spent so much time focussing on his studies in applied computational demonology and his new job as a civil servant that he hasn't had time to think about socializing. And that's before he takes into account his personal affliction: seropositive for V syndrome, and all it implies. Alex could meet Ms. Right tomorrow and he'd be too paralyzed by anxiety and existential dread to ask her out for dinner. It's not that he wouldn't *like* to meet someone, but he is hemmed in by ominous circumstances and oppressed by uncertainty.

The problem with The Question is that, short of hiring an actress for the evening, it's unanswerable. Furthermore, he can't see any way to defuse the ticking bomb of expectations without causing his mother deep existential pain. (Dad too, he suspects, but Eric has always been so emotionally constipated that it's impossible to tell what he thinks.)

Alex doesn't want to hurt his parents. The easiest option is to avoid seeing them, and for the past few months he's been very successful. But he's rapidly running out of time, and what's a young vampire to do?

Wednesday finds Alex on an early train to London for a training day. A *really* early train—a six a.m. departure from Leeds, arriving in King's Cross just in time to dive down into the underground before the morning light blisters the tender skin on his cheeks.

He arrives at the New Annex and heads straight to the second floor—the half of it that is back in service, that is—and the office he shares with Pete. It's more like a windowless broom closet, but there's room for a pair of desks and two chairs in slightly better nick than the rubbish in the Lawnswood bunker. He's about to log into the secure system and check his email when the door opens. "Alex? Do you have a minute?"

It's Jez Wilson. Rangy, short-haired, and in her late thirties, she looks more like a country and western singer than his idea of management. Nevertheless she's his assigned line manager, she knows more about the taxonomy of tentacled horrors from beyond spacetime[*] than anyone else he's met, and if she wants to soak up the half hour he's allowed himself before the training kickoff he can't really say no.

"Yes, I think so," he says, pantomiming a glance at the wristwatch he isn't wearing: "I have a course starting at nine . . ."

"You *had* a course at nine." She manages to look faintly apologetic. "I'm afraid there's been a slight change of plan overnight. Let's grab some tea and I'll fill you in on what's going on."

Jez's office is upstairs, on the fourth floor, formerly the exclusive stomping ground of Mahogany Row except for a handful of uncomfortable meeting rooms. But changes are afoot in the New Annex. Rumor has it that the executives or wizards or whatever they are have already abandoned their top-floor roosts, departing to more secure premises. Some support departments have also moved out, notably Harry the Horse and his basement arsenal—someone decided it was a bad idea to keep it at a site that has been compromised. And the survivors have been making use of the suddenly-less-crowded premises: for the last months before the site shuts down, Ms. Wilson has inherited an office considerably above her station.

"Grab a seat, any seat," she says, walking across the thick pile carpet to an oak sideboard that appears to be made of the reclaimed timbers of a Nelsonian ship of the line. "I'm sorry I'm cancelling your training course, but you can probably get most of what you need from the books and this is more important."

---

[*] And the PRINCE2 project management standards for dealing with them.

Alex perches on the chesterfield and leans forward as she fiddles with a copper samovar that has been polished until it glows as if it's about to catch fire. Atop the sideboard rests a fine china tea set, so delicate that he's almost afraid to pick up his cup: Jez adds milk, then pours. It is at this point that Alex realizes he's in trouble. His manager has pre-empted his training course? That's fine, and in truth he didn't really need a refresher in eigenvector transformations, even with the footnotes on their utility for banishing higher-dimensional horrors back to flatland. But she's pouring the tea. Everything he's learned about the Civil Service tells him that having tea poured for you is one of the ferociously guarded signifiers of rank, like the grade of paintings from the Government Art Collection hung on your office wall, or the quality of your carpet. Never mind the dodgy gender politics of female deference implied by the order in which cups are filled. Given their respective places in the office pecking hierarchy this can only mean that *Jez wants something from him.* Something she expects him to be reluctant to give her, at that. She knows about his caffeine habit and she wants him off-balance: Is this a subtle softening-up?

Jez hands him a cup and saucer, then retreats to the wing-backed armchair on the other side of the fireplace. (The fireplace in her temporary office is a minor mystery. The New Annex doesn't have chimneys, apart from the flue from the central heating system. And there's the mystery of the perpetually drawn curtains, and the geometry of the floor space—he's sure it's impossible to fit a room this large into the building on this side of the fourth-floor corridor—but no matter.) "Tell me about CASE NIGHTMARE GREEN," she says, then waits.

Alex shudders so violently he nearly spills his tea. "Wh-what?"

"Come on." She smiles, almost pityingly. "World's worst-kept secret and all that, at least within the agency." She shelves the smile. "Tell me what you've inferred, Alex. I want to get some idea of how much you've gleaned before I fill in the gaps. Your clearance came through this morning."

"Clearance? For what?" He's having trouble keeping up.

"For CASE NIGHTMARE RAINBOW, of which GREEN is, shall we say, part of the spectrum. C'mon, tell me what you've figured out by yourself."

"Uh-huh . . ." Alex grabs for the mental gear-stick and tries to jam his aching cortex into action. It's hard work—he's on normal office hours today after a week or more of night shifts, and it feels like it's three in the morning. "Okay, let's see. The computational density of the noösphere has been rising non-monotonically since about 1800, and on top of the population bubble—now slackening, but still adding about 10^{20} additional synapses per second to the ensemble—we have the Moore's Law bubble, with upwards of twenty microprocessors per human being—again, on the order of a billion operations per second, even the embedded controllers in your washing machine—and so, given that magic is a side effect of applied mathematics, we're approaching the Twinkie singularity."

"Twinkie sing . . ."

"*Ghostbusters*," he says, flapping his hands desperately, "*too much magic.*"

"Go on."

"There's a, a thixotropic aspect to it. The more you do, the easier it gets. So not only is there more magic out there, it's getting easier to perform. A year or two ago we passed the threshold at which it went from being something you did using custom summoning grids and microcontrollers, and a very few ritual magicians doing it in their heads until the K-parasites turned up to eat their brains, to the point where unwary mathematicians can accidentally stumble into . . ."

He flushes. Jez nods. "You can skip OPERA CAPE if you want," she says, and he draws a shuddering breath. He's still sensitive about his unwelcome and inadvertent transformation into a blood-sucking fiend.

"Okay. Then we also have the pervert suit problem. Random members of the public developing *superpowers*." He pronounces the word with distaste. "There's a power law in play, isn't there? We're on an up-slope. This is going to get worse, much worse. How bad can it get?"

Jez thinks for a moment, then puts her cup and saucer down, untouched. "So far so good, Alex, but you missed an angle. We're not the only sentient tool-using species we know of, not even the only one on this planet. BLUE HADES are worried about it too—the Deep

Ones? You must have met Ms. Random at some point? We know of other once-inhabited planets, too. No, we don't have a magic space telescope, or any other *Star Trek* shit up our sleeves, but we've got the capability to open portals to places compatible with our type of underlying causal logic, where the same laws of mathematics—and physics—hold true. Such gates tend to go preferentially to places that once held intelligent ritual-magic-using life: I say *once* because when we find them they're mostly extinct, and when they're not extinct . . . let's just say we have a *really strong rule* against opening portals at random. How to do so, and how to do a risk assessment first so that it doesn't kill you, was in the next stage of your personal development plan until late last night, by the way."

"Whu—" Alex bites his tongue. They've gone from *Ghostbusters* to *Stargate SG-1* in five minutes. He has an uneasy feeling that if this keeps up he'd better speed-read his way through the entire TVTropes wiki. "Really?"

"Yes! Did you ever wonder why successive British governments spent decades killing off anything that looked as if it might develop into a space program? They gave up about a decade ago—but only because the horse was already over the horizon and the stables had burned down behind it. Today we've got a shiny new national space agency, but for about four decades Mahogany Row had an unofficial policy of trying to ensure that we didn't accidentally blunder into a real-life version of *Quatermass* just because some glory-hound prime minister wanted a photo-op with an astronaut." Jez picks up her cup and takes a discreet sip. "Go on, Alex. What else do you know?"

"Um." He shakes his head. "I think you just blew a few fuses there. You mean we know about other worlds? Other *inhabited* worlds?"

"Yes, several of them. And you will be pleased to know that most of them feature alien ruins. The ones we can still get to are all dead, except for the Pyramid of the Sleeper, and nobody's going *there* in a hurry. That's GOD GAME BLACK, by the way, you can look it up later but you might have trouble sleeping afterwards. The thing is—"

She puts her teacup down, empty.

"—Those ancient alien civilizations didn't die of old age, Alex; they were murdered."

DEAR DIARY:

I suppose my punishment for being too nosy about CASE NIGHT-MARE GREEN is entirely appropriate. They let me in on the secret, and I wish they hadn't.

Let's see if I can put all the pieces together coherently, starting with the big picture:

As we all know, the Earth is not the center of the cosmos. It orbits the Sun at roughly 47 kilometers per second; the Sun in turn is orbiting the center of our galaxy at approximately 220 kilometers per second; and we can infer, from studies of asymmetry in the cosmic microwave background, that the Milky Way galaxy itself is moving in the direction of the constellation Hydra at roughly 550 kilometers per second.

But on a larger scale, the *entire cosmos* is far from stationary. Our four-dimensional universe is embedded on the surface of a higher-dimensional membrane, or brane, which is moving through a twelve-dimensional foam of other branes that play host to an infinity of pocket "universes." Higher-order resonance effects between our brane and some adjacent ones allow information to leak between universes. We, the structures we collectively refer to as "life," are patterns of information—temporary reversals of the arrow of entropy within our universe—and conscious minds are the most concentrated such patterns we know of. We're making an increasing amount of information, generating magical noise and simultaneously weakening the structure of spacetime by *thinking too loudly*. And sometimes other patterns in neighboring universes can sense us, and some of them think we're edible.

Back in the 1940s, Enrico Fermi asked a question which has subsequently become more famous than the discovery which won him the Nobel Prize.[*] During one bull session at Los Alamos, the conversation turned to the prospects for extraterrestrial life. One of the

---

[*] He induced radioactivity through neutron bombardment, and synthesized a hatful of transuranic elements.

other scientists proposed that there must be intelligent life elsewhere in the universe. Fermi's retort was, famously, "Why aren't they here?" If the conditions in our universe are promising for the formation of stars and planets, and for chemical reactions to proceed with increasing complexity, then—given the age of the universe—we should expect alien intelligences to have evolved long ago and colonized our own solar system. Their absence is a smoking gun, pointing to the existence of a Great Filter: some sort of extinction process that prevents intelligent life from spreading throughout the cosmos.

If we are lucky, the people who worry about this sort of thing opine, then the Great Filter lies in our past. It'll turn out to be something that kills off life forms before they get to the banging-rocks-together stage. Candidates include gamma ray bursters or asteroid impacts, or just the rarity of evolving opposable thumbs and fractional reserve banking. In this scenario, we've survived it already if we've got this far. Which means we're the first, and we're going to go into space and become the punch line to everyone else's version of the Fermi Paradox.

But if we're *not* lucky, they add, then the Great Filter still lies in our future. It's some sort of extinction-inducing process that has been running for billions of years and which kills off sentient space-going, tool-using species with brutal efficiency. It's an existential anthropic threat: the mere act of apprehending that it's *possible* for such a threat to exist means you're in the firing line, and if you fail to deal with it correctly your species will die.

I can now tell you that the Laundry has an answer to the question of whether the Great Filter lies in our past or our future, and the answer is neither—the Great Filter is *now*.

Let me tell you about some of the highly disturbing documents I've been reading, which synopsize our organization's response posture to the actually arising class of solutions to the Fermi Paradox.

CASE NIGHTMARE is the superclass of contingency plans the Laundry maintains for dealing with the end of the world. Jez said they're all based on studies of specific inhabited exoplanets that underwent extinction events before they were discovered: then she dropped a pile of file references on me for bedtime reading. (I've only just started ploughing through them, so this is an aide-memoire for future research.)

CASE NIGHTMARE GREEN is the Twinkie singularity: magic gets so trivially easy that everyone's doing it, which creates a bit of a problem when looks really *can* kill, your average *Strictly Come Dancing* fan can call down a plague of locusts on their least favored competitor, and a sufficiently large congregation of Bible-thumpers can bring about the Apocalypse by summoning up something they've mistaken for Jesus. It's like letting a Primary One class mainline Sunny Delight, then handing out brightly colored semiautomatic grenade launchers. Outcome: we exterminate each other, either retail or wholesale (the latter by inviting in the Elder Gods—I'll come back to that subject later).

CASE NIGHTMARE RED is invasion by aliens. The aforementioned excess of magic we're making creates a signal that's causally entangled with the human noösphere, the totalization of human experience that we generate and contribute to by thinking. This signal is detectable at a considerable distance by various entities, who interpret it as a flashing neon sign saying *all-you-can-eat buffet here*. They might be incorporeal parasites like my V-symbionts or the feeders in the night, or they might be physical invaders: but either way, we're into necromantic *War of the Worlds* territory, which doesn't end well.

CASE NIGHTMARE YELLOW is the geek apocalypse. During the Twinkie singularity stuff begins to come alive, and to think: mostly stuff that shouldn't. Stuff like Facebook, or Vodafone, or your teacup—the Internet of Things That Go Bump in the Night. Invasion by superintelligent hostile cafeteria fixtures, if you like. (At least, I *think* that's what Jez was getting at. My brain had halfway shut down by the time she got to YELLOW.) It's your classic nerd-rapture hardtakeoff singularity, but it's a lot less fun than the Silicon Valley set seem to think when it sprouts tentacles and sucks your brain out through your ears. This one doesn't end well either.

There are a number of other NIGHTMARE cases for which remediation protocols exist. Viral SETI signals. Weaponized memes—Rickrolling didn't come out of nowhere, you know. Lunatic cultists waking up GOD GAME BLACK, whatever the hell that is. (There's always some idiot who thinks that after the revolution they'll be the one sitting on top of the hill of corpses, dining on caviar served out of a bowl made from a chromed baby's skull.) But the one thing they've all got in common is that, left to play out in accordance with their internal logic, *none* of them end with anyone getting to live happily ever after.

The big problem with all of this is that the CASE NIGHTMARE remediation protocols haven't been tested—by definition they *can't* be tested ahead of time. The risk of mass civilian casualties is unacceptably high. (They go so far into Thinking the Unthinkable territory that some of the cleanup strategies include—well, if you ever wondered why successive British governments have insisted on retaining the capability to nuke London until it glows in the dark, you're on the right track.) But on the other hand, the cost of failure is infinite: with an existential anthropic threat you don't get a second chance. *Everybody* dies.

How does this affect me?

Well, apparently we're *already* in the early stages of CASE NIGHTMARE GREEN. The shit *is* hitting the fan as previously forecast, as witness all the Marvel Comics wannabes who are showing up in the news. So the organization is hitting the gas pedal, and ramping up in anticipation of wartime-level operations within the next twelve months. Normally they'd have taken two years to train me before letting me anywhere near an active duty assignment ("the organization is very careful about embedding feral sorcerers," as Jez put it), but it turns out that they simply don't have time.

So:

- The Laundry is going to move into Quarry House in Leeds, whatever I may think of the wisdom of the idea. It's close to the geographical center of the country, it's defensible, it was designed as a center for continuity of government after World War Three, and we don't have time to build something better. So fuck me, I'm screwed (family spare bedroom, here I come).
- I'm going to be given an accelerated self-study course in higher-dimensional portal management, ley line construction, and existential

anthropic threat analysis and countermeasures. Then they're going to send me on a firearms safety course so that I qualify for a firearms license, because Health and Safety say they're mandatory for all personnel who can cause explosions at a distance, and the "countermeasures" bit in my training course is a euphemism for what fantasy writers call "battle magic" or "throwing thunderbolts." In fact, once I've finished the course and have been certificated I'll be entered in the books as a light tank for purposes of international arms control treaties.

- Then they're going to assign me a code name and an active duty role . . .

Alex is still new to the Laundry. He hasn't yet realized that training for the end of the world is an ongoing part of the job. Or that however senior the managers he's working for, there may be stuff that they haven't been briefed on either.

Six months before Alex has cause to moan in his diary about the end of the world, another briefing took place for various initiates of Mahogany Row, up on the third floor of Audit House.

Audit House, name notwithstanding, is not in fact the name of an office building from which the Laundry's audit department operates. It was originally a Georgian town house, which served as the home of a particularly stuffy accountancy firm during the late Victorian period. Requisitioned by the Ministry of War in 1915, it has remained a Crown property ever since. Too small to serve as an actual agency headquarters and too architecturally notable to rebuild—it's a grade one listed building—it serves as a conference retreat within the city. Which is why, on a rainy Thursday afternoon, Jez Wilson, Gerald Lockhart, and several other senior officers are there to attend a lecture on variant hominid cladistics and the implications of early FOXP2 gene expression for ritual magic.

With tea and biscuits, no less.

"Tesco's Value range," Lockhart remarks disapprovingly. He's a middle-aged man in a three-piece suit, balding, his posture stiff. "An oldie, and not so much of a goodie."

"Don't even mention the tea," says Ms. Hazard, who is gracing the event with her presence. She looks as out of place as a peacock among squabbling seagulls: she's dressed for a diplomatic reception, or possibly a royal garden party. She shudders delicately. "They used *bags*."

"Don't worry, it'll all be over in a couple of hours." Lockhart is the very soul of solicitude. "Then you can go back to . . ." He trails off, as if uncertain. (A very rare situation indeed for Gerry Lockhart.)

"Wining and dining the younger brother of the Emir of Dubai," she says with an enigmatic smile. "Doing my bit for the balance of trade deficit and the shareholders." A momentary flash of steel in the smile: "Got to keep the toy chest overflowing, haven't we? Shall we take our seats? I'm sure Kylie will be with us shortly—"

A door leads from the reception area into a Georgian drawing room, done out in tasteful period decor, with a seventeenth-century lacquered harpsichord in one corner facing a half-circle of conference hall chairs, as if waiting for a recital. Beside it, there's a much more modern table supporting a video projector that looks as out of place as a hovercraft at a tall ships race. The dozen invitees file in and take their seats, in some cases still munching furtively on bourbon creams and Hobnobs. Then a serving door at the far side of the room opens and a staffer walks in, leading a stranger. "Hello," the gofer says diffidently, as if he's not used to addressing this many top brass simultaneously. (Maybe he isn't—he's young enough that he clearly finds it an exciting challenge to drive a shaver around the volcanic range of zits gracing his right cheek—but if he's lucky he'll have time to grow into the job before his internship runs out or a necromancer eats him.) "I'd like to introduce this afternoon's seminar lead, Professor Kylie McPherson from the Natural History Museum. Professor McPherson is an individual merit researcher in the Department of Paleontology, specializing in the origins of cognitive psychogenetics in genus *Homo*. She's here to talk to us about some recent findings in hominid evolutionary biology."

Kylie McPherson is in her late forties, wears a no-nonsense tweed suit with her hair tied back, and clearly Mahogany Row is of no more significance to her than a pride of unruly baboons or a class of undergraduates. She walks to the table, taps her laptop trackpad to ensure it's awake, and starts.

"Good afternoon!" She hits the spacebar and the projection screen throws up a skull. At least, Lockhart supposes it's meant to be a skull: it looks more like a child's clay model of a skull that's been dropped on the floor, shattered, and inexpertly glued back together again with missing pieces replaced by guesswork. It looks crude, the brow ridges heavy and the jaw powerful enough to crack walnuts. "Meet your great-to-the-nth-grandfather, Jim. Jim is a well-preserved specimen of *Homo erectus*, a species of hominin—our closest living relatives—that lived from roughly two million years ago until they became extinct around 70,000 BC, at around the same time as the Toba supervolcano erupted. There's some argument about how closely Jim's people are related to us; some of the earlier specimens have been categorized as *Homo ergaster* or *Homo habilis*, and it's not clear whether he's a direct ancestor of *Neanderthal man* and *Homo sapiens* or an extinct offshoot.

"However, I want you to be *very* clear that Jim is neither an Australopithecine nor an Ape. He's an early modern specimen of genus *Homo*, the family of species of which our kind is the only survivor to this date."

Kylie pauses, raises a bottle of water for a sip, and remarks drily: "In this business we get to deal with a lot of 'begats.' It can feel a bit Biblical at times—especially the holy wars over cladistics."

They're still chuckling when she lowers her bottle and hits the trackpad again. Another slide, another skull: going by the ruler next to it, this one shrank in the wash. She leaves it on the screen just long enough for the audience to spot it, then brings up another slide: now the infant-sized skull is joined by a full-sized adult one. "These are both grown-ups. The one on the right is a Neanderthal specimen, and the one on the left is LB1, a well-preserved adult specimen of *Homo floresiensis*, Flores Man. You may have heard them described as hobbits: one thing I'd like to put straight right away is that Professor Tolkien was making things up—the name was applied to them after the fact, and it's a bit embarrassing to those of us in the field because of the misconceptions it comes with. Names come with baggage. Some of my colleagues thought at first they were dealing with island dwarfism—Flores is an island, and species on islands frequently suffer from deficiency diseases. There's also evolutionary selection pressure for small size. (Think of Shetland ponies, for example.) But we've recently confirmed that LB1 is a distinct subspecies of *Homo*, one that lived from about 90,000 years ago right up until the end of the last ice age, around 11,000 years ago. Fully grown, she'd have been about one meter ten tall—that's three foot six in old money—and there's evidence that the hobbits of Flores used fire and Upper Paleolithic hand tools. Small skulls and small brains don't automatically imply lack of intelligence: we've used X-ray tomography to measure her brain volume, and it turns out that the dorsomedial prefrontal cortex, an area associated with higher cognition, is about the same size as that of a modern human.

"That's another key point I want you to hang on to: intelligence isn't purely a function of brain size. Albert Einstein's brain wasn't notably huge, and LB1 wasn't obviously backward compared to her full-sized contemporaries on the continent.

"Now, let's move swiftly on. Our friend *Homo neanderthalensis* appeared about 300,000 years ago and disappeared about 40,000 years ago. He's your prototype ape man, courtesy of Hollywood, but frankly if you put one in a business suit and met him or her in a meeting like this you probably wouldn't realize. Neanderthals were heavily built with thick bones and heavier brow ridges than most of us have today—but there's some debate as to whether they're even a different species, or just people like us, *abapted*—that is, selected, rather than adapted—by living in a period of intense glaciation. We recently acquired a complete genome sequence for this guy, and they definitely interbred with our ancestors about forty to sixty thousand years ago. They also buried their dead with grave goods, cooked their food, and we think they made dugout canoes as well. Unfortunately other traces they left behind have had enough time to decay, so we don't know for sure if they made clothing and had other modern cultural practices—painting and decorating, speaking and singing. The first definite evidence for cultural goods that we've got is from early *Homo sapiens* inhabitations in arid areas, going back 70,000 years. But we can't rule it out for Neanderthal man."

She pauses for another mouthful of water.

"Our ancestors began to diverge genetically from other members of genus *Homo*, notably our friend Jim, about half a million years ago. By about 200,000 years ago, recognizably modern humans co-existed with Neanderthals and hobbits. Our ancestors interbred with their contemporaries, but there is no trace of any other hominids in the record of the past 10,000 years. Until recently we thought we were the last *Homo* standing.

"*Very* recently. Then we discovered we were wrong."

4: INTERLUDE: FORWARD RECON

Most Honorable Agent Second, Doyenne of Spies and Leader of Liars, prostrates herself in front of All-Highest's throne and wonders, coldly terrified, if her father intends to kill her. Less than ten days have passed since she was revived from hibernation to join the High Command in horrified contemplation of the wreckage of their world. A lot has changed while she slumbered, including, disastrously, her father and his favorites.

Before she slept, her father was merely a general: elevated above thousands, privileged to command, but still just a slave beneath the sandals of the Morningstar. But now he has become the All-Highest— or the mantle of All-Highest has descended upon him—and to lie to the All-Highest is to die, horribly and painfully. The *geasa* by which he compels submission entangles everyone in the empire in a lethal web of power, for the weak are bound by the strong who know their true names, and the strong are bound by the strongest. Each level of *geas* reinforces the next one down. If there were any weaknesses or inconsistencies in the bindings, All-Highest would already be dead, overthrown by an ambitious subordinate; and so she abases herself before the greatest Power in the empire, and hopes not to die.

Agent Second has never been high in her father's esteem, but while she lived her mother was able to provide some shelter from his mercurial temper. His young new consort (who even now stands by his right hand) is another matter, and can be expected to want to secure the succession for her own children. Agent Second's life is thus in peril from more than one direction.

"Speak to me, Oh Agent, of our ears and eyes overground, of your readiness to walk among the ape men beyond the ghost roads, learn their weaknesses, and ease our campaign of conquest."

Agent Second's ambitions are limited to not dying on this day. *He called me* Agent, *not* Most-Favored Daughter, *but he still solicits my opinion.* It sets an ominous precedent, to withhold recognition of her privilege and title. But on the other hand, All-Highest still wishes to hear her insights. So there is room for hope. She pushes herself to her knees before the charnel throne, eyes still downcast, and steels herself, preparing to speak.

"All-Highest, I stand ready to lead your Spies and Liars out to learn their secrets as you command, and to mislead and entrap them should you so desire. Please recollect that our numbers were depleted by the last counterinsurgency sweep—we lost many of our best inquisitors when the Eastern Devils penetrated our web of trust, discrediting the previous Agent First." Translation: *You executed them during the confusion after the meteor strike because you thought that they'd been suborned and were telling you lies.*

Speaking truth to power is mandatory on pain of death among the vassals of the Imperial Autarchate, enforced by the *geasa* superiors impose on subordinates. Unfortunately, honesty provides no immunity from the consequences of bearing bad tidings. But efficiency in turn requires that vassals of rank must have some discretion in interpreting their orders. Agent Second is not Doyenne of Liars and Leader of Spies for nothing: her tongue is deft with delicate meanings, soft with subtleties of inflection.

"The subsequent decision to take only warrior caste vassals into the future has further reduced the corps of Spies and Liars available to the Host." Translation: *You left them on the surface to die of old age with the rest—or more likely to be eaten by nightmares from beyond the sky while we retreated into hibernation underground.* "And so, our strength is woefully reduced."

"What remains, Agent?" All-Highest's tone is as chilly as the breeze that whispers through the streets of the necropolis, sucking the moisture from the mummified corpses of the unfortunate.

"*I* remain, Father." It is a desperate risk, reminding him of their relationship, but a calculated one: at this point she has nothing to lose. "I hold the fealty of my honor guard, six bodies warm and true that I can vouch for." Bound by her own personal *geas*, they will obey her unto death: this is how authority is exercised among the people of the Morningstar Empire and their fellow not-entirely-human sapients.

"Knowing I could take only my honor guard to sleep with me," Agent Second continued, "I hand-picked the most adroit in the skills of my order. I have preserved in this way Agent Third, Agent Fourth, and Agent Sixth, along with three others skilled in the arts of assassination." Agent Fifth, swollen with a surfeit of personal ambition, had failed to convince Agent Second of her loyalty. After the second poisoning attempt she had left the woman screaming and naked on the surface, her empty eye sockets leaking tears of blood as the barrel-bodied and be-tentacled horrors circled overhead. "I strove to preserve the capabilities of my office to the utmost extent permitted. And so, of the Command of Spies and Liars there remains to you the four most proficient of your agents, and a half-lance of Silent Executioners beside."

All-Highest is quiet for a long time—almost fifty beats. Agent Second kneels before him, frozen in tension. The only betraying sign of her anxiety is a twitch of the tip of her left ear, hidden by the folds of her cowl. Her father is thinking, calculating, weighing prospects. Beside him, the dragon bitch who murdered her mother stands tall in burnished armor, the high crimson plumes of her helmet-crest waving in time to her breath. Her father's new wife's face is outwardly expressionless, but Agent Second recognizes the searing hatred behind the mask. Agent Second's continued existence is an affront to the Liege of Airborne Strike Command, a reminder that she is only a replacement in All-Highest's affections and can be put aside as easily as Agent Second's mother. If Agent Second survives this audience and is to live on, she will have to settle the affair with her stepmother one way or another: to submit and be bound by her *geas*, or bury a hatchet in her back.

Finally, All-Highest speaks.

"Daughter. We are well pleased by your foresight in preserving the rump of your command." (She could weep for joy. *I'm going to live!*

I'm going to live!) "However, we are concerned by the weakness of Spies and Liars, and we command you to rectify this deficiency as soon as possible. You are now our Agent First of Spies and Liars." (She suppresses a reflexive start, a reflexive jolt of pure happiness running through her from skull to sternum. There is no cause for complacency in this battlefield promotion: her standing in her father's esteem is still far from certain.)

"It is our intention to heed Second Wife's proposal to take to the ghost roads in search of living room. First of Diviners and Records has lately unearthed the path to a world that matches both our requirements and the constraints imposed by these straitened times. It was explored some centuries ago but discounted for habitation because it was overrun by an infestation of verminous underpeople. They are ugly, crude and artless, lacking in all understanding of the principles of leadership through like-thinking, and we shall cleanse them in due course. But for now it is enough to know that they are weak and of many minds, disobedient and disorganized, unbound by *geasa*.

"Our magi are preparing a path through the land of ghosts and shadows to the designated target. The Host is being awakened and the magi will widen the road until it can accommodate them. When they are ready, we will ride through and conquer this new realm.

"The lands above us are no longer ours to hold. While we have slept the centuries away, all other kingdoms have fallen before the onslaught of the Ancients. First of Diviners confirms that we are the last of our kind—that the Morningstar Empire dwells here, that we are the last of the Autarchate on Earth. Therefore if our kind is to survive, we must move in force and establish our dominion before the vermin realize the precarity of our numbers and rally against us. Daughter, you will go before us as pathfinder, to walk among the vermin. You will learn their tongue, comprehend their ways, and identify their strengths and weaknesses in preparation for our invasion. Your agents are yours to command; for your part, you will report your findings personally to the throne. The future of the empire, indeed, of the People, rides with you: we salute you."

5: THE DOOM THAT
CAME TO HAREHILLS

Six months earlier:

Professor McPherson taps the trackpad and conjures up another slide on the screen in the drawing room of Audit House.

No more skulls on stainless steel trays: this one is a photograph of an archeological dig. The excavation proceeds beneath a wild, cloud-swept sky, somewhere where the grass grows emerald green between huge slabs of bone-white stone, the soil is a dark peaty brown-black, and skeletons are buried lying on their side. The one in the grave at the center of the screen is curled headless in a fetal position, its broken skull placed before its rib cage, a reddish-brown spike of rust plunging through its ribs.

"This photo was taken at a dig in The Burren, in County Clare—that's out in the west of Ireland—two years ago. It's a limestone karst pavement with low hills, and there are a lot of ancient megalithic burial sites in the national park. Portal dolmens, hill forts, Neolithic sites—you name it, they've got it. This excavation was part of a field course by the Archeology folks at the University of Bradford. They thought this was going to be the usual early Dark Ages tribal chief's burial site with lower-ranking household members around it, but when they saw this, they realized they'd found something else."

Another slide. Close-up of the skeleton, half-excavated, still in the grave. Jez Wilson clears her throat. Lockhart sends her a quelling glance, but Professor McPherson has other ideas: "You have a question?"

"Yes." Jez peers at the photograph. "Is that a containment circle around the remains? And an iron spike?"

McPherson's eyebrow rises minutely, then she nods. "Correct. The archeologists got excited at first because they thought they'd uncovered a new-to-this-culture ritual sacrifice practice. Then they got around to thinking it was a more recent prank, because the spike through the ribs is wrought iron, and the carbon dating dates the burial to the late ninth century AD: wrought iron was very valuable in that place and time, much too valuable to leave in an executed felon. But then they noticed the other morphological anomalies, and that led them to call me in."

Now it's Ms. Hazard's turn to interrupt: one perfectly manicured finger goes up, then she glances at Jez rather than the professor. "You're thinking PHANG, aren't you?"

Jez shrugs noncommittally. "Professor, is there a folkloric tradition of vampires in that part of Ireland?"

"Good try, but you're on the wrong track." McPherson smiles faintly. "Let me cut to the chase. The skeleton is *wrong*—it's *Homo*, but not *Homo sapiens*. It's closer to us than old Jim, our *Homo erectus*, but further away than LB1 or our Neanderthal cousins. There are anomalies in the structure of the inner ear, in what remains of the left hemisphere—the right side of the skull was stove in—and the hyoid bone looks wrong, too. The jaws do not show the typical dentition of a PHANG, with retractable canines; in fact they don't show human dentition *at all*: they're narrower and there is no evidence of wisdom teeth. Cranial volume is comparable to *sapiens*, long bones are somewhat lighter and thinner, and the digits are elongated, almost like a human with Marfan syndrome. But the real surprise came to light when we extracted samples from the long bones and conducted a preliminary genome sequencing exercise." She winces slightly. "Expensive, but for a new member of genus *Homo* that survived into the near-present . . ."

She brings up the next slide. It's some sort of incomprehensible bar chart—incomprehensible because the bars are more like a bar code than a meaningful chart, snaking back and forth across the screen in loops like a demented tapeworm. Then she taps again and another tapeworm joins the first, striped in color-coded bands to highlight areas where their segments differ. "Behold, the mitochondrial genome of *H. sapiens*—that's the lower one—and a similar map for Specimen B.

This was the first surprise we got solid data for. There's a difference of 292 base pairs between us and Specimen B. This compares to a 202 base pair difference between us and Neanderthals, 385 base pairs between us and the Denisovan hominids of Siberia, and 1,462 base pairs between modern humans and chimpanzees."

Now Lockhart raises his hand. "There's no chance this is a mistake?" he asks, almost pleading.

"None whatsoever." McPherson crosses her arms. "Mitochondrial DNA is much easier to sequence exhaustively than the general genome, and we got this one nailed down. She's definitely not a modern human female—yes, two X chromosomes—but she's a close cousin. But that's not the interesting bit. You see, exhaustively sequencing a human being is still pricey, but you'll notice the burial format: the head was detached and laid alongside the torso in a circle bearing ritual inscriptions. The neck was damaged, but enough remained intact for it to be clear that the hyoid bone was abnormally formed. That suggests some sort of developmental divergence involving the larynx, so among other areas of interest we looked at one particular gene, FOXP2, because it's a hot area of study in hominin evolutionary biology."

She brings up another slide, this time showing a bizarrely knotted big molecule. "Forkhead box protein 2 is required for proper development of language and speech in humans. There are some hereditary conditions in which it's absent, and people born with these conditions suffer from really severe language impairment. Chimps have this gene, too, but significantly, *Homo sapiens* FOXP2 differs by just two point mutations from that of chimps." She takes a deep breath. "Specimen B has a mutant FOXP2 gene. There are three single nucleotide polymorphisms that differ between it and chimp FOXP2, and they're different from ours.

"So, let me summarize. We did a full cladistic work-up and it looks like Specimen B's people diverged from our ancestors around a third of a million years ago. You're looking at a hitherto unknown subspecies of *Homo sapiens*. Gracile—lightly built—with elongated digits and toes. It developed language quite recently, about 50,000 years ago, despite which the dorsomedial prefrontal cortex is about thirty percent larger than in modern humans. We're looking at strong theory of mind, possibly an abaptive response to not being able to use speech as a proxy for grooming in extended family situations. That's also the area that gets chewed up most in cases of K syndrome—it's implicated in the practice of ritual magic.

"Specimen B was beheaded and buried with an expensive cold iron stake through her heart inside a crude ward, some time around 950 AD. This happened in proximity to a much older structure that had been abandoned centuries earlier. A long way away from where anyone lived at the time, in other words. There are no grave goods or clothes, suggesting they didn't have any or, more likely, their property was sufficiently valuable to be stolen. But." Professor McPherson smiles triumphantly. "There's one remaining clue that really got the archeologists' attention—although it made them think it was a hoax at first, before they carbon-dated it on principle."

Another photograph, this time of a fully excavated mandible sitting on a display tray, and now McPherson's got everybody's undivided attention because the gold fillings are unmistakable.

"Baby's got bling, and the dental caries they plug show the characteristic abrasion pattern of a diamond-tipped drill.

"*So.* Are there any questions?"

After his midweek meeting with Jez Wilson, Alex returns to Leeds on an evening train. On arrival he heads for the Arndale Centre, where he spends the hours until midnight reading briefing papers that can't be removed from organization premises. Whenever he gets bored he wanders the empty office corridors. There are bulletin boards for non-classified organization-related material, such as vacancies and out-of-hours activities. One of them is reserved for personal ads, including flat shares. This one he scrutinizes. When he finally tires of being the last night owl in the building (apart from the night watch body in the stairwell) he lets himself out and rides his moped back to the room he's renting in an old red-brick hotel on The Calls.

He has a lot of food for thought. But for the time being, he confines himself to writing up his worries in the diary HR told him to keep—he saves it on an encrypted thumb drive—then duct-tapes the curtains firmly shut, hangs out the do-not-disturb sign, and crawls into bed.

One of the disadvantages of being a vampire on the night shift is that you never wake up in time for the cooked full English breakfast. But it's early spring and Alex's hotel is in the city center, in a clump of densely packed late-Victorian buildings five and six stories high, interleaved with newer slabs of glass and steel. They form a canyon-like maze, and on an overcast day it's possible to go out with no more protection than heavy-duty sunblock and a wide-brimmed hat. So Alex showers, shaves, covers his face and hands in skin-toned theatrical latex paint, and gives thanks to the Lares of street fashion for decreeing that hoodies are de rigueur this decade.

First things first: it is nearly noon, he has the day off work, and there is a tantalizing "roommate wanted" ad on the bulletin board at the office. Even with the organization's bargaining leverage working to his advantage, the hotel is costing an arm and a leg compared to his share of the rent on a house. It is beginning to look as if he may be stuck here for the foreseeable future—not just a couple of weeks— and the beckoning bedroom in his parents' house holds all the appeal of a rusty man-trap. So before he ventures out Alex screws his courage to breaking point, checks the photo of the ad that he snapped the night before, and dials a local number.

"Yo. Who is this?" The voice is male, and has a naggingly familiar accent lurking behind the reserve with which unidentified callers are invariably received these days.

"Um, this is Alex Schwartz? I'm answering the room for rent ad on the bulletin board at the offices in the Arndale Centre?"

"Oh, right!" The voice warms several degrees. "Are you one of the London exiles?"

Alex assesses his existential state. "I guess so. Are you—"

"Yes, me, too. What it is, Brains and I found a five-bedroom house for rent near Harehills Lane"—Alex winces, and begins to think of a polite formula for saying *don't call me, I'll call you*, but the speaker is continuing—"not *in* Harehills exactly, just close enough to be affordable. It's got everything we want except it's a bit too big for just the two of us, so we're looking for someone to rent the two rooms on the top floor for, oh, five hundred a month plus bills? It's fully detached, parking out front and a back garden, central heating, fiber broadband, and plenty of room. We can probably get Facilities to ward it and certify it as a class two safe house, if we can just sort out the rent and ensure it's entirely occupied by agency bodies."

Five hundred a month for two rooms is admittedly very cheap, and it's far enough away from his parents to offer a line of defense in depth. Sharing with a couple of guys could be very uncomfortable if they have bad habits, but on the other hand, they're co-workers. They've presumably passed their security vetting, and a class two safe house with co-workers would mean not having to worry about keeping the curtains shut at all hours.

"What's the story behind it?" he asks.

"It's a family home. Something happened, and they relocated to Scotland, I think, and they're looking to rent it out long term. They gave us a standard twelve-month let, and I think they'll be happy to extend it—it had been vacant for three months when we got it."

"Is it available for viewing? This evening? Uh, what did you say your name was?"

"I didn't, but you're welcome: I'm Pinky, your other hypothetical housemate would be Brains. You're the guy we were tracking around Whitby last weekend, aren't you?"

Fuck me, Alex thinks dismally. "Yes," he says. He's almost ready to make his apologies right now, but he can't rent a whole fully detached house by himself—that's the minimum Facilities will look at, for security warding—and it's not as if Leeds is crawling with potential flatmates who are happy to cohabit with a creature of the night. At least these two jokers are unlikely to nail cloves of garlic to his bedroom door or install UV flash bulbs in the fridge. What can possibly go wrong?

"I'll text you the address. Say, are you in the office today? How about I pick you up from the Arndale car park when I clock off, backside of six?"

Alex pulls his jacket on and picks up his backpack, then hangs out the room service card and heads downstairs. The hotel lobby is painfully bright: as the lift doors open he puts on a pair of tinted glasses and then his hat—not the current hipster-fashionable trilby, but a well-worn homburg he found in a charity shop in Epping Forest. There's nothing like a full-face helmet for keeping the sunlight off your skin, but eating while wearing a helmet or a hooded robe tends to get you odd looks.

Leeds's city center is densely packed and walkable, but not very car-friendly—it grew from a village to a regional metropolis in fifty dizzy years starting in the early nineteenth century, before the automobile was a thing. The local red brick buildings (still smut-stained by a century of coal fires) rub shoulders with pompous municipal edifices carved from imported sandstone. Glass-fronted modern structures fill the gaps like bridgework spliced between rotten teeth. Leeds was blitzed in 1941, and the damage is especially visible south of the river, where the bomb sites were finally filled in during the 1980s with strip malls, windowless modern retail parks, and warehouses. It's a thriving, bustling city, but not exactly high-rise. The only skyscraper on the horizon, the Dalek-shaped carbuncle that is Bridgewater Place, rises a mere thirty-two stories above the city center.

Alex heads into the pedestrianized shopping maze between Lower Briggate and Call Lane, works his way round to Neon Cactus, and dives into the back room. He finds a table as far from the daylight as he can get. It's still early, and he's hungry. (He's always hungry, thanks to the V-parasites, but at least he's learned to distinguish between the need to eat and the need for a more recondite repast.) He orders chimichangas and a decaf, then he pulls out his tablet and starts to catch up on his unclassified reading. He doesn't keep work documents on his personal tablet, but he likes to fantasize that he still has a working life outside the Laundry, and there are plenty of interesting preprints in higher-dimensional topology to keep his delusion fed.

He's two pages in when his phone rings. It's the family-SOS tone. *Damn,* he thinks, pulling it out. "Yes?"

"Alex?"

It is not his mother—or his father—for which he is grateful, but it's still family: Sarah, his kid sister. "I'm in a restaurant. Where are you?"

"I'm in the student union bar at uni. Listen, Mum says you're coming to dinner the Saturday after next. Is that right?"

Something about her tone clues him in that this is not a casual call. "I don't know. Did I agree to that?" he asks warily.

"Well, that's what *she* told *me*, and you know what she's like? If you don't come she'll be ever so disappointed. And I wanted to ask you a favor? I mean, you're in Leeds right now, aren't you? Is the bank moving you there?"

"Not—not exactly." Alex chickens out. He knows that if he had any sense he'd use Sarah as a back-channel, confess that he doesn't work for the bank anymore and that his new employer wants him in Leeds full-time. Sarah would then fill in the mater and the pater and they'd get their disappointment out of the way by proxy, long before the uncomfortable silence over dinner . . . but Alex is a wimp. "I'm in Leeds for a, a course. Mum phoned yesterday to invite me to dinner and I"—*I can make that Saturday,* his memory replays him saying, not entirely helpfully—"I didn't say 'no' in time."

"Oh." There is silence on the line for a moment, during which the waiter—check shirt with buttoned collar, tidily barbered full-set beard/mustache, the ends of an intricate tattoo peeping out from his shirt-cuffs—plants a latte featuring a neatly drawn teddy-bear's face in front of Alex, checks him out for signs of approval, and departs, disappointed. "Well, um. Are you going?"

"Mum said something about—" Something in Alex's memory short-circuits and dredges a traitor phrase to the surface. "You have a friend? Mack? Are you bringing—"

"Yes, that's why I was calling." Now it's Sarah's turn to sound evasive. "I'm bringing Mack to dinner and, well, I was hoping you'd be around? You know how awkward it is, introducing—"

No I don't. Alex cringes reflexively. "I guess so. Um. So you want backup. Right?"

"Right," she says, a husky note of gratitude bubbling up.

"Oh my, this is serious, isn't it?"

"Yes. Yes, I guess we're serious, you could say that." A pause. "You were worried about Mum and Dad leaning on you, weren't you? Are you seeing anyone, Alex?"

"N-no." Somehow it's easier to confess this personal failing to his kid sister. "Not right now. How long have you known Mack?"

"Oh, we met in fresher's week, but we only got serious around the end of last year's summer term."

Alex does the numbers and his eyes bulge. "You've been hiding it from the folks for nearly a year?"

"Not *hiding*, exactly: I just didn't know what Mum and Dad would make of . . . It's different for boys."

Alex takes a deep breath. As he does so, he spots the waiter returning, bearing an overflowing plate. "Food's coming, got to go. You want me to run cover with the parents then? How about if we both aim to arrive around seven o'clock? That way we can split their attention."

"Yes, that would be perfect! I'll see you then! Thanks, Alex. You're a champ."

That evening, Alex is waiting in the car park after dark when a familiar white van noses in and the passenger door opens. "Wotcher mate!" Pinky is surprisingly bouncy for a middle-aged guy, Alex thinks. "Hop in, let's go to see the wizard."

This had better be worth it, Alex thinks as he clambers into the passenger seat. "If you could drop me in town afterwards, that'd be great. I'm pretty sure I can tell you if it's going to work as soon as I've seen it." Every week he spends in the hotel room, he's bleeding the equivalent of a month's rent in Leeds. (At least he's still being paid a salary with a London weighting, which lessens the pain.) He's already made up his mind to take the rooms unless there's something badly wrong with the whole house-share. He can always move out after a month or three if he finds somewhere better. Can't he?

There is a satnav on the dash, tucked away amidst a clutter of less mundane electronics, and Pinky makes extensive use of it as he hurls the van along some alarmingly steep backstreets and through commuter rat-runs plagued by a rash of sleeping policemen that rattle Alex's teeth every time they jolt over one. As Pinky drives, Alex studies his co-worker. He's in his late thirties or early forties, with shaven head and a slightly demonic goatee, like a younger Walter White. Alex gathers he's something to do with R&D, or maybe field ops tech support—but sticking your nose in your co-workers' business is strictly discouraged in the Laundry: loose lips don't merely sink ships, they summon krakens with too many tentacles.

"How long have you known, uh, Mr. Brains?" Alex asks as they hurtle across a small roundabout and bounce over another speed bump. He's trying to make conversation in a half-hearted effort to get to know/bond with a possible flatmate, but when you can't discuss work and you don't have a hobby there's not much to talk about.

To his surprise, Pinky guffaws. "Long enough to know better!"

Oh, very helpful. Alex sinks back in his seat, irritated.

"Years ago we used to share a safe house with Bob Howard," Pinky volunteers abruptly. "Since then we've gotten used to living together with nobody else around. But we don't have time to sort out a mortgage and go house-hunting up here, and the market's stagnant anyway, so we're going back to renting for a year or two."

Alex boggles slightly. He is not a fan of Mr. Howard. The first time they met, Bob tried to zap him with some kind of banishment taser. Subsequently he learned that it could have been a lot worse: Howard has heavy mojo in Ops, having trained under the semi-legendary Angleton, the Eater of Souls. According to the org chart Alex sneaked a peek at, Howard is a systems necromancer, whatever that means. Maybe he raises dead mainframes?

Pinky takes a few seconds to concentrate on a particularly ominous roundabout. "We wanted this house because there's a decent cellar—we need space for Brains's lab and my workshop."

"Ah, right." This is probably safe conversational territory, Alex decides, because Pinky raised it first. "What sort of stuff do you make at home?"

"Oh, hobbyist stuff: nothing classified. We got our wrists slapped for taking work home once too often so these days it's just maker noodling. Lately, Brains made a 3D printer out of a TIG welder and I've been using it to repair—it'd be more accurate to say remanufacture—a half-track motorcycle Bob stole from a bunch of undead Nazis in Amsterdam."

Alex's brain shuts down. There are words coming out of Pinky's mouth and they sound as if they ought to mean something but they don't parse. "That's interesting," he says politely. *Undead Nazis in Amsterdam?*

"You ride a moped, don't you? And the Vicar's a biker. Maybe you'd like to test-drive it? We've got a two-seater hovercraft as well, but the house is on a hill so it'd be an all-around bad idea to take it out on the road, we'd never get it back up to the garage. Oh look, we're nearly there."

Pinky ushers Alex through a cramped porch bolted on the front of the house like an afterthought, into an asymmetric hallway with a staircase on one side and doors to the left and front leading into two reception rooms and a kitchen. The back room is cluttered along two walls with machine tools. Alex recognizes a lathe and a surprisingly professional 3D printer; a full-height equipment rack is stuffed with recondite electronics, and other, less familiar lab gear lies scattered around. The kitchen is at least a kitchen. There's a wooden table, and a fridge, and a bunch of fitted units around a cooker. The central heating boiler bolted to one wall emits odd gurgling belches from time to time. It's all slightly grubby, and Mum would have a fit if she saw him living in such squalor, but to his surprise Alex realizes that it feels *comfortable*: as if he could put his feet up on one of the chairs, or leave the boxes from last night's takeaway out on the counter, without being told off. It is, in short, a man cave.

"Let me put the kettle on. Then I'll show you around upstairs and out back, and we can talk about it over a cuppa."

Opening off the first-floor landing are a toilet, a bathroom, and two bedrooms, one of which has been turned into a field-expedient server farm. (They don't spend long there, for it is occupied by Brains. Alex has a confused impression of a pasty-skinned man with a shining, bald head and a mustache the size of a bog brush. He's crawling around on his hands and knees with a bag of cable ties, muttering bitter imprecations about too-short ethernet cables. Evidently relying on wifi in a Laundry safe house is considered about as acceptable as walking around with your trousers at half-mast.)

There's also a mystery staircase which disappears into what was originally the attic.

"Some time back, the previous owners fitted dormers and turned the top floor into two bedrooms," Pinky explains as Alex follows him up the steep and narrow stairs. Alex oohs and ahs appreciatively. "There are blackout blinds on the Velux skylight, and for now there's a wardrobe in one room and a bookcase in the other that you can use to block the windows until you get curtains."

Two whole bedrooms is more than Alex needs: he'll be rattling around like a pea in a walnut shell. On the other hand, after living in student digs in Oxford and then rented rooms in London, the idea of having so much space to himself—and so cheap!—seems like an indecent luxury.

Alex follows Pinky back down to the kitchen, where Brains has migrated. He's busy filling some sort of alarmingly teapot-esque contraption with freshly boiled water: at least, Alex *thinks* it's a teapot. It could be a prototype Vohlman-Stephenson soul reactor, for all he knows. Certainly the intricate occult circuitry sketched on the outside of it looks alarmingly functional. "You said there was something out back to look at," he says diffidently.

Pinky nods and bounces up and down on his toes. "Yes! There's a garage, but you can't park in it. The van and bikes go out front because we're using the garage as a repair shop."

"Repair—"

"Give me a countdown," Brains demands abruptly, as he lowers the lid on the teapot. "Ninety seconds to initiation!"

Pinky sighs theatrically and pulls out an antique stopwatch. "This is *which* test number, dearie?"

"Isolation teapot model three, test eighteen." Brains sounds pessimistic.

"He's been working on this one for absolutely *years*," Pinky confides; "he has a long-term obsession with extreme kitchenware. You know how isolation grids are useful for temporal containment as well as spatial isolation? He's convinced it's the perfect way to keep the tea from stewing, if only he can just get it right . . ."

Pentacles. Alex shudders slightly. Yes, you can use a properly energized grid to keep out tentacle monsters, or to keep them *in* if you're deranged enough to think summoning them is a good idea—and you can use them to isolate the contents from the rest of spacetime, either for a really airtight conferencing suite, or as a kind of occult fridge (because you're a psychotic vampire elder who doesn't want your V-parasites to chow down on your prey too fast) . . . but any way you cut it, Alex has never heard of a use for a summoning/containment grid that gave him the warm fuzzies. Building one into a teapot feels just a little bit too close to lighting your campfire by burning crumbs of C-4 explosive.

"What's in the garage?" Alex asks, hoping Pinky will extricate him from the kitchen before Brains's brew is complete.

"Let me show you. This way." Pinky unlocks the back door and starts down the steep brick steps that lead into an unkempt back garden that seems to be mostly occupied by a slowly crumbling shed and a flat-roofed garage.

"Hey, my countdown!"

"Time's up," Pinky calls. Alex hurries after him. "Don't worry about the teapot," Pinky assures him, "Brains does this sort of thing for a living. Safe as houses, really, as long as he doesn't forget to earth the grounding strap again." They reach the side-door to the garage. Pinky unlocks it, lets Alex in, then flips the light switch. "Behold, the chariot of the gods! Or rather, the Ahnenerbe-SS. We've been hauling it around for over a decade, and it's nearly ready to ride again."

There is a four-wheeled trailer in the garage, with a vehicle parked atop it. At first, Alex can't make head or tail of what he's looking at. He can't even tell which direction it's supposed to face. It resembles a cast-iron bathtub, if bathtubs had caterpillar tracks and the front forks of a motorbike bolted to the end where the water spigot belongs. A bench seat spans the back of the vehicle, going by the location of the bike handlebars; inside the tub there's an old-school saddle, and between the saddle and the bench seat there's— "Is that a *radiator* cover?"

"Yup, it got pretty cold on the Russian Front in 1943. Nothing like as cold as it got on the ground in OGRE REALITY, mind you, which is where Bob found it. The original engine's by Opel, a 1.5-liter water-cooled four-cylinder job that puts out about 36 horsepower, but it was seized when we got it—vacuum welding, not to mention differential thermal contraction when the atmosphere froze during the Fimbulwinter."

Pinky walks around the trailer, idly running a finger along the rim of the bizarre vehicle. "I did a lot of welding on the hull and replaced most of the track pins, Brains rebuilt the transmission, then we completely replaced the wiring loom and dropped in an engine from a Volkswagen Polo." He gestures theatrically: "Behold: the world's smallest half-track, and only the fourth Kettenkrad in the UK! Plan is to get it roadworthy, then use it to haul the hovercraft around on a trailer. It's technically a classic, so it's exempt from road tax—although you need a special license endorsement for tracked vehicles to drive it on the highways." His gesture finishes in a flourish as he points at the rear wall of the garage, where something that looks like a leaf-blower humping an outboard motor boat leans against the wall.

Alex closes his eyes, then opens them slowly again. There are no windows in the garage, and plenty of cobwebby dark corners. There is even an inspection trench in the floor, between the trailer's wheels. Not that he's going to need it—or have room to stash his moped in here—but it's nice to know there's somewhere to take shelter if the teapot explodes.

"Okay," he says. "I've seen enough." He pauses with a hand on the door. "About the rooms. I don't need two bedrooms to myself, but I've got a colleague who has a family down south—he probably won't be moving up here full-time, but he can certainly use a room for the night when he's in town. If you're okay with the idea of me occasionally parking a friend in the other attic bedroom, I think we can do a deal."

"Sure!" Pinky says brightly. "Let's go back inside. I'm pretty sure the tea should be brewed by now, and we can hammer out the details over a cuppa." His expression turns to one of worry. "Assuming this time he's managed to keep the teapot haunting-free . . ."

DEAR DIARY:

I have come to an agreement to rent the top floor of the house off Harehills Lane for six months. I'm getting it semi-furnished for five hundred a month, plus my share of the council tax and bills. Pinky and Brains have already got a BT Infinity connection, and I'm getting to share it, so I will have internet access. It's going to be secured as a class B safe house as soon as we're all listed as living there by Human Resources, which means we get wards installed by Facilities and a secure landline. Also an intruder alarm. I emailed Pete and he's interested in using the spare top room when he's in town overnight. P & B want to meet him but they're okay with this arrangement in principle because he has already been vetted by HR.

I have some minor reservations, and I may not be staying there after the first six months, because something about P & B smells funny.

I don't care that they're civil partners: that's none of my business. Nor do I mind them keeping a hovercraft and a half-track in the garage and a lathe in the living room: that's pretty normal for a geek house. But something doesn't quite ring true. They work in tech support ops, Q Branch, playing with exotic toys, and they know about PHANG syndrome. That's really quite hardcore, when you think about it. They've been in the organization for more than fifteen years—Pinky said in passing that they used to share a house with Mr. Howard and Mhari Murphy. That's time to accrue quite a lot of seniority. So what are they doing in Leeds, rather than down in one of our research sites in Milton Keynes or Oxford?

I'm sure there's a story behind it, but it's a bad idea to ask questions. I guess I should just check with HR before I sign that contract and hand over the deposit and the first month's rent. I'll do it tomorrow.

Hmm. While I'm on the topic of Human Resources . . .

HR have given me a Story. I'm required to roll it out if anyone asks what I've been doing, *including* the parents. I'm not allowed to tell them The Truth, on pain of spontaneous human combustion. (At least, it would be spontaneous human combustion if I wasn't a PHANG. In my case, it's on pain of a black mark on my personnel record, because the standard formula for *geases* doesn't work very well on us.) Unfortunately the cover story they gave me is very badly constructed. I've requested a better one—one that won't get me disinherited, at any rate—and Mr. Jenkins said he'd work on putting together a package, but I could tell from his expression that it's a low priority.

This is what I'm supposed to tell people if they start digging into my background and occupation:

I am Alex Schwartz, PhD in mathematics, University College Oxford. I was headhunted from university by a certain bank, but my entire team was downsized in a round of cost-cutting following the parent institution's indictment over the LIBOR rate-fixing scandal. *Not* my fault, not my team's fault, but the bank had to make adjustments to its overhead to deal with the scale of the fine they got landed with. The bonuses we were due at the end of the year made us a fat target, and after our unit's head, Oscar Menendez, was murdered by a drug dealer in Essex, we had nobody to defend us from a spurious stack-ranking exercise . . .

I'm not bitter. Okay?

Actually, about half of that story is true. The bits that aren't: Oscar was murdered by a crazed vampire hunter who happened to be a catspaw working for the incredibly ancient vampire elder who actually owned the bank. Said elder died, but not before he was maneuvered into making a spectacularly lethal raid on the New Annex by his rival for the title of vampire elder of London. Oh, and my team were downsized because we'd already been recruited by the Laundry— thank you, Ms. Murphy, for saving our collective ass—and someone on Mahogany Row had a quiet word with someone senior at the bank before our annual bonus came through, dammit.

Back to the cover story:

Banking having proven to be a suboptimal career choice (on top of requiring me to work fourteen to eighteen hours a day, seven days a week), I was invited to attend a recruitment open day held by the Civil Service. They decided that I was a good fit for their needs and hired me on—

This makes no sense!

—Firstly, only an idiot would take that kind of pay cut, wouldn't they? An idiot or somebody expecting to receive some *very special* benefits in kind.

Secondly, if the bank had *really* downsized my department, we'd have been headhunted as a team by Goldman Sachs, HSBC, or Morgan Stanley before the ink was dry on the papers, no-competes or not. No-compete clauses in employment contracts aren't legally enforceable in the UK, and if your new employer is a blue-chip investment bank and wants you badly enough, they will throw lawyers at the contract until it breaks under the weight of briefs.

But let me go on:

I have apparently been hired by the Ministry of Defense to work on the quality assurance program for flight software procurement in the F-35B fighter program, which is why I supposedly can't talk about what I'm doing. This is such a transparently stupid lie that a *Daily Mail* reader could shred it in seconds. Yes, it's true that automated theorem provers have a role to play in software QA for writing test harnesses designed to deliver proof of formal correctness, so my background isn't totally implausible . . . but the Pentagon have publicly said that nobody outside the USA is going to get their hands on the source code to the F-35's avionics. And this was in response to a UK request some years ago, reported in all the papers! It's as if they *want* any random person I meet with an IQ above room temperature to see through my cover.

And the best bit? The reason I don't come out during daylight hours is apparently because my work requires me to be online and available for telephone meetings during daylight hours in Japan— except the JSDF are not buying the F-35 at all!

On the train up from London I came up with three different cover stories, none of which contain holes big enough to sail a container ship through. But I am not allowed to use them until they have been approved by HR, because HR is required to provide a documentary and paper trail to substantiate my lies if anyone asks. Coming up with a new (even if more coherent) bunch of lies requires someone to get off their arse and do some work, so it's a lower priority than dreaming up a new mess of transparently stupid falsehoods as a cover for the next employee to come on board.

If I go and see my parents for dinner, then they *will* ask how things are going with my job, and I'll have to confess that I don't work at the bank anymore. Then they'll ask what I'm doing now, and I'll be required to roll out the red carpet of lies—which they will probably see through before I finish speaking. And then I will have to choose between telling the Plumbers to come and clean up the mess and bind my own parents' tongues, or let them think they've raised a bad liar.

I don't know what to do.

"This is a K-22 thaumometric spectrum analyzer. It measures the gradient of the ambient thaum field, and outputs an energy spectrum giving you some idea of the flux in a given area, its rate of change over time and distance, and how penetrating it is based on its excitation level. It's highly directional, so you need to take three readings at each logging point: X, Y, and Z axes."

It's six o'clock on the Monday evening after the Thursday when Alex visited Pinky and Brains's house. He and Pete are the last guys through the door of the briefing room in the Arndale Centre office. Dave, the technician who's giving them the orientation, stumbles through his spiel as if he's sleepwalking: he's obviously been repeating himself at two-hour intervals and he's got an advanced case of teaching assistant burnout.

Alex shares a brief glance of mutual frustration with Pete. Pete has agreed to stay late in the office because after work Alex is taking him to see the house in Harehills, and they'll sign the rental agreement jointly if it looks okay. Starting the training course on the K-22 at four in the afternoon seemed like a good idea—it was supposed to take two hours—but that was before they realized that it was just a version of the lab gear they've been using for months, packaged with a battery in a messenger bag. Nevertheless, Trainer Dave is determined to run them through the entire manual and subject them to a quiz at the end, even though he's clearly suffering from narcolepsy.

"Dave." Pete interrupts, but keeps his voice calm and slow. "Dave, we're both familiar with the K-22. We've been using them on the proving ground at Dunwich and in lab work for the past six months. Why don't you just skip the rest and see if we can complete your multiple-choice right now, so we can go home?"

Trainer Dave yawns and wobbles on his feet, then gives Pete a dirty look. "How do I know you're not secret shoppers auditing me for compliance with training delivery standards?" He puts down the bag containing the K-22—it looks suspiciously like a cheap Android tablet connected to a plastic project box with some LEDs sticking through the front panel—and picks up the training course folder he's reading from. "This is dangerous stuff! If you get too close to a steep thaum gradient you can accidentally precipitate a cascade—"

Alex has had enough. "Excuse me," he begins.

"—cascade chain in which any grid patternings you're carrying become activated, like inducing eddy currents by putting a metal container in a microwave oven. Only they'd be *magical* eddy currents. In which case you can attract—"

Fuck it. This is Thaumotechnic Safety 101 stuff. Never mind knowing it: Alex is qualified to teach it. He's only been on the inside for six months but he has a natural aptitude for applied computational thaumaturgy. He soaks it up like a sponge. "Look into my eyes," he says tiredly.

"—you could be eaten alive from the inside out by K-parasites . . . What?" Trainer Dave stops reciting the canned safety spiel and makes the fundamental error of locking gazes with a PHANG.

Persons afflicted with PHANG syndrome are not, in fact, the living dead. They can't turn into bats or mist. However, they *do* have a number of traits associated with the vampire legends of yore. PHANGS can move superhumanly fast and exert great strength . . . and the mythical vampire mind-control trick is *entirely* true.

Trainer Dave is wearing a standard-issue Laundry field ward on a chain around his neck. It looks like a small silver charm pendant, and it's designed to protect the wearer from everyday magical threats, or at least provide enough warning that they're getting in out of their depth to give them time to run away. However it offers about as much protection against the gaze of a pissed-off PHANG as a bicycle helmet offers against an onrushing tank. Dave stands slack-jawed for a couple of seconds as he stares into Alex's eyes, then he twitches vio-lently and grabs at his shirt collar. A moment later the shorted-out ward is on the floor, emitting a thin trail of bitter-smelling smoke. And Dave is *still* gazing into Alex's eyes like a love-struck puppy.

"Dave," Alex licks his lips. The familiar hunger, ever-present, sharpens abruptly. *Damn it, I'm not due for another blood meal until next Tuesday!* He feels a momentary urge to go for Dave's throat but suppresses it ruthlessly: he'll just have to tough it out until HR deliv-ers the next sample tube. "Dave. You can *trust* us. We are not auditing you for quality purposes: we are *exactly* what we seem to be. But we're all wasting our time here. Let us take the workbooks away and we'll return the completed questionnaires when we've read the books from cover to cover. You can go home and get some sleep. We're done here, aren't we?"

Trainer Dave nods jerkily, his head puppet-like; he picks up the K-22 demonstrator and slings it over his shoulder. "Well, if you're sure, it's your neck on the line when you're out in the field. Let's call it a day: send me your worksheets through the internal post by next Wednesday and I'll sign you off." He bends down and picks up the ward. "Huh. What happened? It got really hot . . ."

"I think it might be defective." Alex catches a sharp glance from Pete and shrugs. Pete's eyes narrow, but he nods imperceptibly. "You probably want to tell Facilities. Sign out a replacement tomorrow. I gather they're issuing higher-powered ones to everyone now: the old class two wards just aren't much use."

"I'll say." Dave yawns again. "Well, I'll be going then. Gosh, is that the time? How did it get to be so late?"

Alex watches their trainer flee, then sits down and massages his forehead. He has a mild headache. Cracking a low-powered ward by sheer willpower isn't something he does very often. It's got his V-parasites riled and they're whooping it up, an insectile chittering of eldritch tinnitus resonating at the back of his head.

When they're alone in the decrepit conference room Pete takes a deep breath and holds it for a count of ten. *"You. Should. Not. Have. Done. That."*

Alex rubs his brow again. Abruptly he realizes he's shivering and hot, angry and scared with the adrenaline flood of reaction. It's as if all his frustration and stress came bubbling up in a rebellious outburst. "Nope, I shouldn't have! And he shouldn't have been wasting our time. It's made me *hungry*!" He glares. Pete blanches, and Alex blinks, cringing inwardly as he realizes how he must look from the outside. He backpedals furiously: "I'm sorry, I'm crabby because I only did breakfast around two o'clock. Let's go grab a takeaway—no, wait, there's a pizza place across the road, how about we sit down and eat?"

Salvo's is brightly lit, brash, and a fine example of what happens when a family of Italian restauranteurs in Yorkshire cross breed a mid-fifties American diner with a Neapolitan pizzeria. While they're waiting for the food, Pete (who has been wearing a positively consti- pated expression ever since leaving the office) has another go at get- ting things off his chest.

"Mind control is . . ." He stumbles to a stop and glares at Alex.

Alex takes a deep breath. "I'm a very bad boy, yes. It's unethical, naughty, and as my mentor you're supposed to shout at me, agreed. But the flip side of the coin is that he was wasting our time, we've got important stuff we should be doing instead, and hey, pizza. Where *exactly* is the harm in what I did back there?"

"Saying it's unethical is beside the point." Pete picks up his fork and bumps it on the table, using it for percussive punctuation. "You don't need a lecture on ethics. You're not *really* a bad boy, otherwise the organization wouldn't be going to considerable lengths to keep you alive." He stares moodily at the wallpaper behind Alex's head. "What worries me is that it's a contravention of HR regulations."

Pete taps the table again. "I know why you did it, and I sympa- thize, up to a point. We've both got better things to be doing—you should be studying, I should be monitoring nominally Nicene Creed– compliant doomsday cults—it's a make-work job and a distraction. Also, you were telling him the truth—all you did was nudge him to agree you weren't lying to him. And I think you got away with it, too, unless we're under active investigation by the Auditors. But if we are, well, from their perspective you broke a really serious regulation for an entirely trivial reason." Alex blinks: that possibility hadn't oc- curred to him. "If they catch you messing with employees' heads, even if it's for *good* reasons, they'll throw the book at you. Their thinking is, maybe this time he did it to cut short a pointless training course that had already overrun its time slot, but what if next time he does it because he's bored and wants to cut short an important mission briefing, and people get k—get into trouble as a result? What if he does it for *bad* reasons, to cover up some impropriety?"

Alex looks into Pete's eyes and sees something new there: Pete is scared. And not scared *of* him: he's scared *for* him.

"Shit, man, I wouldn't do—"

"I know that! But the organization doesn't." Pete's voice is pitched low and urgent. "These are desperate times. There have been issues with internal penetration by opposition factions—not just you-know-who." Alex shudders again. His experience with you-know-who put him in a locked hospital room for a week, *and* he got off lightly. It could have been ever so much worse. "*They* have to go by capabilities, not avowed intentions. If you ever, *ever* mess with the insides of an employee's head again, you had better have evidence and witnesses to prove that they were a clear and present danger, or it'll be the Black Assizes for you."

He stops lecturing abruptly. Alex's shirt is cold and clings clammily to the small of his back. Oblivious to their conversation, a pretty, dark-haired waitress approaches the table and places two pizzas before them, asking, with a smile, if they need any pepper or condiments. Her accent is Polish. Alex stares at her fixedly for a moment, before he realizes that she asked him a question and is expecting a reply. He shrugs. "Sorry," he says, embarrassingly unsure what's expected of him.

"That will be all, thanks." Pete gives her a sunny smile. As she walks away, hips swaying, he murmurs, "You don't need to stare."

"What? Sorry!" Alex twitches violently. "I was away with the fairies. Thinking about what you said," he explains defensively.

Pete picks up his knife and begins to saw at the thin crust of his del' padrone. "You're doing a decent job most of the time," he says quietly. "But you've got to learn to think like a state if you work in the Civil Service. Organizations are not human beings and they don't obey the same priorities. They're hives. Like the bank you worked for,

I suppose, but you were too specialized, working at too low a level to see the politics going on around you. Hives run on emergent consensus and policy. And there are still people in the Laundry who think that leaving any PHANGs alive—much less hiring them—was a really bad idea. You need to make sure you don't give them any excuses to challenge the consensus."

Alex picks at his quattro formaggi despondently as Pete disassembles his own pizza. He's still hungry, but he's lost his appetite for food. Across the room he notices the pretty Polish waitress flirting with the maître d' behind the front desk. He looks down at his plate, focussing on the tines of his fork. They stand out in steely relief against the blurred background of his pizza. *I need to eat,* he thinks dismally, feeling ashamed of himself. After a minute, he forces his hands to move. *I'm not a bad boy,* he tells himself, unsure whether it's a statement of fact or an instruction. But if it's true, why does he feel this way?

After pizza, Alex takes Pete over to visit Pinky and Brains's house. Pete is duly appreciative of the benefits of a nearly unfurnished top-floor bedroom, a lathe in the lounge, and a half-tracked motorcycle in the garage. Pinky and Brains are duly appreciative of the benefits of a second roommate with the right security clearance. A lease is signed, and Alex and Pete hand over deposit and rent cheques. Brains proposes that they celebrate by opening a bottle of his home-brewed tea-wine; Pete leads Alex in gracefully declining (by reason of the need to be sober for the ride home to the hotel), and the evening comes to an end.

The following evening, after dark, Pinky meets Alex with the van and they make the entirely predictable and deterministic trip south to the big IKEA warehouse store just off the M62, where Alex spends the thick end of another five hundred pounds—it feels like a lot more money than it did during his banking days—on a desk, an office chair, a futon, bedding, and some blackout curtains. He's up most of the night hammering, screwing, and swearing as he tries to interpret furniture plans drawn by M. C. Escher. To his astonishment his new housemates sleep through the racket and do not rise to remonstrate angrily with him. Finally, by about four in the morning he has the beginnings of a vampire lair in place. He might have to sleep in a Lycksele instead of a coffin, and sitting on a Torbjörn in front of a Micke desk and a cheap Dell is a step down from the gothic throne flanked by pulchritudinous undead brides that he feels he truly deserves, but at least he can call it home. And maybe in time it'll come to *feel* like home? Who knows: stranger things have already happened in his short adult life.

Alex crawls into bed and lies there with the lights out, staring at the ceiling. The blackout curtains are drawn but the LED on his phone charger floods the room with a ghostly green radiance that, to his PHANG-sharp eyes, is almost bright enough to read by. It's cold— the central heating timer is off until shortly before dawn—and he doesn't want to reach an arm out from under the covers and throw a discarded sock across the charger. But it comes to him that he's neither tired nor contented. So in the end he sits up, shivering, grabs a tee-shirt, checks the time—4:33 a.m.—and phones the only person he can think of who might relate to his predicament.

"Yo, Alex?" John answers on the second ring. Like Alex, he's one of the survivors of the small band of PHANGs who have ended up in the Laundry, dragged along in Mhari's undertow.

"Yo. Can you talk?"

"Oh, sure. I was just finishing some paperwork, thinking about fixing myself some lunch, then hitting the gym as soon as it opens: I can be home before sunrise. What's up?"

Alex can't honestly call John a friend, but they share a certain number of unique life experiences. Heavy math background, worked for the bank, contracted PHANG syndrome together, survived the massacre at the New Annex. Now they're both scurrying around auditing courses on advanced computational thaumokinesis between seemingly purposeless training assignments. When they're in the same city they sometimes go to the pub together after work because bitching about the job is always easier in the presence of someone else who's been there and done that. They're foxhole buddies rather than real friends, but that's okay because it's exactly what Alex needs right now.

"I was just wondering: Have you guys been tapped for rotation through Leeds yet? I'm trying to get a handle on what's actually going on. There are rumors about it being a permanent relocation target for the entire organization."

"Really? You'd do better to ask Janice. If it's that big, the sysadmins will be up to their ears in plans for the server migration"—unlike a commercial operation, or even a regular civil service department, the Laundry cannot outsource its IT infrastructure to third parties—"won't they?"

"Janice." Alex doesn't need to sigh.

"Okay, so you're afraid of her. Who else—Dick?"

"I wouldn't cross the road to piss on Dick if he was on fire. Anyway, he's about as reliable as the *Daily Mail*. On a good day."

John chuckles humorlessly. "Hey, I heard a rumor about Dick. Think you can keep it to yourself?"

"Dick's an animal! When we were exploring the envelope—"

"Dick is in trouble with HR."

"What?"

John pauses. "Listen. About our condition—what do you know about it and sex?"

"Know about—" Alex's train of thought falls apart messily. What Alex knows about sex is entirely theoretical, to such a degree that he gets panicky when another man asks him about it—the long-ingrained fear of being found out by the high school gossip ring still haunts him. Alex doesn't so much wonder about sex as have a fully developed five-year post-doc research program in mind, assuming he ever finds a willing collaborator. "What about it? Apart from how it got Evan into a shitpile of trouble . . ." Evan was one of the PHANGs who didn't make it. (A self-identified pickup artist, he thought developing vampire mind-control skills was the best thing ever to happen to him, right up until the night he picked up a vampire hunter by mistake. It had been a closed-coffin funeral.) The penny finally drops: "Wait, is this about Dick and the night club—"

"HR sent a memo, did you get it?"

"A memo? I get a lot of memos from HR. Mostly about the correct use of stepladders and how to fill in time sheets correctly. Which memo?"

"So you didn't read the memo about sexual contact being a contagion vector for V syndrome?"

"About *what*?"

"Oh geez. You mean you didn't—well." John pauses. "Let me give you the TL;DR version. Your blood meal: you get it in a nice sample tube once a week, like methadone, and you don't really have to think about where it comes from or what happens to the, the donor, right? But when you drink the blood, what happens is that your V-parasites use it to establish a link to the brain at the other end, and they start eating holes in it. Well, the word from HR is that you don't need to *drink* the blood. You just have to mix enough of it with your own circulation for the V-parasites to go to work. Blood-to-blood contact is enough, no drinking necessary. Just like—"

Alex is neither stupid nor slow. "You're saying it's *actually* like HIV."

"Yeah."

"You're saying that PHANG syndrome is *sexually transmitted*?"

"*No.* I'm saying that V *syndrome*, the degenerative side effect we inflict on our hosts, what our victims *die* of, is contagious via blood-to-blood contact with a PHANG. So if you have sex, the only way to avoid killing your partner is to use condoms religiously. Or to choose someone who's already infested with something that stops the V-parasites moving in. K syndrome–induced dementia, for example: they're already loaded with extradimensional parasites. Or maybe another PHANG: it looks like we're immune to each other. Probably."

"Oh God, Janice will fucking *love* that. I can hear Dick's new chat-up line already." Janice is a PHANG: she's also a no-nonsense lesbian. "She'd punch his nuts through the wall."

"Well, she might if Dick dared to say anything. But he's in real trouble this time. They caught him shagging a zombie on the night shift."

"Gross! Where? I mean, wait, what happened?"

The Laundry can find a use for anyone and anybody—often literally: death doesn't always result in release from service. The dead bodies on the night shift have mostly been soul-killed by exposure to summoned nightmares. Physically intact, they are set in motion by captive Eaters and bound to obedience. In organization parlance these are Residual Human Resources: the grim joke is that HR likes them because they don't take vacations or ask for pay rises.

"I'm not sure of the exact details," John continues, "but apparently they caught him down in the archive tunnels under Dansey House one night with a female former employee. I mean, a former female employee. Um, whatever. *In flagrante.* He went down there and used his warrant card to order the zombie to follow him into a storeroom and, well."

Alex shuffles uncomfortably. "Right. Forget I asked. But. Um. What happened?"

"Suspension on pay pending an enquiry. The Auditors are looking into it."

"Oh dear God."

"They're talking about bringing him up before the Black Assizes, if they can work out what charges apply. Awkward."

"Jesus. Fucking a zombie. I feel sick."

That's not all Alex feels: despair at the unfairness of the blow that has just been dealt to his hope of ever having a normal sex life is also a factor, not to mention a mortifying, burning curiosity that he dares not admit. But he's not about to expose his emotional underpants to John, not over the phone and without prior consumption of enough beer to render all statements plausibly deniable. *Quick, change the subject.* "Um. Moving swiftly on. The *real* reason I called—the Leeds thing."

"What, the move? So far I think it's admin only. They want Quarry House, that's for sure, but they're going to need outlying bases all over the country for rapid reaction forces. Is this about your family thing?"

"Yeah, you could say that. I was trying to work out if I could avoid being posted here permanently."

"Well, my guess is the answer to that is a yes, *if* you can figure out some way to make yourself indispensable elsewhere."

"Thanks a million!"

"Tell you what, if I hear anything useful down here I'll call you? I mean, there might always be an internal opening in Cheltenham that requires an expert in higher-dimensional transformational topology who's allergic to sunlight, right? You never know."

"Yeah, you're right! Thanks."

But even before they end the call Alex knows it's not going to happen. He is doomed to be dragged back into the infantilizing maw of his family's expectations. Nothing he can imagine will ever challenge his parents' iron-clad expectations, or allow him to break out of the claustrophobic mold they've spun for him, without shattering them entirely. Forever the dutiful son, Alex can't see any way to create a life of his own unless he can first escape from the city of his birth. You can take the boy out of Leeds, but you can't take Leeds out of the boy: the strongest manacles are born in the blood.

And so he lies awake an hour longer, until the central heating lurches back into life with a distant groan and a throbbing gurgle of pipes. And when he finally dozes off in the predawn gloom, he dreams of a green-haired, mad-eyed girl who can shatter his world with a fingertip touch.

About a month before Alex visits Whitby, Gerald Lockhart attends another briefing—this time in a windowless basement storeroom in a grungy satellite office in Catford.

"Forget everything you think you know about the pointy-eared fuckers," Derek the DM says genially, dropping a meaty hand with casual disregard on the grease-stained cover of a first edition *Monster Manual* that occupies pride of place on his desk. "It's all moonshine and bullshit."

The DM has taken a special interest in Professor McPherson's Specimen B ever since the briefing at Audit House five months ago. He's been particularly evasive for the past two months, closeting himself with Forecasting Ops' spookier haruspices, and asking lots of pointed questions about ley lines (such as the geodesic linking The Burren with certain prehistoric sites in Yorkshire). Lockhart, who makes a point of keeping an eye on what his External Assets are doing, is perturbed: not so much by Derek's more eccentric interests as by his secretiveness. But he's finally invited Lockhart into his den, and Lockhart is determined to get to the bottom of the matter.

Lockhart winces slightly as the DM pulls a book off the shelf behind him—a late impression Allen and Unwin copy of *The Fellowship of the Ring*, its paper jacket slightly foxed—and drops it on the AD&D rule book. "No fucking Legolas here. They're your classic forties Übermensch: Nazis with pointy ears and death spells."

"You're going to give me chapter and verse on what you're doing," Gerald says firmly, crossing his arms and leaning back on the swivel chair with the broken gas strut suspension. It creaks ominously. "Or I'm leaving." *Life's too short for your role-playing melodrama* is the subtext, although Lockhart is warily aware that calling the DM's bluff is generally an unwise strategy. He's the Laundry's very own Prisoner of Zenda, except that after his escape and revenge he came back into the fold willingly, in return for a lavish budget and the organization's tacit cooperation in staging his fantasy scenarios. Which makes him, in Lockhart's world view, a dangerously loose cannon with the ear of Mahogany Row and the goodwill of both Forecasting Ops *and* the Auditors (which is bad enough), and a tendency to pull brilliantly polished rabbits out of suspiciously beaten-looking hats (which only makes things worse). "Explain yourself."

"I began investigating after I got the briefing pack on Specimen B," the DM says smugly, his voice deep and gravelly as a hundred-and-fifty-kilo toad (to which he bears a passing resemblance). "And it bore some structural . . . *similarities* . . . which got me digging, as it were."

He leans forward, confidingly. Lockhart manages not to flinch. "Let me give you a scenario. Imagine you're, oh, I dunno, Doctor Impossible and you've just come out of your time capsule from the year 1940. You're looking forward to unleashing your Vril-powered clone army and taking over the world, but before you can get your marching mojo on it's a good idea to do due diligence and figure out who you're taking over the world *from*." Lockhart nods. "Well now, you don't take long to discover that the USA is top dog, right? And you're going to go up against them eventually. But first, you want to figure out how they're going to react. I mean, why start a land war in Asia when you can just pay off a couple of corrupt customs officials?"

Lockhart's eyes narrow imperceptibly. "Go on."

"Well, thanks to Specimen B we now have confirmation that they've been out there for a very long time indeed, if not so much in the past few hundred years. And what I figure is that everything we know about these pointy-eared fuckers has been filtered through medieval monks from word-of-mouth accounts by terrified peasants. Who *escaped*, meaning they weren't valuable enough to the aforementioned PEFs to be worth keeping. It's like, I dunno? Trying to work out the mechanics of K Street lobbying and beltway politics and the US State Department by listening to an illiterate goatherd from Kandahar who got kidnapped by US Special Forces and was released when they confirmed that, no, he didn't know where the Taliban received their subscriptions to *Penthouse* and *Guns and Ammo*." The DM pauses for breath. "We're reading what the monks thought was worth writing down, the edited accounts of goatherds nine hundred years ago who had the great good luck to be seen as too harmless to be worth a bullet the night SEAL Team Six blew through the village."

"And the body?"

The DM shrugs. "Everyone gets unlucky sooner or later. And we know the pointy-eared fuckers stopped operating on our patch, in our world, not long afterwards. Reports just stop *dead*. Like they gave up on us as too poor to be worth enslaving. Or maybe the folks back home threw their equivalent of World War Three. Or they decided to regroup . . . or something."

Lockhart thinks for a minute. "Let us stipulate that those are the facts. What do we know about Specimen B's people?"

"Let's see." The DM leans back in turn and stares at the ceiling tiles. There's a disgusting brown-edged stain where something has leaked from above. "They got speech later than us, but that doesn't mean they're unsophisticated. They had to spend hundreds of thousands of years longer than our ancestors making do with hand signals and guesswork—which means they had theory of mind, working out what everyone else in the tribe was thinking by observing their behavior and ascribing intent to it, long before they got words. Silent killers who worked in packs, because that kind of brain-work requires a high-energy metabolism and unless they were a tropical-only band of peaceful fruit-eating hippy fuckers, they were hunters. They got speech late, maybe less than fifty thousand years ago if Processor McPherson's cladistic analysis is right. Hell, they might even have developed writing first."

The DM absent-mindedly picks up a set of translucent dice from a stationery organizer on his desk and begins rolling them on the blotter. The decaying thaum field of a thousand hopeful gamers' wishes, harnessed by the DM's occult paraphernalia, slows to local lightspeed when the dice hit the blotter: they glow ghostly blue with Cerenkov radiation.

"Go on," prompts Lockhart.

"Let's say they get speech, and they got theory of mind, so they get religion pretty soon, too—an emergent side effect of ascribing intentionality to aspects of their environment. Animism, polytheism, whatever. They probably discover ritual magic pretty fast because their brains are predisposed to modeling complex entities. Abstract thinking." Lockhart begins to sit up. "But they're not like us psychologically. They've got a much shorter history of selection for social living with non-relatives. What kind of society would a species of smart, fast, predatory ritual magicians come up with?"

The DM smacks his hands down on the dice, locking them to the desktop as he stares into Lockhart's eyes. "They're going to grab each other by the mind and *squeeze*," he announces, gripping the handful of dice in one meaty palm. "You're going to get a society based on cognitive binding. *Geases* all the way down. It'll make Feudal Japan look like an anarchist utopia. Either you're a master—a sorcerer—or you're a slave. Or a less powerful sorcerer: a vassal." He blinks rapidly. "They're smart, too, so they'll make progress. Hierarchy holds them back: a Dark Lord is a single point of failure for the Dark Empire. If you can stick a dagger in his kidneys while he isn't looking you'll trigger a feeding frenzy among the First Circle. Possibly they'll go high feudal, with reciprocal obligations and a great-chain-of-being shtick, so everyone knows how the succession works. Or maybe they'll go full Aztec, and offload all the magic onto a succession of high priests driven mad by blood. But I see no way these fuckers are going to be perfect floaty Tolkienian peaceniks."

"I hear you." Lockhart is laconic. "But if that's the only reason you've been hiding for the past five months . . ."

"Nope." Derek shakes his head. "Because the question I've been asking is, what happens now? We're hitting peak thaumaturgy. We're sending up the bat-signal loud and clear: we've got magic and we're using it. Back when the PEFs last poked around this neighborhood we were in the dark ages. There was nothing to steal but our fleas. Only now . . . if they're still out there, are we suddenly going to get our very own personalized answer to the Fermi Paradox?"

Lockhart's eyes go wide. "What did Forecasting Ops say?"

"Forecasting Ops read the fucking tea leaves and did a double-take, my son. Forecasting Ops are deeply unhappy. You know how it goes when they try to predict the future and someone else is doing the same thing, how the interference effects mess with them and turn it into a muddy blur? Well that's happening."

"Oh dear."

Lockhart's mustache twitches unhappily.

"You can say that again." They sit in silent contemplation for almost a minute.

"You have a plan," Lockhart nudges.

"I have a plan."

"But . . ."

The DM sighs lugubriously. "FO's best projection is that shit's going to kick off in the next month, somewhere in the north."

"Yorkshire. Leeds, even. Right." Lockhart nods. He's been involved in the Leeds relocation planning for nearly a year.

"It could be." The DM glances at him slyly.

"So what do you want me to do about it?" Lockhart asks, losing patience.

"Cameras." Derek smacks his lips. "We need a way to spot them if they show up, don't we? *Cameras*. Forecasting Ops were very definite about that: it's all about the peepers." He blinks rapidly, then looks at Lockhart again. "They couldn't be any more direct. The closer they get to telling me what to do—"

"The less reliable the forecast becomes, yes, I understand." Lockhart dry-swallows. "What exactly do you need?"

"All the street camera time in the world. A technical team. And a bunch of feet on the ground who don't have enough of a clue what they're up against to run away. One set of feet in particular: I've been reading his file and I think he'll rise to the occasion nicely once I set him up." The DM stretches expansively. "Three to two nothing happens. But that remaining forty percent contingency? You'll thank me later."

"Write me a memo: I'll make sure you get everything you ask for." Lockhart stands to leave. "But you'd better be right," he adds off-handedly.

"What? If they're not out there it won't cost you . . ." He trails off, catching Lockhart's icy stare. "What?"

Lockhart slides his half-moon glasses off his nose, and very deliberately pulls a lens cloth from his breast pocket. He begins to polish them, considering his response carefully. "This isn't a game, Derek."

"I know it's—" The DM pauses. "What do you mean?" he asks in a thin, worried voice.

"Games iterate. You win, you lose, you get another throw of the dice." Lockhart examines the surface of his spectacles in minute detail, looking for dust motes. "In real life there are no health potions, no respawns. People play for keeps. You should play this one as if the Auditors are going to drag you away and cut your throat if you lose the round." His gaze flickers back to the DM, a myopic blue-eyed squint: "Because what you've just described to me is not a game, Derek: it sounds more like CASE NIGHTMARE RED."

6: INTERLUDE: ENEMY TERRITORY

Agent First of Spies and Liars dances along the shadow roads that lead through the timeless void of the eternal now.

In her gloved right hand she holds a mace of power; with her left she swings a thurible of burning incense, its chain fastened to her bare wrist by an iron manacle. The velvet choker she wears around her throat is fastened with a clasp bearing gems of memory and a rare, precious oracle stone to help her distinguish destiny from lies. On her fingers she wears rings of power. Her target is a shadow world, one of a myriad of alternate realities that can be molded to the will of the People. It is a penumbral land of ghosts, bereft of law and lore alike, its primitive denizens defenseless before the Host's invading might. Her orders bind her to steal their names and faces and, eventually, their truths: she is required to ensnare them in a cunning harness of lies and present them to her father the All-Highest, that he might tie them to his will.

It does not occur to Agent First that the denizens of this shadow world might defy her father's *geasa*, much less that they might do so successfully. It has never happened before. In all the shadow worlds, her kind have never encountered a subspecies of People who can defy the Host. Not only is it unthinkable, a considerable body of philosophical/religious thought holds that it is impossible, a nonsensical proposition. The People are the pinnacle of primate evolution, for if it were otherwise they would already have been discovered and subjugated (or exterminated) by a more aggressive, dominant subspecies. That they have not been brought low already demonstrates that such an outcome is impossible: obviously no such alien conquerors exist.

The People *are* the master race, the Autarchate of the Morningstar Empire *is* their greatest creation, and the Host of Air and Darkness is the highest and last surviving expression of their martial prowess. Failure, it follows, is not only not an option, it would be indistinguishable from treason. Or so she has been raised to believe.

At least her assignment to this mission removes her from the baleful purview of her father's consort. Out of sight means out of mind. Or so she can hope.

The road Agent First travels spirals through a higher-dimensional space, to which she has been granted access by the Host's magi. There is a vestibule in one of the subsurface caverns, its floor paved with artificial coral shot through with veins of semiprecious crystals, grown *in situ* in the form of a grid to channel the magi's power into a gate to the shadows cast by spacetime itself. The road before her has the semblance of a glowing pathway stretching across a stark plane of darkness. An infinite distance above her, a ghostly manifold of points of light glitter coldly. These are not stars but singularities opening off the edge of the alien fractal that gives access to the universes compatible with the Host's physical laws. Each pinprick of light is a gate leading to another shadow land. (The darkness between them contains an infinity of points representing entrances to members of the set of worlds with physical laws incompatible with existence. This is the dark anthropic zone, universes within which life cannot survive.) As she dances, the stylized moves carry her along the road in strange bursts of motion, the landscape shifting and reconfiguring around her. You do not travel the ghost roads by walking, unless you are willing to die of old age. Here, geometry is an expression of power: the ritual dance of the shadows manipulates distance.

Agent First follows a seldom-traveled route, abandoned these past thousand years. It leads to a shadow inhabited by round-eared brutes, ignorant and easily domesticated. Long ago Agent First's predecessors sent reconnaissance teams hither, hoping to find lands fit for conquest. The place they found was indeed inhabitable, but so dismally bereft of anything worth taking that nobody in their right mind would consider it a fitting home. The natives fled in terror, or fought wildly and viciously with crude iron weapons. Some few were captured, bound, and transported to the empire for interrogation (and to provide cruel but short-lived entertainment for their captors). When the Duke of the Western Lowlands subsequently terminated the exploration program, some of the surviving prisoners were expelled back to the world of their birth, as living testimony to the unwisdom of meddling with the People: hopefully they instilled a healthy fear of their betters among their fellows before dying.

It is Agent First's privilege to be the first of the People to set foot in this shadow realm in a thousand years and spy out the lay of the land for the invasion to come. As likely as not, this will be her only such opportunity. She goes first, as befits her rank. When she sends for her command (what remains of it) the rest of the Spies and Liars will follow her. Far behind, her father's magi continue to chant, pumping *mana* into the road, stabilizing and broadening it. Once their preparations are complete, the Host will emerge in all its glory.

Agent First is equipped as befits the leader of a forward reconnaissance team. Her choker is encrusted with memory jewels, containing a full transcript of her predecessors' experiences of the target realm, and empty gems waiting to receive her own reports. At the front she wears a splendidly mounted fire opal, a thief's stone. The rings on her fingers and thumbs are of purified rare earths, packed tight with wards, crammed with invocations ready to release—so energized that her metacarpals hum. Around her back and upper arms runs an intimate, intricate tattoo of power that binds a glamour to her skin. It will blind anyone looking at her to her true nature: unless they have strong occult protection, they'll see only a pretty young female of their own kind, pleasing to the eye, harmless and instantly forgettable. Later, when she finds a suitable victim, she will use most of her *mana*—stored power—to steal a true name by force and assume the owner's identity, memories, and personality (meanwhile sending the victim back to her father's redoubt as a slave bound by her *geas*). But for now, she is anonymous. By the standards of the People her attire is inconspicuous and dowdy, if of a richness and quality that would be taken for signs of royalty by the awestruck captives retrieved on one of the earlier raids. They are the garments of her caste: boots, a robe and trews of dark green velvet edged with lace, black gloves and hose spun from the silk of false widow spiders and shot through with charms. Over it all she wears a black hooded cloak, fuliginous and dull as death.

The meta-space through which the shadow roads lead lies beyond time and space but not beyond fatigue. Agent First is flagging, her reserves dwindling. There is sweat in her axillae, a slow burn in muscles and tendons, and her joints ache as she dances on. The pungent astringency of the incense in her thurible helps somewhat, keeping her focussed and active. It also lays a tenuous smoke-trail that will linger, allowing those who eventually follow her to sense the correct road. She follows in the footsteps of Messenger Seventh of Polaris Ascendant, the last courier to come this way. His memory diamond is clenched between her teeth, a bitterness goading her on as her body jerks and pirouettes, replaying the exact moves of his ritual dance. Even her breaths and pauses are perfect echoes of his motions. To deviate would be a disaster, until she has reopened the closed portal at the other end of the path and anchored it in place. Once that task is done any member of the Host who has been granted the Keyword will be able to follow her back and forth without effort. But for now she is performing the dance of the opening of the way, and if she falters or stumbles she will be lost forever among an infinity of worlds.

Agent First dances ever onwards until eventually she glimpses the end of her path in the distance. At first it is little more than a vanishing point. It slowly brightens, glowing like a pale blue dot hovering in the infinite depths of the space above the plane the path traverses. Finally it seems to descend, approaching the level of the horizon. There is a humming sense of power beneath her feet, the barely leashed strength of a ley line resonating with the similar conduit buried beneath the evaporated sea on her own world where the Host have made their final stand. Now the ghostly blue radiance grows brighter, and from the semblance of a vanishing point the end swells into a circle.

Agent First pushes herself onwards, chest tight and muscles burning. The circle swells before her until she sees it as a silvery arch that rises above the path, engraved with symbolic bindings. Its glow is a brilliant flare of ghost-light, the radiative emission of photons slowing abruptly as they cross the membrane separating this not-space from the shadow universe beyond.

Up until this point, Agent First has painstakingly kept her mind clear, empty of verbalizations and any thought that might contaminate or undermine her determination to see this path through to the end. But now she can barely contain a flash of fierce triumph: *Mine!* she thinks, embracing with her will the world beyond the gate. There is an undernote of fear, of course—notably the fear that her new stepmother will have contrived to corrupt her path. But that would require subtlety: and the mistress of dragons is not noted for her discreet approach to disposing of obstacles.

Agent First lowers her thurible to the not-ground beneath her feet, unlocking the bracelet that chains it to her wrist. She licks her parched lips, and coughs, and then she speaks (or more accurately croaks) the Keyword, pronouncing the phrase of binding that will lock the thurible to the gate. She raises her mace of power and lightly thrusts it into the center of the blue-glowing void.

And then—

Agent First steps out of the shadow roads, her night vision damaged by the Cerenkov radiation thrown off by the portal. As the portal closes behind her darkness descends abruptly. She takes stock, using her other senses. The ground beneath her feet is hard, level, and flat. The air is cold and damp, speaking of rain, but there is a horrible dead taste in the roof of her mouth—there is no vegetation here, it's like a cold, damp desert—and it is noisy, so noisy, a background roar like a distant waterfall and, approaching, a thunderous growl and bright lights—

She leaps backwards into darkness, nearly trips over her cloak, and catches her heel on a stony uprising. She tumbles and recovers in a roll, her heart hammering. And so it is that by tripping on a curbstone Agent First narrowly avoids being flung across the road by a BMW whose driver is more interested in his cellphone than in avoiding pedestrians wearing dark clothing at night.

Hyperventilating on the cusp of a fight/flight reaction, Agent First leaps to her feet and spins round. She searches her immediate vicinity for other threats. She finds herself standing on a narrow path of poured stone slabs that flanks a broader, lower roadway. Thundering wheeled carts with glaring lights and angry faces rumble past in orderly queues, their pasty-faced occupants squinting into the darkness through curved windows. The carts screech and grumble and stink like the smoky oil lamps of a slave barracks, powered by some cryptic force. After a second, shaky glance Agent First realizes they are not a threat to her as long as she stays out of their path. They are confined between the raised strips at either side, guided along the road bed by painted glyphs. Furthermore, the stone buildings to either side bear signs in an inscrutable script, oriented to be visible to the occupants of these carriages. Such are the hallmarks of civilization, regulation, and traffic: they're not *her* kind of traffic (and the carts seem to her to be sluggish, smelly, noisome, and potentially dangerous), but it's a far cry from the wilderness populated by savages that she'd expected to find.

Clearly the centuries since last a member of the People traveled to this place have brought changes.

On the side of the footpath opposite the road of carts, Agent First sees a wall of rough-hewn stone bricks held together with mortar. Branches overhang it from behind. Opposite, across the cart track, rows of cramped houses built from baked red clay bricks display locked doors and curtained glass windows to the road. They are all offensively ugly, although the darkness of night—pierced by a sullen amber glow from lights on metal poles—draws a merciful veil across their exteriors. Agent First slows her breathing and tugs her cloak into place around her. There will certainly be changes after the conquest, and for the better: the buildings hereabouts are so grotesque they're not even fit for a slave barracks. All-Highest will have the architects responsible crucified in due course. In the meantime, Agent First shudders fastidiously and nerves herself to ignore the pervasive crudeness which seems to be a hallmark of this world.

Some of the buildings close to the footpath display wide glass frontages, illuminated from within as if to deliberately display the contents. These must be public warehouses of some sort, where the serfs can come to collect their rations. Waiting in the shadows she observes as a cart rumbles and slows, amber lights blinking lazily on one side before it turns into a sidestreet and comes to a halt. An occupant climbs out—heavily built compared to one of the People, dressed in well-made but extraordinarily drab clothes, all in shades of gray and black. He walks up to the door of the nearest ration store and goes inside: a bell tinkles. Perhaps two hundred heartbeats pass before he emerges, bearing a nearly flat, square box of cunningly molded wasps' nest. *Do they domesticate insects?* she wonders. (That would explain the buzzing and roaring of their carts.) A smell reaches her, the aroma of hot fresh bread and cooked meat. He climbs back into the cart, starts it again, and it moves off into the stream of traffic. *I will come back here later and sample the food,* Agent First decides, willing her hunger pangs into submission. Like the rest of the Host she has subsisted on time-frozen rations for too long. The smell of hot food, even if only the provender of the cattle-folk, is insidious and seductive. But it will have to wait until she has acquired a face, and memories, and identity—to say nothing of a grasp of the locals' Low Tongue.

Agent First walks swiftly along the path beside the main road, nerving herself for the next step. There is a weakness in her character, one that she has successfully concealed from almost everyone— trainers, competitors, superiors, subordinates, and, above all, her father. It is a weakness she shared with her favorite elder sister—or did, until Eldest Sister was condemned as a weakling and paid the penalty. Usually, in most circumstances, Agent First's weakness is no weakness at all. Indeed, to a Leader of Spies and Liars the ability to empathize with one's prey is a valuable asset. But it is a vulnerability—a weakness—that is unacceptable among the nobility of the People. And it affects her now, for what Agent First is required to do in order to commence her mission grinds painfully upon it, causing her deep discomfort. She is already shivering with pangs of nausea, the price of an emotion with no name in the High Tongue, but which she will later learn the cattle-folk call *guilt.*

It is one thing to steal the face of a serf who has been bound and placed before you in the training pits, their life already forfeit. It's one thing to do it beneath the unblinking scrutiny of your trainers, knowing that if you display any hesitation at all it will cause them to question your fitness to serve the All-Highest. Eldest Sister's disgrace has taught Agent First the consequences of revealing weakness, and among the Host empathy *is* weakness, and weakness means death.

But it is an awful thing to have to hunt down and steal the soul of an innocent who has done you no harm, merely because this is what is expected of you and you are bound to obey the iron will of a distant power.

Agent First drifts aimlessly through the stony canyons of the shadow city, waiting to encounter a suitable victim. In the back of her head she is compiling a map, storing it in her memory palace for later transfer to her gems. She's observing and explicating the mores of this land, inasmuch as she can do so while functionally illiterate and unable to understand the language. The city is very densely constructed by the standards of the People. The buildings are ugly and cramped, the gardens tiny and badly maintained, the costumes of the round-eared natives are drab and uncomfortable-looking. There is little sense of *mana* here, no sign of constructed conduits for power, no sign of industrial civilization—but there must be *something*, some eldritch force that causes lights to glow and carts to snarl and rumble through the poorly maintained streets. This is clearly a land that languishes in the grip of a dark parody of civilization, and perhaps if she could get a glimpse of one of the overseer class she would be able to better understand what she is seeing. But in her frustration and distress she decides that the round-eared cattle-folk of this shadow land truly deserve the name her kind uses for such ugly subhuman slaves-to-be: *urük*.

Hours pass as Agent First walks. She passes many people and sees many sights. Her perambulations carry her deep into concrete canyons lined with buildings of a scale that might be described as palaces were they not so utterly bereft of beauty. Some of them are clearly storehouses, possibly clusters of many storehouses gathered together under one roof. Some of them have no obvious purposes, but through unscreened windows she sees many *urük* in curiously drab, uniform clothes sitting in chairs before tables topped with glowing mirrors. As the night deepens, the lights dim and the many-windowed labor-sheds gradually empty. It comes to Agent First that soon there will be few enough people on the streets that she will have no excuse for foot-dragging. If she shirks her duty, the All-Highest will hold her to account sooner or later. Her heart sinks and she retreats into darkened side streets, passing doors lit by brilliantly colored signs from within which waft peculiar smells. Barking, babbling, ugly cattle-people: *Which one of you will I become?*

Her chest feels hollow with a dread that dares not speak its name when she finally sees a likely target. Three young adults have stumbled from the doorway of an establishment that smells of stale beer and buzzes with raucous discourse. It's clearly a tavern or brothel of some sort. They wobble unsteadily along the street ahead of her. She is still learning to parse the dress code sufficiently well to tell genders apart—beards are male-only, long hair is *usually* female, females *often* wear high shoes, and she has yet to see any eunuchs or freemartins at all—but two of them, one man and one woman (or so she thinks) are the worse for wear. They stumble towards one of the curious open-sided glass shelters and huddle beneath a sign, evidently waiting for one of the large carts that sluggishly rumble around the city, picking up serfs and dropping them off elsewhere. Their single companion is less drunk, and Agent First is pretty sure that this one is female—the length of hair and the sway of hips betray her. She says her goodbyes to her friends at the cart-stand then walks on, slowly heading uphill towards a district where many-windowed labor-sheds rub shoulders with more taverns: it seems to be a center of activity among younger adults.

Agent First follows her target along a well-lit road. The target seems aware of her presence, but unalarmed by another solitary female. Finally an opportunity presents itself. There are no pedestrians nearby as Agent First readies the rings on her left hand and accelerates, overhauling the round-eared girl from behind. Catching up, she reaches out with her gloved hand to tap her target on the shoulder.

The woman whirls round. Her expression of momentary alarm fades as she peers into Agent First's face. Agent First stifles her unease, steels her will, and stares right back. The woman is of roughly the right age and build. She wears dark leggings and practical boots, a short kilt around her waist and a short leather coat thrown over baggy layers of knitwear above. *"What is it?"* the woman says. *"Do you need help?"* Puzzlement creeps into her expression as she registers Agent First's lack of comprehension. Now is the moment: Agent First's oath of allegiance tightens its grip on her will and she obeys instinctively, unleashing the power stored in her rings.

It takes much power but barely a heartbeat to suck the target's memories and appearance into the thieves' stones that hangs from her necklace. It is the work of another heartbeat to touch the woman's eyes, mouth, and chest—cardinal points all—with her harshly glowing ringed fingers and utter the Keyword to dispatch her back along the shadow road, screaming silently. The binding she has placed on the woman will carry her to a cell beneath the limestone pavement, where Agent Second will supervise her interrogation. Meanwhile Agent First collapses to her knees beneath a torrent of foaming memories, the raw stuff of identity flooding through her mind and energizing the glamour that disguises her features.

She allows herself a single sob of horror at what she has done. Dread and a sick, nameless emotion fill her for a few seconds, then she forces her treacherous feelings back under control and immerses herself in stolen imagery. Words in an unfamiliar tongue come to her lips unbidden. She lifts her left hand, and turns it in front of her face, struggling to remember her victim's true name, the stolen key that will give her access to everything. It's on the tip of her tongue, waiting for her: then everything she stole from the *urük* girl comes flooding in.

She turns stiffly, taking a deep breath. The kebab shop she saw when she first arrived is barely half a kilometer away, and business will be slow half an hour before pub closing time. It's an easy walk, and the guys behind the counter will give her a large döner without questioning if she flashes them her glamour-enhanced smile and tells them what she wants.

"My name is Cassiopeia Brewer," she tells herself, the English phonemes rough and misshapen in her mouth, the curiously flattened Yorkshire vowels a vexing puzzle (for in the tongue of the People, regional accents are unthinkable deviations from the will of the All-Highest). "I am twenty-two years old. I am a scholar—no, a *student*— studying *Performance* at *Leeds Beckett University*." She smiles painfully, forcing her traitor knees to tense, leaning against the wall of the hospital car park as she rises to her feet. "Yes Yes! And my friends call me *Cassie*."

PART 2

MEETING DR. RIGHT

7: MEET CUTE

The next Monday morning, Alex is scheduled to attend an orientation meeting at Quarry House, the proposed new headquarters building in Leeds city center. He isn't too enthused by the prospect of being out and about in daylight, but he manages to combustion-proof himself against the miserable gray overcast that passes for early spring in West Yorkshire by means of a hoodie, gloves, dark glasses, and a pancake-thick layer of theatrical makeup. (Summer is going to present an entirely new set of obstacles if they insist on him working here, but summer is still months away.) Rather than risking his neck on a moped in rush-hour traffic around the Inner Loop, he walks down the hill and catches a bus to the proposed new office. It's easy enough to reach, being right opposite the central bus station, just north of the river, in the rotting concrete armpit between York Road and Marsh Lane.

Quarry House squats menacingly atop the same low hill as West Yorkshire Playhouse and the Leeds College of Music. It was built in the early 1980s as the headquarters of the Department of Health and Social Security, and it's hardened by design against the twin shibboleths of that period—race riots and a nuclear war with the Soviet Union. It's nicknamed the Ministry of Truth for good reason: there are no windows on the first or second floors and there's a bomb shelter in the basement. (The previous building on its site was earmarked by the Gestapo for their Headquarters, Northern England, after the planned Nazi invasion of Great Britain.) Surmounting its central atrium is a peculiar landmark—a tower not unlike a giant stainless steel syringe needle on which is impaled a chromed metal toroid supported by flying buttresses—purpose unknown. Its overall aspect is brutal, a modernist bureaucratic fortress.

"No, seriously Alex, how could you possibly think there's anything inappropriate about a classified entity planning to move into the Ministry of Truth?" Pete asks, when Alex expresses this thought to him as they wait for their coffees in the cafeteria queue. "Next you'll be asking if it's true about the swimming pool!"

"Swimming . . . pool?" Alex blinks at Pete. He's been up all night, grappling fruitlessly with a maze of twisty little expense claim forms (supposedly the organization will be paying his hotel bill—if he can fill out all the paperwork correctly) and he's slightly frazzled this morning.

"The health club in the basement has a swimming pool," Pete explains.

"The health club." Two coffees materialize on the counter: a flat white, two shots for Pete, and a gigantic mocha, capped with a swirl of gradually deflating whipped cream, for Alex. (Ordered with decaf: Alex isn't *that* tired.) "There's a health club?"

"Yup, and quite a nice one. They built in back in the early eighties when they were trying to give London-based DHSS staff an incentive to move up to Leeds. Complete with a pool—it doubles as a water reservoir and radiation shielding for the bunker in time of civil disorder or war. It's open to the public these days but"—Pete touches the side of his nose—"I gather we've got plans for it."

"Plans." Alex blinks. Something tickles his memories. "You don't mean BLUE HADES?" A few weeks ago he was on his way into the New Annex when he had to step aside to make way for an extremely pretty blonde in a motorized chair. Then he looked at her a second time and realized there was something really odd about her skin. But she was talking animatedly to the terrifying Dr. O'Brien, and if *she* didn't know she was chatting with a Deep One in a bath chair, then clearly there was no hope, so . . .

Pete shrugs. "Health and safety regs. If they send us liaison officers, we've got to provide them with suitable office accommodation, you know what I'm saying?"

"Liaison officers." Alex tries it on for size. "The Deep Ones are sending us liaison officers."

"Ssh, there are civilians about." Pete takes his flat white and scans the room for a spot as far away from the windows—and neighbors—as possible. They take a spindly designerish table in an unpopular corner close by the kitchen entrance. He sits down. "Doris dropped it on me via email this morning: we got the lease."

"We got the—" Alex stops. "Oh right."

"Yes. The Department of Health folks are being shipped out to a new purpose-built campus around the back of St. Jimmie's, with plenty of space for private insurance companies to set up shop." Pete sips his coffee. "As for the DWP, I'm not sure *where* they're going. Probably Manchester. But the point is, both departments should be out the door completely by the end of the year. Meanwhile, *we* have got office space in here from the beginning of next week—we're moving out of that fleapit in Headingley." He means the Arndale office. "So we have to establish an internal security perimeter to SOE-approved standards, set up and deploy perimeter wards for the site, survey the hell out of the entire neighborhood, and *really* make sure any inactive ley lines in central Leeds are identified and capped off."

"We don't want to leave any open back doors?"

"No kidding." Pete shudders slightly. The last two major head-quarter sites had disastrous weaknesses, and people died as a result. People Pete and Alex knew. "We've got a briefing in room 424 today. Then we get to walk the grounds with K-22s, looking for anomalies—we're dogsbodies on this one, but I think the idea is to familiarize us with the floor plan while having us do something boring but useful."

"Happy joy."

"Don't you start again." Alex does a double-take: the normally sunny and open Pete looks quietly frustrated—almost angry. "Sandy is back home looking after a colicky baby by herself, I'm shamefully neglecting my parish, I've got a backlog of reports to process, and now this! I should jolly well tell—" Pete stops, but not without a visible effort. "Sorry. Must think happy thoughts."

Alex is set back in his seat. He stares at his mentor. Pete doesn't *do* angry, as a rule. He's a vicar: he's an expert not only on Aramaic apocalyptic scriptures but on helping people deal with life's major milestones. Grief counseling, marriage guidance, deaths in the family, all the emotionally demanding situations that Alex has never had to face (for which he is extremely grateful, when he gives the matter time for thought). Pete has had to comfort so many people for whom things are going terribly, unbelievably badly that he keeps his own personal life in an emotional containment grid. So to see it bleeding over into his attitude to work shocks Alex rigid. "Are you—" Alex licks his lips. "Are they going to make you move up here?"

Pete knocks back his coffee, and grimaces. Alex takes a mouthful of his own and his lips curl involuntarily. The coffee is diabolically bad, as if the espresso machine's nozzles haven't been cleaned in living memory. Presumably the permanent staff know better than to drink the overpriced swill in the canteen. Hoping to salvage it, he picks up one of the paper tubes of sugar but fumbles as he tears it open, spilling grains of Demerara across the table. "Shit," he says, trying to tear his eyes away from the mess. He can't help himself: he begins to count. Quietly, anxiously: *"Shit."*

"What's—oh, I see." Pete peers at Alex for a moment as he sits there staring at the spilled granules, trapped by stochasticity. "Let me—"

19. 20. 21. "Wait," Alex manages to say. *25. 26. 27.* The sugar granules fill his vision, urgently enumerating, hyperreal, pulsing for attention. "I need to figure this out."

"Figure out what? If it's just the arithmomania again, I can tidy—"

"No." Cold sweat prickles on Alex's forehead. "This keeps happening." *42. 43. 44. 45.* "I need a better solution. Not sweeping it under the rug." *52. 53. 54.* "It's debilitating."

"Is it getting worse?" Pete asks gently.

"I think so." His forehead turns hot. *66. 67. 68.* "I had a mild case of the counting bug before, uh, before I turned. But this is much worse." *70. 71. 72. 73.* "I know it's part of the folklore about vampires, but it's a real thing, too. Compulsive counting." *79. 80. 81.* "It's in my *head*, damn it, the V-symbiotes *want to know how many*—"

"You're a programmer, aren't you? Can't you come up with a way to count it for them?"

"It's not that simple, counting isn't just—" *A recursive integer function: Come on, how hard can it be?* Alex shakes his head, as if irritated by a passing fly. "Wait a moment." *95. 96. 97.* Alex forces the numbers to stop, pinning the grains of sugar to the melamine table top by sheer force of will. He mumbles to himself under his breath, haltingly, hoping he's got the syntax right. He's speaking Old Enochian, the ancient formal language the Laundry's necromancers use for bossing unruly mindless horrors around. It's not much of a numerical language but it's good at semantic interpolation and you can do basic arithmetic with string substitution, it's just lousy-inefficient—

"Alex?" Pete asks quietly.

"Wait. Metaprogramming." Interrupting his flow takes conscious effort and Alex starts again, but this time it comes easily to mind: a short looping construct wrapped in a conditional proposition that hovers and writhes in his visual field. It's a trivial piece of ritual magic, a mere cantrip. The trick is the recursive element, because if you can distract a vampire by forcing him to count grains of sugar or salt or rice linearly, you can brute-force his attention by dumping a huge sack of the stuff on him—but not if he uses a chunking algorithm. To a normal human magician this sort of usage would be unacceptably dangerous, attracting the eaters that cause K syndrome, but Alex is already infested with V-symbiotes: things can't get any worse. And now he has an answer: "Two hundred and thirty-six," he says contentedly, then sweeps the spilled sugar onto the floor. "*Thank* you, Pete. That was brilliant."

"I didn't do anything." Pete looks distant, unhappy. Alex feels a flash of disappointment. Then he remembers his question, right before the spill.

"Are they going to try to move you up here?" he repeats.

"I should hope not," Pete says flatly. "Because if they do, I shall have to ask my bishop for guidance. I can't continue to neglect my parish duties. It's actively damaging."

Boss fight between the Church of England and the Laundry: Who wins? Alex shakes his head. "Let's go and get started on this bullshit work assignment," he suggests. "Then we can get set up in a secure office and you can go yell at HR. Maybe they'll listen this time?"

"They're idiots," Pete grumps. "Sorry. I mean they're not idiots: they're overworked, understaffed, under-budgeted, and their morale is in the pits, just like the rest of us. They're mostly doing the best they can. *But*—"

"Never attribute to malice that which can be explained by incompetence or overwork?" Alex asks, rising.

"Something like that. But there's a point at which sufficient incompetence *is* malice."

Alex, remembering his sometime co-worker Basil Northcote-Robinson, follows him to the lifts in silence.

And now for a flashback:

Cassie walks through the sleazy studentland of Leeds late at night, eyes wide with wonder. Around her, everything old is new again, and strangely enchanting besides. It's familiar from memory but she feels as if she's seeing it clearly for the first time. *This* is a dustbin; *that* is a parked motorbike. She's simultaneously entranced, contemptuous, and horrified, her hidden second identity lending a strange parallax to her perceptions, crowding and jostling with the fresh insights of an alien abroad in a new world.

Inside her head two distinct sets of memories mingle uneasily; behind them, other half-remembered ghost identities wail and rattle the bars of their cages. Agent First has stolen identities before, but after the task was accomplished she suppressed them with relief, retaining only faint impressions of their original owners' lives. But Agent First has drunk deep from the well of Cassiopeia, as this is not a normal mission. Most masks need only be worn for a handful of days, but Agent First has no idea how long she will have to be Cassie. It might be for several moons, or even longer: if the unthinkable happens, it might be for the rest of her life. So she has taken a far deeper imprinting than is customary or even safe, and her sense of her own identity is dangerously fragile.

Cassie believes that she is Agent First of Spies and Liars, daughter of the former General-Overseer of the 14th Western Host of Air and Darkness, who is now the All-Highest of the Morningstar Empire (or what remains of it, all other claimants to that status having been crushed by the ancient horrors that ate the moon). But at the same time she is also Cassiopeia Brewer, aged 22, a cheerfully extrovert art and drama student. Her work: theatrical management, lighting effects, set design. Her hobbies: costuming, music, and a heavy paranormal romance reading habit. Her personal life: plenty of friends, a handful of BFFs, no sultry smoking vampire boyfriends on the horizon. Her upbringing: from the backstreets of Hull to breakout and departure for the bright lights of the nearest metropolis by way of an academy school. Next stop: London or LA.

This is the cause of no little perplexity to Agent First. Agent First understands *work*, of course: she is trained and prepared for infiltration, assassination, and skullduggery. But there's more to Cassie than work alone, and the linked concepts of *fun* and *hobby* strike Agent First as perversely indulgent, alarmingly decadent, and dangerously frivolous. Such things are at best a distraction from the urgent demands of survival. (As to *friendship*, there is no one word in the High Tongue that can express the concept. Her upbringing was a single-minded death march dedicated to training her for this particular type of mission, and her current life a desperate struggle to assert her value in the face of her stepmother's implacable hostility. Next stop: incredulous envy.)

Cassie has a loving but work-weary mother and a laid-back, drily amused older brother with *no ambitions whatsoever* (interests: beer, football, cars). She had a father she secretly worshipped behind her mask of teenage disdain, before a premature heart attack carried him away when she was seventeen. She has student loans which she refuses to worry about, and she supplements her income with casual jobs in pubs and cafes. Latterly she's acquired an unpaid acting gig—grist for her CV—which will take her to Whitby and (who knows?) perhaps even into the Playhouse for an amateur run. But what she really wants is to get into set and costume design and, eventually, build a career in television production.

Agent First finds all of these concepts profoundly disorienting. There is a fetish called *money* that the *urük* are obsessed with, for they collect and exchange it at every opportunity. They use money to *pay* for goods and services, as if they have no clear way of understanding hierarchy and obligations, that which is demanded by those to whom submission is due. Worse: they have social axioms like *love* and *friendship* that denote circumstances in which the normal traffic of obligation is suspended for purely emotional reasons. Their family groups are incoherent and preposterous, their relationships chaotic and insecure, no vassals owing allegiance to their betters, no nobles owing—

Well, there *is* a queen. Cassie has memories of seeing her on television, waving and smiling. Waving and *smiling*, not smiting. It's a mystery. How does this ancient and undoubtedly powerful sorceress compel the obedience of so many millions of subjects, if she refrains from smiting?

The part of Agent First which is Cassiopeia Brewer accepts with equanimity the apparent randomness and chaos of the *urük* empire (which is not, it appears, one end of a continental peninsula, but merely a large island off the coast of the continent, isolated by some ancient deluge). To Cassie, this is simply the way things are. Cassie is cheerful, happy-go-lucky, and so totally uninterested in politics, diplomacy, geography, war, history, or necromancy—the key areas Agent First has been tasked with reporting on—that for Agent First's purposes Cassie might as well be an illiterate serf. Her head is cluttered with nonsensical lies, legends, fashions, and folklore: stories told for entertainment, not enlightenment. Indeed, Agent First ruefully wonders whether it might be better to set aside Cassiopeia Brewer's mask and steal another face. If only she had enough stored *mana* to perform the ritual again! And if only being Cassie wasn't so much more fun than being Agent First.

Cassie walks home in a light-headed daze, marveling at her surroundings. Things that she was taught to be afraid of (dark alleyways, damaged streetlights, drunken strangers) pose no threat to her now: Agent First can deal with situations that would leave the original Cassie puking in terror. Meanwhile, Agent First is reveling in Cassie's alien aesthetics, memories that paint the space around her with a wash of comforting familiarity. *That* is a bus; *this* is a taxi; you cross a road safely *like so*.

Eventually she finds her way back to her digs. Rather than one of the system-built student flats, Cassie has a room in a shared Victorian terrace house in Headingley, on the edge of Woodhouse Moor. She lets herself in silently (for along with Cassie's face and memories she took her handbag, purse, keys, and phone), pads upstairs to her room (a part of her sniffs irritably at the sink full of dishes and the empty pizza boxes on the kitchen table), and falls into bed. Then she spends the next six hours in a dream-wracked, uneasy slumber, as the two halves of her raveled memories knit themselves together.

Agent First awakens to a dilemma, brought about by her appreciation of the full extent of Cassiopeia Brewer's ignorance. To be honest, Cassiopeia Brewer was not merely a poor choice of identity to steal, but a terrible one. If she is true to her mission, Agent First should rectify this oversight as soon as possible. But it takes a lot of *mana* to steal the face and memories of an unwilling victim: *mana* that Agent First does not have.

The Host is desperately low on supplies and equipment—and, indeed, on spies—thanks to the war that smashed the moons, invited in the Ancient Ones, and destroyed most of the Morningstar Empire and all its rivals. The Host is also low on *mana*, the stored form of thaum power, thanks to All-Highest's attempt to conserve his force by out-hibernating their foes. Agent First was sent forth with a barely energized mace (doubtless the consequence of her stepmother's machinations) and she will have to scrabble for what power sources she can find by herself. She is proficient in the grand patternings that can draw *mana* from the land, but to perform such a rite will draw the attention of any magi within a hundred leagues.

There are ley lines in every world that connect power points and deliver a trickle to anyone who has the wherewithal to capture it stealthily. And she has the mace by way of a storage vessel. So when she awakens on her first day as Cassie—careful not to disturb her flatmates, who are either attending lectures or still abed—she follows her instincts and the number 93 bus route to the city ring road and beyond. A tree-lined main road leads out of town towards Bramhope and Golden Acre Park. There is an upwelling here, and she walks some distance into the park. The daffodils are just beginning to unfold their golden trumpets beneath the still-skeletal branches of the oaks and birches as she follows the prickling in her fingertips towards the strongest flux. She's almost dancing on the tips of her toes: it's a lovely cold spring day, a good day to be alive. The sky above her is reassuringly stable, not lit by the summer lightning of meteors, the in-falling bones of the murdered moon beyond the horizon. Laughter wells up at the back of her throat as she looks around in delight. Her fingers and toes lead her to one side of a muddy path, where a bed of crocuses flower. Here, after quickly checking that nobody is watching her, she bends and plants the stem of her mace among the bulbs soaking up the life and power of this new world. Then she squats and meditates, pushing her awareness into the amethyst she wears at the base of her throat.

The oracular charm is hazy, distanced from her awareness as if shrouded by gauze. But there is a sense of *rightness* to her presence here. She is in the correct place, the stone appears to indicate. She is in the right body. Or at least not in a body inimical to her future. She is still capable of making progress, of obeying the *geasa* she is controlled by, if only she can see how—but Cassie's memories are infuriatingly vague. She knows nothing of the powers that rule this realm, let alone their true names. Oddly, she *does* know some legends that, stripped of their more nonsensical accretions, might reflect folk-memory myths of captives released by the People—but Agent First is reassured to note that they are so garbled as to be worse than valueless.

Cassie was scheduled to attend a lecture and a tutorial this afternoon, so as a test of how well she has internalized her new identity, Agent First goes to college. She joins in the idle gossip and amiable chatter of her fellow students, sits through an hour-long talk on the subject of theatrical accounting—she finds it unexpectedly riveting and makes copious notes as she tries to understand what these alien concepts *mean*—while around her Cassie's classmates fight to stay awake by making snarky comments on Snapchat. Her head is spinning pleasantly afterwards (money: oh yes, it's a concretized form of accounting for obligations, but *how* does it compel you to obey your owner? Does it carry some sort of *geas* of its own?), but there's no time to work it all out. Instead she has a tutorial with Ronnie (basic blonde but too sweet to call a bitch) and Tiger (male, shaggy, queer as a three-bob note, *rowwr*) and a couple of other cast members from the am. dram. group they're setting up to do *Dracula* at the goth festival. They're meeting with their facilitator, Dr. Chesley, to go over the plans for the dress rehearsal in Whitby next weekend. There are a ton of jobs to finish before then: costumes, timing, the route between scenes, what to do in event of bad weather. And while listening to her castmates discuss these things, Agent First has her epiphany.

Cassiopeia Brewer's memories and training are useless for Agent First's purposes, and her identity and role do not lend themselves to infiltration. In many respects she's a complete liability. But Cassie is good at *people*. What's more, in this strangely childish culture where people are allowed to *like* one another and be *best friends forever* instead of competing to avoid punishment, Cassie is *bubbly* and *popular* and *likeable*. She may not have enough *mana* to steal another face, or enough local knowledge to even know whose face is worth stealing, but all Agent First needs to do is ensure that Cassie meets as many people as possible. Sooner or later, she will meet someone useful and important. And when that happens, she'll *make* them like her.

"Listen, this is weird," Alex is telling Pete as Jez Wilson pauses in the office doorway. They're peering into the murky depths of a desktop monitor that is displaying a map with topographic overlays. "I swear I didn't spot anything when I was doing the walk-through the day before yesterday but this"—he points at an indistinct blob on the screen—"should be showing up like a . . ." He trails off uncertainly as he notices Jez waiting for him to notice her. "Hi," he says, as nervously as a schoolboy caught with his hand in a sweet jar.

"Hi yourself." She nods at Pete. "How's it going?"

"I think Alex has found something." Pete sounds uncharacteristically self-satisfied.

"Found what?"

"A new ley line," Alex mumbles.

Jez leans close to the screen, squinting. "Tell me," she says. She's in Leeds for three days this week to check up on the security ward extension survey and to meet with the site security planners. Alex is walking the streets around and just south of the river, checking for residual thaum eddies and abandoned invocations. The area around the River Aire has been settled for centuries, and many generations of hedge witches have left their mark on the landscape.

"Here." Alex points at a street map of the surrounding square kilometer or so south of Quarry Hill. It's centered on a complex of buildings alongside a lock used by canal boats traversing the river. "We expect ley lines to join major prehistoric sacrificial sites and to track the local geophysics model, don't we? And we've got a complex cluster here on the hill, connecting us northwest to the Yorkshire Dales, northeast to York, and south to the cluster around Doncaster—"

"Yes." Jez nods. "Well?"

"Well, this morning I was logging an outer perimeter walk, out towards the Hunslet Road, when I got an anomalous thaum spike. So I walked Black Bull Street and Carlisle Road and picked it up again, and when I plot it, I get this." He points to the map on the screen. Three points show up in red along a line running due south of the government offices on Quarry Hill. "What's interesting is I *didn't* get a reading on East Street or Duke Street. If it's a ley line, it's a new one since the last survey, and it terminates somewhere around here." His finger hovers over Clarence Dock, a small rectangular harbor a couple hundred meters south of the office. "Near the museum."

Jez frowns. "Yeah, it's a new one. Any ideas?" she asks, looking at Pete.

Pete shrugs. "Anomalous readings, but it doesn't look like faulty equipment to me," he says. "The river's been used for transport since the Norman invasion. Could that be something to do with it?"

"Maybe. Or maybe a geophysical shift somewhere else has opened up a new fault line. Can't remember hearing about any earthquakes, though." Jez shoves back a stray lock of hair and glances at the clock on Alex's computer desktop. It's nearly lunchtime. The weather is overcast and cloudy, threatening rain this afternoon. She's acutely aware that Alex's pancake of sunblock conceals reddened and peeling skin. "Do you want to check it out this evening, after sunset?" she asks.

"I've got an idea it's something to do with the museum," Alex volunteers.

"Really?"

"Ley lines are associated with graves and sacrificial sites as well as topography. When they're not emergent geological phenomena they're usually necromantically powered," Alex points out. Pete's face freezes, but he holds his peace. "The museum is, uh, it's the Royal Armouries, right? It's full of swords and stuff, much of which has been used. If there's a strong concentration of blooded weapons under one roof, close to an existing nexus—like the hill, here—wouldn't that maybe tend to set up a secondary resonance? Could that have attracted some wandering power source and given it a route to ground?"

"Huh." Jez runs a hand through her hair, shoving it back from her face. "Yes, that's possible. You ought to talk to Vik Choudhury about secondary sites, and maybe email Mr. Howard"—Alex twitches at the name—"in case there's something about it in the nonclassified wiki. Hmm. The museum covers quite an area, doesn't it? How would you like to nip round there after lunch and take some informal readings? If it *is* a local secondary resonance, rather than something to do with the river, that'll give us something to work with. We need to know if it goes anywhere useful."

The museum is indoors and mostly windowless. Jez can send him there with a clean conscience and a good chance of answering the question. He's right: weapons that have drunk deep of human blood are a good bet for a ley line disturbance. Just as the sites of unquiet deaths tend to be associated with ghosts and hauntings, the paraphernalia and tools of torment can generate occult resonances. "Do you have anything else you're working on that's a higher priority?"

"I've got plenty of training courseware to keep me busy in the background," Alex admits. "And a meeting about internal marketization of outsourced technical support services at four." He rolls his eyes.

"Then you ought to get out of the office for a couple of hours after lunch." Jez smiles wearily. "Go on, go visit the museum. It can't do any harm, can it?"

And so it comes to pass that, instead of lunching in one of the Quarry House canteens and then slaving over a stack of training worksheets for a couple of hours, Alex scuttles out beneath a rain-heavy sky and spends the first half of the afternoon taking discreet thaum flux measurements on his smartphone while gaping at one of the largest collections of murder cutlery in the entire world.

The Royal Armouries collection was originally housed and stored at the Tower of London, where since time immemorial the monarchy (and subsequently the British armed forces) maintained a magpie's nest of all things bright and stabby. But by the end of the twentieth century the collection was overflowing, and only a tiny fraction could be put on display. In the early years of the twenty-first century various national museum collections were moved away from London and its suburbs, on the not-unreasonable theory that improving the cultural life of the nation was a good thing. (In reality, the overheated property market in the capital meant that the Crown Estates could sell off central London sites, build and stock palatial new museums in outlying cities, and make a tidy profit at the same time.) The Royal Armouries were one of the collections that got the treatment. So a shiny new national museum was built in the Luftwaffe-flattened industrial wasteland of south Leeds, next to the Leeds Docks arts and cultural complex: a concrete invader from the War Dimension, with an entry corridor lined with heavy machine guns.*

(At least, that's the cover story.)

Alex makes his way in, past signs advertising a huge animated film festival that's coming to town later that month, then walks the main corridor. Ahead of him a circular staircase spirals up a five-story-high tower lined with porthole-like windows. As he approaches it the

---

* The complex is more than just a museum. The British government has obsessively collected firearms since 1631—maintaining a complete working example of every single handgun and small arm under the sun. The national firearms collection known as the Enfield Pattern Room was formerly located at the Royal Small Arms Factory in Enfield. But when the new museum opened in Leeds, the contents of the Pattern Room were relocated to a very discreet secure building close to the museum site. But Alex is unaware of the NFC at this time. Which is perhaps all for the best.

thaum flux display on his phone rises alarmingly. In the middle of the floor, right below the stairs, sits an odd display case. He sidles up to it cautiously—it's uncomfortably well-lit by daylight streaming through the ports above—and he tugs his jacket cuffs down over his gloves as the skin around his wrists dries and tightens painfully. It's *not* a display case, he realizes, with growing astonishment: it's an octagonal array of polished mirrors, angled upwards to show the reflected walls of the tower, a tower lined with—

"Holy shit," he subvocalizes, awestruck. *We're going to need swords: lots of swords.* The towering inner walls of the stairwell of the Hall of Steel are lined with cold iron. Halberds and spears and swords and arrows bristle at the sky, floral wreaths of death brandished triumphant at the ceiling. As he walks around the central reflector, peering into each mirror in turn, Alex sees two-thirds of a millennium of war hanging overhead. Almost without thinking, he invokes his counter cantrip: it reports three hundred and sixty-four blood-soaked items hanging on a wall. You can clean the stains off the metal, but you can't erase the memories of souls swallowed: his V-parasites are excited, chittering in the back of his skull at their proximity to so much death. They're not very clear on the flow of time: he senses an edge of frustration to their noise, for the food in question is centuries past its use-by date.

The thaum flux measured by the bluetooth widget in his pocket spikes as he stands in front of the reflector, then drops as he walks back towards the elevators. He rides up to the first floor in thoughtful silence, then through the darkened tunnel of Ancient and Medieval Warfare that leads to the War exhibition. The flux spikes again, and stays high, then the monitor begins to pick up the characteristic fingerprint of a ley line. His pocket dongle isn't as sensitive and directional as a K-22, but it's enough. *I'll have to come back here with Pete,* Alex decides. As he walks past a display of horse armor through the centuries, the thaum flux continues to spike higher. Many of these pieces have seen blood spilled, he realizes. Some of those holes were not made by rust.

It's easy to lose track of time in the windowless maze of weapons, and Alex forgets the outside world for a while. He's gazing, increasingly disturbed, at an exhibit on the horrors of trench warfare when his phone vibrates. *Meeting in fifteen minutes,* it reminds him. "Shit," he mutters, and goes to hunt for the way out. *I'll come back later,* he resolves, and not just to map out the local ley line endpoint and isolate whatever unquiet piece of bloodthirsty history is powering it. The museum is only a ten-minute walk from the new offices: he wonders vaguely if it's the sort of place you could take a date.

It's Tuesday afternoon and the sky is covered by a slate-gray slab of cloud, the vanguard of a frontal system blowing in across the Pennines. The canyonlike pavements on the south side of the city center smell of rain and dogshit, and Alex is footsore and irritated as he nears the end of his beat. He's carried the K-22 scanner out past the Royal Armouries, around a chunk of the Inner Loop, and almost as far as the strip mall on the site of the old Tetley's Brewery. Now he's working his way back to Quarry House. His eyes ache, the skin on his face feels hot and dry beneath his factor-200 sunblock, and the logging app on his phone has barely budged the whole while. This part of Leeds is stubbornly dead. Yes, there was a spike in the car park at Staples—old breweries were often built on the site of springs—and there was another, stronger one on the side of the canal lock behind the Armouries, but the Armouries isn't on his route today. Anyway, it'll probably get assigned to someone else as soon as the team from Exorcism Services in Liverpool arrive on Wednesday.

In the meantime, however, Alex—whose contract of employment stipulates that he is not required to go out in daylight at any time unless under exceptional circumstances meriting hazard pay—has just racked up *four hours* of stumbling about in overcast daylight. To PHANG senses this is as searing as high noon in the Sahara desert. He's in a profoundly bad mood as he trudges across the Playhouse car park towards the side entrance to Quarry House. It occurs to him to wonder whether he has grounds to file a formal complaint against the idiots who assigned him a daylight task that could perfectly well have been carried out after midnight. *It's ableist at a minimum, displaying a lack of sensitivity for diversity in the workplace—*

"Hey, Quincey! I mean, Alex! What are you doing here?"

Alex's train of thought derails instantly under the impact of a sparkling smile framed by verdigris hair. The owner of the smile is wearing a black biker's jacket over a polka-dot dress, black leggings that terminate in giant Doc Martens laced almost up to her knees, and electric blue bootlaces. Her hair is the color of church bells left out in the rain, tied up in pigtails that reveal multiply pierced ears rising to adorable little points. For a moment he can't work out why she looks familiar: then he flashes back to Whitby, the Brides of Dracula, and his borrowed jacket.

"You're, uh—" He racks his brain, aghast at how easily his traitor memory let slip her name.

"Cassie?" she says, still smiling brilliantly.

His throat clenches. It feels as if his ward is burning—but that's obviously psychosomatic because the back of his brain is shrieking *Help! A girl is smiling at me! I don't know what to do*, and he seems to have forgotten how to breathe. But after a second he manages to say, "Hi, Cassie," and then he contorts his face at her, *almost* like a normal human being grinning or baring his teeth or something. *Oh God don't show her your teeth.* "I work in that office. What are *you* doing here?"

"I work"—a toss of her head indicates the squat windowless block to the left of Quarry House, a Mini-Me to the government building's Dr. Evil—"there! At least right now, I mean, I'm enrolled in a course in theatrical design and management and we're doing practical work backstage at the Playhouse."

They stand in the half-empty car park and smile at each other like amnesiac star-crossed lovers who know they're supposed to say something but who have both lost the script. But what is going through their heads in those few seconds couldn't be more different:

For Alex, it is as if the gray heavens have briefly parted to admit a single perfect sunbeam, focussing on the patch of pavement in front of him where Cassie is standing. She's a girl, and she's smiling at him, and she remembered his name from a brief encounter more than two weeks ago, and if his brain was a computer it'd be throwing segmentation faults and dumping core because this is so utterly outside Alex's lived experience that he doesn't know what to do next. Unlike the late and unlamented Evan—the PHANG pickup artist—Alex is somewhat introverted, timid, and under-socialized. Cassie is out of his league: but she's being *friendly*. And, truth be told, standing in a car park smiling at her like an idiot is the most fun that he's had for days. Even though it's beginning to rain, and the ward around his neck feels like it's choking him.

For Cassie, it's as if the dark and turbid mists of destiny have blown away to reveal a coruscating finger of prophetic brilliance, lighting up the asphalt car park around her. The oracular stone of power at the base of her throat is shrieking in the back of her head, *This is the one*, as she smiles, awestruck, at the young magus standing before her with a puzzled smile on his face. Agent First is attuned to *mana*, and Alex is full of it. She sensed it briefly along the cliffside path in Whitby, but she'd been unsure: she'd left the stone back in her room in Leeds, unwilling to risk it as part of her stage costume. She'd invited him to the party in hope of getting a closer look but he never showed up, and she'd gradually persuaded herself that she'd been wrong, jumping at shadows after so long alone in the field. But now she can see him with the oracle stone against her skin, and her toes and fingertips are on fire with his power. Alex is clearly a practitioner of considerable power. The refrain of one of Cassie's dad's favorite songs runs through her head—*bait the line, set the trap, catch the man*—and her knees weaken, an outcome bred in the bone by five hundred generations of selection for deference to power. But she forces herself to face him down, keeping her smile-mask intact, showing no sign of terror or adoration.

And so they stand and smile at one another, both unsure what to do next, until Alex's "I've got to check in at the office—" collides with Cassie's "Fancy a coffee?" And they stall.

"Coffee?" Alex echoes.

"Office?"

"There."

"Where?"

"Second floor, west wing, uh, I *really* need to drop this file off before I go home for the day but I can be out in fifteen minutes—"

"That's okay, why don't we meet up in the Playhouse bar?"

"Where—"

"That door there." Cassie points vaguely. She's afire with his power. Alex burns by daylight, metaphysically, and although he dresses like an accountancy clerk and his skin's a mess there's a strength to him that makes her certain that everything Cassie thinks she knows about the *urük* empire's masters is wrong. "I'll wait around."

"Uh, okay. Yeah, be right back, don't go 'way . . ."

Alex nearly trips over his own feet as he stumbles hastily towards the side entrance to the government office complex. *What,* he wonders bewilderedly, *is happening to me?* He's more used to summoning demons, drinking blood, and consorting with vicars than he is to being invited to join cute green-haired girls for coffee. But as he rushes back to room 424 to drop off the K-22 kit and download his readings, he can't help feeling a strange, light-hearted hope that this chance encounter might mark the start of another stage in his life.

Oh, Father. Cassie waits at the Playhouse bar, trying not to tap her toes impatiently as the barista polishes glasses by the dishwasher and natters to one of his heavily tattooed buddies. *Let me be right about this one. Just this once.* She forces herself to stillness, calling upon resources that Agent First has learned over the course of a lifetime of deadly lessons. *He must* come! *He* must!

In Whitby she'd expected him to follow her to the party, englamoured—she'd seen her own eagerness reflected in his eyes, the attraction of power towards its own reflection—but then he'd evaporated into the night, leaving her swearing, without even a hair or drop of blood for her to track him by.

Now she's let him go *again*—but at least she knows: second floor, west wing, Ministry of Truth. *Alex works for the government.* Which, as she now understands, is a proxy for the exercise of power by the unseen sorcerers who rule this nation from the shadows. They are curiously diffident, these magi, for ones who only a century ago ruled an empire upon which the sun never set. In recent years they seem to have stepped back behind a curtain of silence, making a pretense of delegating their power to a strange, toothless commonwealth and a queen of no particular magic. They leave the steel gauntlets of martial glory out for younger upstart nations to play with: but they are still here, lurking in the background. Of that much Agent First is utterly certain. If it were not so, Great Britain would have fallen long ago, wouldn't it? In Agent First's world, the ineluctable law of power is that you rule or you die.

To Agent First, the puppet show of democracy that Cassie believes in is obviously a child's tissue of attractive lies, set before the cattle to enable the secret rulers to dominate them without fear of uprisings. It obviates the need to instill *geasa* of binding upon every individual subject, making possible huge economies of scale in the application of *force majeure*. (Subjects whose mind-bogglingly vast numbers beggar Agent First's imagination: it makes no sense, who *needs* that many slaves?) But to rule effectively from behind the stage curtain, the unseen theatrical directors that call the tunes in this production must send actors out among the audience to work their will. Alex shows every sign of being such a person. Outwardly he wears the guise of a gray man—deliberately average and forgettable. But he is robed in tremendous power for those with an inner eye with which to see him—an inner eye which most of the *urük* appear to lack. And he works for the government. What else could he be, but an agent-magus serving the secret rulers?

He's got to come, he's got to— The barista notices her. "Venti soy mocha with an extra shot, cream *and* cinnamon on top," she rattles automatically—*come, he's got to*—

"Hi!" Alex squeaks behind her shoulder, his voice breaking bat-high with nerves.

Cassie jumps. He moves surprisingly silently: he's close enough that she can feel his breath. "Hi!" She sparkles back, then forces herself to get a grip. She's not sure whether to be embarrassed or terrified at the way he sneaked up on her, and the way her heart pounds in his presence. Her next words are a huge bluff: "What are you having?"

"I'll have a"—he hangs fire, stuttering silence for a few seconds— "a decaf latte?" Another pause. "I'm paying?"

"You don't need to." She's not short of spending money: one of the skills she mastered on her first day as Cassie was walking up to a man in a suit, pointing at the nearest bank machine, and saying: "Give me a hundred pounds." Their eyes glaze as they push the buttons for her, completely defenseless before her will.

"You're a student, right?" He meets her eyes, but there's no soul-gaze there: just a wide-eyed smile. Either he isn't trying (*He suspects nothing!* a reprehensibly dutiful part of Agent First howls triumphantly in the privacy of her mind) or she's adequately shielded. "I'm working. Let me buy this one?"

"Okay!" It's a strain trying to stay bright the whole time, but she manages somehow. The part of her that's Cassie is engaging in some weird etiquette negotiation that she doesn't quite understand, about gendered social interactions and the relative status of scholars and sorcerer-lords, but he seems well-intentioned and it's too transparent to be an attempt to trick her into a transfer of fealty. "Did you finish your work?"

"Yeah, I'm done for the day." As he says it a certain tension fades from his shoulders, and he relaxes very slightly.

Oh look, he's remembered to be human, Cassie's shade remarks acidly. Seen through the eyes of the unenhanced Ms. Brewer, Alex is pretty much a dead loss in the charm stakes. It takes Agent First's uncanny perceptions to see how much more there is to the boy than meets the eye. She studies Alex at close quarters. For an *urük* he's not totally ugly, and his skin isn't bad: but he's wearing an implausible quantity of theatrical powder for some reason. Cassie's memories suggest that this is *not normal* for a male office-worker in this place. Especially as the rest of him, apart from the *mana* that oozes from his every pore, seems determinedly mundane. "Huh," she says, "I've finished work, too." She pauses for a beat. "Are you in rep as well?"

"In rep—" He freezes again. (Original Cassie would find his zoning out hopelessly uncool. Agent First thinks it fascinating, as if he's pausing while he works out how much he's allowed to tell her. Like a parasitic wasp larva moving under the skin of an unwilling caterpillar host, the real Alex is struggling not to emerge prematurely.) "Oh, you mean acting? Sorry, no: it's just my skin, I burn really easily."

"You mean, sunburn?" She raises an eyebrow at that. "In *this* weather?"

Two coffees appear on the bar behind her: Alex produces a banknote, somewhat rumpled and sweaty from spending time in his trouser pocket. As he pays she takes her cup and walks towards a table, putting a little primate-signaling jiggle in her stride, glancing over her shoulder to see if he's paying attention. She doesn't dare attempt to englamour a magus—she's not suicidal—but the *urük* appear not to castrate their magi to render them tractable, which leaves them interestingly open to other forms of manipulation.

"Sunburn." Alex follows her as if hypnotized, but then sits opposite her and stares moodily down at his coffee. Then he glances up at her and his expression softens. "I came down with, with a medical condition about six months ago," he admits. "I'm hypersensitive to sunlight, among other things."

"Like a vampire," she jokes.

He startles and nearly spills his coffee. "Vampires don't exist!"

She stares at him. "If you say so." She picks up a sachet of sugar and pauses for a moment, frowns. "What about Dracula?"

"Dracula's a cultural archetype. A legend."

Cassie opens the sugar and pours most of it into her coffee. The last few grains she allows to scatter on the table between them. Alex freezes for a couple of seconds. *Got you,* she thinks triumphantly. But then he looks up, faster than should be possible.

"Dracula's not real. I mean, the turning into a flock of bats thing, or a mist, the aversion to crucifixes—it's all rubbish."

She's said or done something wrong: an invisible barrier has risen between them. *Was it the sugar? Did he notice?* "Okay, so they're fictional." *Or is it the narrative?* She shrugs. "But they're fun in films or to read about. Smoking hot and scary at the same time."

"There's nothing hot about them," he says with world-weary conviction; "it's, if it existed it'd be a nasty disease, that's all. One that kills most of its victims and makes life a misery for the survivors. One that prevents them having normal relationships and forces them to—" He stops dead, eyes bulging slightly as if he's a sworn liegeman running up against the edge of his discretion and thinking better of what he was about to say. "Gack. Just joking." He smiles weakly.

Agent First narrows her eyes, exaggerating her natural suspicion: she *knows* that expression. Any remaining doubts she might have harbored evaporate. *Yes, he's a magus, master of blood magic and darkness and bound servant of power. Even if he's resistant to the counting trap.* "Forget it, I was being silly," she says, and smiles back at him. "Are you in town for long?" He nods lugubriously. Her stomach churns. She's perilously close to losing him: every time she tries to turn the conversation somewhere productive she accidentally says something that disturbs him. *What am I doing wrong?* she wails. "I, I wasn't expecting to run into you," she says haltingly. "But if you work so close"—she gestures through the far wall in the direction of the building he disappeared into—"why, we're practically neighbors!"

"I guess we are," he says, and his expression slowly brightens. "I'm here on a temp assignment from London, but it seems likely they'll make it permanent. I wasn't looking forward to it, but I suppose every cloud has a silver lining. How about you?"

"Oh, I'm here for the rest of the year. And I guess next year, too"— a flashover oracular vision of *next year* tells her otherwise, flames roaring skyward, despairing screams from beneath wrecked buildings, the sky a roiling black vortex of smoke—"if nothing bad happens. We're going to do *Dracula* at Whitby for real next week, and they've offered us a one-week matinee run at the Playhouse if it goes well, but Easter vac is coming up, only I'm not going home—"

"Home?"

"To Hull."

"Oh God." His fingers are warm and dry against her hand, and at last she's made a connection. "You have my deepest sympathies."

Got you . . . "Where are *you* from?" she asks, frantically trying to keep up with this unfamiliar game of empathic bridge-building. (It's quite unlike anything she's experienced among the People: nobody would *dream* of speaking so. It's not merely undignified, it's degrading and leaves one vulnerable.)

"I'm from Leeds," he admits glumly.

Cassie can't help herself: she giggles, shocked. "You should run away while there's still time!"

"I tried. They sent me back. There is no escape."

"Listen, it could be worse." Words rise from her stolen memories, an ancient prayer: "From Hell, Hull, and Halifax may the Good Lord preserve us, right?"

"I guess Leeds wasn't around in those days. Otherwise they'd have included it." He realizes he's holding her hand and twitches as if to pull back, but she tightens her grip.

"You're not getting away that easily," she tells him, and she means it. (In her experience the truth is *always* better than a lie: the truth is unlikely to get your eyeballs melted in your head when it's found out, unless your liege is having a particularly bad day.) Anyway, she has a feeling that she'd quite like to see him without his false skins, both the heavy makeup and the slowly dying caterpillar-caul of his Mister Normal disguise: she's certain they conceal a spectacular butterfly, even though (she's upset when she remembers this) she's *geas*-bound to break it on her father's wheel. "You stood me up at the after-party! I had to put up with that ass Jeremy droning on for hours about the Lair of the White Worm. It was no fun!"

"Um, I'm sorry—"

"How would you like to make up for it?" She smiles as she looks him in the eye and pushes just a *tiny* amount of willpower into her gaze. It's enough, because he sits up. "It's pretty fucking dull around here after hours, and my homies are all pissing off for a month in two weeks' time—Easter vac, like I said—and I'm *not* going home to Hull!" She pouts, draws a deep breath, and pushes her chest out just a little.

Alex's eyes don't glaze over, but they lose the tight focus as he visibly makes an effort not to let them drift south towards her chest. "How would you like to go see a movie together after work some time?" he asks.

"I'd like that a lot!" She pulls out her phone. "Hmm. Busy Thursday. A week next Friday I'm off to Whitby for the goth festival . . . how are you for tomorrow? Wednesday?"

"Tomorrow? That would be"—he blinks, surprised—"good."

"Me too! Text me your number and Facebook name," she says, and he turns his phone towards her: there's an address book entry in the name of *Alex Schwartz*, and a menu option to send contact details. *Bingo!* Agent First thinks triumphantly as she keys in her own mobile number. She can barely believe it: Has he really told her his true name? (The *urük* seem oddly fearless about identity theft.) A moment later her phone vibrates. "YesYes!" Cassie beams at him like an out-of-control searchlight. "We have a date!"

8: INTERLUDE: INVADERS MASSING

That night, Agent First returns to the location whence she first arrived in this world. The actual spot is inconveniently close to the middle of Burley Road, which carries more traffic than she is comfortable with, so she waits until the backside of midnight, fuming. It will be necessary to relocate the anchor spot to a more convenient location, one connected to the local ley lines, but she doesn't yet have enough *mana* to do so. Finally the traffic subsides enough to allow her to walk into the road, reopen the portal, and call the first of her agents through from the shadow roads where they have been waiting.

As luck would have it, the cloaked figure steps out of the glowing portal and begins to look around just as a late-night delivery truck rounds the bend, headlights flaring against the darkness. Agent First swears and bundles her disoriented minion out of the way before he's flattened.

Hell of a way to run an invasion, she thinks distractedly. *"Agent Second, report!"* she commands in the High Tongue.

"I hear and obey, mistress." Agent Second stares at her oddly, the whites of his eyes showing all around his dilated pupils: then he shudders and pulls himself together. *"Salutations from All-Highest, and you are to forward your report immediately. I bear a courier beast for your convenience . . ."*

Agent Second throws back one side of his cloak and relaxes his grip. The coatl tastes the smoke-fouled air and hisses vehemently, then raises its hackles. The beast is venomous and can lash out if it feels threatened, even against those it is bound to. Agent First doesn't flinch. *"Good,"* she says. She reaches into the top of her dress and tugs one of the memory gems loose from her necklace, then holds it in front of the courier. *"Excellent creature, bear my offering to All-Highest with all available speed."* A forked tongue flickers out, sampling the air again. Evidently satisfied, the beast's feathers droop slightly and it extends its neck, jaws gaping. There is a trickle of moisture and her hand lightens infinitesimally as the coatl swallows the crystal. It will reside in the beast's gizzard while it makes its way through the shadow roads to All-Highest on his charnel throne, waiting for news from the enemy land. *"Release the beast,"* Agent First commands. Her subordinate makes obeisance to her, then carefully releases the coatl from beneath his garment. There is a flittering of scaly membranous wings and a diminishing hiss, then a flicker of light so far into the violet that it approaches invisibility as it returns to the unreality from which it was summoned by the Host's magi.

She takes a deep breath and focusses on Agent Second. *"Come,"* she commands. *"We have much to discuss."*

"I hear and obey, mistress." She looks at him through half-human eyes, seeing to first approximations a tall, thin man, delicate-boned; the corners of his eyes smoothed by epicanthic folds, the helices of his ears stretched towards points at the top. His lips are plump, his long hair gathered in a braid—gender signifiers among their kind are not as they are among the *urük*. Like most of their species his skin is the brown of almonds, his hair black. The human tongue Cassie speaks has a word to describe him: *elfin*. It is no mere metaphor.

"Follow." She turns downhill towards Kirkstall Road, leading him along a side street past rows of hunched red-brick dwellings and trees that are still barely recovering from winter. Something, she thinks, is not quite right. *"Walk with me on this raised pavement: do not venture into the road lest"*—she is nearly bowled over as Agent Second leaps aside in shock when an elderly hatchback shoots past his right elbow—*"that."*

"What is-is—" Agent Second stutters.

"Our historic records of this world are defective." Agent First is secretly pleased that her own reaction to this realm is not untypical. She is less pleased by her Second's wild-eyed look. She hasn't worked with this man for long, but something about his attitude seems subtly

off. *"These are not savages: there is a civilization here, but it is very strange. They use very little mana, but they are not without powerful artifices—as you just saw, artifices that they make available even to serfs. They lie extensively and willfully, even to their lieges, using obfuscation and misdirection to conceal what is true—I have met only one individual who seemed bound by geas."*

"Ah." Agent Second is silent for a while. They pause at a street corner until there is no sign of traffic, then Agent First leads him on a mad feline dash across the road. Once they gain the safety of the opposite sidewalk, Agent Second asks hesitantly: *"Then these wheeled carts that speed so—they are used by* serfs?*"*

"There are too many of them, far too many. Their breeding has spiraled out of control, and they live in huge hives and barrack-cities of which this one is far from the largest."

"All-Highest will certainly wish to thin the herd," Agent Second opines.

Agent First's stomach lurches at the idea. Cassie has a word for what she feels—*squeamish*—but the High Tongue lacks the concept. She pauses. *"What news of home?"*

"The situation is desperate," Agent Second reports. His head swivels ceaselessly as he scans his surroundings: *"One of the supply depots was found to have been incorrectly sealed when we retreated into slumber. Those responsible have paid for their error, but the Host now have barely enough fodder on hand to feed the heavy brigade's mounts for another tenday. After that time they will have to deploy the cavalry, or start eating the serfs."*

There is a third option, of course, but Agent First doesn't even bother to enquire after it. Slaughtering the mounts is a non-option, for without the heavy brigade the Host will be unable to conduct offensive operations. She knows her father well enough to know what he will do. *"When is the attack scheduled for, and where?"*

"All-Highest has not seen fit to confide in me, my lady. But the Intelligence Section is tasked as a highest priority with capturing and returning to headquarters a magus or other officer with credentials sufficient to gain access to the enemy palace. Bound to All-Highest's will and alive for questioning. I suspect he plans a swift assassination

under cover of a decoy offensive: conquest by subterfuge." Agent Second glances up and down the road, taking in the brutally oppressive buildings of fire-baked clay and stone. *"Are we alone?"* he asks.

Agent First pauses at another pedestrian crossing, glancing both ways along the road. Her sense of danger crystalizes in a split instant. *"I believe so,"* she says, careful not to look directly at Agent Second. *"Why do you ask?"*

A grunt. *"Alas, I am bound and commanded to deliver the fond salutations of your stepmother—"*

A dagger plunges through the darkness but misses its target. Agent Second grunts, falling into a defensive crouch. His movements are jerkily over-controlled.

Cassie's grief and rage mingle as she pulls the veil of darkness tight around her and steps behind her former subordinate. That he *was* loyal to her she does not doubt: nor is there any doubt that Second Wife has chained him by power of her rank and turned him into an weapon. She can hear the tension in his panicky gasps as he finds his body compelled to perform actions that threaten to tear him apart, making an oath-breaker of him regardless of outcome. Agent Second cannot disobey the *geas* of the wife of the All-Highest, she who in other times could call herself Empress of the Morningstar. But the wages of treason are death: if his blade drinks Agent First's blood his own life is forfeit under the *geas* she holds him with. It's elegantly cruel, Cassie realizes: if Agent Second kills her he, too, will die, and thereby serve her stepmother's purpose, but if *she* slays *him* her command will be weakened.

"Stop this," Cassie commands, casting her voice to echo off the damp brick walls behind.

Agent Second spins warily in place, unable to see her. *"I can't,"* he hisses, pained. His face is creased in anguish. *"She won't let me."*

"If you persist, we may both die."

"Then you will have to slay me, my lady, for I cannot help myself." He lunges and lashes out again, his eyes screwed shut. Cassie dances backwards a step, two: she recognizes the tactic. Darkness will not be sufficient. She begins to spin a web of mist and night, muffling sounds. *"I am sorry,"* he adds, knife tip circling.

She risks everything on a question. *"Does All-Highest know of this treachery?"*

"I know not." Agent Second moans faintly, a string of drool dangling from his lower jaw. *"His wife ordains your death, my lady. I am sorry—"*

For a moment he rallies. Tendons stand out in his neck as his back arches, fighting the dragon lady's *geas*. He stumbles, arms thrown wide, and Cassie recognizes a gathering rumble behind them.

The moral calculus is hazardous, unavoidable. She darts forward and punches his shoulder, shoving him off-balance.

"I'm sorry, too!" she mouths, as a horn blares and brakes screech. Agent Second seems to fall forever, but it can only be a split second before he vanishes beneath the wheels of the articulated lorry. She doesn't stay to watch, but whirls and runs, horrified, metallic-tasting stomach acid rising at the back of her throat. *It was one or both of us,* she rationalizes, trying desperately to un-see what she witnessed, to un-hear the sounds of Agent Second being dragged beneath the wheels, the driver's face a pale circle glimpsed through the windscreen—

After a couple of minutes, Cassie slows to a walk, panting. Her mood, uncharacteristically light until recently, is now tainted with fear and apprehension. It is not because she mourns for Agent Second. He was demonstrably incautious, and allowed her stepmother to corner him in isolation for long enough to impose her murderous compulsion. His weakness brought its own reward down upon his neck. But at the end he rallied, resisting the enemy's will for long enough to give Cassie an opening. She recognizes that she is alive through his act of self-sacrifice, and that her position has gone from marginal to precarious. She is still under orders, charged by All-Highest with gathering intelligence on the *urük* empire's occult rulers. She can no more fight that *geas* than she can still her rebellious heartbeat by will alone. But now she knows for a fact that the mistress of dragons wants her dead. She can be certain that any aid that will be granted her is tainted with treachery, voluntary or compelled. Her own command has been compromised and her own agents can no longer be trusted. She is alone in this place of exile with only the knowledge of the coming invasion to reduce her isolation to something she can comprehend— and the invasion itself will imperil her.

Perhaps the report she dispatched via Agent Second's coatl will serve to redeem her name in her father's esteem. But somehow she doubts it. In truth, she's even coming to doubt her sanity, or at least the value of her stolen memories.

The messy decentralization of Cassie's world is a calculated affront to the intellect: it makes no sense to one of Agent First's kind. They *know* that there can be no society without *mana* to provide power and *geasa* to bind the weak and empower the elevated. All-Highest is as likely to be offended by the ugliness of her report as he is to be persuaded by her insight. At home, everyone can see the intricate web of obligations that connect them to the great chain of being, all the way from All-Highest at the apex to the lowliest slave at the bottom. But Cassie feels the imprint of no such will upon her memories and upbringing. Nor does she recognize the pattern Agent First is seeking. Cassie's queen is not a terrifying sorceress presiding over her empire from a moonlit throne atop a tower of skulls, but a figurehead in a pink twinset and pearls, smiling and waving. She presides over a raucous parliament of self-important men in suits: the only thing they can strike dead with a glare is a sound bite.

Agent First might reluctantly credit Cassie's understanding of her world if there was truly no *mana* here. But there *are* magi: she's met one. She senses it on Alex's skin, smells it curdling on his breath. If he'd show her his teeth she could see it for herself. She has walked the streets around Quarry House and every footstep set her skin crawling, raised the hairs on the nape of her neck with the numinous power embedded in the fresh concrete paving slabs. The only explanation she can see that fits the facts is the hand of a hidden puppeteer, animating the ministries of state through the strength of their will-to-power and their magically enforced oaths of fealty. There *is* magic here, and where there is magic and will there *is* power, and where there is a source of power there *is* a ruler, and a ruler *is* a single point of failure that can be dominated and controlled. But finding that ruler, and a weakness by which she can reach them? She barely knows where to begin.

Whether All-Highest will even bother to review her full report, or hear her thoughts on this subject, is anybody's guess. The only way to convince him would be to present him with incontrovertible evidence—nothing less than a captured enemy magus would do. And she is on her own, with no way to get word home before the invasion force itself arrives.

What's a spy to do?

In his pale throne room beneath the bones of a long-dead sea, All-Highest awaits the report of Agent First of Spies and Liars. Honorable Second Wife, Highest Liege of Airborne Strike Command, occupies the lower throne to his left, chin propped on fist. To his right stands Her Excellence, Highest Liege of Heavy Cavalry. Arrayed behind them are the various members of their staff and assistants.

Their attention is focussed on a chair of limestone where Cassiopeia Brewer sits, fettered with bonds of iron. Skin stinking of terror, mouth stoppered with a gag of leather to muffle her shrieks, she cuts a pathetic figure: clearly the *urük* place little weight on displays of stoical fortitude in the face of inevitable martyrdom.

"*The message.*" All-Highest gestures languidly at the slave woman in the stone chair: "*Put it to her.*"

"*Yes, Highness.*" Honorable Second of Analysts and Communicators steps forward, robes swishing against the floor. He bears a skullcap to which is wired the memory jewel so recently borne across the shadow roads by the coatl. The *urük* female squirms in the chair, trying to slither away from him. Tears trickle down her cheeks as she shakes her head violently, trying to mewl in her barbarous tongue.

All-Highest regards her with disfavor. Her noises are an irritating distraction. He would have had her tongue removed if he had not been waiting for this message from his daughter.

Second of Analysts grips the back of the barbarian woman's neck and forces her to submit. As he lowers the skullcap atop her shaven head—she sports a tonsure, a recent imposition made necessary by the process in hand, but one which fails to make her look any less stupid and brutish—she stiffens as if in a seizure. Her eyes roll up in her head, and her neck becomes limp, so that her head is held up only by Second of Analysts' grip. Then the spasm passes. The woman lifts her chin, a new intelligence glowing in her eyes. The mewling stops. *"Remove the gag,"* commands All-Highest.

"Father." The woman ducks her head briefly, as great a gesture of submission as her bonds permit. *"My memories are yours to command."*

All-Highest permits the merest ghost of a smile to flit across his lips. His daughter's soul is fearless, even in such dire circumstances— entangled with an *urük* slave before a committee of all the powers. He is not unaware of the way Agent First's stepmother glowers. This is to be expected. He would be astonished if she did not have plans for the offspring of his previous whelpings. Behind his right shoulder loom the golems of Punishment and Exemplification of Obedience, ready to excruciate any who should question his will. His new wife is not stupid: he trusts her to leave Agent First alone until she completes her report.

"Tell me, daughter, of the world you have found."

For the next few hours Cassie's mouth labors awkwardly around the unfamiliar lilting tonal phonemes of the High Tongue. Her accent is slow and barbarous, but behind the mangled words a keen intellect delivers news of its labor. Agent First speaks of lies and paradoxes, of a civilization without *mana* and a hidden empire that denies its own manifest existence. Much of her report is profoundly shocking to the staff of the Host of Air and Darkness: she sings of a dirty, terrifyingly overcrowded land where contrivances of mere mechanism run riot and a foul culture has taken root, showing signs of barbaric vigor but bereft of beauty. She sings of a monstrous, seething anthill capital that is in turn the regional hub of an even more populous center to the southeast. And then she sings of a fastness of honey-colored stone surmounted by a gleaming metal spire reeking of *mana*, that stands atop a hill in the midst of the city: a fastness surrounded by wards of power within which secretive magi work by day and night at tasks unseen.

This last captures All-Highest's attention. *"Speak now of this hidden master you have identified,"* he demands, as Second Wife leans forward attentively beside him.

"He is a magus of their kind, an initiate of the blood-feeding brood, touched by power but left uncut and whole. I am unsure how they control him, but presumably they hold their magi in thrall through other means. I met him at dusk on the steps of the theater beside the regional palace of the hidden overlords, beneath the shadow of the steel spire. I am in the process of learning his background and gaining his trust: this is, perforce, not a process that can be hurried. Once obtained I intend to enter the palace under cover of his office, to seek those who rule from the shadows. I shall report further on their identity so that the Host shall be aware of their true nature and location, and I will then proceed as ordered . . ."

All-Highest is aware of his wife's pensive frown as his attention drifts from the prisoner's halting monologue. *"What troubles you, fairest?"* he asks idly, reaching to take her scale-gloved hand in his.

Her fingers curl into a tight fist, betraying tension. *"I dislike the gamble thy Host is drifting towards,"* she says—the word for *gamble* in the High Tongue refers to wagers on natural outcomes, not games of skill, for no wager on a game of skill can be truly free from the risk of interference. *"That one's report is vacuous and lazy, a work of purest imagination scribed to cover a lack of diligence. The urük prisoner"*—she gestures at the subject—*"is clearly a useless mouth, a serf so ignorant of authority that it seems to this one that Agent First deliberately chose her in mockery of thy instructions. Her account of an empire ruled from the shadows, with neither will-to-power nor an immediate descent into anarchy, is a fairy tale to frighten infants. It adds naught to our understanding of the enemy. That we gain nothing from this is a sign that there is nothing to be understood in the first place: it is a sign of treachery, not of insight. If All-Highest will permit this one to send her task group to examine the territory from above, we will rapidly learn the truth about this so-called civilization without mana or authority."*

She smiles at him fiercely. It is an expression of shared complicity and ambition that fills him with pride. *"We will review the matter on the morrow,"* he replies. *"How many of your wing are available to fly?"*

"Two can take wing immediately; the other six can be awakened at your command. All we await is word that the road has been widened sufficiently to accommodate them."

All-Highest makes a snap decision: *"Then you must make haste to awaken all your riders. Of their mounts, prepare two for flight as soon as the shadow road is ready—Second of Magi shall serve as your guide. Hold the rest in reserve, ready to awaken and support the Host when we are ready to ride forth together. It would please us if you were to prepare terrain maps of the target city that Agent First spoke of, assuming it exists outside her imagination. If it is not simple confabulation, then it will be an ideal target for our first thrust: we will find the urük leaders there, and use Agent First to open a traitor's gate so that we may bring them to the path of obedience through stealth while the Host holds their attention."*

His gaze turns back towards the prisoner on the limestone throne. *"Return this one to her cell."*

DEAR DIARY:

There is a department on the fourth floor of the New Annex that does not exist.

Or rather, it exists conditionally, paradoxically. Sometimes it's there; at other times it has never been occupied. Until two years ago, its state of neverness was localized on Dansey House, the Laundry's former headquarters building—now a bulldozed sinkhole of thaumaturgic contamination surrounded by construction hoardings. More recently it has migrated without authorization to another building. And it is a vital part of the agency, for all that many people don't believe it's even real.

This is the Forecasting Operations Department, where one is supposed to imagine that crystal-ball gazing precognitives may or may not tickle the tummy of Schrödinger's cat while juggling ampoules full of hydrogen cyanide and giggling madly at the whirling fogbank of the uncertain future.

I've never visited Forecasting Ops, but I've been given a back-grounder about what they do, and it's fascinating stuff when it isn't boring. Fascinatingly boring, in fact. On the one hand, they claim to be able to foretell the future. That, on the face of it, is insane. It would allow them to create and operate a Turing Oracle, an abstract function that can resolve undecidable problems (including the Halting Problem) in $O(n)$ time. NP-complete? No problem! P-Space- and P-Time-complete functions? Trivially soluble. Put me in charge of Forecasting Ops for a month and I'll cure my annoying V-parasite infestation in one easy computational step—and break any public/private key pair you care to point me at for an encore. But no: they're not interested in curing Krantzberg syndrome or its relatives. They're just in the wholly mundane business of *predicting the future*.

I find this deeply, offensively foolish. As if the future is predictable at that level! But abusing the Oracle is a *political* imperative, or so I am informed. They send reports around on a regular basis, discussing the most mundane matters with a lamentable lack of abstract insight. Mostly they make for terribly dull reading ("status is green: no existential threats anticipated"). Sometimes they're just perplexing ("the rain of fish over York Minster next Thursday lunchtime has been cancelled"). And sometimes Forecasting Ops *doesn't exist*—this is apparently a rare but critical paradox that emerges when the existence of Forecasting Ops will itself lead to a detrimental outcome, resulting in the department retroactively cancelling its own establishment until the threat is past.

(I am not convinced by the underlying metalogic of this proposition; it appears to be undecidable even in P-Time. But that's what you get for playing with Turing Oracles, I guess.)

It is Wednesday, and I am back in the windowless office at the Headingley Arndale Centre, catching up on my paperwork. I will confess I am finding it somewhat difficult to concentrate: I have a date this evening and I am not sure what I'm supposed to do—Wikipedia is maddeningly uninformative on the subject, and other sources range from unreliable (citation needed!) to actively misleading. However I am conditionally confident of the accuracy of the advice Pete gave me, which was to treat any behavior showcased by the male lead in a Hollywood romantic comedy as dangerously abusive. (*Do not*: follow her home; break into her house to watch her sleep; put spyware on her computer or phone; send giant bouquets of flowers signed YOUR SECRET ADMIRER; boil her family's pet rabbit; and so on.) I am therefore using paperwork as a distraction from life, rather than vice versa. And that's why the weekly update from Forecasting Ops catches my attention:

FORECAST: PERIOD BEGINNING MARCH 29TH
SEVERITY: RED
CONFIDENCE LEVEL: HIGH
SPECIFICITY: LOW

An extremely low probability front is incoming from the northeast-unseen, dimensionality approximately Re($1.026 * 10^{-16}$), associated with a high-level thaumotropic phase transition from high density to medium density.

Intrusions from a variant parallel reality are possible within a 50/50 confidence radius of approximately 25Km around Huddersfield town center. The intrusions may include, but are not limited to:

- Outbreaks of idiopathic macroscopic cryptobiotic infestation
- Outbreaks of paranormal enhancements up to an order of magnitude more frequent than normal background level, including 3–4 sigma power spectrum deviations from normal
- Statistically significant anomalies in probabilistic outcomes
- Thaum flux variations in ley lines throughout the region

There is a low-to-medium (<20%) probability of a major extradimensional intrusion occurring at this time. In event of intrusion taking place, severity of outcome is estimated as medium to high.

Recommendations:

- First responder assets within a 40Km radius of the epicenter should be placed on major incident alert for the period March 29th to April 2nd.
- Precautionary deployment of an OCCULUS unit and associated personnel to a suitable location within 60-minute deployment of the epicenter should be considered, unless high-probability/high-severity incidents in progress elsewhere demand all available response capacity.
- Notify regular emergency services to cooperate with OCCULUS unit on deployment, provide cover story referencing "possible hallucinogenic chemwar agent leak" or similar.

I find these recommendations troubling.

I've worked with an OCCULUS unit before—six months ago, during the debacle at the MAGIC CIRCLE OF SAFETY storage warehouse in Watford—and the idea that Forecasting Ops think it would be a good idea to deploy one within sixty minutes of Huddersfield makes my skin crawl. Huddersfield is just down the road from here (along the M62 motorway). It's part of the western extremity of the West Yorkshire conurbation which peters out in the foothills of the Pennines, just before the motorway crosses the border into Lancashire.

I'm not sure quite what a "major extradimensional intrusion" means when it's translated from the FO jargon, but if Forecasting Ops are suggesting that an armed response unit equipped with heavy thaumaturgic firepower ought to be deployed on our doorstep, it can't be anything good.

I wonder if this has got something to do with the urgent requirement to reinforce the security wards around Quarry Hill this week?

9: ALEX IN LOVE

Alex's experience of dating is similar to his experience of string theory: abstract, intense, and entirely theoretical due to the absence of time and opportunities for probing such high-energy phenomena. He is therefore understandably nervous when he walks into the Playhouse bar after work and looks around for Cassie.

Unbeknownst to Alex, Agent First's experience of dating is no more extensive than his own. The *original* Cassiopeia Brewer has indeed been dating since secondary school and spent her first eight months at university partying, drinking, and sharing a bed with one of her classmates (then the next eight months pretending not to know him and the former BFF whose bed he had switched to). But the original Cassiopeia Brewer considerably outstrips both Alex *and* Agent First in terms of sexual experience. Casual sex is common among the People, but courtship tends to be abrupt if not invariably brutal, and longer-term relationships are cold-blooded political alliances. The idea of approaching the subject gradually, bonding over dinner and dialog and shared experiences, is perplexing. On the other hand, such an approach serves Agent First's needs perfectly well.

Agent First started a secret diary in the back of a Moleskine notebook right after she met Alex for the second time, on the Playhouse steps. She has a to-do list: *Get to know the urük mage's mind. Ask about his liege and his responsibilities.* She records her notes using the cramped syllabary of the High Tongue, her handwriting spiky and somewhat hesitant. Knowing nobody else in this world can read them is reassuring. *Discover what he knows of the High Tongue and who taught him,* she notes. (It is inconceivable that a magus of his evident power can function without a working knowledge of the metagrammar that permits the direct manipulation of reality.) She writes in pale violet ink, using a gold and lacquer fountain pen she fell in love with in a shop window. (The proprietor gave it to her spontaneously, thanking her for her role in some film she had never heard of.) And that part of her which is forever Cassie adorns the margins with pictures of daisies and elder signs.

Agent First is nearly as nervous as Alex when she walks into the Playhouse bar. She pulls Cassie tight around her shoulders like an invisible security blanket as she looks around. Alex is perched on a stool at one of the bar-style tables alongside the back wall of the room, eyes swiveling restlessly. In a desperate attempt to psych himself up, he ordered a medium cappuccino; he has nearly finished it already, and he's wired.

"*Eee!*" Cassie squeaks. With Cassie's fashion sense, Agent First sees that he is dressed extraordinarily badly. It's not just a matter of drab ill-matched colors or poorly fitting office-casual: it takes hard work to clash that loudly. From the ankle-skimming cuffs of his navy blue M&S chinos to the randomly cut tips of his hair, by way of his brown tweed sports jacket and button-down shirt, no single aspect of his ensemble is remotely flattering. On the other hand, his will-to-power washes over her like a blast of heat from an open furnace door. To Agent First's inner eye he'd seem like an emperor even if he was wearing a grocery sack. "You look great!" she half-lies.

Alex's smile goes goofily up to eleven. "Hi!" he manages. He regains control of his larynx and repeats himself, in a lower register: "Hi. You're just as beautiful," he says, then his tongue stops working and his cheeks flush as his brain catches up with his mouth. "Er . . . nice dress?"

Cassie tries not to jump out of her skin. "I want one of those," she says, looking pointedly at his coffee. Some raptorial instinct prompts her to bat her eyelashes at him as she climbs onto the bar stool opposite. "Get me one! And another for yourself, *please*," she adds, clamping down on the glamour with a frisson of fright. (It's dangerous to use glamour on a magus: they can sense the flow of *mana*, and she doesn't want to discover the consequences of being caught trying to suborn a blood sorcerer. If it provokes anything similar to the reaction it would get from one of her father's magi she can expect it to be drastic and probably fatal.)

But Alex doesn't notice her momentary slip. He looks befuddled for a moment, or perhaps star-struck. "Okay, I'll be back in a minute," he says nervously. "Don't go anywhere?" He gets up and heads towards the counter at the front of the room, moving like a sleepwalker.

Cassie watches his receding back, captivated and terrified. *He likes me!* she realizes, trying the idea on for size. On the one hand, this is as it should be: after all, Agent First wanted to get his attention, and what Agent First wants she usually gets. But on the other hand, becoming an object of fascination for an *urük* magus might be a bit too much of a good thing. The skin on her neck and wrists prickles and the tips of her ears stand on end, for she can *feel* the strength wrapped around the armature of his will, just as she did at their last meeting. Alex is remarkably unassuming for one with such vast potential. In the empire, he would be a Magus of the First Rank, terrible and puissant, his ambitions held in check only by the *geas* of a powerful noble and the enforced tranquility of castration. But she will eat her diary, card covers and all, if Alex is a eunuch. She crosses her legs restlessly at the idea of a virile male blood-mage. Such a thing would never be permitted in the empire: it brings visions from Cassie's bookish fantasy habit to life, uncomfortably detailed visions, unaccountably attractive. *How do their rulers control them?* she asks herself, desperate for something to distract her from the fruits of Cassie's overheated imagination. She racks her brain: but Cassie has no memory of ritual castration as a tool of management in this place, unless it's symbolized by the neck-wrappings many male *urük* wear as part of their uniforms.

Alex takes a couple of minutes to get served, during which time Agent First calms down enough to be mildly perplexed. Perhaps his failure to use his power to demand obedience from the servants is a sign of compliance to whatever directive of secrecy requires him to hide his light under a bushel? It strikes her as sweet but faintly ridiculous. At home, any duke or baron with such a powerful magus among their retinue would parade them around in their robes of office, accompanied at all times by an armed retinue of bodyguards, to trumpet their own wealth and power. But the rules are different among the *urük*, and while Alex is pretending to be a humble desk-bound bureaucrat, Agent First manages to settle her apprehension, regains her outward poise, and allows Cassie to quickly check her lipstick in a compact mirror.

Alex returns to the table, bearing two cups of cappuccino: they clatter as he sets them down, one of them splashing into its saucer. "I don't normally drink this stuff," he says apologetically, "caffeine doesn't agree with me."

"Really?" Cassie bubbles, despite his downbeat tone: she can't help herself. "Then we won't be able to hang out here all evening! Did you have anything particular in mind for later?" Her heart pounds. Dating, with its conventions of multiple social encounters as a prelude to fucking, seems absurdly complex to her, like cooking your own food rather than having servants and poison-testers prepare it for you.

"I was thinking, um, I don't know, what movies are worth seeing? Have you eaten? Or we could find a pub—"

"Movies." Cassie blanks for a moment. This is a *date* and *people on dates* often go and *watch movies* together, at least among the *urük*. She has only warped second-hand memories of motion pictures, none of them her own. It seems like a fantastically unproductive use of her time with Alex, staring vacantly at an elaborate visual lie. At this point, if he were one of the People they'd already be getting down to business.

But he persists: "Would you like to see a movie?"

The penny drops: *This is one of those* bonding experiences, *isn't it?* "YesYes! That'd be great!"

"But, um, the Odeon is half a mile uphill from here—" He takes a mouthful of coffee, pulls a face as it burns his mouth. "Yes well, we could do that. Um. But um there's this problem I have um caffeine doesn't agree with me and c-can we wait until sunset?" he asks.

"Sunset?" His pupils are dilated, and she fancies she can hear his heart pounding. *Caffeine doesn't agree* with me seems like a massive understatement. She smiles encouragingly: "I can wait. Do they sell beer here?"

Two gassy pints of Tetley's Bitter take the edge off Alex's jitters and relax Cassie pleasantly, then it's time to go. Theatergoers are arriving for tonight's production and the bar is filling up behind them.

They end up at the Odeon. Most of the smaller screens are running anime and other cartoon movies in the run-up to the comics festival down by the dock, but one of them is showing a movie that's on Cassie's hit-list: a Jim Jarmusch romantic comedy starring Tilda Swinton against Tom Hiddleston, vamping it up as a pair of immortal star-crossed lovers. To her surprise Agent First enjoys it, although she is certain that she's missing some of the sardonic jokes. She's acutely aware of Alex's presence in the seat next to her, even as her eyes and ears drink in the lights and sounds that dance across the screen in front of them. He twitches a couple of times during the blood-drinking scenes, almost as if it makes him uneasy, which is perplexing. (If he can't cope with a little bloodletting why did he become a magus?)

Eventually they stumble out onto the pavement. The air is cool but the rain clouds have blown away towards the east, and the sky above them is darkening from azure to indigo in the north. Venus drifts overhead, a bright and lonely promise of the starry night to come. "Walk with me?" Agent First asks as she takes hold of Alex's arm. She leans on him for balance as they descend the slope down Vicar Lane, heading back towards Quarry Hill. She's wearing a pair of ankle boots with spiky heels that Cassie's memories prompted her to buy, but balancing in them is challenging.

"Let me show you the river walk," Alex offers.

"Yes, let's. Which way is it?" she asks, wobbling slightly. She likes hearing his voice. It reminds her that she's not alone in this drab, *mana*-bereft world.

"Back the way we were, past the Playhouse . . ." He leads her along the side of Eastgate, half-deafened by buses and cars, under the old railway viaduct and past the shiny glass and concrete hotel. "Not far to go."

"You work in Quarry House, don't you?" she asks. "Are you really a civil servant, then?" The nest of twisty concepts behind the term baffles Agent First: as if it's possible for abstractions to command minions to serve them. "A servant of the, the Crown?"

"I—" He pauses for a moment. "I suppose I am." He sounds surprised and slightly depressed, as if she's shocked a confession of guilt out of him. "I'd rather not talk about it," he adds apologetically.

"Then don't," she says. Normally she'd find this reluctance irritating, as it threatens to prolong her mission. (It's already getting late, and if she wants to maintain the pretense of being a student she'll need to go home soon and get some sleep before lectures.) But instead she finds herself warmly happy at the excuse for a second date, an opportunity to spend more time in his company. "What did you think of the movie?"

"I thought it was—" Alex pauses. There are steps here, leading down to a path alongside the river, which is as thoroughly walled-in as an artificial canal. "It annoyed me," he admits as he helps her descend.

"Why?" she asks breathily, leaning on him a bit more heavily than is strictly necessary for balance.

"Vampires—" He stops again, as if a distant instructor is reading lines for him to repeat: almost as if he harbors a secret narrative, Agent First recognizes with a shiver. "Bah." The air alongside the river is moist and cool, and there's a faint shimmer of activity in the air by some bushes. "Midges."

"Midges—" The haze dances closer. "They bite, don't they?"

Alex glitches again. She squeezes his fingers encouragingly. He takes a deep breath, preparation for the confessional: "Midges are vampires."

She looks at him sharply, but he's not smiling. "What?"

"Midges and mosquitos are blood-suckers, but nobody thinks they're sexy, do they?"

"YesYes, but . . ." Cassie's head spins as, abruptly, she sees Alex on the edge of self-disclosure—not the insight she'd asked for, but an important one nonetheless. "What do you mean?"

"Insects. Bats." They pick their way hand-in-hand along the tow path, past a mooring where a narrow-boat is tied up, light leaking from behind curtained portholes. "Blood-suckers. They're not sexy, are they? Not like Adam and Eve." The stars of the movie, star-crossed ancient lovers. "There's a species of leech, you know? *Placobdelloides jaegerskioeldi*, the hippo arse leech. Leeches come in all shapes and sizes and are adapted to feed on different hosts. Hippos have thick skin, so the only place *jaegerskioeldi* can suck blood is inside the hippo's rectum. They *breed* in there, if you can believe it? And if you ever wondered why hippos spin their tails when they shit, it's to throw the leeches as far away as they can. *That's* what a vampire is," he adds, either bitterly or enviously—his tone of voice is distinctly odd. "A hyperspecialized parasite. The only sexy blood-suckers are ones that look like us—and they don't—" He coughs. "Well. What I'm say-ing is, real vampires are *nasty*. You want to avoid them." And he lets go of her hand.

"Well, thank you very much for spoiling what was shaping up to be a really good evening!" Cassie fumes. She stands in the path and glares.

Alex looks stricken. "Oh gosh, I didn't mean it like that," he says with a deer-in-the-headlights look that makes him seem a decade younger, "I wasn't trying to gross you out, honest. I was just . . ." Finally his brain catches up with his mouth. "I should stop talking now, shouldn't I?" he asks nobody in particular.

Agent First thinks rapidly. *So you aren't allowed to talk about what you are, and it's a source of shame, is it?* She can work with that, although it makes her feel dirty. "Well, now I feel sick, which means you owe me another date!" she announces, letting the tension bleed out of her shoulders. "One without leeches," she adds, keeping a wary eye on the river passing hippopotami. "How about Saturday?"

"Why, uh, yeah, yes! I can do Saturday!" He's transparent, she thinks sadly, and so appealingly vulnerable, if occasionally disgusting in the manner of a cute puppy that hasn't completely mastered the finer points of toilet discipline. She gets it now: she's dealing with great power coupled with total dorkish innocence and an unaccount-able sense of shame.

"Great! I'll text you!" Agent First leans forward and briefly kisses his cheek. She forces herself to ignore the impulse to grab his ass, nibble his neck, and see if he's up for helping her explore Cassie's torrid fantasy life: she doesn't want to spook him by moving too fast. But she's breathing faster as she pulls away. "You'd better show me back to the bus station now. It's definitely time to go home."

Another day, another meeting in the DM's basement man-cave. Lockhart is afraid he's getting used to it: it's sordid, but no worse than what you often find in the way of living circumstances when a squaddie musters out and falls off the map.

"So," he says, "what have you got for me?"

"Plenty." Derek smiles faintly, maybe a touch enviously. "He's a lucky bastard, our boy."

"Maybe so, but I want a full situation report."

It's a reminder, not an order, but the DM gets the message. There is some sighing and grunting as he shifts his belly into position behind the edge of the table, then rummages for the paper files. It's all on neatly gridded graph paper, drawn with a Rotring 0.5mm technical pen and a variety of propelling pencils. Maps, names, probabilities, flow charts.

"Alex Schwartz, Whitby. The changeling, Whitby. *Not* a coincidence, oracular nudging is highly likely. Whether by ours or theirs is unclear: the inference fog is obscuring almost everything. But anyway, they run into each other and proceed directly to boy-meets-girl stuff, desirable from whichever side of the wall you look at it, theirs or ours." He slides a couple of CCTV stills across the table towards Lockhart, whose expression of stiff-lipped disapproval deepens. "There's no need to be like that," Derek adds; "our boy had no way of knowing who or what she was."

"That's beside the point: it's still Fraternization with the Uncanny, and the Assizes will take a dim—"

"I *know*, but when life hands you honey, you build a honey trap." The DM shrugs. "She's here on her own in a strange world, surrounded by people like—" His gesture takes in the other photos, the Victorian cosplayers and strolling goths and street theater. "And if what we can infer about her background is right she must be suffering from massive cognitive whiplash right now. You know how many agents the Soviets lost, trying to gain traction in the United States during the cold war? About three thousand. They figured out how things worked, did a double-take, and then they dived underground— not just into deep cover, they actually cut their ties and hid. The KGB thought the FBI were ruthlessly efficient at rounding up and shooting spies, but in reality, the kids from the Kolkhoz were living the American dream. They worked out they'd been lied to about the evils of capitalism, so why put out?"

Lockhart rolls his eyes but doesn't say anything. After a few seconds to savor his self-derailment, Derek gets back on course.

"Anyway, we set Alex up to meet cute with her, as agreed. It worked. Now we need to give him room to run. Serendipity: he has a mentor who specializes in counseling, awkward conversations, relationships, that sort of thing. Less serendipitous: he's inexperienced and he's got PHANG syndrome. Well, the bathroom cabinet is well-stocked with condoms and lube, that's all we can do for him without it being obvious. Oh, and we got her phone's IMEI and SIM ID so we can man-in-the-middle their lovey-dovey texts and Snapchats and whatnot *pro re nata*. If he clams up and goes shy we can poke her until she talks to him, or vice versa. Main thing is to get her on a string and reel her in. Then apply Stockholm syndrome proactively."

Lockhart twitches. "I do not think Stockholm syndrome means quite what you think it means."

"What, the tendency of people—usually women—in unfamiliar societies to enculturate rapidly?"

Lockhart inclines his head. "Point."

The DM summarizes. "It worked on the Eater of Souls. If we're lucky it'll work on whatever is walking around wearing the late Cassiopeia Brewer's face. Then we can milk her for information and prepare a suitable response, hopefully before the full-scale incursion Forecasting Ops are screaming about takes place. It's our job to ensure Alex doesn't end up too moon-struck to do *his* job. And to make sure the beehive is positioned close by the rhododendron bushes and busily accumulating poison honey, of course, and position a company of archers just beyond the ridgeline. Or Apache Longbow gunships. Whatever it takes . . ."

*   *   *

After that one chaste kiss—to which Alex had so little idea of how to respond that he simply froze in place—he walks Cassie to the bus station before heading up Briggate towards the bus stops for Harehills Lane. His head is spinning; butterflies are shooting up crystal meth in his chest. *Oh God a girl kissed me, what does it mean?* Well, in the abstract, Alex knows *exactly* what it means. He's old enough to know better, too. He got the memo, after the late-night chat with John. *Oh crap, I don't know what to do.*

He's completely mesmerized, and suddenly frightened for his future. It's not as if he's had much of a chance until now, but somehow he has internalized the ur-cultural narrative: you grow up, go to university, get a job, meet Ms. Right, get married, settle down, have kids, grow old together . . . it's like some sort of checklist. Or maybe a list of epic quests you've got to complete while level-grinding in a game you're not allowed to quit, with no respawns and no cheat codes.

But a few months ago Alex found a cheat code and now he's infected with the thaumaturgic equivalent of HIV. He's locked out of the normal player mode, pressing his nose against the plate-glass window of reality and peering inside longingly, wondering what the hell happens next—when Ms. Right shows up, with blue-green pigtails and a smile like the sunrise he no longer dares to face. And *she's* a bit weird, too, but that's okay . . . that's entirely okay . . . if only he wasn't a PHANG . . .

Alex's brain is still spinning around these imponderables as he walks into his bedroom and lies down. He is asleep almost instantly, because he's working days this week and it's past midnight. But morning brings no surcease, and his previous befuddlement is replaced by a low but pervasive sense of anxiety by the time he gets to the Arndale office for a morning briefing.

Pete is waiting there with a mug of decaf helpfully lined up for him. "We were going to go over the take from the K-22 survey of the Armouries, weren't we," he says by way of introduction. "Then report on whether we need to do anything more on-site. Tomorrow's a training day, and . . ." He frowns. "What is it?"

Alex looks perplexed. Something is missing, something important. "Just a sec." He puts his phone down on the desk, then fumbles with his unbuttoned shirt collar. "Just want to check something." He pulls out his ward, unclips it from the lanyard, and puts it beside his phone.

"What?"

"I think I felt a surge yesterday evening, near Quarry House," Alex says, "and now I can't feel it. It's cold." The inscribed crystal feels like a lump of stone, lifeless and dead.

"Really?" Pete leans back and sips his own coffee as Alex fidgets with the OFFCUT app on his phone.

"Yeah, I'm getting nothing. Can you check it for me using your own phone? This isn't working."

"Okay . . ."

A minute later they're both shaking their heads over the duff ward. "You'd better indent for another one," Pete tells him. "That's not supposed to happen. Do you remember breaking it?"

"No." Alex frowns. "It might have been at the RA. They have a lot of blood-soaked history there, and there's that anomalous new ley line node down by the river. But it could have been any time, really. I normally check it weekly."

Pete shakes his head again. "They're not supposed to just die on you. I mean, if something burns out a ward, it gets hot, right? Eddy currents or something. You'd know about it, unless you were completely away with the fairies."

"Well I wasn't." Alex is mildly defensive. "So, um. What should I do?"

Pete sighs. "Nothing right now. So let's go over the survey first and see if we can get these wandering ley lines nailed down, then when we're done you can email Facilities for a new one." His face brightens. "How did your date go?"

Alex twitches. "We went to a movie," he says tentatively. "And we're meeting up again on Saturday." The less said about hippo arse leeches, the better.

"Oh excellent!" Pete smiles. "I thought you looked a bit distracted. Jolly good."

"Work," Alex nudges his mentor. The last thing he wants is a forensic examination of his personal life.

"Okay, work. Did you get enough readings to generate a heat map of the ground floor of the museum . . . ?"

They finish the post-mortem on Alex's trip to the Royal Armouries, and Pete wanders off to another busywork session—a meeting about the ongoing headache of how to replace the MAGIC CIRCLE OF SAFETY public information campaign, which passed its use-by date some time around 1980. Alex returns to the office alone, and finds a familiar internal post package waiting in his in-tray.

He sits down and stares at it for a minute, stomach cramping. Then he stands up again, walks stiff-legged to the doorway, and flips on the DO NOT DISTURB lamp outside. He locks the door, sits back down, and reaches for the package. His hand trembles slightly.

It's a day early, which is slightly upsetting if he stops to think about it. Somewhere in England (he doesn't want to know where) a ninety-something Alzheimer's patient is going downhill, feverish with a pneumonia infection that will kill them in the early hours. (*No, probably not Alzheimer's. That would damage the gray matter.*) Or maybe they're a middle-aged man, wracked by terminal cancer and dosed up to the eyeballs on morphine. (*That's better: more likely, too.*) But maybe they're a woman in her early twenties, lonely and depressed, who burned her liver out with a handful of paracetamol tablets in a mistaken call for help; the ambulance was too late and she won't live long enough to receive a compatible transplant organ because suicides go to the back of the queue. (*That's the worst. All the wasted years ahead . . .*)

Alex takes a shuddering breath and pulls the rip-tab along the edge of the padded envelope, then shakes it until the box drops out onto his blotter. He tosses the envelope in the bin, then leans over the desk, hands to either side of the box, and forces himself to wait.

This is a personal ritual. Making himself wait, despite the hunger pangs cramping his stomach and twisting around his spine, sending needles of lightning-like cold up and down his arms and legs to gnaw on his extremities. It seems to Alex that every time he consumes one of the "ration tubes" he loses part of his claim to humanity. They taste of sinful complicity, of the willful shortening of a human life. It doesn't matter that the donors are already dying, so that his feeding will merely add a haze of confusion to their final hours. It's still a reminder that what keeps mankind alive involves gruesome death. And it comes in a Civil Service mailer, as if to say, *Remember that you owe your life to the state.*

He meditates until he feels he understands what he's about to do. Then he slides open the catch on the box, pops the seal on the plastic tube, and upends it onto his tongue.

There is a faintly ammoniacal tang to the blood: it tastes slightly off, teetering on the edge of decay. Yes, definitely a suicide. (Or liver cancer, but that's rare.) He shudders at the sense of release as his V-parasites latch onto the link to another unprotected brain and flit across to feed on it. It's better, the other PHANGS tell him, than sex. But the relief he gains from feeding does nothing for the numb sense of grief that outlasts his hunger, and leaves him so fragile that he has to sit for half an hour before he is ready to unlock the door and switch off the DO NOT DISTURB sign.

Meanwhile, the invaders are refining their plans.

With the arrival of the coatl bearing Agent First's preliminary report, clear confirmation is received that the shadow road to *Urükheim* is open and anchored barely six leagues from the enemy's northern palace. The report contains Agent First's sketchy map of the ley line endpoints around the enemy hive—*city* seems too dignified a word for such a grotesque chaos—and close scrutiny offers up some promising snippets. There is an endpoint very close by the palace, down by the river. Less plausibly, it appears to be completely unguarded, which bespeaks either terrifying indifference or total incompetence on the part of the defenders. There's another one near an abandoned fortification and a ritual corpse disposal site a league and a half from the end of the shadow road, and *that* one links in turn to a powerful line that terminates at the counterpart of the Host's garrison: a large limestone outcropping in the foothills of the low mountain range that forms the spine of the *urük* kingdom that is All-Highest's target.

This matter of ley line arrangement is of considerable interest to All-Highest's staff. Once they secure control of the far end of the shadow road, the Host's magi can, with some effort, move it around the local ley line endpoints. And ley lines are vital for logistic support and mobility, for they are the Morningstar Empire's chief form of long-range transport, permitting the rapid movement of armor, infantry, and provisions without risk of interdiction by enemy forces. The usual problem with using a ley line to move troops through enemy territory is that unless the enemy are smoking poppy juice, they'll notice the sudden drain in *mana* in the middle of their stronghold and smash the anchor stone, thereby consigning the unfortunate expeditionary forces to perdition. (Spies and assassins are one thing, heavy cavalry battalions are another.) But if the anchor stone is surreptitiously moved to a defensible forward location, the Host can pour through and attack across the last few dozen leagues by conventional means, taking the enemy by surprise. And this suggests a plan to All-Highest.

First, the magi will carry the shadow road anchor to the ley line node by the abandoned underground fort. Then they'll shuffle it out of the enemy city, to the limestone outcropping. At which point the Host can pour through and marshal in strength, under the watchful eyes of Airborne Strike Command.

It is decided early on that the first aerial reconnaissance sorties will cautiously skirt the city-hive itself, hidden by terrain and distance from the air defenses that sweep the skies around the enemy palace. These early flights will seek to confirm the substance of Agent First's report. If confirmation is forthcoming, Highest Liege of Airborne Strike Command will obtain local air superiority above the limestone outcropping, then the Host's heavy armor and forward reconnaissance units will pour through and strike en masse at the enemy city, traveling over land, using the ley line for energy and communications once they reach the outskirts.

The worst case All-Highest envisages is that the armored spearhead will draw the defending forces out from wherever they're hiding. (If fate smiles upon him, the cavalry strike will take the enemy completely by surprise and roll through their defenses, taking the palace.) Meanwhile, while the enemy are distracted a smaller force of combat magi will seize the unsecured ley line terminating on the river by the enemy citadel. The plan is to penetrate its perimeter wards by treachery, kill the sorcerer queen within, grab her empire's controlling *geasa*, and add them to All-Highest's string. Next stop: planetary domination.

It's a desperate plan with many imponderables, but to the Host these are desperate times. They're running perilously low on food for the cavalry mounts; they can't return to hibernation under hill, and the oracles all predict a fate four point two degrees worse than death if they try to retake the surface territories of the Morningstar Empire. The probability of a successful outcome in *this* venture is far from certain, but the oracles all agree that the enemy witch queen will not triumph over All-Highest. (So there's that.)

Days pass.

The four remaining Assassins of Spies and Liars, bound now directly by the will of All-Highest, travel the shadow road unsummoned by their leader. It is their privilege to escort a pair of forward assault geomancers, whose job it is to seize the anchor of the shadow road and relocate it to the marshaling point, then fuse it to the local ley lines.

In the upper caverns of the redoubt the slave-technicians of Airborne Strike prepare two firewyrms for service. Bringing the dragons to combat readiness is a painstaking business. Rather than slumbering in envenomated sorcerous suspended animation while their human riders slept away the years, the siliceous organisms—distant relatives of the war basilisks that provide the Host with heavy fire support—have been encouraged to binge on fluorspar and rock salt, then placed in a powerful summoning grid to sever them from the passage of time. The beasts are quiescent and relatively harmless while in a digestive torpor, and the ground crew are well-trained: few slaves lose limbs this time round as they fettle and irrigate the wyrms. Meanwhile, their riders awaken in their cocoons. Less disposable members of the ground crew prepare the mission plans and retrieve munitions from the deep storage bunkers.

Finally, the riders and their passengers—the magi of Airborne Strike Command—are briefed, and the dragons are delicately prodded and chivvied towards the tunnel leading to the road to *Urükheim*, waiting for the all-clear.

The dragons travel in convoy with their forward ground crew, behind a double lance of light cavalry, their gold-chased wrought-iron armor burnished to a refulgent gleam. Helmet plumes nod gracefully as their mounts high-step onto the road between the worlds. Following at a safe distance, the steady thudding hoofbeats of a tactical air defense group rumbles in their wake, ready to protect the forward base from insurgents.

The full might of the Host of Air and Darkness is still working up to operational readiness, but Airborne Strike and Forward Reconnaissance are about to sweep the ground around Malham Cove clear of *urük*, preparing the staging area for the invasion force.

Alex is alone in his cramped, windowless office, writing up his report on the Armouries in a vain attempt to settle his free-floating unease, when the source of the anxiety he's been holding at bay all morning reveals itself to him. Comprehension is heralded by a familiar SOS ringtone.

Alex stares at his phone. It's Mum. For a couple of seconds he stares at it, half-intending to let it ring through to voice mail: but he's self-aware enough to recognize the futility of attempting to delay the inevitable. He finally picks up, guts churning. She's going to ask him the Question again, isn't she? Only this time . . . "Hi, Mum?"

"Hello, dear! Are you busy right now?"

Alex's eyes swivel furtively, a habit ingrained through long experience of sharing offices and cubicle space with others. "I'm at work, Mum." Honesty compels him to add: "But I'm alone right now."

"Oh good! I can never tell whether you're on night shift or terribly busy or—" And she's off, into a three-minute monologue about family friends he hasn't seen since he was in school, about his father's sciatica, and about Aunt Emmy's creaking knees and his sister's exam results. Terminating abruptly in: "—but you *are* in Leeds this weekend?"

A moment's hesitation and he's lost: "Yes, Mum."

"Marvelous! Then it's settled, you're definitely coming for dinner on Saturday. What is she called, by the way?"

Oh fuck. "I haven't asked her."

"You haven't asked her *name*? Alex!"

"No, I mean"—Alex scrambles for a diplomatic way to admit that he's completely forgotten about the dinner on Saturday, and that he has made alternative plans for the evening, if he can barely remember what they are—"I haven't asked her to dinner."

"Well, Alex Mansfield Schwartz, you can fix that right away!" His phone buzzes like an angry wasp. "Tell her she'd be ever so welcome, really, it's no trouble whatsoever to feed another head—" He translates mentally: *Are you trying to hide her from us? Is there something* wrong *with her?*

It's getting worse by the moment. "No, Mum, honest! It's just I'm not sure we're on meeting-the-folks terms yet," he says. "I don't want to take things too fast—"

"What's she called?"

He stifles a sigh. "She's called Cassie."

"And what's she like?"

"She's a final year student at Leeds Met," he says reluctantly, try- ing not to pass ammunition to the enemy. He saw what happened when Aunt Emmy's daughter Patsy got engaged to a rather damp solicitor from Wakefield: it wasn't pretty. Mum is all fired up to stage- manage a dream wedding that will put right all the perceived wrongs Gran inflicted on her own nuptials (and lay to rest forever her sense of mild insecurity relative to her older sister). It's only a matter of time before either he or Sarah get to draw the short straw. Exposing Cassie to Mum on a second date is almost certain to ensure that there won't ever be a third date. "Listen, Mum, I think she has other plans for the weekend—"

"Well ask her anyway, won't you? Just for me?"

"I'll think about it," he says. "I'll definitely see if it's possible."

And there he submits to another ten minutes of chirpy monologu- ing about the weather, his deplorable haircut (Alex's hair is *always* deplorable), whether he and Cassie are going to dress up for dinner, and a promise that as they're all grown-ups now there will be wine with the meal.

Finally he's had enough. It takes him a couple of minutes more to get a word in edgeways: "Mum, I'm at work—"

"Oh, I quite forgot! Well, not to worry. Remember what I said? Ask Cassie to come along? I'm sure we'll get on like a house on fire!"

Visions of shrieking and jumping out of upper-floor windows dance in his mind's eye. "Yes, Mum. Bye . . ."

Alex puts his phone down with a shudder then shoves it to the far side of his desk, like the corpse of a particularly large cockroach. He stares vacantly at his computer. His fingers, poised over the keyboard, make minute twitching motions, but no words appear on the screen. His body is present but his mind is far away.

Mum expects to meet the Girlfriend. This has been made clear in no uncertain terms. Worse, Sarah expects him to show up and support her, with or without partner. There was something fishy about little sister's call the previous week. (Is she concealing an agenda of her own?) In any case the prospect of introducing Cassie to his family so early in the getting-to-know-you game is excruciating. They're like the anti–Addams Family; if Cassie has any sense she'll take to her heels and not stop running until she hits the North Sea.

But then he remembers something else. Cassie is heading off to Whitby the weekend after next, isn't she? For the goth festival. And Cassie is—if he's not making a wild error of judgment—something of a goth. She'll be in her natural habitat there, with a bunch of party-animal thespians and a superabundance of sexy creatures of the night for her to throw herself at if she is inclined to forget about him. And he'll be stuck in Leeds, tied down by work.

"*Oh God,*" he moans quietly, "*I'm screwed.*" Cassie expects to see him on Saturday. Dragging her along to meet the potential parents-in-law might be a scary big deal and a good way of ensuring that it's the last time he'll see her. But if he goes to dinner and doesn't bring her along, or if he blows off Mum's arrangements, both Mum *and* Sarah will be pissed off at him. And if he doesn't see her on Saturday he may not get another chance before she goes traipsing off to Whitby for a week, at which point he can be certain she'll forget him.

What's a boy to do?

*   *   *

The morning after her date with her nerdishly cute prince of darkness, Cassie is scheduled for a lecture at nine o'clock. She blows it off because life's too short and anyway the world is going to end in about two weeks' time, when the Second Heavy Cavalry Brigade rumbles into town accompanied by skies that rain wyrmfire and the death spells of combat magi. If she's lucky she'll have a chance to find out whether the goth festival is as much fun as everyone says it is before that happens. But first, she has to arrange another date with cute boy, identify his weaknesses, conquer him, and use him to get her inside the fortified palace on Quarry Hill. Only then will her father's *geas* allow her to turn her ingenuity to more urgent priorities—such as saving herself from her stepmother's murderous attention, partying with cute boy, and performing in *Dracula* at Whitby.

This is all very bothersome. Over the course of her weeks in *Urükheim*, Agent First has discovered that the architecture is ugly, the road traffic offensive to the eye, and most of the fashions are unsightly—but it is surprisingly relaxing to wake up in the morning knowing that one's day will not be taken up by avoiding assassins and enslaving new minions for the greater glory of All-Highest. The *urük* obsession with money, which she can obtain in any reasonable quantity by snapping her fingers and asking for it, makes life easy. Her studies are trivial but absorbing and enjoyable, the flowers are blooming, the skies are curiously lacking in barrel-bodied bat-winged horrors hunting human prey, and Alex has agreed to take her out on Saturday. Life would be good, if only the world wasn't about to end.

But she can't do anything about that, so there's no point worrying.

Around lunchtime Cassie's phone vibrates. Agent First pokes at it warily. These things work on some sort of eldritch *urük* craft, *mana*-free and alien: scrying crystals powered by the chemical properties of matter and stored lightning, rather than clean and simple magic. Over the past few weeks she has become accustomed to using them, but they still confound her from time to time. Now she sees that her phone has received a message, from Alex. She begins to smile as she reads it, then her face freezes in puzzlement.

> Saturday: really sorry but I promised my parents I'd do dinner with them. Can I come to Whitby with you instead?

Agent First shakes her head. This is *wrong*. Incompatible with her orders. She *must* gain access to the enemy palace and breach its protective wards before the strike force deploys. She can see no better way to do this than by suborning a magus who works there, and the only blood-mage of her acquaintance in this world seems to be trying to back out of their date . . . *this cannot be.* And so she rapidly thumb-types her reply.

> I'd love to meet your parents! On condition you come to meet mine some time. Yes you can come to Whitby with me too afterwards? :-)

Alex replies barely five minutes later:

> Yes to both Qs. But Sis is introducing her boy to parents for 1st time. Mum wants grandchildren. Cld be awkward.

Agent First's initial grin of triumph fades to a frown as she tries to understand the hidden meaning behind the message. She's unclear on the significance of the comment about grandchildren, and she didn't know Alex had a sister, but it is becoming clear that his family might be relevant to her mission. A mother *and* a father—she suppresses a brief flash of envy—who want their children to attend a family audience? Are Alex's parents members of the occult elite who rule the secret Britannic world-empire from the shadows? She briefly contemplates the mirror-image problem. If she were Alex, tasked with intelligence-gathering among the Host, she'd definitely need to meet All-Highest, especially in the role of his child's chosen consort. *Need*, of course, not being the same thing as *want*. Meetings with powerful enemy sorcerers are fraught with danger at the best of times. But if

Alex's sibling plans to introduce *her* chosen one at the same time, then there is an opportunity for diversion, and evaluating Alex's parents is clearly an important milestone.

> I don't think so. Your sis will take heat. Let me come. We can have fun afterward!

It takes a while for Alex to reply. Agent First nervously suppresses the twitchy urge to pick up the phone and let Cassie talk to him, just to hear his voice and reassure herself that she hasn't caused offense. But then, just as she's really beginning to worry, he replies:

> OK. But don't say I didn't warn you! Mum can be a bit overwhelming at times. PS: Want me to pick you up?

Cassie sends him her address book card, then pauses.

> What shld I wear?

What indeed. She is accustomed to audiences with her parents, and the elaborate etiquette of hierarchy that infuses the People leaves her clear on the honors due to various grades of liege, all the way up to the Empress-All-Highest (albeit in the twilight days before the fallen moon). But knowing the sumptuary laws and rules for carrying edged weapons in the presence of royalty at home is no help in this situation, and Alex's reply gives scant guidance:

> Mum asked me to dress up but this is just dinner with the folks: plz don't make a big deal of it or I'll die, just wear something fancy but not over the top.

At this point Agent First runs straight into Cassie's awareness that men of a certain age and gender orientation are actively discouraged from paying too much attention to their appearance.

> YesYes!!! Pick me up at 6:30! I'll be waiting.

She sends the final text and resists the urge to bang her forehead on the table. *Dinner with the folks* could mean *anything* because Cassiopeia Brewer's bubblehead memories contain no record of ever attending a formal dinner with a partner's parents. Just a vague apprehension that it's a big, possibly irrevocable, step (not that this means anything in the run-up to the end of the world). *Wear something fancy* could mean anything, too. Cassie's school held a prom dance for the sixth form—a recent import, she remembers—but Cassie went full gothic, dyed her hair crimson, and punked out her school uniform. Somehow Agent First suspects this would be inappropriate. Nor can she rely on her glamour, if Alex's parents are thaumaturges as powerful as their offspring. She briefly considers not wearing anything at all, but it's too early in the year and it still gets chilly at night, and anyway, the *urük* have lots of tiresome body taboos.

Oh well. She doesn't have any lectures to attend until four and the weather's nice: she might as well go to college and raid the theatrical wardrobe for something fancy to wear to the end of the world.

10: INTERLUDE: MALHAM

Agent First's description of the terminal of the shadow road proves accurate. The geomancers wait beside the cold iron spike that anchors it to the not-ground of the blue-glowing void between the worlds as First Liege and her escort approach.

Although she rides a cavalry mount for the time being, First Liege wears the silver-and-ivory fluted light steel plate of a rider of firewyrms, as befits her command. Instead of a crest her helmet is crowned by a golden circlet, jade power gems blazing balefully. As she stares coolly down at First of Geomancy, they flare so brightly that they cast the shadow of her mount's head and neck across the magus's face.

"Why the delay?" she asks, her tone deceptively light. *"Is the road not yet re-anchored?"*

"High Lady." Magus First of Geomancy bows deeply, but does not fully prostrate himself before her: court etiquette is onerous and time-consuming, and is therefore abbreviated in the field. *"The road is indeed open, but the gate is not yet re-anchored. I desired to complete the move before Your Excellency ventures across its threshold."*

"Not yet re-anchored?" First Liege's ear flaps hinge subtly backwards in response, a reflexive expression of anger and scorn. Magus Second cringes visibly, having felt the wrath of First of Airborne Strike Command's mercurial rage in the past, but her superior is made of sterner stuff and stands his ground, even as the All-Highest's wife hisses: *"Pray explain."*

"High Lady. The gate was anchored by Agent First of Spies and Liars when that one came this way. If she was plotting treachery even

then"—it is clear to all present that First Liege bears Agent First no love, and obvious that the sentiment must be reciprocated—*"she might well have sought to booby-trap the exit. And the failure of Agent Second to return hither evinces the plausibility of this supposition. Also, she used excessive mana in the process of securing its far end in Urükheim. Pray grant this one the gift of a tenth-day to re-anchor the gate with care, moving it from this end, and not only will you be guaranteed a safe transport; the treacherous one will be unable to find it and sneak behind your back."*

The magus's case is unassailable, and although First Liege is deeply annoyed by the delay, she yields to his logic. *"Yes, then make it so. We shall wait while you proceed."*

The magus clears his throat delicately. *"There is one thing."* He gestures at the glowing oval of the gate. *"We will expend considerable mana of our own in this operation. I and my Second require sacrifice, lest we are left exhausted when you need us subsequently."*

First Liege stares silently from atop her mount for so long that First of Geomancy suspects he has made a fatal misjudgment, and composes himself accordingly. But he is mistaken. First Liege bottles up her anger and frustration and beckons one of her troopers closer. His mount sidesteps, snorting angrily as her own mount hisses and lowers its horn, challenging the intruder until First Liege yanks on its reins. *"Do we have any sacrifices in train?"* First Liege demands of her lancer. *"My magi hunger."*

"My Liege!" The knight dips his head, peacock-feathered plume bobbing: *"We brought none such, anticipating forage beyond the road."* The unspoken, unspeakable truth hovers in the starry void: the Host is already desperately short of serfs, having left so many behind when they entered hibernation. They expected to find the road already re-anchored in underpopulated wilderness, a hub from which they could harvest bodies at will. *"The useless urük mouth can be spared."* He means the prisoner, manacled and blindfolded, who shuffles along with their tail of slave-technicians and body servants. He pauses delicately. *"Or if my Liege requires it, I or any of my lance stand ready for the ultimate sacrifice—"*

First Liege raises her chin, dismissing the offer. *"The urük will do,"* she says. *"Bring it hither."* To First of Geomancers, she explains: *"We have but one blood offering. Use it wisely. Your first duty once the road is re-anchored and secure is to find provender for your second."*

First of Geomancers bows deeply, while his Second prostrates herself before First Liege. *"Your will shall be made stone,"* says the first magus, as two dismounted lancers step forward, frog-marching the stunned *urük* prisoner. She's shaking her head dizzily, as if trying to wake from a dream: *geas*-bound, of course. The soldiers force her to her knees, remove her blindfold, and pull her head back. She looks up to see First of Geomancers smile at her.

First Liege makes a complex gesture, unbinding the fog that wraps the *urük* woman's mind.

Awareness dawns almost instantly. The *urük* woman looks away from the magus and instead stares angrily at First Liege. She hisses, in Agent First's voice: *"Your life will be mine!"*

"I don't think so." First Liege's ears go up in satisfaction as she gives First of Geomancers the signal. He steps forward. The sacrifice struggles, but with two lancers holding her and her arms manacled her resistance is ineffectual. First of Geomancers bends towards her, as if to kiss her exposed throat: then he bares his teeth.

Cassiopeia Brewer's body screams for a long time. Then the blooded geomancers go to work.

With the road lifted and re-anchored in a flare of false lightning, the scouts of the First Lady of the Host trot forward onto ley lines less well traveled, a branching network that stretches beyond the newly moved gate. First of Geomancy tiredly conjures up a map of the network and points at the widest path, signed as being anchored to the node on which they stand: *"Hither lies the abandoned enemy bunker and the path adjacent to their palace."* He breathes deeply, almost panting with effort. *"We came through it. Forward scouts would . . . would . . ."*

First of Geomancy fed deeply, consuming the life-energy and *mana* of the *urük* prisoner barely an hour earlier, but he is gray-faced and tired from the effort of moving the shadow road anchor-point and binding it to the ley lines. His Second is even worse, lying supine, his stretcher borne by two apprehensive servants (neither of whom wishes to become the object of a mage's bloody thirst). As the soldiers move forward, another two servants ease First of Geomancy onto a palanquin, draw blackout curtains, and shuffle forward beneath his weight.

Highest Liege of Airborne Strike nods at her Second: *"Send scouts to secure that ley line,"* she tells him. *"Now let's see what we have here."* She rides forward between her escort of knights, straight and proud, and as her steed snorts and steps off the ley line onto solid rock she looks around at the marshaling area in her new demesne for the first time.

It is early evening in the Yorkshire Dales. Grass and scattered rocky debris render the surface treacherous for her mount, but the war-steeds of the Host have excellent night vision. Scrubby trees grow here, spaced well apart, their bark gnarled and twisted from the winds that blow over the low mountains to the west. Highest Liege inhales deeply: the night air smells of grass and moisture. Turning her head— her helm and gorget make this tricky—she sees a horseshoe-shaped waterfall of pale stone frozen in flight behind her. Plants grow from its surface, their outlines indistinct in the moonlight shed by the dwarf planet floating overhead.

This world is *alive*. Highest Liege smiles. If her idiot stepchild spoke truth in her report—and she has yet to catch Agent First lying— there is little *mana* here. There are no priests of darkness to shatter moons or invite in the undead horrors from beyond the walls of the universe. There are pitifully few magi, too, and those that exist are in hiding for some reason. Overhead an owl hoots, and in the bushes below small things quiver for cover. Her smile tightens. There is little sign of habitation here. The Second Lance scatters swiftly, hooves pounding on grass as they spread out to secure the perimeter. The horseshoe-shaped valley will do nicely, she decides, once they secure the crest of the cliff. She turns and looks at her First of Lancers. *"Inform my staff that we have a defensible area and they are to bring Strikers One and Two forward. If your scouts find nothing untoward, then Air Defense will deploy on the clifftop yonder, accompanied by Third and Fourth Lances for security. I want them dug in before the daystar rises. Prepare shelter from daylight for our magi at the foot of the cliff—there are caves, I can feel them below us."*

She pauses. *"If you find any urük here, take two alive; kill the rest. Our magi need to feed."*

Her mount snarls softly beneath her, and she feels it tense and flex the great hinged scythe-claws that fold alongside its hooves. Its head dips towards the horizon. She sights along the fluted spiral of its horn towards the distant light-glow on the horizon. That must be the *urük*-hive Agent First tried to describe, she realizes. *"Tomorrow, all this belongs to my Lord,"* she observes, and her knight salutes, fist raised to forehead. *"You have your orders."* He wheels and rides back towards the troops who guard the gate, already waving hand signals. *And the day after* that, *all that is his will be mine,* Highest Liege resolves. Then she raises a hand to pull down the crystal visor of her helm and prepares to dismount her ground steed, because there is a commotion near the ley line and if she is not mistaken that means that her servants are about to bring through her *real* mount: Striker One.

As the huge moon sets and the sky darkens towards true night, the ground crews in Malham Cove prepare the first two firewyrms for flight.

Strikers One and Two are fettered, quiescent, upon the cracked limestone and grass below the cliff face. The dragons' barrel-shaped thoraxes rise and fall slowly, air pumping through their air sacs. Their legs, weak and hollow-boned, are splinted with a filigree of titanium trusses to stop them shattering under the weight of riders and weapons payloads. Woven copper wire hoses vanish into mouth and rectum, driven by moaning ventilator boxes to keep the corrosive fumes away from anyone who might approach them. Once airborne the deadly fluoritic acid (a decomposition product of wyrmspit) will diffuse away naturally, but close to the ground it can dissolve the bones inside the ground crew before anybody notices.

The dragons' necks stretch forward from their bodies, eyeless heads twitching from time to time. The anesthetists stand to either side of the lipless, circular maws, chanting softly as they cautiously raise the creatures from their thaumaturgic slumber. The firewyrms' lumbar ruffs, folded masses of tentacles as fine as any jellyfish's, pulse slowly within the safety sacks that the ground crew use to avoid accidental contact with the lethal stingers. Huge bat-wings are hobbled carefully in bags of spider-silk to prevent the creatures from momentarily unfurling their control surfaces and sending the ground crew flying. And the slender counterweight spikes of their barbed tails rest between V-shaped safety brackets, lest the dragons lash out and slice an unfortunate in half. Even the cavalry mounts of the Host—with their blue-glowing eyes and fangs and horns, slobbering bloodstained drool and snarling for flesh—step lightly around the sleeping firewyrms of Airborne Strike Command.

The armorers are busy strapping the riders' thrones and their payloads to the monsters. The dragons' shiny skin, color-shifting chromatophore scales coated with a slippery fluorinated wax that can resist the effects of wyrmspit, makes it difficult to secure anything to them. It takes bonds of dull metal alloy, locked tight around legs and neck and tail, to hold weapons and riders in place. When the harness has been adjusted and stores hung from either flank, the pilot and battle magus's howdah is bolted to the creature's back. Tandem saddles sit within a cage of steel and transparent crystal, warded to resist not only the wyrm's own fire but the arrows and death spells of an evenly matched enemy. Not that they are likely to encounter magic countermeasures in this backwards and unsophisticated land.

A thin frost rimes the blades of grass beneath their boots as First Liege and her back-seater approach Striker One. Their eyes are wide and dark, pupils fully dilated. They move with confidence because the night vision of the People far exceeds that of the *urük* of this world. Behind her, the crew of Striker Two follows suit. The pilots wear light armor, but the magi are only robed and hooded against the light. They lack the protection of cold iron, for the metal that might absorb and disperse the *mana* of an attack can also prevent a practitioner from delivering a blow. Slaves scurry to position mounting blocks beside the howdah, then abase themselves before their lords and ladies.

Highest Liege turns and looks up the crest of the cliff. For all her keenness of eye she sees no sign of the dug-in perimeter guards, or of the earthworks they are preparing for the arrival of the air defense basilisks. She raises her chin in satisfaction, then climbs the short ladder and raises her arms while servants strap her to the saddle. At last she waves at her crew chief. The woman waits by Striker One's head, holding a heavy jar sealed with occult symbols at arm's reach. Now the crew chief dips her head, then turns the jar towards the back of Striker One's neck and taps sharply on the bottom with a silver wand.

The brain leech emerges, blindly seeking shelter from the chilly air. Highest Liege closes her eyes and smiles rapturously, feeling the smooth power of the leech's muscles as if they are an extension of her own body. It's eager to bond with her mount, for the dragon's blood is heady and satisfying and the familiar ulcers are barely scabbed over from their last flight, even though many years have passed in stasis. The leech squirms home behind the firewyrm's skull and Highest Liege takes up the mental reins with a sense of relief. Yes, everything is as it should be. She raises her hands again, makes a corkscrewing gesture. Ground crew rush to pull the drain hoses from the dragon's mouth and anus, then remove the tentacle bags and release the wing leashes as she urges her mount to lumber to its feet and begin to turn, dragging its tail away from the safety cleft.

"Magus, your status if you please."

She feels her back-seater shift his balance through the frame of the protective howdah. *"I am ready and my wards are prepared, Highest."*

Highest Liege opens her eyes and looks at the landscape around her, then at her mount's scaly neck. She frowns, then wills it to shift color. Chameleon-like, the dragon responds, fading into the scenery. This is only the first of its defenses; before the People found and domesticated them the ancestors of firewyrms were prey to basilisks (likewise domesticated and turned to martial use). *If you can be seen, you are dead* is the watchword of dragonriders everywhere. As the blood-drinking sorcerer in the seat behind her begins his chant, Highest Liege finds herself increasingly unable to detect her mount, her seat, or indeed her own hands. She seems to be made of glass, and this amuses her enough to draw a brief, delighted chuckle, for she knows it to be a symptom not of psychosis but of the power of her back-seater's defensive countermeasures. She takes a step forward, then another, driving her mount's body via the brain parasite entangled with her own will: and she becomes huge and powerful and lighter than feathers. The breeze tickles her naked skin, an unbearable provocation, and she stifles the urge to draw breath and bellow a roar of challenge at the sky.

"*Striker Two, prepare to follow.*"

Her helm takes her words instantly to the ears of her Second, who acknowledges, promptly: "*I obey and follow, my lady.*"

Highest Liege drives her awareness deep into the senses of her mount, and it seems as if it is *her* wings with which she catches the breeze, and *her* will by which she begins to fall into the sky—for dragons are far too heavy to fly like birds or bats or coatl: it takes much *mana* to lift a ten-ton monster and its cargo of death. The sunken valley drops away below, the world spreading its apron, shadows crossed by strings of amber lights stretching into the distance in all directions.

Striker One spreads its wings and soars, spiraling up and out from the marshaling zone beneath the frozen limestone waterfall, while Striker Two rises to take up position astern and to port. Then the two dragons commence their night patrol, while beneath them the first light cavalry battalion rides out of the shadow road.

PART 3

MANEUVERS IN THE DARK

1 1 : WHAT TO WEAR
TO THE END OF
THE WORLD

On Friday evening, Alex belatedly realizes that if he's going to take Cassie out for dinner with his parents he can't ride his moped. The rear suspension is rubbish, it wheezes asthmatically with just one rider on board, and if it rains tomorrow evening she'll get wet, which would be bad, wouldn't it?

So he goes downstairs to the back room, where Pinky is fiddling with a compact milling machine and a chunk of wood, and clears his throat. "Uh, do you think it'd be possible for me to borrow the van tomorrow evening?"

"Nope." Pinky doesn't even look up.

"Oh." Alex rethinks his approach and tries again. "I, um, it's because I have a date tomorrow and I need to pick her up and get her home afterwards. A taxi will cost an arm and a leg, the busses don't go there, and my bike's no good. Any suggestions?"

Pinky straightens up and turns away from the workbench. "Coffee," he grunts, and goes through into the kitchen. Alex trails behind. *Coffee* isn't *yes* but it isn't *no* either. Pinky picks up an elderly aluminum stovetop kettle, fills it from the tap, and puts in on the gas ring. "Decaf for you, I think," he says thoughtfully, then begins to rummage in the cupboard. Bits of caffeine-related detritus rain down on the counter: an AeroPress, two chipped mugs, and something that looks like a prototype artificial heart with a trailing mains lead. "The van's a works motor, and the contents of the back office—you didn't say she's staff, did you?"

"No." Alex shakes his head. "Civilian."

"Then you can't drive the van." Two more mugs appear on the worktop. "You're on decaf, but the Vicar's on full-fat, isn't he?"

"What, Pete? He takes his coffee regular—" Alex looks around. "Where is he?"

"Out with Brains, fetching the tank from the MOT test center down the hill."

"The—" Alex flashes back to the bizarre machine in the garage. "It's *running*?"

"Not only is it running, it's legally roadworthy." The kettle begins to whistle, and for a minute Pinky is busy pouring, filling, and finally pumping. (The artificial heart or whatever it is makes an alarming repetitive gurgle-sploosh noise as it sucks near-boiling water and crams it through some sort of filter cartridge.) "You could borrow it, I suppose."

"Is that even legal?" Alex ponders the possibility.

"Sure. *Technically* it's also a company car, but there's nothing secret about it except for a Fuller-Dee Tetragram to power a glamour that stops other drivers from crashing when they see it. And that's just a bit of random graffiti in the leg-well until you plug your OFCUT device into the cigarette-lighter socket Brains installed and fire up the see-me-not app."

"But, but driver's license!"

Pinky thrusts a mug towards him. "Relax. Sure you'd need a category DM license endorsement—tracked vehicles—and you've only got a moped license. But"—his eyes swivel side to side, cartoon-conspiratorially—"you've got a warrant card. With the see-me-not ward nobody's going to notice you—they'll just see a totally forget-table car, and if you *do* get pulled over you just hand over your war-rant card when they ask to see your paperwork."

"Um." Alex sips his decaf cautiously, gears spinning in his head. What Pinky is proposing is bad, naughty, and wrong—but he's right. The van's off-limits, his moped is no good, and as for Pete's big bike . . . *what if she wears a skirt?* Alex asks himself. And anyway, Pete will probably be riding it home to London tomorrow morning. He's got family, after all.

Alex also has a vague idea that the kind of girl who studies drama and dresses as a vampire in Whitby on Halloween might be amused by his turning up for a date driving an antique half-track: or at least take it in her stride.

"If you don't like it, you can borrow the hovercraft," Pinky says, as a rumbling noise outside heralds the triumphant return of the Kettenkrad. "But you might have some trouble with the hills."

Agent First dreams uneasily in the early hours of Saturday morning.

She dreams of standing, stiff-legged, on a darkling plain beneath a sky of tattered, speeding clouds. Behind her stands a frozen waterfall of stone. Her feet rest on a limestone pavement much like the landscape above her father's redoubt. But this is not her home. There is no flicker of in-falling meteors lighting up the night, no vast disk of snowy dust and rock arching overhead to occlude the southern half of the sky. She wears the clothes of a young woman of the *urük*, but her wrists and ankles are fettered with cold iron and her stomach is as empty as a slave's. Two of her father's soldiers hold her upright between them: her knees are too weak to support her. They drag her before her stepmother, who is flanked by a pair of magi. From their leaden expressions she can tell that they're half-starved, exhausted by the working of great art. First Liege smiles contemptuously at her.

Oh, thinks Agent First, *this can mean only one thing.* She tenses leaden limbs that feel too short, too weak to support her. *"Your life will be mine."* She rallies, mustering what defiance she can for her death-curse. Not that curses work, as a rule, but—

"I don't think so." Her stepmother's ears go up, signaling smug satisfaction, and she motions the elder of the magi towards her.

Agent First tries to pull away, but the soldiers hold her in place when the thin-faced eunuch leans close, his grimace revealing razor-sharp canines. He locks gazes with her, and her shreds of bravado slip away in the face of the hangman's horror in his eyes. She screams in fear as he yanks her head back and sinks his teeth into the soft flesh at the base of her throat, then in pain as the blood flows. Too bad he hasn't ripped an artery: there is no abrupt gout of merciful release here, just the hungry lapping of a soft-tongued parasite suckling on her venous circulation.

Barbed appendages latch onto the surface of her mind, tearing and compressing, and she shudders, horrified as her self-image contorts and shrinks.

"*Before you depart, your father gave me a sending for your true self,*" says First Liege, leaning close. She peers into Agent First's dying proxy's eyes with hungry fascination. "*Deliver this dream tomorrow at dead of night. Time is running out. You received your orders from your Second. Present yourself and your prize*"—clear-eyed contempt shines through First Liege's words—"*to All-Highest no more than thirty hours from now.*" (As the People count time, there are twenty hours to a day.) "*Find the nearest ley line, it will take you to him. He is eager to see what you have accomplished. As am I.*"

"W—*w*—" Agent First can't feel her lips or toes and fingers. The pain is subsiding now, supplanted by a tingling chilly numbness in the periphery that is nevertheless exquisitely sensitive and unpleasant, as if the edges of her being are dissolving.

"*He will arrive tomorrow,*" says her stepmother, almost sympathetically. She takes Agent First's sagging head between her hands—the magus is holding her upright, arms around her chest and his face nuzzling against her throat—and now she, too, gazes into Agent First's raw and battered soul as it recedes, stabbing a mental image at her. "*Be present by noon on the morrow or your loyalty will be questioned, little rabbit.*"

There are many things Agent First would say to this if she was present in her own person, and not dying, palsied and shaking, in the grasp of a magus. But her mind is not her own: she can feel pieces of Cassie Brewer slipping away into darkness, the ground crumbling beneath her identity. She can't feel her hands and feet anymore, and her tongue is a huge and cumbersome block of timber between the numb white steles of her teeth. Even the vampire's grip is fading from her awareness as his parasites suck the life from her brain, all memories fading. The last to go is the dark poisoned well of her stepmother's gaze.

* * *

It's Saturday evening.

Alex has spent the afternoon in a nervous tizzy, worrying about what to wear. He's combed and re-combed his hair in instinctive fear of Mum's reaction, ironed a shirt and run straight into the question of what to wear with it. One of his office suits from the bank would be overkill, jeans and a hoodie would be underkill, and as for in-between . . . to tie, or not to tie? In the end he chickens out, goes for chinos and a tweed sports jacket, shoves a tie in his jacket pocket *just in case*, and finishes it off with a cashmere scarf and a matt-black motorcycle helmet with mirror-finished visor. Daft Punk meets Stephen Fry.

Finally he goes downstairs. Brains is sitting at the kitchen table, doing something on an iPad. "Do you have the k-keys?" he asks, all but breaking into a stammer.

"Keys?" Brains looks momentarily lost. "Oh, so you *do* want to borrow Ilsa?"

"Ilsa?"

"The Kettenkrad. C'mon, I have to check you out on the controls."

Five minutes later, Alex is sitting on an ancient motorbike saddle in a steel bathtub, with a petrol engine gurgling busily behind him. He sets his phone to vibrate: there's no way he could hear it through his helmet and the engine and track noise. "Clutch pedal on the left, brake pedal on the right, handgrip throttle on the right handlebar," Brains points out helpfully. "The gears are like a car—three forward, one reverse, and this lever selects the low ratio. You'll need to double-declutch because there's no synchro—*ouch*," as Alex stuffs it into first gear with a grate of gear teeth. "Headlamp, indicators, hazard flashers. (We added that.) To steer, pretend it's a car: at low speed the handlebars engage the track brakes, at high speed the front wheel provides steering input."

"Right, right." Alex eases up on the clutch pedal carefully. The bathtub shudders, jerks forward, and the engine stalls.

"It helps to release the handbrake." Brains chides. Alex nods rapidly; he can see that another sixty seconds of this is going to cause Brains to re-evaluate the wisdom of lending Alex his toy.

"How about I back out of here, then take it down the hill for a spin around Potternewton Park?" Alex asks. "That way I can get used to changing gears in low ratio without risking it in traffic." The park is off-limits to vehicles, but with the no-see-em in operation he should be safe enough.

"That's a good idea. But first, see if you can get it out of the driveway."

Alex gets Ilsa started again, engages first gear without any hideous crunching noises, and eases out into the quiet residential street. At the bottom of the hill there's a sharp right turn onto Harehills Lane—a commuter rat-run plagued by speeding idiots in hatchbacks—then an immediate left through the park gates. At this time of evening the park is mostly empty of joggers and dog-walkers. For the first minute, Alex gingerly experiments with the throttle and sticks to the footpaths. Then he pinches himself—Ilsa is an off-road vehicle, after all—points the handlebars at the grass, and guns the throttle.

Clattering around the grassy slopes of the park in a pint-sized half-track is tremendous fun, and the tracks (which rumble and grate on the road) are nearly silent. Alex finally gets the hang of shifting gears. But time is getting on, the light is fading, and the address Cassie gave him in Headingley is a few miles away. Luckily it's en route to his parents' place. So he drives back up to the park gates, turns onto Harehills Lane, and sets off in search of his date.

By some miracle, he does not crash.

Ilsa grunts and squeals like a pig humping a farm tractor. She sways at speed, shimmies worryingly above forty miles per hour, and vibrates excitedly until Alex eases off the throttle in a cold sweat. The heater is rubbish, the suspension is antediluvian, and the instruments rudimentary. Most of the creature comforts he expects of, say, a third-hand Honda moped, seem to have been replaced by things better suited to the minion of a particularly demented supervillain: it's not as if he expects to get any mileage out of the set of snow chains that clutter up the tiny baggage compartment, or the pintle-mount for the air-cooled machine gun. A few idiots honk their horns at him or flash their lights at him, but it's his speed they're complaining about, not his tracks or the Wehrmacht insignia painted on the fuel tanks. He drives past a parked police car without attracting any notice; the no-see-em glamour is clearly doing its job.

Google Maps takes him to the door on time, and he parks around the corner. Then, taking his courage in both hands, he raises his helmet visor and rings the bell.

The door bursts open: "Alex? Eee! I thought you'd forgotten me!" Cassie grabs him and drags him inside. She kisses him on the mouth, and by the time his circuit breakers have reset she's wrapped her arms around his waist. "I'm so glad you came," she says breathlessly.

"Er . . ." Alex's larynx seizes up as his mental circuit breakers trip out once more.

"Which way to your chariot, my lord?" She relaxes her grip, giving them both room to inhale.

"I'm—I'm parked round the corner. I brought you a spare helmet," he adds hesitantly as she opens the door and drags him out onto the pavement again. "Are you going to be okay like that?"

"YesYes!"

His pupils dilate as he sees what she's wearing. "Um. That's very— striking. When I said fancy, I, uh, wasn't expecting fancy dress . . ."

Cassie squeezes his hand. "My flatmates are going to a costume party late tonight and I was looking for an excuse to wear this! You should come too! Isn't it great?" She twitches an ear-tip at him.

"Yes, but what are you? I mean, who are you supposed to be?" Alex asks, mesmerized.

Cassie strikes a pose. "I'm a high-born lady of the Host of Air and Darkness! A child of the All-Highest of the hidden people, a courtier at the Unseelie throne!" She lets go of his hand and twirls quickly in place, nearly bowling over a passing dog-walker with a flare of her heavy black cloak. "It's very *me* isn't it? YesYes?"

After a couple of fruitless hours spent trying to second-guess Alex's occult and powerful parents, Agent First had a clever idea. She went out to Golden Acre Park to repossess her semi-charged mace of power, then she used what *mana* she could spare from it to implant in some of her more suggestible classmates the idea that they're going to dress up as fantastic, mythical beings and go clubbing later that evening.

So today she is wearing her traveling outfit, which she dry-cleaned after her arrival and stored in a dress carrier in the back of Cassie's battered wardrobe. Her closely tailored jacket and leggings are of emerald and black velvet trimmed with lace; gaudy glowing gemstones shine from the rings she wears on every gloved finger and the choker clasped around her throat. A jeweled mace dangles from one side of her belt, opposite a long dagger of questionable legality. It's the perfect disguise, for it gives her an excuse to drop the glamour she normally uses to conceal her unusual features—there is no telling how perceptive Alex's mother and father might be, if they are sorcerers of sufficient power to have spawned this one. So she will allow them to see her as she truly is: her high cheekbones, slightly slanted eyelids, hair worn in a glossy black braid falling almost to her waist, and the tall, expressively mobile ears of her kind.

Alex cocks his head in thought for a moment. He manages to simultaneously look disconcerted and poleaxed by her beauty. Finally he mumbles, weakly: "If I'd known we were going to a party afterwards I'd have come as Dracula!"

"Oh, there's still time for you to change if you want to!" she tells him airily. "I took the keys to the wardrobe room and borrowed the most dashing silk-lined opera cape and tailcoat for you! They're upstairs. But first, I want to meet your parents."

It is nearly seven o'clock. Thanks to his test-drive around the park, Alex is running late. So he leads Cassie around the corner to where Ilsa the Kettenkrad sits parked, helps her get settled on the backward-facing bench seat, then hits the road.

It's only about four or five miles to Alex's parents, but they include a nerve-racking drive up a busy dual carriageway, followed by circumnavigating the big roundabout at the intersection with Leeds's outer ring road. Halfway around the roundabout Alex's phone vibrates, the family SOS ringtone translating into an angry buzzing that's barely audible over the rumble of rubber-shod tank tracks on asphalt. He ignores it because he's busy maneuvering a slow, unwieldy vehicle across four lanes of high-speed traffic, trying not to throw Cassie off the back of the half-track as he dodges BMWs and minicabs that seem to see him as an agile motorbike. Ilsa's engine roars like an injured she-wolf, vibrating so much that his vision blurs. A minute later his phone rings again, but there seems little point in answering because now that he's passed the junction of doom it's a simple five-minute run to his parents' front door.

Alex recovers from the gut-watering terror of driving a half-track around a roundabout just in time to recognize a familiar suburban close. He drives slowly between rows of densely packed semi-detached houses, each fronted by a neatly groomed lawn and (in most cases) one or more parked cars. He has to make an effort not to let his over-eager enumeration cantrip predigest the house numbers. *Number twenty, number twenty-two . . . twenty six.* He gingerly noses in alongside the pavement, sets the handbrake, then kills the engine. He sits for a moment and stares at his hands, which are shaking. In the sudden silence, he hears a whoop from behind: "That was fun! Do it again! YesYes!"

Oh God, he thinks. He removes his helmet, clambers over the side of the bathtub-shaped carrier, and walks round the back to offer Cassie his hand. She steps down daintily, unstrapping her own helmet and dumping it on the bench seat. "Are you sure you want another lift?" he asks doubtfully: "I was afraid you were going to fall off . . ."

"No, it was wonderful! I haven't had that much fun since I borrowed one of Daddy's sparkle ponies for a joy ride!" Her face is such a picture of innocent joy that Alex can't bear to tell her how scary the hell-ride across the roundabout had been. "I must take you to meet my father soon, YesYes?"

"Of course," Alex agrees.

"Promise?" she persists. "A third date, third time lucky?"

"I promise." He pats her wrist, and she smiles triumphantly.

"Is this it?" she asks, looking around.

"Er, yeah. Yes." His parents' house sits precisely twenty pre-metric feet back from the pavement, slightly downhill, behind a cement foot-path and a lawn as carefully manicured as AstroTurf. The house itself is faced in red brick, with cellular double glazing and about as much character as one of the night shift zombies. Alex leads her to the porch and is about to push the buzzer beside the fiberglass-paneled front door when his phone vibrates again.

Once is happenstance, twice is coincidence, but three times means a family crisis. He glances at the screen: it's Sarah. "Yes? I'm on the front step right now—"

"You're late!" Her voice is odd, as if she's trying not to be over-heard. "Help! Mum's having a seizure or something and Dad's trying to drink himself to death—"

Alex goes cold. "Have you called an ambulance?" He stares at the door. "Let me in, I've got some first-aid training—"

"Not that kind of seizure, I think the penny dropped—she's just met Mack." There's a click as the door unlatches from the inside. It swings open just as Sarah says, "Bye," and drops her phone. It clatters noisily on the front step, unnoticed.

"Hello?" Cassie says from behind Alex's shoulder. She waves her left hand hesitantly. Sarah stares at her wide-eyed and open-mouthed for long seconds, until Alex remembers he's supposed to do some-thing other than wait for the doorstep to grow teeth and a digestive tract beneath his shoes and swallow him whole.

"Uh, Sarah?" he says carefully. "This is Cassie. Cassie, this is Sarah, my sister. Sarah, Cassie's my, uh, my—"

"Consort," Cassie volunteers helpfully just as Alex manages to force the word "date" past his suddenly too-large tongue.

Sarah's eyes roll up in her head. "Saved," she says fervently, "we're saved!" She takes a step back, blinking dizzily. "Come on in, you can help with damage control."

The front room of the house is a combined living room and dining room. At one side, the TV is blatting a content-free soap opera in the direction of the three-piece suite. (Probably *EastEnders*, Alex guesses. It's his family's favorite window into a world of excitement and glamor.) At the other side, the over-polished dinner table* is laid with settings for six.

---

* He remembers how—years ago—next door's cat got indoors, leapt on the table, and slowly slid across it and fell off the far side, despite futile front-paw backpedaling. It had worn an expression of profound outrage the whole time, much like a child summoned to the sink-side to do the washing up.

Dad is sprawled on the sofa. His eyeballs are pointed at the screen as if blind to the world around him. He's wearing his usual work suit, minus jacket and tie, plus gray wool cardigan and tartan slippers. A half-drained tumbler of gin and tonic dangles precariously from his left hand.

"Where's Mum?" Alex quietly asks Sarah.

"In the kitchen, hiding."

"And your . . . ?" *Mick? Mack?*

"In the bathroom, hiding."

Oh God, he thinks again, just as Cassie skips into the living room like Zelda on crystal meth, all cloak and boots and pointy ears. As she registers the presence of his father her manner suddenly shifts toward uncharacteristic diffidence: it's almost as if she's nervous about something. "Uh, Cassie, this is Dad—"

He points helplessly. Then Dad, hearing his son's voice, opens his eyes.

"Hello?" Cassie says quietly.

Dad flails and sits bolt-upright, drops his G&T, and shouts, *"What now?"*

"Dad!" Alex winces. "This is Cassie, my"—he swallows— "girlfriend."

Dad sits up unsteadily and looks at Cassie. "Oh good," he slurs, "this one's *normal.*"

Cassie shoves her cloak back, endangering the table setting in the process, and delivers a sweeping bow: "I am at your service, oh liege and master," she declares. "Life, power, and the blood of your enemies poured on the altar of your gods!" She finishes with a salute, her gloved left fist clenched before her beating heart.

"We're going to a fancy-dress party later," Alex announces to the disbelieving silence, his heart speeding. "She's an elven princess—" His tongue stumbles into shocked silence as he recognizes what's been under his nose all along. *Those ears,* he thinks, still enchanted despite the shiny new protective ward hanging against his breastbone, *they're not falsies.* "And I'm a vampire," he adds, unsure whether he's courageously outing himself or merely supporting Cassie's conceit.

Dad raises a hand. "Son, get me another drink? This one's broken."

Sarah looks at Alex in mute appeal. He takes a deep breath and shrugs, then looks back at her helplessly. She's about one-sixty centimeters tall, with short, mousy hair and mild brown eyes. Right now she's filling a pair of jeans with torn knees and a checked lumberjack shirt. Her DMs are adorned with tiny multicolored daisies. Another penny drops. He's lived in the big city long enough that despite his sheltered upbringing he's learned what this particular dress code means. He nods, minutely: "I'll get it," he says.

"Do you think that's wise—" Sarah begins, then notices Cassie. "Make it a double. You'd better get me one, too, and a Coke for Mack. She doesn't drink alcohol."

Alex potters over to the sideboard, where he finds a half-empty bottle of Gordon's and a couple of bottles of Schweppes sitting beside a bowl with half a lemon in it, neatly pre-sliced. Cassie is kneeling at his father's feet, as if she's about to perform an elaborate ritual prostration. *Okay, deep breaths,* he tells himself. *The worst is over. Dad's drunk and Mum's in hysterics because Sarah's girlfriend is hiding in the bathroom.* Mum and Dad aren't narrow-minded, but they lack imagination . . . when it comes to their children they have curiously rigid ideas. Coming right after their daughter coming out, breaking the news to them that their son is a vampire and he's dating a self-identified elven princess should be a walk in the park. *Just don't mention the pay cut,* some residual sense of self-preservation prompts him.

He lines up a row of four tumblers, divides the remains of the gin bottle evenly between them, throws in a curl of lemon and a couple of ice cubes, then tops them up with a drop of tonic water. Then he picks one up and nods at Sarah: "Is Mum still in the kitchen?"

Sarah nods and clutches her drink like it's the last one in the world. So he turns and goes in search of his mother.

Mum is fussing around the kitchen, multitasking between a hot oven and a variety of serving dishes with vegetables keeping warm on the hob. She's in twinset and pearl necklace, evidently having felt the need to raise her game to tax audit levels in preparation for meeting both her children's partners simultaneously. Her movements are fussily precise and over-controlled.

"Mum." He puts the tumbler down on the butcher's block with a deliberate thump, to telegraph its presence despite the risk of sloshing the contents. "Mum?"

"Alex?" She turns to him with a sniff, eyes wide. She opens her arms. "Come here! How you've grown."

He hugs her. She seems to have shrunk, or he's taller, or something: he can almost rest his chin on her head. She's vibrating with nervous energy. "It's all right, Mum. I brought you a drink."

"Oh, you good boy! Have one—" She pauses doubtfully. "Are you driving?"

"Yes, Mum. Is there a Coke? And a Diet Coke for me?" There are always a couple of cans in the recesses of the family fridge, pining for company.

"Of course!" She lets go and looks at him. "You bought a car? Did they pay you a bonus?"

"Not exactly." It's now or never. He resolves to tell the truth this evening, or as much of it as his oath of office will permit: it's a huge weight off his conscience. "Uh, Mum, the bank—they, uh, they downsized my unit."

"They what? But they can't do that! There must be some mistake." She looks bewildered, all the certainties of her carefully curated family picture thrown askew.

"It's all right, Mum," he says wearily. He's rehearsed this in his own head so many times that now he's got his back to the dishwasher it's almost a relief to get the prerecorded spiel off his chest. "They could and they did, but I got a good job with the Civil Service. It's in the defense sector and it's technical so I can't talk about it, but it's much more secure than the bank. You win some, you lose some. They're threatening to relocate me up here."

"Oh." She sniffs again, then takes a deep breath and sighs. "Be a dear and pass me that drink, will you? This seems to be the day for disappointments." He hands her the tumbler, silently angry on Sarah's behalf. "I suppose next you'll be telling me that your Cassie is an imaginary friend like *Gregory's Girl*, and you just made her up to get me off your back."

Alex shrugs uncomfortably. "I wouldn't do that, Mum."

"Oh, you know your father and I just wanted you both to do well. So perhaps we leaned on you a bit too hard with our own ideas of what would be a success story. But really, it doesn't matter. Why did the bank fire you?"

"They fired my entire *team*, Mum, it wasn't just me. There was a scandal. Our manager Oscar was, uh, he had something over the chief executive. It all fell apart after Sir David killed himself—I'm sorry, it went that high—the rest of us were collateral damage. An institutional embarrassment to be swept under the rug." He gets creative: "I'm probably blacklisted for life from the entire investment banking sector. But I guess I got lucky because I was unemployed for less than a week when I got an offer."

His mother's expression turns mulish. He knows that look. It has been known to make headmasters and company secretaries wet themselves. "You got an offer within a week? *Really?*"

"There was—" He swallows. "Listen, we were doing cutting-edge mathematical research. It came to the attention of certain people and they made us an offer. It seemed like a good idea to take it at the time."

He's careful to avoid the idiotic, broken, no-good F-35 software story, and to *also* avoid telling her any lies—Mum has a tax inspector's built-in lie detector—while not overstepping the red line of his oath of office.

"You mean GCHQ, don't you?" she asks, a sudden quiet respect creeping into her voice.

"Not them, exactly, no. Uh, I can't tell you anything about who I work for. Just, it's defense-related and it involves mathematics." He pauses. "The pay's rubbish, but the job security is high. And the rest of the security. Security is high *in general* where I work—" He realizes he's babbling and manages to stop.

"I see, I think." She turns away and opens the oven door, throwing out a blast of heat and an odor of cooking beef brisket that nearly makes Alex involuntarily extend his fangs. "Hmm, I think it's done."

She bends down and lifts the roasting tray out. "Would you be a dear and carry the vegetables? We're ready to eat, and it would be a shame to let the food go cold."

Dinner is not obviously a total disaster at first.

While Alex is talking Mum down from the trees and Cassie tries to engage Dad in small talk, Sarah scrambles upstairs and bangs on the bathroom door. The result is that by the time Alex backs into the dining area, bearing a steaming hot dish full of boiled frozen peas and identically formed bright orange conic sections ("carrots" in Mum's culinary vernacular), he finds a stranger seated at the table at Dad's right hand, listening attentively as Dad apologizes stumblingly for something or other he may or may not have said earlier. By a process of logical deduction he recognizes that the stranger must be Mack. She's glammed up for the event in a navy blue polka-dot dress and enough makeup to notice but not overwhelm. Obviously this is her way of trying to make a good impression on the partner's parents. Her hair is longer than Sarah's, which reminds him that the last time he saw his younger sister she sported a bushy mane. "Hello?" she says quietly.

"Hi, I'm Alex." He deposits the serving dish and offers a hand: she shakes it firmly, surprising him with her grip. "This is Cassie—"

"I got that." Mack smiles reassuringly. Her voice is a little husky.

Cassie looks excited. "Alex! You didn't tell me your people have ceremonial eu—"

"No," Alex interrupts hastily. But he's too late.

Sarah smiles, icily. "You do not call Mack that," she says calmly. "I don't care whether you're staying in-character for the evening; her gender identity is none of your business. Are we clear?"

Cassie looks away and nods. "YesYes," she mutters sheepishly. Louder: "I'm sorry. I was just excited because I had been wondering where your kind keep your—" She stops abruptly.

Alex wishes the dining chair would swallow him up. The prickly tension between Mack, Sarah, and Cassie is mortifying. He gets that Mack is trans and that Sarah is coming out and he's supposed to play a supporting role in kid sis's family drama, but at least she could have *warned* him before he brought Cassie into this without notice—

Dad takes a big gulp of G&T as Mum enters, bearing the beef joint.

"Is she always like this?" Sarah asks Alex challengingly.

"Cassie is studying acting and drama at Leeds Met," Alex says defensively. "It's just method acting isn't it, Cassie? Your character . . ."

"I'm a princess-assassin of the Unseelie Court!" Cassie agrees enthusiastically. "Not human, not even *slightly* human. So *of course* I'm weird and I make horrible social blunders when I try to pass for human! Faux pas is my middle name and I don't understand human social mores *at all*!" Her smile is blinding and utterly sincere. "I am sorry for your discombobulation! We're going to a fancy dress party later," she confides.

"Huh." Sarah smiles, not entirely nicely. Mack, for her part, is as impassive as a poker player, clearly unwilling to contribute further to what promises to be a family reunion that will be remembered for all the wrong reasons. "How did you get here, then?"

"Oh, very easily!" Cassie giggles: "Alex stole a Nazi half-track motorcycle from a mad scientist he knows through work! It was most exciting!"

Alex sighs. "I did *not* steal Ilsa," he explains before Dad can throw a drunken hissy fit at the hint of impropriety: "Brains lent her to me for the evening."

Sarah stares at him. "I'll swear someone said 'Nazi half-track motorcycle.' And 'mad scientist.' I must be hallucinating, right? Tell me I'm hallucinating."

Mack opens her mouth, then pauses thoughtfully for a moment. "Would it happen to be an NSU Kettenkrad?" she asks. "If so, was it wartime or postwar manufacture?"

Mum clears her throat diplomatically. "Alex, your father is a bit sleepy. Would you do the honors and carve the brisket?"

"Wartime," Alex says, his feet carrying him on autopilot towards the sideboard and the dish with the carving set. "How did you know?"

"I made a model of one when I was a kid. The Tamiya 1:35 scale precision one." Mack sounds just slightly wistful. "I used to make lots of models before I grew out of it. It was something I could do by myself and I was good at it."

"Half-track," mutters Sarah. "So you're driving?"

"Yup." Alex picks up the carving fork and pokes the brisket hesitantly. As usual for Mum, it's slightly overcooked but just the right side of burned. "So I'm not drinking." He can feel eyeballs drilling into his back like gimlets. "I'm not making this up," he protests defensively, "it's parked outside!"

"I believe you," Sarah says after a moment, as Cassie chirps: "It's all true! Even the mad scientist!"

"He's not mad, he just works in Technical Operations," Alex says as he begins to carve. After the first slice: "Well, he's not *very* mad." After the second slice: "By Tech Ops standards."

"What does your mad scientist friend do for your employers, dear?" his mother asks.

"He does quality assurance testing on death rays." *Please, dear God, don't ask me about the coffee maker.* "Also, he repairs stuff for a hobby. Like the Kettenkrad. He's working on a hovercraft right now."

"My hovercraft is full of eels," Dad slurs, but nobody pays any attention to him except Cassie, and Alex is too busy trying not to slice his left hand off to look round.

Presently he has six plates stacked with what he hopes is enough burned cow's arse to feed a dysfunctional family, so he turns and begins to deliver them around the table.

Things go all right until he gets to Mack, who looks perturbed. She turns and whispers something in Sarah's ear. Sarah responds, audibly: "I *told* Mum . . ."

"Told Mum what?" Alex asks.

"Mack's vegan," Sarah confesses.

"I said not to make a big fuss," Mack touches her wrist. "I'll be okay." But she's leaning away from the plate in front of her as if Alex has deposited a great steaming jobbie on it.

Mum's smile freezes in place. "Do vegans eat fish?" she asks. "Because I've got a couple of salmon fillets I can microwave if it's any help—"

Mack takes a deep breath, then visibly bites her tongue. "Not really," she says quietly.

Cassie looks confused, then her left ear twitches, telegraphing enlightenment. "Oh! I know, you need tofu!" Then her ears droop. "I didn't bring any. No pockets, sorry."

"Those prostheses are *amazingly* responsive," Sarah says brightly: "Are they those Japanese toys that can sense brain-waves? Can I touch—"

It's either kid sister's revenge for Cassie putting her foot in it with Mack earlier, or a brilliant attempt to redirect the conversation, but before Alex can work out which (or Sarah can tug Cassie's ears) Cassie sweeps the offending burnt offering from before Mack. "Be right back!" she trills, and makes a beeline for the kitchen.

Mum takes a deep breath, smiles tremulously, and lifts the lids off the vegetable dishes with a flourish.

British domestic cuisine spans the gamut from the sublime to the abysmal. Alex never really questioned Mum's culinary efforts before he left home—they came off well when compared to school dinners—but exposure to a broader diet has taught him how close she sticks to her 1970s Domestic Science lessons, raiding Tesco's and Asda's chiller aisles for variety. Mum is not an adventurous cook, and faced with the prospect of catering to two grown-up children and their guests she has panicked slightly and retreated into the comforting certainties of meat and two (frozen) veg. One of which is still frozen.

"Um." Alex stares at the brick of broccoli florets, ice crystals glittering under the dining room chandelier. "I'd better just take these through and heat them up . . . ?"

Mum blinks, then with no warning whatsoever her eyes overflow and she starts to sob.

Sarah, Mack, and Alex watch in paralyzed silence. Dad is no help whatsoever, muttering inaudibly into his nearly empty tumbler: he's out for the count. Alex looks round and realizes he must have put away a quarter of a bottle of gin. The crashing and clattering of an enterprising alien foraging for who-knows-what echoes from the kitchen. Across the table, Mack clutches her chair's arms as if she wants the floor to swallow her. Sarah leans towards her protectively from the next seat, but her eyes are on Mum, and she's as appalled as Alex. Mum is a tax inspector: she has nerves of steel. She doesn't lose her shit like this, she just *doesn't*. But there she is, at the far end of the table, quietly weeping tears of desperation and unhappiness. Alex has no idea why, or what to say.

The silence is broken by the scrape of a chair being pushed back. Alex realizes he's standing beside his mother's seat. "Mum. Mum? Come on, let's get you some tissues and clean up. Hey, it's going to be all right—"

She stands up and leans on his shoulder. "I'm being silly," she sniffs.

"C'mon, Mum, over here." He guides her towards the sofa. There's a box of Kleenex on the coffee table. He glances past her, back at the table, as Dad's head tips slowly backwards and he begins to snore. Mack's shoulders are shaking and as Alex turns back to focus on Mum he sees Sarah hug her. *Good for them,* he thinks, then a loud crash and a musical tinkling from the kitchen remind him that Mum is only Crisis Number One on his bucket list. "You can sit down and have a good blow and tell me all about it. What's wrong?" Because even to Alex's untrained male sensibilities it is obvious that something badly unhinged Mum right before he and Cassie arrived. Whatever it was, it hit her so hard that she burned the brisket and forgot to defrost the broccoli.

A possible explanation suddenly occurs to him: Could it be the V-question? *Work. Did Security interview her for my enhanced background check?* "What's wrong?" he repeats. Quietly: "Was it me? Did you get any, uh, visitors? From my new employers?"

"Visitors?" Mum blinks bewilderedly. "No dear, it's your sister."

"Mum." He holds a bunch of tissues out for her and she takes them, wipes cheeks, blows her nose. "You know that's kind of bigoted?" He treads carefully. Mum has never been particularly religious, other than filling out the census forms with Church of England—it's the default option—but you can never tell, and while he's never seen her as a homophobe before—

"No, it's not that! It's her degree course." Mum honks mournfully into her wad of damp tissues.

"Her course." Alex's brain freezes. "What about her degree?"

"She's changed her course"—she'd been studying for a BA in Business Studies and Accounting, Alex recalls—"to study *history*." Mum begins to tear up again. "History! *Why?* What use is *that*? How is she going to earn a living with a *history* degree?" And she's off again.

Another crash, this time barely distinguishable from a smash, interrupts his confusion. *Oh God, Cassie,* he thinks. "Stay here?" he implores his mother; "I need to see what that was."

He finds Cassie in the kitchen, surrounded by the shattered wreckage of dessert. A glass pudding basin lies in pieces on the floor; the tortured corpses of fruit, viciously flayed and seeds eviscerated, sprawl around the worktop. "I know it's supposed to go together!" she protests. "I just can't get them to fit properly." There is a supermarket spongecake base in a plastic container, along with the makings of a liter of raspberry jelly, an unopened carton of custard, and a jar of whipping cream. Mum was evidently planning to make a sherry trifle before Sarah's educational catastrophe dismayed her and drove Dad to drink.

"Don't bother." Alex takes everything in at a glance. Cream comes from cows, custard contains egg, and as for the jelly—*Isn't gelatin some kind of kryptonite for vegans?* he thinks, then surrenders to the inevitable. "We're done here; I'm calling in the professionals."

He goes back to the living room and clears his throat. Sarah and Mack disengage, somewhat bashfully. "I know what this looks like," Mack says before his sister shushes her.

"Not my problem." Alex drags Mum's chair round to face them. Puffy-eyed, she holds a bundle of tissues to her face and sniffs mournfully. "Listen. First, is Dad okay?" Before anyone can answer Dad supplies an answer by beginning to sing the refrain to "With a Little Help from My Friends," in a new and creative key. "Fine, that just

leaves us in need of something to eat. I've got a takeaway app—
Mack, you're vegan, I know what Mum and Dad will take, Cassie is
easy, do we have any other restrictions?"

Sarah shakes her head. "Alex, I don't know what Mum's told
you—"

"Food before inadvisable career choices." He pulls out his phone,
locks it into guest mode, and fires up a takeaway menu finder. "Let
me guess, South Indian or Mexican are good bets?" Mack nods.
"Okay, see if you can find something that appeals to you and fill in
what you need. Then I'll order for the rest of us, can you do that?"

"I'll try."

Mack takes his phone, just as Cassie bounds out of the kitchen on
the tips of her toes, announces, "I'm done!" in a loud stage-whisper,
and drapes herself over Alex's shoulders. She stares wide-eyed at
Mack. "What's he—she—doing?"

If looks could kill, Sarah's glare would reduce Cassie to a pile of
cinders as she replies: "Magicking up dinner for six. And please don't
misgender, it's rude."

Alex forces himself to breathe. Cassie is doing unprecedented things
to his neurohormonal system—she seems to be an amazing antidote to
his creeping sense of inhumanity—but right now he feels as if he's
caught in the middle of some sort of alpha-female threat display between lionesses. (And there's the matter of her own inhumanity to
address, but not in public.) He concentrates on Sarah. "Mum said
you'd changed your degree."

His sister nods. "That's right. Mum thinks she's more broad-minded
than she is, and she's having a little trouble adjusting to the idea. As for
Dad—"

Mack glances up. "It's his fault," she says defensively. "He shouldn't
have asked if he didn't want a straight answer."

Alex closes his eyes. "Do I want to know?"

"You probably need to, for your own good." Sarah's lips are a
tight line. "There's an FAQ, things not to ask trans people on first
acquaintance. I sent him the link but he obviously didn't read it."

Alex opens his eyes, with an effort. "Hence the gin bottle."

"Hence the gin," Sarah agrees. "Maybe you should read it, too?" she adds, pointedly making eye contact with Cassie.

Cassie tenses. "I apologize for any offense I may have caused, but your *urük* ways are alien to me. I will read this FAQ if you direct me to it. I am of the Host," she says stiffly, "and although we do not like to unintentionally give offense I am still finding my way among you . . ."

Alex glances down at the table. Mum has laid it with the good cutlery, he notices for the first time. It's a wedding present from his grandparents, silver-plated and a complete pain in the neck to clean. She obviously did it because she was making a special effort. He reaches round with his left hand and touches Cassie's wrist, but she's wearing a glove and she's behind him so he can't look her in the eye. He feels a telltale tingling and a sense of urgent desire from her, and he's sure there's something he ought to say, although it's on the tip of his tongue. But then he looks up and sees Sarah aim a guarded nod at Cassie and a certain tension goes out of their posture.

"Here," says Mack, passing his phone back to him. "It says they can deliver within half an hour once you place your order: you've probably even got time for a drink while we're waiting—a small one, seeing you're driving." She smiles disarmingly.

Alex sends the order. "I need to check on Dad," he says, and Cassie lets go of him as he stands. Dad is still singing quietly to himself. "C'mon, Pa? Let's get you to the recliner." It's an overstuffed armchair that matches the sofa's crumpled floral velour. It is Dad's habit to nap in it for half an hour each evening when he gets home from work. Unlike the dining chair there's no risk of him sliding off it. Paternal relocation completed, Alex confiscates his near-empty tumbler and refills it with ice and tonic water. As he positions it on the occasional table by his father's right hand, Cassie materializes beside him.

"This is your father," she says quietly.

"Yes." Alex puts the glass down.

"But he's *harmless*."

He glances at her sidelong, and remembers the question he's been saving up for some time. "Can you tell a lie?" he asks.

She meets his gaze, unblinking. "Not to *my* father."

"Your father." He thinks for a moment. "The food won't arrive for at least half an hour. It's time you and I had a little talk about your family, isn't it?"

Cassie draws breath to reply, then nods abruptly and stands. "Outside," she says, "where the stars can stand witness to my truth."

12: LA CAGE AUX FOLLES

Alex stands in the open front doorway. Cassie squats on the front lawn, clutching her knees, her back tense. They are serenaded by distant traffic and barking dogs. For a moment he's torn. He ought to help out with the mess indoors, make sure Mum is all right and that Mack (who is clearly having a terrible time) isn't traumatized. But he has a horrible feeling that if he doesn't talk to Cassie right now he'll be making a huge mistake.

He comes up behind her and kneels. "You're not human, are you?" he says.

"No. Are you?"

"I'm—" He stops dead, rephrases what he was about to say. "I used to be."

"Well then. What would you do if I said I'm *trying* to be? I mean, I like it here. Only I'm not very good at faking being one of you."

"You're good enough for me," he says, carefully feeling his way through the swamp of assumptions.

"Oh, you poor fool," she murmurs sadly, leaning back against him.

Alex thinks very hard for a few seconds. Then he asks, "Why are you here?" Meaning, *Why are we having this conversation?*

She is silent for a few seconds. "Alex, when I asked you to come with me to meet my family I did not mean you ill. But I *have* to take you, do you understand? I am forced to do so. An obligation—I'm not sure that's the right word? A compulsion that I can't break, perhaps." She falls silent again. Then, just as he's about to ask her to explain, she continues: "I don't like my father, and my stepmother hates me and wants me dead. At best they will try to use you against me, or me against you. Do you understand?"

Alex understands let's-you-and-him-fight games all too well, but something about Cassie's vehemence scares him. "Not really. Why do you have to introduce me if they're so bad?"

"Because he's my—" She shakes her head and half-turns towards him. Her expression is one of mute misery. Alex wraps his arms around her and she tucks her chin into the side of his neck. Her ears quiver like a frightened rabbit's. She's warm, and he can feel her heartbeat, hear the hiss and sigh of blood in her arteries, the ebb and flow of air in her lungs.

She's not human, he thinks. *But neither am I.* And he's torn in multiple directions by his own ignorance and the urgent sense of impending crisis. How did she find him? *Why* did she find him? (Because he can't kid himself that this is nothing to do with work.) What is she, and have her kind been living in the shadows all along, or—did she come here from somewhere else? *What*— He stops. There's no safe way out of this. "What kind of person are you?" he asks, half-afraid of what she'll tell him.

"I'm a—" She pulls back slightly, frowning faintly. "I'm of the People. That's how our name for our own kind translates into your tongue: not very helpful, is it?" He nods encouragingly. "In our tongue we would say *alfär*. We are distant relatives, closer than your Neanderthal cousins. But prehistory took a different path in my homeworld. Speech came late to my ancestors, and when words arrived they already had the makings of magi. Your kind have many names for us: fae or unseelie. My father is the All-Highest. Everything I told you is true. But your legends about my People are nonsense and confusion." She pulls back further, raises a hand to his face, and pokes at his upper lip. Alex flinches. *"Magister,"* she says, peering into his eyes.

Alex meets her gaze. Cassie's irises are a dark, muddy brown, turbid as a bog pool. Her pupils are slightly elliptical, almost catlike, but in the streetlight it's hard to be sure because they're also dilated. He feels a glamour pressing on his mind, but held carefully in check. He pushes back, and her pupils dilate wider as he feels a matching resistance. Then, before the mental shoving match escalates, she leans forward and kisses him on the lips.

Alex recoils. "Wait!" He takes a deep breath. "It's not safe, I'm a, a . . ."

"Vampire?" Shocked, he lets her take his hands. "You aren't going to suck my blood, are you?" she asks suggestively.

"But I'm infectious—"

"Not to me and those of my rank: only those of us who embrace the blood feeders become magi." She pulls him close. "*We* control the mage-power: we do not allow *it* to control *us*."

Alex's head spins. "How?" he asks desperately, then wishes he could swallow the word: *Wrong question, nerd-boy.*

But she doesn't seem to notice; instead she kisses him again, and this time he doesn't try to escape, or even to hold his breath. He loses track of time until someone behind him clears their throat. At the second throat-clearing he opens his eyes. Cassie is still there but she's looking past him. Alex turns sideways just far enough to see Mack holding his phone out at arm's reach, as if she's afraid of getting too close: "It's for you. Your work, I think?"

Cassie smiles smugly but relaxes her grip to allow Alex to stand up. He takes a deep breath. "Thanks," he says, breathing heavily as he extends a hand.

Mack passes him the phone, then retreats. Her cheeks are flushed, and Alex wonders, mortified, how it must look to her. *Way to make a good impression on kid sister's girlfriend*, he thinks, looking at the caller ID, then doing a double-take. A wash of fear settles over him. It's the Duty Officer in the control center in London.

"Schwartz here," he says. "I'm in public." He looks round. "Among civilians," he adds quietly. The urge to report his latest discovery is strong, but he holds back for the time being: obviously head office wouldn't be calling unless there was a matter of overwhelming immediate importance, he rationalizes—

"Alex, this is the DM." The harsh, grating voice is instantly familiar from a rainy night in Whitby. Déjà vu stabs at Alex, and he feels a pang of fear for Cassie. "You are in Leeds, correct?"

"Yes."

"Harrumph." Only the DM can make a throat-clearing sound like an accusation. "Did *you* conduct the ley line survey around Leeds docks last week?"

"I was part of it, yes—" Alex does a double-take. "You know I'm not on duty right now?"

It's water off the DM's back. "Was there a proximate ley line end-point in the vicinity of Leeds Docks, connecting to the Lawnswood vertex? Did you successfully traverse—"

"Yes there *was* and no I *didn't*. It was just a site survey with a K-22, establishing signal strength and geometry. Also, for the last time, I'm not on the clock and I'm with *company*." Alex is firm. He's had co-workers like the DM before, driven types with no life of their own and a tenuous grasp of work/life balance. "It's a family event."

"Oh. Well, Dr. Schwartz." The DM sounds more than slightly irritated. "Would this be your parents at"—he rattles off their address—"or some other family?"

Alex tries not to choke. "Dinner. With my parents."

"Well then, you may return to your family repast for now. But can I suggest *as a matter of urgency* that you check whether the ley line between the Lawnswood bunker and Leeds Docks is active, and let me know as soon as possible? Forecasting Ops were most insistent that *you* should investigate it this evening. I believe it is adjacent to the shortest route from your parents' house to your own lodgings, and the matter is of *some* importance. Thank you."

The DM hangs up, leaving Alex staring at his phone.

"Who was *that*, sweetie?" Cassie clutches his left arm possessively.

Before he can think of an answer Mack clears her throat. "Are you coming inside?" she asks. "Because you'll get awfully cold if you plan on waiting out here for the takeaway, and"—she lowers her voice—"Sarah says Mr. Green opposite is a creeper and he's got a set of binoculars."

"That was work," Alex mutters despondently at Cassie. To Mack, gratefully: "Yeah, we'll come inside." Then, to Cassie: "Let's eat. Then how about we go find your friends' party?"

"I'd like that! Yes Yes!" And suddenly she's as chirpy and bouncy as before—almost as if there are two different Cassies inhabiting the same skin. "If we go via my house we can pick up your costume?" She makes it sound so like a salacious invitation that Alex shuffles uneasily.

"Okay. I've got to pay a visit along the way, but it'll only take ten minutes. And then, party time!"

Cassie might as well be a cardboard cutout of a girlfriend as far as Mum and Dad are concerned. They're perfectly polite to her but it's as if her weirdness makes everything she says and does slide right past them. Cassie isn't using a glamour or any form of magic to hide herself as far as Alex can tell. Some people are just better than others at noticing things that don't align with their concern, and Mum and Dad are simply oblivious to elves, vampires, vegans, and other esoteric manifestations of modernity. All they care about is a sensible career development path and a solid pension plan. Alex figures this is all for the best, because expecting them to cope with a manic pixie dream girl while they're still figuring out how to respond to having a history student and a civil servant in the family is a parental trauma too far. But it doesn't make for easy dining table conversation. Sarah and Mack seem to realize there's something weird about Cassie, but they're at pains not to make a big deal of it, proving that *they* can behave like civilized adults even if *she* can't. *He* can't talk about work, and the more Cassie smiles and the less she says the better. So the conversation around the table veers wildly between willful vacuity and long, awkward silences until the takeaway arrives to put them out of their misery.

The arrival of food is a blessed relief from the pressure of conversation. Alex and Sarah manage to keep Dad's glass topped up with plenty of soda water and lemonade until he shows signs of recovering from his sobriety excursion, which he does just in time to dive into the dosas that Mack magicked up on Alex's phone. Mack's mastery of the latest smartphone fast food app scores her brownie points with Mum, and Cassie's blinding smile seems to charm her, so by the end of the evening it is only Alex and Sarah who are in the doghouse.

The meal is over all too soon (or perhaps not soon enough). Luckily Alex's counting cantrip saves him from the sucking attention vortex of the channa dhal, so he is present in mind as well as body to hug his mother goodbye when it's time to go. "You look after yourself," she warns him. "And see if you could get your girlfriend to do something about her hair? It's very striking, but . . ."

"Yes, Mum." Alex manages not to roll his eyes, and feels very grown-up. "I've got to get her home now." *Via a party.*

He finds Cassie in the hall, deep in some sort of furtive exchange with Mack. "Hey?" Mack says, seeing him; Cassie startles, looking faintly guilty.

"Hi." His helmet sits on top of the coat rack like the skull of a vanquished enemy war-band leader: he grabs it and pauses. "Are we ready?" he asks. "Do you need more time?"

It's Subdued Cassie who answers: "I'm ready to go." Unexpectedly she swoops in on Mack and kisses her on the cheek. "You be careful! Remember what I said!"

"No fear." Mack looks at her, then at Alex, her expression wary. "We were just leaving anyway."

"Leaving?" Alex looks between them, just as Sarah comes downstairs, carrying a duffel bag. "What's going on?" He blinks. "I don't think there's room on board to give you a lift—"

"We're going back to Nottingham," Sarah says briskly.

"What, right now?"

"Yes. We can just make the last train if we call a minicab." She gives Cassie a hard stare. "I hope you know what you're talking about."

"So do I." Cassie is uncharacteristically low-key, and this in and of itself puts Alex's back up. "Alex, can we go? Right now? Please?" She's almost bouncing up and down with tension, but there's nothing happy-go-lucky about it: it's as if she's just learned there's a terrorist bomb threat in the vicinity.

"I guess so." Alex nods at his sister. "Uh. Talk later?"

"See you around." She manages a faint, slightly shaky smile. "Go on. I'll sort out the leftovers and talk Mum and Dad down from the trees while we're waiting for our car. You don't need me around."

"I don't—" There is subtext here, but Alex can't for the life of him work out what it is.

"Go on. Scram."

He opens the front door. *Kid sisters.* He feels Cassie following close on his heels. "Don't stop," she urges him. "We should not stay here! We should not leave our scent behind!"

"Our scent." He stops dead.

Cassie hisses impatiently. "Wait one moment." She pulls out a fat black marker and goes to work defacing his parents' front door.

"Hey!" he manages, just as he recognizes the design. The runic script she annotates it with is unfamiliar but the star-within-a-pentagon of a Petersen Graph is frighteningly familiar, as is the trailing Elder Sign.

"This will hide your parents for a while, I hope," Cassie says quietly. "They are good people, they do not deserve to be caught up in what's coming." She makes the marker vanish, then pulls out a pin from somewhere in her cloak and stabs the ball of her thumb.

Alex's mouth fills with saliva. Her blood smells silvery, *different*— he forces himself to step back as she fills in the nodes of the graph with the reddest ink of all. "Take me home," she says again.

"Hide them from what?"

"The wild hunt. Take me home, please?"

Alex stands very still. "If I do that, you're going to answer all my questions," he says.

Cassie thinks for a moment, then nods.

Alex almost drives as far as the Otley Road before he remembers he promised the DM he'd check out the ley line linking the Lawnswood bunker to the center of town. The bunker is indeed just off his route home. Ilsa is chugging and rattling along happily, and Alex makes a snap judgment call. Having a heart-to-heart with Cassie is important, but he doesn't want to have to drive out here tomorrow just because the DM's got his knickers in a twist about a weather forecast from the department of oracular obfuscation. So as he nears the driveway concealed by the row of poplars he pulls off the road, parks, and clambers over the side of the half-track.

"What is it?" Cassie hops down behind him.

"Work asked me to check on something," he tells her vaguely. "I'll only be a minute or two. Damn. I don't have the keys . . ." He looks at the chain holding the gates shut, and sees a new and very shiny padlock securing them.

Cassie cocks her head to one side, bright-eyed and thoughtful as a magpie: "You need to get inside, Yes Yes?"

"Yes, but—"

She walks up to the gate and grabs the padlock with one hand. "Ouch! It's cold." She brings up her other hand and twists the lock round to a better angle.

"You don't need to—"

There's a quiet click and the hasp releases. "Does that help?" She holds it up proudly.

Oh crap. Alex stares for an anxious moment. "Let me drive Ilsa inside. Can you shut the gates behind me?" It wouldn't do to leave the half-track parked on the Otley Road, and he has an inkling this may take longer than expected. Indeed, he has a feeling that he really *shouldn't* be bringing Cassie in on this. If he had any sense he'd be on the phone screaming for backup, and holding her until he can get her into a warded debriefing room. Just because she isn't a many-tentacled thing of horror it does not follow that she is safe to be around. But an odd sense of fatalism grips him, as if everything is already determined. Whatever's happening here has already happened. Something is *wrong*, and he's not sure what it is, but he can't get away from it by walking out now. It'll follow him, snuffling along his trail in search of the bloody spoor of his magic—

He zones out for a while. When he comes back to his own head he swears under his breath. He's in Ilsa's saddle, parking up at the end of the drive in front of the decaying shed that squats above the nuclear bunker. Cassie crouches at the top of the steps, motionless, her cloak blending in with the shadows. She's deep in a dangerous stillness: he almost misses her, his eyes gliding right past, even though he knows what the front porch looked like on his last visit. A light blazes through one of the windows. It's probably only candle-bright but to his PHANG-sharp night vision it shines like a beacon. He kills the ignition, and in the sudden stillness he feels his fingertips prickling. He can rarely feel the proximity of a ley line directly—he needs a

K-22 or similar unit to be sure it's there—but this one's really strong. Much stronger than it was last time he visited.

Alex climbs off the Kettenkrad, steps clear of the mass of cast iron and steel, then checks his phone. His pocket OFCUT dongle isn't very accurate but it says the thaum flux is almost off the scale, as if a flash flood has turned the trickle of muddy water at the bottom of an irrigation ditch into a turbid torrent. He swipes a quick text message on his phone, attaches the OFCUT readings, and fires it at the Duty Officer's number. "Cassie," he says quietly, guessing that those pointy ears must be good for something, "we ought to leave—"

She waves him to silence, her hand gestures urgent and expressive. Her ear twitches as she leans close to the door, motionless. Then: "Get *down*. There are guards."

Alex drops and rolls towards Ilsa's tracks. The ground is dry, and he is fastidiously grateful. He doesn't have time to take his helmet off, but with the visor up he can see well enough and his face is in shadow.

He hears them first, footsteps on earth accompanied by an odd jangling clanking sound. A squeal as of bare metal surfaces rubbing reminds him of a display at an Army recruiting day when he was a kid, minus the hammering of the power pack in the Challenger tank. Whatever they are, they aren't stealthy, and they're *close*—

A pair of armored knights step around the edge of the building.

Alex stares. No, they're *not* knights. At least, they're not wearing classical European armor. He saw enough suits of very posh Renaissance plate in the Royal Armouries the previous week that these guys look *wrong*. But not wrong in a theatrical, this-is-for-show-not-work way: just unfamiliar. There is gothic fluting on the pauldrons and cuirass and other parts he can't put a name to, but the articulation is different and the helmets have wide, high earpieces, and in particular there is a visor with some sort of crystal or toughened glass so that he can see their eyes, alert, scanning the shadows. They have swords slung from their belts, but they hold short truncheons that are naggingly familiar, until he recalls Cassie's mace. When he looks at them they make his eyes hurt, like staring at a powered-up summoning grid for too long.

THE NIGHTMARE STACKS 213

Fuck me, it's the medieval cybermen, he thinks, then tenses because they're bound to spot Ilsa in a second and then they'll see him—

But they don't spot Ilsa. Ilsa is blanketed by Brains's heavy-duty no-see-em ward, and Alex lies in her shadow. Instead they walk right past her, around the front of the building, armor clattering softly with each step (soldiers in full steel plate can move surprisingly quietly), and then one of them notices Cassie.

There is no shouting and no wasted motion, but both soldiers act as if controlled by a single mind. Their truncheons come up simultaneously, one of them bearing on Cassie while the other spins round, moving unbelievably fast for a man who's wearing at least twenty-five kilos of steel. He hasn't seen Alex but he's raising his weapon in anticipation of another intruder: they're well-trained, alert, and all hell is about to cut loose.

Alex reacts without thinking. He shoves himself off the ground with a surge of power that comes unnaturally easily, drawing deep on his V-symbiote's energy. He kicks off towards the nearest man. Time slows down as the ground recedes below him. The mace begins to glow blue-white as he stretches his arms out towards the prey and opens his mouth, teeth expanding painfully in his gums—

Something punches him in the sternum, hard. There's a bang as his beefed-up defensive ward explodes, fragments slicing into his chest as he jumps. A wash of pure rage ripples through him, shockingly unfamiliar in its arrogance: rage at the spam-in-a-can who has the sheer *effrontery* to aim an occult weapon at him. He's still trying to make fists of his slow-moving fingers when he hits the soldier with a brain-rattling crash, knocking him off his feet and sending them both sprawling in the dirt with Alex on top.

Something is happening on the front steps but Alex doesn't have attention to spare because his own target is fast, strong, and demonstrating a keen interest in murdering him. If Alex was a normal, pencil-necked nerd of mathematics geekery, he wouldn't even have gotten off the ground before the soldier gave him a lethal zap with the thaum capacitor in his truncheon. But Alex is a PHANG, and although he's not remotely well-trained in hand-to-hand mayhem, he's a lot stron-

ger than he has any right to be. He's also inhumanly fast when his
V-parasites take over. This is not the first time people—soldiers, even—
have tried to kill him. The first time it happened he froze; the second
time he rules-lawyered his way out of it; and this time it just makes
him *angry*.

Alex's first punch doesn't achieve much except to make a truly
impressive noise and send a silvery shock of pain through his knuckles.
But his second punch is so strong his victim's breastplate buckles. And,
for a miracle, tank-guy stops trying to get his gauntlet-clad hands
around Alex's throat and instead moves his forearms across his gorget
and pushes. Alex can see a face, contorted behind a half-misted visor.
He's shouting something Alex doesn't understand as he squirms, trying
to get away: *Ah, bless, how cute,* he thinks muzzily. His left fist is a
solid lump of throbbing agony and Alex is *hungry*, hungrier than he's
ever been except back in the warehouse right after he'd been zapped
with the backlash from a ceiling rigged with ultraviolet flashbulbs—
and the prey recoiling centimeters away from his aching jaws smells
of fresh warm wet *food*—

—Metal yields and bends beneath the tip of his right index finger,
and the smell intensifies dizzyingly—

"'Ware his knife!" Cassie calls, and everything around Alex flashes
into sharp focus. The prey he's sitting on: one arm is broken, but the
other is raised above Alex's back with a dagger (Alex has no idea how
he *knows* this, he certainly can't *see* it). Cassie: squats on a prone
armored body, blood squirting in rhythmic splashes—

—The prey's knife-arm sags weirdly, shoulder bending the wrong
way as Alex's right hand digs into the steel gorget protecting the prey's
throat and twists, hard. Rivets pop and his fangs pulse in his gums
with ghastly urgency. He bends and shoves his mouth towards the gap
in the armor. The prey tenses, and one steel-capped knee rams him in
the balls with enough force to reduce a normal human male to breathless agony. But Alex is a spectator in his own body, watching as the
things he invited into his head reduce the man beneath him to meat,
convulsing as it dies with terrifying rapidity. V-parasites normally kill
over days or weeks, not seconds. He stretches out his left arm, feels
the shattered bones in his hand slide greasily into position as the swell-

ing subsides. The numbness between his legs also fades. He realizes that he's not hungry anymore, and the body beneath him isn't moving. There was none of the rush that normally accompanies feeding. He takes a deep breath, aghast at what he's just done, and looks up.

Cassie is sitting on the bottom step, using her cloak to wipe down the blade of a dagger that's barely wider than a bodkin. Her eyes track him, unblinking.

"I thought you said you were immune to—"

"I am," she says shortly, sliding the knife into her sheath as she stands. "So are all those of noble rank. We have a, a vaccine? Something like that. Else we could not survive the appetites of our own magi. But not these, not common soldiers. It is their obligation to provide sustenance for the magi, should there be no better source to hand." She looks round. "Why did you attack my father's men?"

Alex looks at the body behind her, then back at her. "Is that who they are? I thought I was protecting you!"

She looks away. "You probably were. I do not think I was supposed to come here or, having come, to leave alive. But why are *you* here?" She takes a wary step towards him. "*Why*, Alex?"

"I was sent—" A momentary look of confusion crosses his face, then clears abruptly. "I don't think I'm allowed to tell you. If *you* are connected to *these*"—he gestures at the fallen guards—"I should be asking you some hard questions. Like, why are they here?"

"Patrolling, guarding . . ." Cassie frowns, looking at him: but Alex is silent. A wall has gone up between them. "If you hadn't killed your man I would have ordered him to tell me everything." She doesn't mention her own victim. "I don't know what they're doing here. I'm not privy to my father's plans."

"Then," his gaze flickers to her knife and the mace she holds ready in her right hand, then back to the door, "why don't we go inside and find out?"

In London, the DM is becoming concerned. So concerned that he's camping out in the office, working over the weekend. So concerned that he's called up a Watch Team and signed for their overtime to keep them in the building, 24x7. So concerned that he's on the edge of sending up the bat-signal to call in the Deeply Scary Sorcerers of Mahogany Row—

—Because something big and very messy indeed seems to be kicking off in Leeds, and while he's set up the parameters of the scenario it's anybody's guess as to how well Alex will perform as bait in a honey trap. After all, if you farm bees on rhododendron flowers you get poisoned honey . . .

The Laundry runs on codewords and committees, and sometimes they overlap confusingly. It's less obsessive about secrecy than most other government agencies; the oath of office all staff swear binds them with a *geas* to act always to further the interests of the Crown authority vested in them, so the presumption is that staff are trustworthy. Consequently secrecy is mostly used to avoid burdening specialists with too much confusing detail outside their area of expertise, rather than as a defense against enemy infiltration. But there are exceptions. Even now, years after the fact, the COBWEB MAZE group are *still* trying to work out how Iris Carpenter subverted her oath of office so thoroughly that she squared running a congregation of the Cult of the Red Skull with her remit as a departmental manager in IT Services. Theories to account for her deviant behavior include an undiagnosed psychopathic personality disorder, an impressive talent for double-think, and overexposure to Windows 2000 Domain Services. Whatever the reason, it is now clear that relying exclusively on *geas*-enforced loyalty is inadequate. Especially since some of the newest high-value human resources (PHANGs, not to put too fine a point on it) respond idiosyncratically—if at all—to all forms of blood binding, including *geases*.

The original cause of the DM's concern was a report Forecasting Ops emitted more than six months ago, during the early stages of preparations for the migration to the new Headquarters North building in Leeds. Forecasting Ops are notoriously vague, sketchy, not to say Delphic in their utterances. But Derek is not in the habit of ignoring strong hints from oracles, and FO's warnings about the consequences of not reinforcing the peripheral security cordon around Headquarters North as soon as possible were far less vague than normal, verging upon the apocalyptic. But when someone on the MORTAR BRICKS working group suggested that perhaps the move to Leeds might be a bad idea, or should at least be postponed pending a full review, Forecasting Ops threw such a collective hissy fit that word reached the Audit Committee and Mahogany Row. A diktat came down the line, backing Forecasting Ops up to the hilt: *something* bony was obviously rattling around inside the locked wardrobe of the unrealized future, but the best way to stop it escaping appeared to be to expedite the move and beef up security. However, the changes to the relocation program are proving extremely costly—and if something doesn't show up on time to justify the ghastly expense, Accounting is going to ensure that heads roll. It is, everyone agrees, altogether too damn similar to the whole Y2K mess.*

So then *another* smoke signal from Forecasting Ops came out, with a prediction of an incursion in the vicinity of Huddersfield. Worst case is NIGHTMARE RED. Unfortunately FO projections have the circular error probability of a fifty-megaton nuke, which really doesn't narrow things down. Moving an OCCULUS unit into the region is a sticking plaster for the bigger problem, which is that since the drawdown in forces triggered by the 2010 defense review, the units the Laundry can draw upon have been depleted. There are now just two SAS squadrons, 120 men in total, to cover all contingencies: and only half of them are available at any given time. If the shit really hits the fan they can draw on the regular Army and the Air Force for support, but there will be delays in getting everyone up to speed. So Derek, playing in the sandpit of Operations Control, is desperately trying to figure out how to counter the FO projection. "Outbreaks of idiopathic macroscopic cryptobiotic infestation" could be anything from the usual tentacle monsters to ice giants or shoggoths or other, less familiar phenomena like the pointy-eared bastards FO have been dropping broad hints about for a while. So the DM just has to hope

---

* Y2K was a *real* end-of-civilization problem. And the people who could deal with it treated it as such, working flat-out on disaster management for the last year-long countdown. With the result that the end-of-the-world scenario *didn't happen* . . . causing everyone not directly involved to conclude that it was a false alarm.

that CCTV will pick it up in time for OCCULUS to get there before it does too much damage, and if it breaks out past OCCULUS and rampages in the direction of Quarry Hill . . . that's what the SCORPION STARE camera network is for.

The idea of firing up an experimental look-to-kill network in the middle of a densely populated city does not fill Derek with joy. It's a desperation move, and could trigger civilian collateral casualties on a scale that would be even harder to cover up than the national trauma of the last Last Night of the Proms.* And that's before considering the 0.3 percent false positive rate during the neural network recognizer test in Whitby—a spike far higher than any they'd seen on other tests using the same software build.

Something about Whitby had nagged at his mind, an untidy loose end: the PHANG, Alex, who was there in his free time. Normally Derek would have dismissed that aspect, writing it off as just another peculiarity of co-workers who insist on "having a life," whatever that means. But the coincidence of finding lots of false positives when there was a PHANG in the test run was . . . suggestive. He'd listened to Lockhart's grumbling about Specimen B, and rerun the video several times, and put two and two together, and is hoping he's made four. Alex is in Leeds, now, and a site he visited two weeks ago has begun showing signs of instability. That's suggestive. Alex is dating the target the DM identified. That's even more suggestive. And so the DM begins to roll his dice.

"Do you think he's a ringer?" asks Vikram Choudhury. He's slumped forward in his chair, elbows braced on the conference table and bags under his eyes. Like everyone present in the suite he's been in the office since Friday morning: they're all getting a bit rank, and very fatigued. "I've met your boy and, unfortunate affliction aside, he seemed sound. A bit inexperienced, but very proficient in his specialty."

"Spellcaster," grunts Derek, rubbing the side of his nose tiredly.

---

* Which has been blamed on Islamist terrorists with hallucinogenic gas by the more tractable media—newspapers and the BBC—although the volume of conspiracy theories is somewhere between deafening and eardrum-rupturing.

With his other hand he massages his dice bag obsessively. "A spellcaster *and* a v—a PHANG. Breaks all the rules." Derek's preferred rules are original Dungeons & Dragons (not even first edition AD&D: Derek is *really* old-school), but he is grudgingly aware that the real world doesn't always reduce cleanly to a set of gamer-friendly stats tables. (Vampires, it turns out, are not abominable undead walking corpses: they're just a character class. He can work with that.) "But according to his file he's very socially . . . inexperienced." The DM doesn't add, *like me*: it cuts too close to the bone. "Is he really up to this?"

Vikram shrugs. "Mr. Howard's late director Mr. Angleton put Dr. Schwartz in the line and he didn't break. With the approval of Dr. Armstrong, I will remind you. This is just conjectural: there might not be anything there."

The DM makes a steeple of his fingers. "I feel a great disturbance in the force . . ."

"Yes, yes, as if a hundred geomancers cried out in frustration and had to rework their topographic maps because the ley line shifted." Vikram's tiredness is overflowing into irritation. "Why don't you ask Mr. McTavish?"

Johnny McTavish is leaning back in his conference chair, eyes closed, booted feet planted firmly on the seat of the empty chair adjacent to the rubbish bin. He is not snoring, but it's pretty obvious that his interest in the proceedings has hit rock bottom. At the sound of his name his eyelids open nearly instantly. "Yer wot?"

Vikram clears his throat fussily. "Derek was casting aspersions on Dr. Alex Schwartz's ability to handle circumstances he's never experienced before, if indeed it transpires that the ley line shift up north has something to do with the recent change in his social life reported by his housemates . . . and with the cause of our current weekend alert status. Given that the endpoint of this particular geodesic is twenty meters below surface level in a Tempest-shielded bunker where our young protégé's mobile phone is unlikely to get a signal, we might have a problem if he runs into a Boojum."

"All right, me old cock." Johnny swings his boots back down onto the floor and sits up. He is, of course, yanking Vikram's chain: this is understood by all present. Johnny doesn't answer to anyone except

Persephone, and he answers to her the way that a fight-trained pit bull usually responds to its owner—as long as it isn't currently trying to bite someone's throat out. "So what you're saying is, you sent our man into harm's way and now you're worried about what to do if he don't come back?"

Vikram rolls his eyes as Derek the DM nods, very seriously. "Yes, exactly that."

Johnny sighs heavily. "'Is mentor's the Vicar, isn't he? And 'e's got the mad science clown crew for backup, and an OCCULUS team, and Catterick Garrison just up the road if 'e wants a conga line. And this bird 'e's smitten with? Seems to me you don't want to get 'Seph out of bed for this. She's still jet-lagged from that caper in Queensland last Thursday."

Vikram shakes his head. "Then we shall let BASHFUL INCENDI-ARY sleep in," he agrees. Sending one of the Laundry's most powerful witches on a wild goose chase is a bad idea: Persephone has a vicious temper when sleep-deprived. "Any other suggestions? Things we can do to help from up here?"

"When in doubt ask a policeman." Johnny winks at Vikram. "'Ow about it?"

Another head-shake. "I can't go calling out the TPCF on a house call either. They're external to our reporting chain and you should see what they bill per hour." The supercops who police the superpowered might have been set up with loaned Laundry personnel and a nod and a wink from the Home Office, but there is a hugely complicated reorganization in process, as part of the fallout from the Albert Hall debacle.

"So what's left?" Johnny asks.

Vikram sighs as Derek looks at him and harrumphs significantly. "I think you'd better telephone the frat house, Mr. Choudhury. Get the Vicar, he's the responsible adult. If he's not there, get Pinky. Tell him to sit up and call back if Dr. Schwartz isn't home by"—he checks his antique wristwatch—"midnight and hasn't checked in by mobile."

"And then?" Vikram asks.

"Then we start phoning the on-call list and waking people up. What else would you suggest doing?"

* * *

"We need to have that talk as soon as we're done here. Sooner," Alex whispers, crouching down beside the keyhole. They've scouted the grounds around the bunker but found nothing. As far as Alex knows, the two dead soldiers and the changed locks are the only signs that anything is wrong. But they're pretty big signs that the DM is right about a major incident kicking off here, and all his instincts are screaming at him that it would be a really bad idea to go inside without knowing more.

"Yes Yes . . ." Cassie stands with her back to the wall beside the door, holding her mace. "I am sorry, didn't mean to"—she swallows—"mislead."

Alex closes his eyes. *My girlfriend is an alien princess and her father's soldiers just tried to kill us,* he thinks, then shoves his doubts aside, because *of course* people like Cassie are imaginary, just like vampires don't exist, and yet here he is and there she stands. He stretches his sensitive hearing as far as it can go, trying to listen in on the other side of the door, but the distant rumble of traffic on the ring road drowns out anything closer to hand. "I'm getting nothing," he says. "Can you hear anything?"

Silence for a moment. Then, "Your heartbeat is too loud. Step around the corner for a moment."

Alex holds his breath, tiptoes to the corner, and stands there for almost a minute. Finally Cassie waves him over. "Yes?"

"Nothing," she says, very positively. Then, less certainly, "At least, nothing that I could hear . . ." Her ear twitches, and an echo of a long-ago seminar on evolutionary biology raises the dust in Alex's memory: gracile hominids with predatory adaptations. *H. neanderthalensis* was adapted for a cold climate, *H. habilis* for ruggedness in a way later hominid species didn't need thanks to their mastery of weapons. *H. sapiens* was adapted for speech, tool-use, teamwork. What would you get if you had a hominid species adapted for thaumaturgy and hunting? Alex looks at her in a new light. *She's on the outside, not briefed on their plans . . . a spy? Or a traitor?*

All of this passes through Alex's mind in an instant as he reaches for the doorknob and says, "Well, then," and realizes—further insights cascading—that these are not questions for *now* but questions for *later*, if he and Cassie make it back to safety. The DM is already alert to a potential problem and doubtless tracking him on the metaphorical game board. Alex needs to phone home or alarm bells will ring. But if he *does* phone home and he has missed a watcher or misjudged Cassie, he'll be giving the hidden adversary vital information. Thinking in these terms makes his head ache. Most of the threats the Laundry is called upon to deal with are brainless gibbering horrors with chitinous claws and wildly waving stinger-tipped tentacles, not Machiavellian strategists with spies to do their bidding. "Well, then," he repeats doubtfully, and twists the doorknob and braces his feet and—*shoves*.

Vampire super-strength is a poor fit for many of the modern world's problems—it really doesn't help you fill in your time-sheet any faster—but when it comes to breaking damp-weakened wooden door frames it's superb. The door crunches, deafeningly loud to Alex's amped-up hearing, and then it flies open so fast that he barely has time to grab it before it slams against the interior wall.

A carefully drawn summoning grid fills the entire floor space of the overgrown shed, surrounding the stairs down into the bunker. The diagram's arcs and nodes are lit up like a radioactive slug-trail left by a mollusk the size of a Volkswagen Beetle. Someone has helpfully poured an outer circle of pristine white salt crystals around it, clearly intended as a vampire trap. Alex looks away from the pool of thaumaturgic energy locked inside the shaft: peering into it hurts his head, and as for the salt, the counting cantrip babbling in the back of his skull is the only thing averting complete paralysis. Cassie is frozen, staring past him into the building, an expression of horror on her face. "FuckFuck!"

Alex grabs her left arm and pulls her back out of the doorway. "Explain," he snaps.

"Is—was there a, I don't know the word for it . . . a road here? A line of power from hither to yon, connecting sacred sites?"

"A ley line?" Alex stares at her. She stares back, her eyes wide and dark in the moonlight. "What if there was?"

"Let me see—" He holds her forearm carefully, as if it'll shatter if he lets go of it. She pivots around him as if he isn't there at all, and looks through the opening. She squeaks unhappily. "*Thought* so." She swivels back out hastily, pushing him away from the door, then collapses against him. "Come, go, sit, stand, *move somewhere else.*"

"Where?"

"Anywhere!" she cries vehemently.

"Why?" he demands.

"If, if we go in there"—she's breathing fast and deep, hyperventilating—"the path at the bottom of this fastness will carry us to my father's people."

"Good." And Alex steps into the doorway.

13: THE BUNKER

The new world's landscape spreads out beneath Highest Liege's wings, impressing her with both its familiarity and its sheer alien weirdness.

She soars high above the ridge-line of the low mountain range that bisects this landmass from north to south, protected from observation by her back-seater's powerful aversive countermeasures, looking down through her mount's incredibly sensitive photoreceptors. The shape of this land is similar to that of her former home. But rather than forming the western extremity of a continent, it is separated from its neighbors by a shallow sea to the east, covering the fertile lowlands and slave plantations she remembers from before the war. To the west, another channel floods the farmland and turns the westernmost fingerling of the continent into a separate island. The land is shrunken by the risen ocean, its shape eroded and warped. And that's not the worst of it.

The terrain Highest Liege and her wingman cruise above has been blighted by the *urük*. Gone are the impenetrable, dark northern forests of the western uplands of the empire. There are scattered stands of trees, clearly coppiced and curated by farmers, but for the most part the ground is carved into a patchwork of fields, slashed through by roads—so many roads!—lit up with chains of amber lamps. The metal carts her husband's idiot daughter described crawl along them, picked out by brilliant white and red lights fore and aft. Hovels pock the sides of the peasant tracks, bunch up into great carbuncular masses every few leagues, and in the distance they form a glowing lump of cancerous tissue so vast that it lights up the underside of the clouds. All the *urük* slums emit the same lurid orange glow, although some shed a pale white glare from open windows. It will take blood and iron to cure this disease, she thinks as she monitors her mount's senses, circling around the smelly masses of *urük* habitation. But it will have to wait until the full body of the Host arrives in the marshaling area and commits to the lightning attack on the enemy palace. Once their autarch has succumbed, the All-Highest will add the *geasa* that control these subhuman scum to his own might and turn their own militia against them. But for now, it falls to her to observe and monitor and scout for signs of hostile intent in the rolling landscape around the Vale of the Bad Village, as the *urük* call the staging post.

Highest Liege of Airborne Strike can find no sign of enemy troops upon the landscape. Such castles as she can see appear to be indefensible, bastions slighted, towers in ruins. She has cruised high above more than one great house, set well among trees and fields surrounded by rambling stone walls: they appear to be built for peace. She can feel no defensive wards around them, and her back-seat magus is becoming increasingly disturbed by the lack of thaumic resonances and ground-works. There are ley lines aplenty, and signs of ancient defensive workings allowed to fall into disrepair, but the lack of power suggests that the dumb *urük* cattle have no mastery of the arts and sciences whatsoever—either that, or this land has been free from war for an improbably long time. The mystery of their spread across the landscape deepens as she spares it the odd moment of consideration. How can barbarians and primitives have multiplied so prolifically?

Also puzzling are the curious linear cloud formations that rip across the dome of the sky many leagues above. In the absence of tribal war bands that might stumble upon her husband's marshaling forces, *that* demands her scrutiny like nothing else she has seen this morning.

Circling for altitude, Highest Liege tells her back-seater and wingman to get a fix on the spearpoint of one of those clouds. *"What, if anything, are they emitting?"* she demands.

Wingman reports: *"The trailing clouds are just clouds, my Liege. Water vapor, from the egg-shaped things under the wings of the . . ."*

"The flying cattle-carts." Highest Liege permits herself a smile. *"You are certain there is no mana in them?"*

She hears the flight-magi conferring in the back of her mind. Presently her back-seater reports: *"They are entirely inert, my Liege. We sense metal and minds,* many *minds—and engines like those of the carts. But there is no trace of science to them, merely brute physical artifice."*

"Then attend," she commands. *"In the past eighty stances I have counted seven of the flyers passing overhead. Mostly from southeast to northwest. Confirm my count and maintain your own while we return to base. This patrol will now conclude."* The *urük* use roads on the ground; it is to be expected that they use set paths through the sky as well. All-Highest will welcome a diversion, and although the cattle-carts fly unattainably high overhead (for the dragonriders carry no bottled air: in the empire's world to be seen above the battlefield is to die instantly, so as a rule they stay close to ground cover) their presence suggests an exciting tactical opportunity to her.

Cassie grabs at Alex but she's too slow to stop him going inside. The strength she found in action a minute before has vanished, leaving her shaky. She takes a deep breath, dizzy, then feels his arms around her like an echo of the hungry magus in the sending. His cheek against her neck is rough and sandpapery, warm to the touch.

"You shouldn't have done that! It's a trap." Her heart flutters in her chest at the memory of her stepmother's sending, the traumatic experience of the death that powered it. She remembers it, and her father's *geas* works through her to latch onto her stepmother's last words with the unyielding pressure of steel handcuffs in her head: *Present yourself and your prize . . . or your loyalty will be questioned.*

"Of course it is. Do you know who I work for?"

"The government." Cassie's words, not Agent First's, although they come ever more easily to her tongue now. "You are a magus, a, a sorcerer who steals *mana* by drinking blood." He flinches in her arms. "And the government has a department, yes? A"—a memory of a childhood book springs into her mind—"a Ministry of Magic, based in Quarry House. Yes Yes? And you are bound by a *geas* of your own, an oath to serve your queen?"

"Not exactly. It's an oath to the Crown, not the queen," he explains. "The Crown is a legal abstraction, not a person. And I have discretion, as an agent of the Crown, as long as I obey lawful orders and act in what I believe to be its best interests." He pauses for a moment. "The oath doesn't bind vamp—ma—people like me very well, either. It wasn't designed with us in mind."

Lawful order is an oxymoron to Agent First—orders *are* law—but Cassie nods all the same. "Well, I *am* bound, and I have been given a direct order to pay attendance on my father, and if I fail to do so—with you—then, that's it." She shivers against him. "My stepmother wants to kill me."

"Where is this supposed to happen?" Alex sounds surprisingly calm. Having met his family, she has no idea why he's taking this so well. They are, even by *urük* standards, startlingly mundane. They cannot have prepared him for confrontations with murderous magical stepmothers; for a moment Cassie wonders if he even understands her predicament. "The, the noon deadline?"

"I don't know exactly—not on a map, but I'm supposed to find the end of the nearest ley line. And there is one such here: I feel it below our feet. We found guards oath-bound to my stepmother: she did not place them here for my safety. If they kill me, she wins, and if they kill you, I will be in breach of my *geas* and she wins. There will be other obstacles. Even if I present you to my father and discharge the obligation she'll find a way to . . ." She swallows. "We should not have come here."

"Too late." Alex hits the send button on his phone, and the text message he wrote to the DM while Cassie was busy at the door is on its way. He feels abruptly light-headed, committed: "You have to present me to your father or die; very well, take me to him." It's dangerously close to reckless, he knows, but he's not going to let this opportunity slip between his fingers. Also: "My—one of my bosses asked me to report on this place." He nods towards the circle of occult energy surrounding the stairs. "We both need to go down there," he adds. And with the implacable strength of a magus, he takes a step forward.

As Highest Liege circles in to land in Malham Cove's sheltered vale—now concealed from casual intruders by a field camouflage glamour powered by no fewer than six battle magi—the vanguard of the cavalry strike force is arriving via the shadow road. High-stepping steeds pace to either side of logistics wagons pulled by great hairy steppe elephants. Their riders work to keep their snarling chargers away from the mammoths, who roll their eyes and swing their great sword-capped tusks towards any steed that threatens to get too close. The chargers glare at them, fury and spite filling their eyes. Ready for war, they wear coats of finely articulated steel plate, engraved with wards to absorb and deflect the death-bolts of *mana*-energized battle magic. The spiral-fluted horns that grow between their eyes glow with power: the Host's cavalry do not ride horses but eldritch war-mounts, equoid horrors bound to service by All-Highest's veterinary thaumaturges.

The soldiers who ride them are also armored and protected by military-strength misdirection glamours and chameleon spells. To an eye equipped with suitable countermeasures, the advancing cavalry troops appear as refractive silhouettes. The landscape is visible through them, rippling and distorted, as if they are figures of glass or super-heated air. To eyes lacking such countermeasures they are imperceptible save by the signs of their passage—broken branches, crushed vegetation. They move at night, for to be visible on the battlefield is to court instant death, and while the troopers of the mobile force bear swords at their hips, these are no more central to their combined arms doctrine than rifle bayonets are to the soldiers of the *urük*. Their real weapons are a barely perceptible pyramid of complex bindings and glamours, systems drawn from a baroque arsenal of mind-burning sorcery that constitutes the apex of a six-thousand-year history of *mana*-powered warfare and mental conquest. While the crudely mechanical aspects of their kit superficially resemble a late medieval knight's, the leashed power at each soldier's command is closer to that of a main battle tank.

Behind the first screening cavalry company follows a long convoy of logistical support and specialized combat forces. Here come the sauropodian air defense basilisks, hooded heads held high as they sniff the alien air, giant paddle-feet thudding on the rocky ground; their support teams trail cautiously behind, riding on wooly pachyderms, wearing armor polished to a mirror-like shine. Four tumbrils of slaves, pulled by the fittest of their own number, stand ready for the magi's replenishment—for combat sorcery eats *mana* a hundred times faster than more typical invocations. A guard of infantry with power maces march alongside them, death's head illusions filling the crystal visors of their battle helms. Two more companies of cavalry ride out of the gate to the shadow roads. And then the first two lances of the All-Highest's personal bodyguard appear.

While all this is happening, Highest Liege walks across to the pavilion where First Lance has established a field command headquarters for the theater air defense group.

First Lance is head to head with three subalterns, poring over a map, when Highest Liege enters. As one, they straighten up, then abase themselves before her. *"Rise, rise,"* she says impatiently. Of First Lance, she asks without preamble: *"Have you observed the high-altitude vehicles of the enemy?"*

"Yes, my Liege. They appear to be of no military significance—"

"Yet they are numerous and consistent in their course, for the most part." While she has seen many smaller fliers traveling in various directions, the southeast-to-northwest track appears to be highest, and home to the largest *urük*-carts. *"We need to determine whether the urük have, in fact, any offensive airborne capability at all. So I have a mission for air defense to draw them out."*

It will, if nothing else, make a spectacular welcoming display to herald her husband's arrival in the new world; hopefully it will also confirm that the *urük* are as defenseless in the skies as they are on the ground. And if they aren't, that's what the headquarters glamour is for.

*   *   *

All-Highest rides into the camp in the predawn darkness the day before the assault: a tall figure encased from toe to crown in the black fluted armor of command, surrounded by the power and the glory of his personal escort—an entire lance of battle magi, two companies of heavy cavalry, and his headquarters staff.

Behind him heavy siege golems trudge, thunder-footed, behind the cavalry chargers. They carry the hollow tubes of thaumic catapults—bolt-throwers able to split the meters-thick stone walls of castles from tens of leagues away. They are followed by other specialized weapons systems: suppressors, the wingless relatives of firewyrms that can drain the *mana* from an enemy battle-mage or combat construct at long range; diggers, lowing like eyeless cattle, that can liquify soil and defensive earthworks; and the walking dead, animated by eaters, bearers of *mana* bombs.

It's a pitiful excuse for an army, All-Highest thinks, but it's all he's got, and it will have to do. Failure is unthinkable, for if he fails it means the end of the empire and the final downfall of civilization on this and every other world.

Which is not an option.

As his cortege winds past munitions dumps and grooming stations, soldiers and slaves stop whatever they're doing and make signs of obeisance: a salute with arms from the soldiers, full prostration from the slaves. All-Highest acknowledges only the most senior officers in passing. Out of the corner of one eye he notices a slave, insufficiently fast to kneel, being dragged aside. Irritated, he turns his head and raises his left hand, palm up. The soldier behind the slave freezes, sword in hand, as All-Highest looks at the miscreant groveling at the trooper's feet. *"That displeases me,"* he says, almost gently, and closes his fist. The slave convulses and drops, blood squirting from ears and eyes. All-Highest turns back to his destination, the shimmering mirage of the staff headquarters tent. As reminders of his authority go, this one is minor, even low-key. But spare bodies are few enough that a true demonstration of his might—a periodic necessity, to keep his more ambitious vassals from seeking to evade the web of his *geasa*—

will have to wait. Once the first stage of the conquest is complete there will be plenty of scope to remind them of his determination.

His procession takes him past an odd spoil heap, a head-high mound of cracked and scorched stone statues. *"What's this?"* he asks.

"All-Highest, these are the remains of urük who stumbled across our air defense batteries today. They are more numerous and more curious than forecast."

He snorts. Ignorant savages, prancing around the landscape as if they owned it. A question occurs to him: *"These are only the ones who saw too much? The glamour holds?"*

"The glamour holds, All-Highest. There were many more of them during the day than was expected of such a remote site—this appears to be a place of some ritual significance to them."

"Well." He looks at the basilisk-stricken corpses again: *"See to it that the pile is secure. I don't want it falling on the tents."*

As All-Highest enters the headquarters pavilion, all assembled bow their heads and salute, fist-to-heart. He walks between their lines to the throne of bones, takes his seat, and looks to his left. *"Honorable Wife,"* he says. *"I believe you have been busy. Report, if you please."* It is no less an order for being phrased prettily, but it is a signal of his esteem that he words it so courteously. Highest Liege of Airborne Strike Command is pleasing to the eye, lively in bed, and eagerly ruthless: all welcome improvements over her predecessor, the sullen cow whose treasonous plotting she exposed. So he smiles, tight-lipped and teeth concealed from view, as she ducks her head submissively, ears back, and launches into a description of what she has seen from the skies of this world.

"There are many sky-carts passing over this land," his wife explains, with an illustrative vision that makes his eyes widen with enlightenment. *"We believe them to be part of the urük society's transport system, but they are extremely vulnerable. They are also highly visible . . ."*

She makes the case for an additional diversion, and All-Highest's ears twitch appreciatively as she finishes. *"That would be an excellent use of your force,"* he says. *"I have been considering our options for a feint, and this will certainly help misdirect the enemy's attention."* He inclines his head. *"I hoped we might have another day or two for final preparations, but in view of the number of urük roaming these hills we must commit our full force to the planned attack no later than tomorrow morning, at the first hour. Accordingly, I am bringing all our plans forward. Honorable Wife, it would please me if you would prepare and execute your plan at dawn tomorrow."*

Highest Liege of Airborne Strike Command displays excellent mastery of her expression, but he cannot help but feel her tension and dismay. *"It shall be as you command, my husband,"* she says, despite the sudden change of tempo: oh yes indeed, she's an ambitious one. *"I should hasten to obey . . . ?"*

"You may go." He reaches out to touch her forehead as she dips her face, ears back and tilted close to her head. He tastes her apprehension and the hot, dry tension of her desire. *"Bring glory to our house, Honorable Wife, and I will remember your deeds this day."* It's an old formula, but she seems pleased to accept it.

As soon as she is gone he turns to his First of Diviners and Records with a broad, undignified grin. *"Well, First!"* he says, now visibly amused. *"How goes our infiltration of the enemy palace?"*

"I believe the plan goes well, All-Highest. A siege is certainly feasible, and perhaps easier than anticipated—these people are rank amateurs at the art of war—but your other scheme is also bearing fruit." First of Diviners and Records dips his head. *"Your wife's animosity towards her predecessor's get has had the desired effect, and Agent First is indeed motivated—and has made contact. The urük lack much in the arts, but they do have a handful of magi. And Agent First has become passing close with one of their number."* First of Diviners and Records looks more than slightly smug: *"So close, in fact, that she has offered the threefold invitation and the sharing of food and drink, and he has accepted."*

All-Highest's ears go up. *"Really?"* he purrs.

First of Diviners dips his chin. *"Truly, All-Highest."*

"Just so." All-Highest pauses for a moment, savoring the impending victory: To capture an enemy magus is always excellent, but to entrap a member of the palace magi without their liege even knowing

is a triumph of subterfuge. His daughter has excelled: he will have to order Highest Liege of Airborne to leave her unharmed, lest his ruthless new wife inadvertently weakens him by depriving him of a loyal and effective spy. He clenches his fist, recalling his daughter's *geas.* *"Let her bring this urük vassal to me, that I may bind him as the first of my new subjects and take his face for our convenience. And then we shall proceed: first with the ground-based strike force, second with my wife's airborne feint—and then with the true strike, into the defenseless heart of the enemy's palace, wearing the visage of one of their own magi."*

Cassie does her best to warn Alex: "This is a really bad idea."

"I know." He renews his counting cantrip, crosses the line of salt, and pauses at the edge of the grid. He pulls out his phone and fires up the occult countermeasures app, sets the thaum field counter to buzz the phone if it detects a spike in the flux reading, then shoves it back in his pocket.

Meeting Cassie was not an accident. That's the most devastating blow; everything else—alien hominid invaders, soldiers trying to kill them—is trivial. That stuff is all part of the job, but he'd nearly mistaken Cassie for part of the jigsaw puzzle of life, or maybe a thread leading back to the tangled hairball world of mundane humanity. It's lonely and cold out on the edge, with no stronger connection than a weekly vial of blood in a mailing envelope, but for a while he'd begun to hope that—well, never mind.

The DM taking an interest in Whitby, and later in the Lawnswood bunker, was not an accident either. Forecasting Ops are notoriously Delphic but they *sometimes* shine a torch beam on dangers lurking in dark corners. Why the DM chose Alex in particular as the tool with which to probe this particular headache isn't clear to him, but then, it shouldn't be: what Alex doesn't know he can't disclose to the enemy. And that, he is very much afraid, is what Cassie is.

His trainers were keen on drilling a particular outlook into Alex, and now he's trying to apply it to his situation: *observe, orient, de-*

cide, act. Well, he's had an eyeful this evening, but what does it mean? It's time to finish observing and get oriented.

Alex's pulse fills his ears as he studies the grid. The notation around the outside is unfamiliar, but consistent with the form of a containment field. It might be safe to cross—it probably is, if all it's for is to distort or divert a ley line—but he can't be certain without further study and that's going to take too long. On the other hand, he has a source right here. He looks back at Cassie, feigning nonchalance: "Where are you from, why are you interested in me, and what were those guys doing outside?"

Cassie's eyes are huge in the darkness. "I wanted to watch a movie with you first, to explain."

"A movie? Which movie?"

"A famous film called *Dr. Strangelove*. Movies are wonderful! My people don't have them but I could sit and watch them all day except *Dr. Strangelove*, which makes me cry because it's so true. I thought it would make it easier to explain. Have you seen it?"

"I've heard of it, I think—is it a war movie?"

"Oh yes, but it's so much more, and I need to show it to you, but there's no time—" Cassie leans close, almost nose-to-nose with him. "It is important because *it is the story of my people*. Except not, because it is about *your* people and their cold war, but what I mean is, it's a *metaphor*." Her speech cadences are shifting slightly, he realizes, her grammar falling into the patterns of an alien language. "After the Sisterhood of the Red Night opened the gateway to the end of the universe by mistake, our All-Highest in her wisdom ordered a, what you would call a strategic attack. She was not expecting the Fellows of the Blind Tyrant to blow up the moon in retaliation, and then the Eaters beyond Time came swarming out from behind the blackened stars to steal the minds of every magus on the surface, and All-Highest and the entire court of the Morningstar Empire were killed by one of the first impactors, and only those of us sheltering deep underground survived the rain of lava when the sky caught fire, YesYes?"

"Um," Alex says, then stops, unsure what he can say that will cause her to slow down and show him the sense behind this demented tirade of names and apocalypses. "Really?"

She clutches his arm and peers at him intensely: "When the empire fell, the chain of command fell also, the oaths of loyalty, the bindings of obedience. My father is now the All-Highest of all that remains of the empire—dust and ashes and his own small command, lurking at the bottom of a mountain thousands of, of kilometers away from the capital. The *mineshaft gap*, don't you see?" Her grip tightens as she leans against him again. "The film *Dr. Strangelove* is like the origin story of my people. It is a parable of our recent history! And what happens next is what happens after, after history ends.

"My father commands the only remaining Host. Barely three thousand knights and their slaves and warbeasts survive, and we are running short of food. Our own lands are lost forever, the world destroyed and the ruins ravaged by monsters. So he ordered his magi to unseal the shadow roads and lead us to a new home. And my stepmother persuaded him to send me first, to probe the way forward. Or to die, she hopes."

"So what am I walking into?" Alex asks abruptly.

"There is a ley line at the bottom of this mineshaft, and this is a defensive spell set to protect it from intruders. Which means it must lead to my people. Hold my hand . . ." Cassie raises one foot, then delicately steps across the edge of the ghostly glowing design on the floor. Alex looks down and realizes: *She's still holding my arm.* "Come *on.*" She tugs him after her. "It is configured to kill anyone not of the Host or accompanied thereby who tries to enter," she explains, "but I am one such and you are with me."

"Well, *fuck.*" He tries to stop as Cassie begins to descend the stairs but his feet aren't listening; and his phone begins to buzz in his pocket, the thaum sensor vibrating a warning. "You've got me caught in a *geas* of your own," he says mildly.

"Yes." Her tone is almost apologetic. "I was sent hither to gather intelligence and find the magi of the enemy and bring him to my father. That is my *geas*. I invited you three times and you accepted, YesYes? But I'm not totally constrained—" She stares at him over her shoulder, an expression of desperation on her face as she continues in another language. "*I set you free.*"

Alex lurches to a halt as she steps off the staircase into the tunnel leading into the bunker. His expression is most peculiar. "I didn't know you spoke Old Enochian," he says. Then he swallows, and walks after her.

"Speak? Of course I can speak, what—what are you *doing*, idiot? You should flee!" She stops dead and stares at him, her expression shocked. "This isn't going to end well! One or both of us is bound to die, and then—and then—"

"You're not getting rid of me that easily." She's vibrating like a live wire as he takes her hand, and he can see the muscles in her neck standing out. He strokes the back of her hand very gently as he speaks, trying to convey the calm certitude she clearly needs. "I thought it was obvious what I'm doing: I'm coming with you to see your father. But first, we need to talk about what we're going to do when we find him . . ."

When Alex hit the button to send his text message on its merry way, he expected it to produce a shit-storm of epic proportions—but he had little or no idea of the sheer *scale* of the events it was about to set in motion.

BUNKER GEO NODE COMPROMISED CODE RED CASE NIGHT-MARE RED

It is 2314 hours BST on a Saturday night in London when the Duty Officer's phone terminal displays the message. The Duty Officer tonight is, as usual, sitting alone in the Duty Office in one of the decontaminated wings on the second floor of the New Annex. First he checks the origin of the message and verifies the caller ID by hand from the official (printed, top secret) departmental phone book. This takes him approximately thirty seconds. Having authenticated the sender, he then looks up a second number. Then he picks up the telephone handset and calls it.

At 2315, the phone rings in a conference room on the fourth floor, where the DM is morosely pondering probabilities, Vikram Choudhury is catching up on a couple of briefing documents he needs to be familiar with in time for a meeting on Monday morning, and Johnny McTavish is snoring quietly, an early copy of the *Mail on Sunday* shielding his face from the flickering overhead lighting tubes. Vikram twitches violently, sending papers flying, and makes a grab for the handset. "Room 414," he says, "yes?" He listens intently for a moment, frown lines forming on his forehead. "I'll tell them," he replies, finally. "Notify everyone on the Red List. We'll be ready when you call back." He puts the phone down, and looks across the table to where Derek is watching him. Vikram clears his throat nervously. "We have a Code Red in Lawnswood," he states. "Report from Alex Schwartz. He's announced CASE NIGHTMARE RED."

Johnny sits up. "Dear me," he says mildly. He pulls out his phone and speed-dials a number. Seconds later: "Duchess? We've got a Code Red in Leeds, and an EAT case report tagged RED to deal with . . ."

A wave of electronic signals ripples out from the Duty Office and the Watch Team in the fourth-floor conference room, lighting up darkened offices across the nation and pulling key personnel back from their weekend retreats.

In Cheltenham, in an office deep inside an anonymous block not too far from the donut-shaped hub of GCHQ, two analysts suddenly find themselves inundated with transcription requests. They feed SIM codes and IMEIs to their secure terminals, provide override authorizations for the interconnects with the phone companies' networks, and begin to replay the past day's conversations to a farm of servers capable of turning spoken words into readable textual transcripts, accompanied by maps and a handy timeline to indicate who said what, where, when, and to whom.

In an aircraft hangar at Filton, not far from the Bristol Channel, a phone that should *never* ring begins to buzz in the ready room office, causing a man who wears a blue uniform to break into a cold sweat as he picks up the handset. He frowns intently as he notes the call in a logbook, pen clenched between white fingertips, not once looking at the sleek white shape that fills the hangar floor beyond his office window. If he did, he'd see a sudden burst of movement as the engineers on the night shift begin the ground prep checklists for a mission that should never fly.

Phones begin ringing in the Duty Offices of peripheral Laundry field installations everywhere from Penzance to Inverness, anywhere big enough to rate a 24x7 desk presence. The Duty Officers retrieve their contact lists from their office safes and begin to call people, working down the hierarchy. (Mobile phones are also displaying text messages, and priority email queues are overflowing—but the gold standard is a confirmation by voice, "message received" on a secure landline number.) One office, in Huddersfield, makes no such calls: instead, the Duty Officer walks out into the ready room next door, raises a protective flap, and pushes the alarm button concealed behind it. (Boots come running.)

Early on Sunday morning, the anthill finishes kicking its on-call elements into a state of high alert, and the ripples begin to spread out beyond the organization.

The first external signal goes to a call center in India, which is operated on behalf of a private security company based in Bradford. This call is started well ahead of midnight by a member of the New Annex Watch Team, but a number of obstacles delay its completion. For one thing, the call center is in the middle of an evening shift change, and the staff are reluctant to stay on line despite a client call. The call has to be repeated three times. For another, Telereal Trinium seem content to employ a subcontractor whose staff have poor language and communication skills and a lackadaisical approach to emergencies. (This issue will not go unnoticed by the Parliamentary Public Enquiry in the months to come.) In any case, it takes until 0014 before a private security guard from the Leeds office sets out to visit the Lawnswood bunker, and they do not arrive until 0028. Inexplicably it takes another twelve minutes for them to gain access, and the eventual call to the West Yorkshire Police emergency control room is logged at 0043, over an hour and a half after the incident.

It's a Saturday night but the pubs have already closed, and the weekly cleaning-up action on the streets of Leeds is winding down. The first responder—as luck would have it, an Armed Response

Unit—arrives on the scene at 0049, and the site is flagged as a homicide case within ten minutes.

While West Yorkshire's finest are puzzling over the discovery of two armored bodies outside a supposedly secure government installation with a glowing green radiation hazard visible through the bashed-in door, phones are ringing elsewhere. In Fareham, a call is received at NATS Swanwick near the south coast, the national-level Air Traffic Control Center for England and Wales. Near Hereford, the Duty Officer in the Pontrilas Army Training Area takes a call and forwards it to a captain running a night training exercise. And elsewhere, calls are being made to various military and sensitive civilian installations that need to know that, in the vaguest possible terms, something big is about to kick off.

One fateful phone call goes unanswered.

The DM stares balefully at the phone as it rings continuously, then diverts to voice mail. "Pick it up," he grates, "pick the damn thing *up*." Then he ends the call and hits redial.

Derek the DM has been war-dialing Alex's mobile phone continuously for close to an hour, hanging up and redialing endlessly. They've requested a trace from GCHQ, but it hasn't arrived yet; there's no way of knowing why it isn't connecting. The Watch Team meeting room is now crowded with the great, the good, and the concerned—Dr. Armstrong was the first of the Auditors to arrive but they're almost all here now, along with those local elements of Mahogany Row who aren't already charging up the M1 motorway in a convoy of police cars with flashing lights. Dr. O'Brien, the newest Auditor, is still on medical leave, but her former unit—the Transhuman Policy Coordination Force, the police agency for superpowers—is represented by Mhari Murphy, ill-temperedly displaying her fangs over being called in on a weekend night. Bob Howard, lately standing in for the Eater of Souls, is somewhere in Japan, and Colonel Lockhart is listening in on the conference line from Leeds, making notes in case he has to brief the Cabinet Office in the morning.

"Pick up the bloody *phone*, Alex," hisses Mhari as the DM dials his mobile number again.

But Alex is not going to pick up the phone that he set to vibrate, not ring, before he headed out for his fateful date. The phone is rattling and squealing like an overtaxed vibrator, its thaum flux warning app overloaded so badly that the regular buzz of an incoming call is swamped. Which is why he remains blissfully unaware that in the two hours after he sent his text message, it has triggered on the close order of half a million pounds in billable overtime hours, hundreds—soon to be thousands—of sleepless nights and abandoned weekends, and a full-dress Police murder investigation.

But that's nothing compared to what's going to happen in the next few hours.

14: THE NIGHTMARE STACKS

The lights are on in drab-looking government offices in Leeds as well as London, and a crisis meeting is in progress in an office in Quarry House.

"He's out late." It's Brains. He sounds both sleepy and irritable, as well he might. "He borrowed Ilsa to pick up his date and do dinner. That's all I know."

"Not good enough." Gerald Lockhart frowns, mustache bristling. "*Why* is he late? He sent that message, then went dark, and now he isn't answering his phone." Gerald Lockhart, External Assets Manager, charged with executing the DM's plan for the missing PHANG in Leeds, is distinctly unamused. "Pinky. What word on his phone?"

"The trace isn't showing up." Pinky twirls a finger across the trackpad of a laptop. He's frowning, too, more in perplexity than disapproval. "It went to his parents' street in Bramhope, then back towards town, but it stopped pinging when he hit the bunker. At least I'm pretty sure he went to the bunker—his last location is solid to within about a hundred meters—"

"So we know where he went, but not where he is. Not good enough." Lockhart's mood is not improving. "What does his activity log show?"

"Well. He ran OFCUT, but it's offline now so it doesn't tell me much. The thaum field it was logging was sky-high, but going by that report on the bunker it might just have gotten contaminated. It's not paired with a high-precision field-effect counter so I can't be sure."

"So." Lockhart taps his pen on the table, cap first. It makes an ominous *tonk* as it hits the hardwood. "Let me summarize. This morning, Weather Control flagged anomalous ley line activity to the east of the Pennines. The DM is on the list, and just under three hours ago he called Dr. Schwartz and asked him to check out the Lawnswood bunker. An hour later our man sent up the red flag. It's geotagged from the bunker, and he reports CASE NIGHTMARE RED—how does he know this? It's a mystery. He then goes off-grid. The police check on the bunker and find two bodies, deceased—"

Pete, who has been reading something on a tablet screen, looks up and diffidently waves his hand for attention. "They're not human."

"What." Lockhart turns his death-stare on Pete, who seems unfazed.

"OCCULUS have been on-site for half an hour now. Sergeant Noakes just sent a preliminary sitrep. Look." He lays his tablet on the table and tap-zooms on a photograph. "What does that say to you?"

Heads crane over the small screen. "What." Lockhart's tone sharpens. "That's an ear? Dammit."

Pinky is peering at the same report on his laptop screen. "There's a cartoon convention in town but that's no cosplayer, not unless cosplayers have plastic surgery and wear several thousand pounds' worth of bespoke steel armor. And get into fights with . . . um."

"Look," says Brains, sounding irritated, "they've got Ilsa."

Lockhart looks at him, then at Pinky and Pete. "So what are you waiting for?"

Pete stares at him. "What?"

"Go and get your half-track before some jobsworth tries to wheel-clamp it," Lockhart snaps. "OCCULUS are busy with the incident scene and the police are as much help as a portion of warm ice cream so I'm relying on you troublemakers to locate Dr. Schwartz and extract him from whatever mess he's gotten himself into. You *might* just need an all-terrain transporter with a solid steel body shell, if Forecasting Ops are right about this one. Go on, get moving." He waits while they leave, then turns to Jez Wilson. "Do you want to call Dr. Armstrong, or shall I?"

"I'll take it if you handle the army and OCCULUS," she says automatically. "What's the message?"

"He needs a full summary so he can report to the Cabinet Office emergency meeting tomorrow—this—morning. Assuming it's not a false alarm." Lockhart sighs noisily. "He's going to have to explain to the deputy prime minister that one of our vampires is missing. And then the shit is *really* going to hit the fan. But first I think I need to talk to site security."

He picks up the handset and dials an extension. "Site security? Colonel Lockhart here. Authenticate me, please . . . good. I am declaring a Code Red for Quarry House and the Arndale Satellite Office in Leeds. I repeat, Code Red, Code Red. Please tell Control that I recommend transferring control over MAGINOT BLUE STARS coverage on the Leeds Inner Loop Road and all approaches to Quarry Hill to site security here, in anticipation of a hard incursion. Then you will call the office of the Commander Land Forces at Army GHQ in Andover and tell them that PLAN RED RABBIT is in effect."

Jez Wilson stares at him, aghast. "You want to activate SCORPION STARE in a city center? Are you out of your mind?"

"I hope not," he says grimly, "I really hope not. I also fervently hope that Forecasting Ops have got egg on their face. But it's best to be ready for the worst. Then you won't be disappointed when it happens."

Cassie leads Alex down the stairs into the bunker, marveling at and simultaneously mourning his misplaced loyalty. She feels a stab of lust and tenderness that surprises her with its intensity. He's following her of his own volition, despite knowing what lies ahead. She may have freed him from her will to obey, but love is also a kind of *geas*, and one that she can't control. (Part of her wonders whether she would have been consciously able to free him from her third-date snare of compulsion if she hadn't been aware of his obsession; probably not, she decides. All-Highest's goals override both whim and reason.)

Agent First understands Alex a good deal better now. She's seen the house that shaped him, and has the perspective from Cassiopeia to recognize the claustrophobia and alienation that drive him. The beginnings of a plan are coming together in her head. It's a plan that would be hopelessly naive and foolish if Alex was of the People, with their candidly nihilistic outlook on life—but he isn't. He's *urük*, and these round-eared folk are gentler and more trusting than her own kindred. So is she. Among these people, the fatal flaw in her soul that she has concealed for so long is unremarkable. But there are limits to trust, and this plan won't work unless—

She licks her suddenly dry lips. "Alex, do you trust me?"

"That's a leading question, isn't it."

"Yes." Ahead of her a tunnel slants down into the earth. The overhead strip lights are out, but the glowing runic tracery of the ward upstairs sheds just enough light for her crepuscular vision.

"Well." He pauses. "If I didn't trust you I wouldn't be following you, would I?" A momentary catch in his voice. "I have an idea, but—what do you think we should do?"

She walks forward slowly. "My father bears your people no particular ill-will; they are simply *in his way* and he'll try to crush them. Our world is no longer inhabitable. My father thought to lead the Host somewhere they can live safely. Stepmother suggested this world. She fed him old reports which were at best wrong and at worst disastrously misleading. He thinks to conquer and compel obedience, as is usual among our kind. I believe *her* plan was to let him, but to encourage him to bleed himself in the process, weakening him to pave the way for her ascendancy." She closes her eyes, seeing in her mind's theater the television set downstairs in her student lodgings, the evening news, the unimagined vastness of this crowded city-hive of humanity overhead, the realization that this isn't even a *large* human city, that it's a provincial capital in a medium-sized nation, the creeping apprehension of scale— "But he's wrong. Your people are far stronger than they expect. He will kill a lot of people, all of his own and many of yours, if he is not made to stop. And she's even worse." She is choosing her words very carefully here, walking along a razor-edged precipice between suicidal treason and rationalized defense of the All-Highest's interests. "I do not want that to happen, Alex, but I cannot stop him because I am bound to obey the will of the All-Highest."

"And your father is the All-Highest," Alex says tentatively.

"Yes. But he wasn't always." Around the curve of the tunnel, she sees an open door ahead. She stops and Alex wraps an arm around her shoulders. "The, the empress died, and her city and her advisors: all the *chain of command*. The bindings and power of All-Highest fell on him then, and nearly broke him. He was a general before. Now he is the empire itself: the *Crown*, as you put it."

"And you can't disobey him or betray him or your head catches fire or something. I get it." His fingers contract around her upper arm and she shifts her balance uneasily in response.

"If he dies, the chain of power that defines All-Highest falls next to my stepmother. It would have been my mother's, if First Liege of Airborne Strike had not denounced her for treason while my father's mind was wandering," she adds with quiet venom.

"Ah." He moves his hand: fingers begin to stroke her tense shoulders in tiny circles. She breathes deeply as she waits to see if he is canny enough to realize what comes next. "And if your stepmother dies, who becomes All-Highest next?"

Yes! Something inside her exults, but she stills the traitor realization instantly, terrified of exploring the possible consequences. "The chain of command continues," she says. "First through the bloodline, by marriage, then by descent; then, if not, to his highest-ranked oathbound officer. That is how he became All-Highest after all." She opens her mouth and chooses her next words very carefully: "It is *very important* that my father must outlive my stepmother."

"Ah," he says again, then hesitates on the brink of further speech. And nods, wordless, clearly understanding what is better left unsaid.

It's time for the final step, for Agent First to place her neck willingly on the block if she has misjudged this boy-man. She hopes not: he certainly seems as besotted with her as she is with him. But trust is a strange currency, and her upbringing has taught her that if she expects betrayal she will not be disappointed. So Agent First closes her eyes, and leaves it to Cassie to ask the final question. "My father has summoned me and commanded me to bring you as the, the enemy magus I have bewitched. He believes that you will then obey me and allow him to gain access to the citadel on Quarry Hill, which he believes to be your queen's castle." She chokes on her own tongue for a moment. "Will you come with me *not* under compulsion, but of your own free will, with volition preserved?"

"You want me free to act as I see fit?"

"Don't tell me what you're thinking," she warns. "If I am aware of any threat to my Liege I am compelled to act."

"Then I'll make no threats," he says, deceptively light-heartedly. "And you'll take me into your father's court without alerting your stepmother's servants, and let everyone assume I'm bound by, by your *geas*?" His hand moves away for a moment as he pats down a pocket.

"Yes. And remember, it would be a *very bad idea* to show them how fast you can count your way past a circle of salt. Or to show any sign of agency. They're not stupid: if you aren't *clearly* in thrall they'll strike immediately." She turns and rests her chin at the base of his neck and licks his ear lobe delicately. "When this is over we will have to spend some time together. My magus." His intake of breath hisses quietly. She rubs against him: "My *special* magus."

"Why special?" he pants.

"Our magi can't count that fast. They can't do this either." She touches the bulge in his trousers: "The men, I mean. They're cut. The women are controlled differently. To make them placid," she adds, then growls in the back of her throat. "Else they would drink us dry. You are different, I think."

"What do you want, after all this is over?" he whispers.

"I want *you*." She lets go of him reluctantly—the lust is rising—and stares into his eyes, seeing the green glow of the tunnel walls mirrored there for a moment, green strands of light writhing behind his pupils. "But first I must slay my stepmother, the dragon."

Hours later:

The white Transit van turns into the open gates at the top of the driveway and stops. A light rain is falling, visible in the beams of its headlights as they illuminate a scene of organized chaos.

Four police cars are parked around the building like toys discarded by a bored child. They've been joined by a scene-of-crime van, and another van full of uniforms who are now swarming around the site like angry bees in hi vis jackets and rain gear. What appears to be a City of London fire service major incident support truck is parked alongside the police cars, and men in what looks at a distance like fire service protective gear are moving between their truck and the door to the building.

"Oi! You can't park here—"

Pinky winds his window down and shoves his warrant card in the cop's face. "Yes we can, we're from the Ministry," he snaps. "This is one of our sites."

"Tough." The constable isn't backing off, and this is a very bad sign indeed when there's a Laundry warrant card in play. Pete, unbuckling his seat belt on the passenger side, looks through the rain-streaked windscreen and sees two more bodies erecting a white dome tent in front of the door to the bunker, while another cop—holding a G36 assault rifle—keeps a wary eye on the new arrivals. "Go through channels, piss off and don't bother us until we've secured the site, this is an armed incident—"

"Excuse me," Pete says mildly, "we're here for our half-track."

"What?"

Pete rests his hands on the dash, sweating. Where there's one armed officer there will be more and if they've brought out the long arms he's willing to bet there'll be one aimed at the Transit right now. "Excuse me," he calls past Pinky, "can we talk to the OCCULUS crew?"

"Stop right—" The cop stops, finally recognizing what's going on. "You're with the spooks?"

Pete slowly opens his door and steps down beside the Transit. He shuts the door and raises his hands as Pinky begins to back up. A couple of the fake firemen are approaching him warily, holding what look like infrared imaging cameras. Pete's skin crawls. "Head office!" he calls, allowing his warrant card to unfold from his right hand. "Ministry of Defense, Officer. This is one of our sites, we're here to help. Take me to your incident commander and I'll explain everything . . ."

"Oh, it's *you*." The cop looks round as one of the ersatz firemen approaches. Up close, he doesn't look much like a fireman: it must be a combination of the army boots, the holstered pistol, or the thaum field radiating from his protective gear that makes Pete's skin itch. "Let them through, Officer, they're ours."

"Mac?" Pete asks quietly as the fireman raises his helmet visor. He's Warrant Officer Gavin McAndrews, part of the SRR team cross-trained in occult operations to work under Laundry guidance in the field.

"Yep." Mac beckons. "Skipper's been expecting you."

It takes a couple of minutes to smooth over Pinky's lack of tact, but sooner rather than later Pete is sitting in the back of the OCCU-LUS truck with the officer in charge of the unit and a tired and edgy detective sergeant, while the others work out how to get the Transit and its tow trailer turned round without reversing into a police car. "We're looking for the member of staff who phoned in the alert," Pete explains. "This is his last known location, as of two hours ago, and he was driving the Kettenkrad, along with one known associate."

"Associate." Captain Hastings fixes him with a skeptical look. "What's that supposed to mean?"

Pete shrugs. "Girlfriend, if you can call it that: it was their second date. Head office asked him to check up on something at this site and at this point you know as much as I do."

The detective clears her throat. "Excuse me, Mr. Wil—"

Pete smiles politely. "That's Reverend Doctor Wilson," he corrects.

"Reverend?" The sergeant gives him a who-do-you-think-you're-kidding look.

"Church of England, on secondment to the Ministry of Defense." Pete shrugs. "Long story. Listen, we're out here to reclaim the half-track and ensure the site is locked down. Captain Hastings has the second part of that in hand. I understand you're investigating the site of a suspicious double-homicide, but if you've looked inside the building—"

"Level six containment ward," says Captain Hastings. He looks as if he's bitten an orange and found himself sucking a lemon. "The bodies aren't human, either."

"Now wait a minute!" the detective says.

"Sergeant." Pete smiles again, even more politely. "What did you say your name was?"

"I didn't." She glares. "Emma Gracie, criminal investigations. Vicar.

Captain. There are two bodies here. You say you were called in by one of your men, but there's no sign of him. And there's some sort of radiation hazard—"

"Yes, that's why we're here," Captain Hastings says with ill-concealed impatience. "But if you'd just pay attention to what I'm saying, those bodies *are not human*. Listen to your own SOCO people. Those pointy ears are not made of latex, their dentition is wrong, and they've got slit pupils. Also," he adds for Pete's ears, "the tinplate they're wearing is carrying a thaum flux fit to burn out a standard-issue ward, and they're armed with some kind of baton that you really don't want to mess with outside a warded firing range. They came out of the bunker, your boy is missing *inside* the bunker, and we really need to take over from the police before we can go see what's down there."

"Lovely." Pete turns to the detective. "Which just leaves the half-track. Do you need to dust it for fingerprints or something? Because if not, we can get out of your hair right now. Unless you need a liaison with headquarters ops?" he adds for Captain Hastings.

"No, that won't be necessary." Hastings runs a hand through sandy, thinning hair. Like the officer in charge of the OCCULUS unit Pete worked with the previous year in Watford, he's wiry and intense, more like a head teacher with a triathlon habit than anyone's idea of an officer in the Territorial SAS. "My men will establish a perimeter around the surface structure, contain any excursions, and stay the hell out of Sergeant Gracie's patch while she does the scene-of-crime tap dance around the bodies." He glances at her and she nods, minutely. "We're setting up camera nodes in the building so that if anything tries to come out, Control can observe it. And—"

"By anything, what exactly do you anticipate?" The sergeant gives him a cold-eyed stare. "Is there a public safety issue I should be aware of? What aren't you telling me?"

Captain Hastings thinks for a moment, then speaks. "Sergeant. Right now you're looking at this as a crime problem. Unlawful killing, yes?"

"Yes, which is why—"

"What if it isn't? Suppose it's a national security problem. Suppose those bodies, for the sake of argument, were Russian Spetsnaz special forces soldiers who were here as pathfinders for an invasion. Here to kill civil authorities, fuck stuff up, and raise hell right before a paratroop assault. Suppose also that they've had the supreme bad luck to try and break into a camouflaged Ministry of Defense installation with lethal countermeasures and got themselves killed. So it's actually not a normal crime, but an act of war. What would your priorities be then?"

Sergeant Gracie stares at him in horror. "You're kidding me."

Pete spots where Hastings is going and pitches in. "We're from the Ministry of Defense: our sense of humor is surgically excised at birth. What Captain Hastings is trying to tell you is that business as usual will be resumed once we know this *isn't* an act of war. In the meantime, it'd be a very good idea if you and your officers would secure the crime scene, do only whatever needs to be done *right this minute* to record the evidence, then clear the hell out and be prepared to handle civil defense in event of an attack. If it doesn't materialize, if it's safe to come back afterwards, you can come back and it's business as usual. If not—well, you'll be one less instance of civilian collateral damage for the captain to worry about."

"Thank you, Vicar." Hastings nods, unsmiling. "It's probably best if you and your associates leave now—as part of the public whose safety Sergeant Gracie is so keen to ensure, after all."

"Absolutely." A thought strikes Pete. "Do you plan to enter the bunker?" he asks. "Because I got the guided tour about two weeks ago, and if you need a guide—I mean, assuming it's not full of eldritch Spetsnaz types—I may be able to save you some time."

Hastings's smile vanishes. "Maybe if we're still here tomorrow, Vicar." He glances at the rack of radios and other instruments occupying one wall of the truck, and the technician leaning over them. "But not now: it isn't safe. If the forecast from London is accurate and something's coming through, I want everything done and dusted and everyone off this site within half an hour."

Across the Yorkshire dales, nightmares stir in the predawn light. Gradually at first, then with gathering momentum, the invading forces begin to move.

Hours before dawn, the heavy cavalry of the Host's armored brigade finally arrive en masse. They thunder through the portal below Malham Cove in file, three abreast. The drumming of their claw-flanked hooves shatters the still night air as they trot downhill, first south, then wheeling to the east across the wooded hillsides of the national park. They continue to track southeast, across the rolling farmland and dry stone walls of North Yorkshire. It takes nearly an hour for the steel-clad riders on their horned steeds to ride out in good order, for there are more than two thousand troopers under arms, led by officers and accompanied by well-fed battle magi in carriages with drawn blinds to protect them from the light of daybreak. Pennants flutter in the predawn air, unit insignia for the riders to form up around; but the Host is eerily mute, only the jingle and rattle of metal and the thud of hooves on stone heralding their arrival. Such orders as are issued are delivered by their officers' will-to-power, directly into the minds of the troopers. They're as inexorable and impossible to disobey as cold iron hooks buried in tender flesh. Visors are lowered, reflective and occlusive, protecting against any glimpse of their wearers' skin: this army rides in purdah.

As the last of the armored brigade rumbles away from the shadow road, trailed by a handful of stragglers (lamed mounts, brain-struck riders), the supply train follows. Long-haired steppe pachyderms haul cargo wagons piled high with fodder for the cavalry mounts. An equoid can devour thirty kilograms of red meat in a day, while a battle magus may consume the souls of a handful of slaves in an hour-long firefight. Keeping the Host engaged with an enemy burns through rations with monstrous speed, consuming the lives of two hundred oxen and a hundred slaves in every twenty-hour day.

All-Highest watches from the top of the cliff as the last of the redoubt's time-stoppered supplies roll after the cavalry. There is enough meat to keep the Host fed for just three days, then they will have to forage for supplies, raiding whatever passes for slaughterhouses and slave farms in this alien land. The Morningstar Empire's armies take as many prisoners as they can seize—but they don't build camps to warehouse and feed them.

All-Highest looks downslope towards Highest Liege of Airborne

Strike Command, who is inspecting her squadron. Eight dragons are lined up below, ground crews scurrying busily to load their chariots with munitions and to pump high-energy nutrients into their bizarre five-chambered stomachs. Pipes run downhill, draining their waste into a nearby stream that bubbles and fizzles, emitting toxic fumes. Again, there is no slack in the supply chain. There is precisely enough food for a single day of high-tempo sorties, enough weapons for a day of operations against a competent enemy. Then it will be necessary to rest the dragons and—with desperate haste—seek local stockpiles of the fluorinated minerals they consume in enormous quantities, lest the mounts turn feral through starvation. They did not evolve in a world like this one or the People's, but in another place, dark and corrosive and toxic. Their tentacles twitch listlessly, narcotized for now, but hinting at the barely constrained power leashed within their barrel-shaped bodies.

The heavy armored brigade will travel cross-country, following an ancient and powerful ley line until it intersects with one of the *urük*'s larger stone highways. Then the ley line diverts south towards the edges of the gigantic enemy hive-city, until it terminates at an anchor point established by the pathfinder magi. (This is linked by a tighter route to the endpoint under the battlements of the enemy palace—but it runs underground, useless for cavalry mobility.)

The cavalry steeds do not run much faster than a horse, but unlike a horse they can keep up a canter or a gallop for hours, their monstrous meat-fueled stamina and alien heat-dissipating metabolism combining to achieve a level of mobility no premodern force could hope to match. When they follow a ley line they can tap into its huge stored power to boost both their offensive weapons and defensive wards. Back home, no defender would be so negligent as to allow an unguarded ley line to exist next to the heart of one of their walled strongholds—but the *urük* are apparently ignorant of the arts of war.

The sun will be nearing the zenith by the time the cavalry brigade reaches the sprawling stone canyons around the center of the *urük*-hive, but a force mounted on horseback would be barely a third of the way there. The task of the air group is to first deny the *urük* access to the skies, then engage whatever enemy mobile forces are drawn out by the cavalry spearhead. With its superior maneuverability and close air support, the Host of the Morningstar Empire is one of the most lethal armored formations ever fielded, in this or any other world. But it is a huge gamble to aim it straight at the heart of an enemy capital without deeper insight into the defender's arrangements. Although All-Highest is desperate, he isn't stupid: he has no intention of betting everything on a single crude spear-thrust.

He turns his helmed head to survey the air defense basilisks behind him. There are four of them, sleeping where they stand in pits dug into the top of the hill. Their long, sauropod-like necks droop, hoods tightly furled around their eye clusters and feeding tentacles by the handling crews. Not far away, the precognitive magi who select their targets are waiting under cover by the stockade where their dull-eyed soul-fodder lies bound, awaiting their sanguinary fate. Forecasting the movement of aviation assets is *mana*-intensive work. Slave blood runs like water before the huge basilisks are induced to open their crystal eyelids and turn their mindlessly lethal gaze towards the eye-warping air knots that mask enemy fliers. But things are different this time round. If Highest Liege of Airborne is right, the *urük* flying devices are little more than cattle-carts, easily detected, defenseless, and sluggish.

Satisfied with this final survey of his forces, All-Highest turns to Third of Infantry and inclines his head. *"Is your force prepared?"* he asks bluntly.

"My Lord." She raises her mailed fist to the base of her throat. *"All are equipped and briefed. Once the cavalry have left I will move my force downslope, ready to march at your command."* Unlike the cavalry with their brilliantly polished reflective armor and anti-cognition countermeasures, the ground troops merely wear dull metal, their layers of mail and protective plates muffled with rubberized fabric. The Host's infantry are not required for the opening stages of this campaign. A single battalion is mustered at the top of the cliff, out of the way of the cavalry, while the rest bring up the rear of the army traversing the shadow road, shuffling under the weight of the final load of supplies. Infantry Third's battalion is the highest rated in the Host, which is why she has been selected for this task. *"All we await is the pathfinder and our occupation objectives."*

"That is in hand." All-Highest's expression reflects his satisfaction. *"You must be ready to move at noon, local time, possibly earlier if readiness permits."* He pauses a moment. *"The guards on the ley line endpoint just outside the hive. Have they reported in recently?"*

Infantry Third doesn't hesitate. *"Two hours ago, my Lord. The ley line was secure at that time; they are next due to report an hour hence."*

All-Highest's near-smile fades. *"Fifth-of-day intervals? That's not good enough. I want you to raise your situational awareness to operational levels immediately."*

"The plan called for that to happen at dawn; I will bring the schedule forward as you direct." Infantry Third's face is impassive, but All-Highest senses her fear as a tightening in the silvery spiderweb of obligations that is an ever-present tingling at the back of his head. *"There is a problem keeping the magi fed: constant contact is expensive . . ."*

"I don't care if you run out of sacrifices. Have a squad round up some natives. Our magi are perfectly able to consume urük blood."

"That will make life easier! It will be as you command." All-Highest feels Infantry Third's relief immediately. *"By your leave . . ."*

"Go." All-Highest gestures. Infantry Third marches over to her team and begins giving orders: her men and women attend, and presently messengers depart towards the magi's pavilion. All-Highest watches for a minute, then turns back to his own bodyguards. *"I have seen enough."* He turns his mount away from the cliff face and rides slowly downhill. From experience he knows that it will take half an hour for the last of the cavalry force to leave the valley, and another half hour for the infantry battalion to get into position. But everyone *will* be in position an hour before dawn, including the onrushing cavalry spearhead—and then it will be time to engage the enemy.

As Pinky pulls out of the driveway and turns onto the empty dual carriageway, Pete glances in the back of the van. Brains is busy with the rack of routers and the picocell base station; it's hard to be sure in the slowly strobing shadows cast by the streetlights, but he looks worried. "Where next?" Pete asks.

"Quarry House car park." Pinky sounds distracted as he gears up, making the diesel engine bellow hoarsely. "We can unload Ilsa there: she should be safe for a while."

"Hang on," calls Brains. "What was that again?" He's talking into a headset, Pete realizes. "Yes, I'll tell them. Change of plan, guys. We're going for a spin around the Inner Loop before we drop everything off at QH."

The Inner Loop is a five-kilometer-long one-way route that snakes through Leeds city center like a particularly demented level from *Grand Theft Auto*, twining between town hall and railway station, alongside hospital and under Victorian viaduct. It's not an actual road: more a succession of loosely coupled street signs that direct traffic around the pedestrianized core, in such a way that unless the driver knows exactly which exit they're aiming at they're locked into a frustrating twenty-minute stop-go detour. "What for?" demands Pinky. "Isn't everywhere closed at this time of night?"

"Yes, but that was Lockhart. He wants us over at the Royal Armouries: he's getting one of the curators out of bed to let us into the special repository. It's going to be"—Pinky joins in suddenly, and they chorus—"*just like Christmas*!"

"Um," says Pete, in the sudden gap as Pinky hurls the van and trailer across the deserted roundabout with the ring road, "am I missing something?"

"Lockhart wants us to raid the nightmare stacks for anything that isn't nailed down. That's the special collection at the National Firearms Centre," Brains adds. "Silver bullets, cold iron, banishment rounds, that sort of thing."

"The National Firearms Centre?"

"The Ministry of Defense has a hobby: they've been buying one of everything ever since Henry VIII's day. They used to keep it at the Enfield Royal Small Arms Factory—it was the Enfield Pattern Room back then—but it got too big and cumbersome, so when they built the Royal Armouries Museum up here they bolted a secure underground archive on the side. That's the NFC. It's basically a reference library for firearms. You've seen *The Matrix*?"

Pete racks his brains. Shiny black latex, bullet-time video, cold-faced agents— "You mean that bit with the guns?"

"Yeah, it's just like that," says Pinky. "Only it's real."

"But what are we going to *do* with a load of guns?" asks Pete.

"I don't know, Brains, what *are* we going to do with a half-track full of guns?" Pinky asks.

Brains chuckles. "Same thing we do every night, Pinky—"

"Fort up and wait for reinforcements," Pinky says flatly. "Because Alex has disappeared, Lockhart is spooked, and Forecasting Ops are convinced the world could end tomorrow."

"But, *guns*—" says Pete, channeling his inner British unease at the idea of prepping for survivalist role-playing games in built-up areas.

"Relax," says Pinky, flooring the accelerator as he drives past Woodhouse Moor Park, "we won't be taking anything too big. Did you know," he adds, taking his eye off the road to grin manically at Pete, "that the original Quarry Hill Flats were designed to be defensible with machine guns from any approach in case of a Communist revolution? That was in the 1920s! I just bet Lockhart's aware of that . . ."

Pinky steers them onto the Inner Loop and then turns off, to crawl through backstreets between red brick warehouses refurbished and given an afterlife as riverside apartments. They come to a halt in a pedestrianized courtyard before a modern building with a glassed-in entrance, incongruously flanked by eighteenth-century naval carronades. "Right, this is it," he says, opening his door and climbing out. "Pete? You're driving Ilsa, we can stack a bunch of extra stuff on her and use the trailer. Brains, you handle filling the van. I think this is our man now . . ."

"Our man" turns out to be female, thirty-ish, and distinctly annoyed at being pulled out of bed at two in the morning. "You," she says, pointing her flashlight at Pinky in a no-nonsense way that suggests a personal history encompassing time in the military, "you realize this is a no parking zone?"

Pinky raises his warrant card. "Jan Downum?" he asks.

"Yes—oh hell, wait. Are *you* why I'm here?" She steps forward until she can see his card clearly. "Bugger. Who are your mates?" Introductions are made. "Okay. I'm the designated keyholder for the stacks. If you'd kindly move your van and park over on that side of the cannon, yes, over *there*, I'll take you in through the side entrance. You all have official ID on you? And you're unarmed? There are metal detectors and we'll have to search you if you set them off."

She leads them through a windowless entrance in a neighboring building, then through a keypad-secured door leading to a corridor with a freight lift at the end. They descend at least two stories before the lift stops. It terminates in a lobby with a uniformed guard on duty beside a metal detector arch and a baggage X-ray belt. He is, Pete realizes with a lurch of unease, carrying a holstered pistol at his hip. *Armed guards at a British museum?* "Good morning," the guard says. He nods at Ms. Downum. "If you'd present your ID, please? Jackets and shoes go on the belt, along with any bags, phones, wallets . . ."

The security check is thorough by airline standards, in line with the flaming hoops Pete has become desensitized to ever since he got himself sucked into one of the more obscure lagoons of the security state. "Remember: no photography, no phone use, no wandering off, and no touching the exhibits without prior permission," Downum warns them once the blue-suiter on the front desk signs them in and signs them off as definitely not carrying anything illegal, immoral, or fattening. "This is a working archive and all the items we keep here are operational, which means they're capable of killing you. Any questions?" She stifles a cavernous yawn, then glares at them.

"Er, yes," says Pete, just as Pinky asks, "Have you been told what we're here for?"

"Yes. Follow me," she says, unlocking another windowless door leading into a white-walled corridor wide enough to take a shipping pallet. "I'm to take you to the special collection and sign out anything you need—" She opens the next door and Pete stops dead in his tracks, heart hammering.

Beyond the doorway Pete sees a windowless room with a high ceiling. Every square centimeter seems to be covered in gun racks; the opposite end of the room is a solid wall of rifles. The floor facing him is occupied by a different kind of exhibit. Eight tripod-mounted heavy machine guns are drawn up side by side, their rifled muzzles converging on the doorway; in the middle, the black cylindrical bundle of an M134 Minigun's six barrels squats atop an electrical ammunition

feed and a battery pack, aiming straight at his face. A laminated plac-
ard dangles from it by a string. It warns: SHOPLIFTERS WILL BE
OBLITERATED.

"Ooh, that'll do nicely!" says Pinky.

"I'm not sure it'll work." Brains bends over the minigun and peers at
its mounting bracket. "Remember it's American and Ilsa is all-metric—"

"But we could weld a mount to the top of the tow hitch!" Pinky
is clearly getting excited. "I'm pretty sure there's room for the ammunition box to fit in the engine cover storage—"

"Children," says Pete, "what are we here *for*?"

Pinky looks up guiltily. "Didn't Lockhart tell you?" he asks Brains.

"Sure did." Brains straightens up, shoves his hands in his pockets,
and looks smug.

"Spill it, love." Pinky's eyebrows furrow minutely, but Brains is
clearly annoyed about something: possibly the idea of his partner
wreaking such indignities on an eighty-year-old vehicle, or perhaps
something else that Pete isn't privy to. "Come on, not *now*—"

Downum clears her throat noisily. "If you gentlemen would care
to stop drooling and step this way, we're *not there* yet." She sounds
more than slightly peeved. "I'm not the only person you've got out of
bed this weekend, and you don't want to keep Harry waiting." She
doesn't wait for a reply, but walks rapidly past a rack of bolt-action
rifles towards a door at the back.

"Harry?" asks Pete, trailing after her.

"Harry?" Pinky echoes, a trace of awe in his voice: "*Harry* works
here now?"

"Whoops," says Brains, his mustache crinkling in a smile, "what a
surprise! Don't tell me you hadn't wondered where he got moved to
after they closed Dansey House."

"I thought he was in the New Annex . . ."

Pete follows their guide through another echoing arsenal that
smells of machine oil and (very faintly) of powder fumes, keeping half
an ear on Alex's two tech support housemates as they bicker good-
naturedly. Surrounded by the tools of violence he feels cold, lonely,
and a million miles away from his calling. This is not for him, he realizes, this callously light-hearted joshing amidst a hundred half-filled

graveyards. He's too used to seeing the other side of the equation, to offering comfort to the numbed survivors and weeping bereaved. It's not that he's a pacifist: the theology of the just war doesn't seem obviously wrong to him, and some of the things the Laundry are called upon to protect humanity from are so unambiguously outside the light of creation that it's an open-and-shut case. When the enemy is the end of all life he can't even object to the use of demon-haunted tools and ritual magic in self-defense. But these aren't tools for blocking the incursion of nameless horrors from beyond the walls of the world: these are instruments of human slaughter. And the bodies at the crime scene outside the ring road might have pointy ears, but they were human enough that the blood puddling around them in the headlights was red.

Downum eventually pauses at another door. She knocks: two slow, then a pause, then three fast. A muffled voice from the other side replies, "Yuss, coming." There's a sound of heavy objects shifting, then the door scrapes open.

"Pinky my son! And your prodigal brainiac!"

The grizzled man stares past Pete and Downum at Pinky and Brains. He looks to be in his sixties: one eye is covered by a piratical black patch, and he's wearing overalls and cotton gloves which once were white but are now stained with gun oil.

"Long time indeed, Harry." Pinky grins. "Pete? I don't believe you've met Harry. Harry the Horse, meet Pete the Vicar . . ."

Brains doesn't smile, or take time for social niceties. "Lockhart sent us. I believe you have a picking list for us."

"I do indeed." Harry backs into the room, wheezing slightly. "An' I've been busy, as you can see." A wooden pallet sits atop a small forklift, piled high with metal ammunition boxes and odd-shaped drab fiberglass carriers. Behind it, the room is tricked out with floor-to-ceiling warehouse shelves, crammed with storage boxes and wooden crates. "Something tells me you've got some ideas of your own"—he finally focusses on Pete—"and your new friend. So tell me son, what's going on upstairs?"

Pinky shuffles aside, then half-turns and hams it up: "Brains . . . what *is* going on upstairs?"

Brains takes a deep breath, then shrugs. "We've got an incursion, but it's not the normal kind." He stares at the loaded wooden pallet. "Long on pointy ears and cold iron, short on tentacles and mindless brain eating. Colonel Lockhart thinks they're heading this way, maybe targeting HQ North. We've got one OCCULUS team in town, but they're busy—another is on its way up the M6 but won't be here for a couple of hours yet. They've got one of our people; Gerry wants us tooled up in case we can get him back—or in case the bad guys come for us."

Harry shakes his head. "Children's crusade. Children's fucking crusade." He taps the pile of boxes on the pallet with one size-eleven boot. "If we are talking about *fair folk*"—his eyes narrow—"then this little lot will only get you so far. But if you come into the back with me, I think I can get you something more useful." He turns and walks back between the shelving units; after a brief shared look with Downum, Pete finds himself following. "Bang-sticks." Harry snorts. "No, you don't want regular guns for dealing with those fuckers. What you want is back here in the stacks, where we keep the really *useful* nightmares . . ."

15: RAIN OF STEEL

While the British armed forces are administered by the Ministry of Defense in London, the army itself has a headquarters complex in Andover, a picturesque town in Hampshire, about forty-five kilometers from the deep water port of Southampton on the south coast of England. Andover is an army town, home to the headquarters of the Defense Logistics Organization as well as the Chief of General Staff. It's part of a sprawling complex of army headquarters bases in Hampshire and Wiltshire, near the south coast channel ports, including the Army Air Corps' helicopter squadrons, the main battle tanks of the Royal Armored Corps, and the Royal Artillery.

(It is possible to get from Hampshire or Wiltshire to Leeds by road, but not without aggravation; it's nearly four hundred kilometers by motorway, the traffic congestion is legendary, and both routes are prone to being blocked by accidents.)

Well-run armed forces do not operate on an office-hours-only basis and close for public holidays in the face of active threats. One of the oldest tricks in the book is to launch a surprise attack the weekend before a public holiday. However, maintaining readiness around the clock is expensive. The British Army burned through huge accumulated stocks of equipment during the turbulent first decade of the twenty-first century, and the draw-down from Iraq and Afghanistan coincided with an austerity-minded government intent on cutting the national budget to the bone. Furthermore, in the wake of the collapse of the Soviet Union nobody anticipated a military attack on the homeland at short notice. (Terrorism is one thing, but you can generally spot a mechanized strike force with air support preparing for operations weeks or months in advance.) So staffing levels fell to the lowest level since the 1920s, and by the spring of 2014, with no clear threats on the doorstep, the Army was unready to deal with out-of-hours invasions. Reserves and active forces were reduced, equipment was not replaced, and by the small early hours of one Saturday night in March, the office of the General Staff is occupied by a handful of sentries, some outsourced cleaners, and one tired and irritable major. The major is staying awake by multitasking, dividing his attention among a stack of procurement process manuals (soporific), a mug of tepid coffee (stimulant), and the website of ARRSE, the Army Rumor Service (distraction).

The last thing he expects is an after-midnight phone call, so when his network phone begins to buzz it takes him a moment to focus. "GHQ duty desk, Major Cameron speaking. Who is this?" He stares at the caller ID display. The call is coming from *somewhere* in the MOD, but it's not an office he recognizes. "Hello?"

A woman's voice speaks. "GHQ? This is Q-Division, Special Operations Executive, Headquarters North. We have a major incident developing, reference PLAN RED RABBIT, that's PLAN RED RABBIT."

"You're *who*?" Cameron stares at the phone, perplexed. The only Special Operations Executive he's heard of was a Second World War sabotage organization, disbanded in 1945 after a postwar turf war with MI5. He has no idea what PLAN RED RABBIT could be, but it's probably buried in his big fat ring binder of coded alerts. Unless it's a prank call, of course. He wouldn't put it past a couple of the sprogs in the mess to set him up the bomb, but— "Please hold," he says, dumps the procurement bumf on the beige-tiled carpet, pulls the desk binder over, and flips pages one-handed. It doesn't take long. "Please confirm that plan again?"

"PLAN RED RABBIT. Focus is Headquarters North, Quarry House in Leeds. We have a major incident developing, confirmed hard contact with enemy special forces in North Leeds, and we need you to activate RED RABBIT *now*—"

Major Cameron's eyes widen as he quickly reads the page. "Let me confirm and get back to you," he says, and hangs up hastily, before the terrifying litany on the other end of the line deteriorates into a series of ancient curses chanted in an alien tongue. He hastily scribbles the phone number on his blotter, then says the first thing that comes into his head, which is: "What the *fucking* fuck?"

It may be four in the morning, but the phone call has reached the parts that coffee cannot wake. He kicks his chair back, yanks a key ring from the key box next to his desk, and rushes into the main office next door without pausing to fill out the logbook. Which is technically a breach of regulations, but if this *isn't* a fucking juvenile prank by a Rupert from Sandhurst it's quite possibly an emergency, and if it *is* a prank the idiot whose idea of a joke this is will be cleaning toilets with a toothbrush for the next decade. Or worse.

Four minutes of rummaging through the pages of another ring binder from the RESTRICTED documents cupboard in the next office convinces Major Cameron that if it is a joke, the prankster is a boss-level overachiever. PLAN RED RABBIT is indeed a thing. It's the current post-2010 strategic defense review update to something that first showed up in the files in 1945 as PLAN BLUE BUNNY, then got updated in the early 1950s to PLAN GREEN GOBLIN and in the 1970s to PURPLE PEOPLE EATER, suggesting a slight shortage of serious intent on the part of the operations planners or their management. But RED RABBIT nevertheless exists, and furthermore, the printed first page of the plan indicates that an alert coming from SOE Q-Division is one of the start conditions. Except that RED RABBIT is a response plan for a *Never Happens* scenario.

The Army has contingency plans for *everything*.* They used to have plans for invading the USA—a counterstrike after the anticipated US annexation of Canada—at least until the mid-1930s. They still have plans for organizing stay-behind resistance after a Soviet invasion, even though the USSR hasn't existed for a quarter of a century. These are half-jokingly classified as *Never Happens (Probably)*.

---

* The plans used to live in a building full of filing cabinets, then they migrated to a dinosaur-era mainframe in an air-conditioned basement, and more recently someone who has heard of the internet has been trying to get the usual public sector procurement suspects to implement a wiki system using Lotus Notes. It's so cumbersome that they keep the first couple of pages of each contingency printed out on paper to this day.

But RED RABBIT is a *Never Happens (Definitely)* case. Its mere existence is probably nothing more than the only remaining evidence of an awful homework assignment handed out to a bunch of Sandhurst cadets as informal punishment for getting too fresh with a visiting lecturer. RED RABBIT is indexed in the classified lexicon on the same page as RED HARE and RED HORSEMAN. RED HARE is the plan for what to do if and when Martian death tripods land on Horsell Common; RED HORSEMAN is the official Army plan for dealing with the Apocalypse of St. John the Divine.*† But RED RABBIT is a little different . . .

Cameron reads the next page, swearing softly in disbelief, then hastily goes back to the key safe to pick out a key to a somewhat smaller steel cabinet containing files that were once marked as SECRET, before the coalition government upended the entire security/confidentiality classification system and replaced it with a multidimensional thing of horror that nobody quite understands. There is a directory of code names that squaddies aren't supposed to know because what they don't know can't scare them. He looks up SOE, then Q-Division, and starts swearing even more loudly. There is a phone number in the directory, and he makes a note of it, then locks the file back in the cupboard before he returns to his desk, and dials the number.

"Ops desk," says a male voice at the other end of the line. Cameron stops swearing audibly: the number he dialed connects via the Ministry of Defense's own internal voice-over-IP network. If it's being spoofed, even for a wind-up mess hall hoax, someone's head will roll.

"Q-Division, this is Army GHQ. I have a caller claiming to be one of yours from, ah, Headquarters North, who is declaring PLAN RED RABBIT is in effect. Can you confirm?"

"Yes, please hold while I transfer you. Headquarters North situation room coming up."

His phone blares hold music for a few seconds—a snatched ear worm refrain that digs its claws into his head in seconds, D:Ream's

* Another unreasonable homework assignment.

† Last updated in 2003 at the request of Tony Blair.

"Things Can Only Get Better"—then the same woman's voice speaks: "Hello? Is that GHQ?"

"Yes," Major Cameron says through gritted teeth, then forces himself to loosen up. His palms are damp. "Can I confirm that you definitely want to activate PLAN RED RABBIT?"

"Yes." The woman's tone is incisive. "We have two dead non-human intruders, missing personnel, and an incursion in North Leeds. An OCCULUS team from 23 SAS is on-site and can confirm through their own reporting chain. This is not an exercise."

"Understood." Cameron takes a deep breath. "Okay, we're under strength right now so I need to go off-line and work the phone tree. Call me back in half an hour if you haven't heard anything. Sooner if you have any further developing contacts." He crosses the fingers of his free hand under the table.

"Wilco. I'll tell London to prep a pre-cleared liaison bod to brief you in person. HQ North out." She hangs up without waiting, and Cameron flips to the next page in the ring binder, then opens the Emergency Plan telephone directory and dials the number at the top of the page.

The phone rings three times before it's picked up. To Major Cameron it feels like an eternity because this can't possibly be a prank, but it can't be the real thing either, and if it's a prank the prankster has gone well beyond latrines-and-toothbrush territory at this point and is now looking at a court martial, and Cameron is looking at early retirement if he's lucky—

"Yes?" The voice is rough from sleep, but clearly awake. "Who is this?"

"Sir," Cameron forces himself to stay calm, "this is Major Cameron at GHQ. I have an authenticated emergency report and am putting the major incident plan into effect. You are my first contact. SOE Q-Division just reported a contact situation in Leeds and have declared PLAN RED RABBIT."

"RED—fuck me. RED RABBIT? Seriously?"

Cameron keeps a straight face: he figures under the circumstances the general is allowed to swear. "Yes, sir, at least they're taking it seriously. 23 SAS is apparently involved."

"Understood. I'm on my way in. Carry on, tell everyone to get their arse in gear and there'll be a briefing at 0500 hours."

The general hangs up and Cameron briefly pauses to wipe his forehead, then dials the next number on his list. He feels *slightly* less tense: if Major General Holmes has heard of RED RABBIT and this Q-Division mob and is taking them seriously, then he's made the right call. "Sir, this is Major Cameron at GHQ. I have a confirmed major incident in progress and the major incident plan is in effect. You're needed at HQ for a 5 a.m. briefing . . ."

After the top five seats get a personal wake-up call, Cameron hits his computer terminal and sends out a priority message to the crackberries of everyone who qualifies for a pager these days (not for secure data, but just to ensure they're on a leash): MAJOR INCIDENT BRIEFING AT 5 A.M. Then he goes back to ruining the colonel's beauty sleep. He has one job for now, and that's to ensure that when Major General Holmes gets to the briefing room it will be full of equally unhappy officers (and a sprinkling of civil servants) and that someone will be there to fill them in on what the hell is going on.

Martian invasion: sure, the Army understands what it needs to do, if not necessarily how to go about it. Religious apocalypses involving the Four Horsemen: pass the holy water and bend over, here it comes again. But invasion by the armies of Middle Earth—who ordered *that*?

Alex leads Cassie down into the Lawnswood bunker.

He pauses a couple of steps down the sloping corridor, briefly adjusting his phone. The OFCUT suite can run a defensive ward, although it's hell on battery life and has an annoying tendency to screw with GPS location. Also he feels the need to collect himself. Cassie isn't keeping her distance anymore, but wraps her arms around his waist and leans her chin on his shoulder. "What are you doing?" she asks quietly.

"Necessary preparation, assuming we're going to do this thing we're not talking about. Hush a moment . . ." He slides his phone away again. "Okay, let's go. Uh, there was a caretaker living here. What do you suppose happened to him?"

"Don't ask." She lets go of him as he takes a step forward. "They *might* have taken him prisoner."

He recognizes a comforting lie when he hears one. "He might have taken the night off, too." He hates himself a little for wanting to believe it, so distracts himself by walking forward.

The blast door looms around the curve of the tunnel, gaping into the corridor. (In event of a nuclear attack, huge hydraulic rams stand ready to pull it closed, flush with the wall, to allow the shock wave to blow past the bunker's entrance.) A ghostly greenish radiance spills from beyond the threshold: there are more luminous grids painted here, and Alex is careful to hold Cassie's hand as he advances. He can feel the energy in the ley line rushing through, far below his feet. *Of course the entry node would have to be in the basement, wouldn't it?* "Will there be other guards here?" he asks.

"Not soldiers. They might have set mage-beasts to guard the anchor instead."

Alex swallows. "And mage-beasts are . . . ?"

"You don't have . . . ? Oh. Of course you don't. Creatures compelled to obedience by a trainer-mage, like guard dogs. Or like"—she frowns—"living sentry guns? From that movie with the woman and the cat who fights the dragon queen at the end?"

"You mean *Aliens?*"

"YesYes!" Cassie is happy with her shiny pop-cultural reference but Alex's heart sinks. His idea of a second date was dinner with family, not a live-action dungeon crawl. Meanwhile he's wearing a sports jacket and chinos and the other side are playing for keeps. "Cassie." He takes a deep breath, trying to control his fright, because if he is certain of one thing it is that he is deadlier than he realizes, and if he knows anything about this baffling, infuriatingly attractive intrusion in his life it is that she is equally capable of looking after herself— *Jesus, she killed an armed guard without breaking a sweat.* "We're on the top floor of three and we're going to have to take the stairs. Are you armed?"

"Of course!" She offers him the handle of a steel knife the length of her forearm. He recognizes it from the assortment of stabby accoutrements the soldiers upstairs had strapped to various parts of their armor: judging by the basketwork hand-guard it's a *main gauche*, a parrying dagger.

"Right. I should have known. Stupid question. Did you bring anything else?"

"Will this do?" she asks, raising the baton that's part of her costume, left-handed. She barely waves it: he can feel ripples of static raise the hair on his arms as it parts the air.

"I'd better take the knife, I don't know how to use that." She hands him the dagger wordlessly. Alex takes it, feeling as light as a feather and sick with a fear he can control as long as he doesn't think about it too hard. *Bottom level. Big corridor. Sentry guns.* "Let's do this." He tenses and opens up his consciousness, feeling a sense he can't quite articulate as he visualizes a blazing five-dimensional fiery knotwork revolving inside his head, fractal gears revolving within skeletal Möbius loops—

His superspeed kicks in and everything around him seems to slow down. The light reddens and dims, and the air thickens to the consistency of water as he sprints towards the other end of the corridor.

He spins round, presenting his back to the wooden door for impact, sees Cassie's mouth slowly open, her eyes widen as she meets his gaze. Everything is very cold and as he draws strength from his V-parasites he hears a mindless chittering sound, as of a million mandibles nibbling at the paper-thin walls of reality. His back hits the door and the wood splinters and shatters, exploding away from him as he finishes his turn: but all he feels is the gnawing maddening hunger in his soul, the hunger of a black hole that seeks to destroy everything he touches. His feet fly out from under him and he skids across the cement floor and out over the first flight of steps, bounces off the opposite wall of the shaft, then begins to fall.

Cassie is running after, but although she's fast she doesn't have his PHANG mojo—or magi power, as she'd put it. She flies down the steps moonwalk-slow, taking them three at a time with her mace held before her. Its tip is glowing violet. He hits the middle floor landing, absorbs the impact with his toes, and gently kicks off, aiming himself at the next flight of steps. His shoes leaving a black rubber slug-trail on the concrete, gently smoking.

Then he sees the writhing luminescence of eaters on the loose beyond the exit from the shaft, and realizes he might have bitten into something too big to bleed.

A wave of blue-eyed equine horror floods across the Yorkshire Dales, but the only human eyes that witness the progress of the Host of Air and Darkness are dead.

The armored column rides six abreast, their ranks stretching back for kilometers behind the spearhead. A cloud of dust and debris roils in the air above them and the earth drums beneath their clawed feet. But the riders who make up the column are curiously hard to see. The unaided and unprotected human eyeball naturally slides past the riders, interpolating less disturbing images: an out of place freight train thundering along a track where no rail runs, perhaps.

To the fore, and spaced to either side of the column at regular intervals, ride the magi in their closed carriages. The sun is still below the horizon, and the magi have windows of subtle crystal through which they maintain watch. They watch the land unroll to either side, and whenever they see an observer they sink ghostly fangs of necromantic venom into the witness's visual cortex. As the column pounds across a B road, a milk tanker returning from an early farm run rounds a curve. The driver blinks, bleary-eyed, and begins to brake: by the time his vehicle has rolled to a halt he slumps dead at the wheel, eye sockets bleeding and empty around the withered stumps of his optic nerves.

There aren't many casualties at first. A few farm workers, up and about in the early hours. Trucks on their way to make deliveries, cars driven by those unlucky enough to have Sunday morning jobs. They screech and skid, spinning and shedding bumpers and metal when they rebound from the drystone walls lining the roads, drivers already dead. But as the column pounds onwards across the countryside, the death toll begins to mount. They die by handfuls at first, then by tens and scores and windrows.

The Host's route bypasses the urban sprawl of the *urük* for the most part, which is a small mercy. They pound across open country until, south of Rylstone, they pick up the Grassington Road. The two metaled lanes provide fine footing for the Host, although it is here that they receive their first injuries: two of the front rank of cavalry troopers are unable to dodge the skidding Hovis Bakery truck that jackknifes side-on across their path as its driver convulses and dies. Their mounts roar angrily, struggling on rapidly healing broken legs, but the riders are less lucky: no amount of armor will save one of the People from a hundred-kilometer-per-hour collision with a Volvo engine block.

As the road bends towards Skipton and the ugly stone hovels grow more frequent, the Host leaves the metaled surface and races across the nearby golf course, bypassing the center of the small market town. At half past six, a couple of kilometers east of Skipton, the armored column encounters the A65. And now the slaughter begins in earnest.

The A65 started life as an eighteenth-century turnpike, but today it is a fast, two-lane-wide main road, running northwest from Leeds to the Yorkshire Dales. In the near-dawn on a Sunday morning it is not heavily trafficked, but nobody has explained the *urük* traffic laws to the Host's marshals. Consequently, the first encounter with a Range Rover barreling along at a cheerfully excessive hundred and twenty kilometers per hour comes as a nasty surprise to the front rank. Angry remonstrations are exchanged; nearing the crest of a hill the column bunches and pauses, and then regroups to continue its march behind a screen of fire magi, their incendiary gaze at full alert.

The drivers of the next fifty-eight vehicles die so suddenly that nobody has any time to raise the alarm. Their bodies are so badly burned that in the aftermath they are only identifiable by dental impressions. Less fortunately, two of the vehicles in question are buses, and this is the point at which the death toll from the incursion rises into triple figures.

There are other side effects: traffic cameras and CCTV installations burst into flames, as do the curbside boxes of any networks carrying data from cameras pointing in the general direction of the Host. The strike force contains specialists equipped with battlefield countermeasures that target observation mechanisms and the brains of watchers alike.

Two hours after leaving Malham Cove, the predawn glow of the rising sun finds the Host of Air and Darkness nearly a hundred kilometers away, bypassing Burley-in-Wharfedale and rumbling through Otley town center, then on towards the outskirts of Leeds. With a population of over fourteen thousand, Otley is the biggest *urük* habitat that the Host has encountered thus far. The troopers make no attempt to hunt down and kill the feral serfs that live here, but they rely now on force rather than camouflage: the death toll rises rapidly as early morning *urük* witnesses fall to the ground, their heads wreathed in sparking purple flames, bodies twitching and convulsing.

There is a little screaming. (But only a little, for death comes fast.)

The Host's path skirts the runway of Leeds-Bradford International Airport. Unfortunately the departure path of this morning's outbound flights crosses the A65, and most aircraft will not have had time to climb above a thousand meters before they cross the road. So it is that Thomson Flight 3748 to Tenerife has the supreme bad luck to be on the runway and accelerating for takeoff as the Host approaches. It's a charter flight but demand has been very slack lately, and today it is little more than a third full, with seventy-six souls on board. There are two pilots, four cabin crew, and seventy passengers: most of them families with young children, on their way to a cheap holiday destination during the Easter school vacation.

The Host's main air defense detachment is far to the rear, emplaced on the heights above Malham to await the reaction to Highest Liege's decoy gambit. Nor are the dragons of the Close Air Support section available right now. The battle magi have never seen a Boeing 737-800 before, and have little idea of what it is capable of, or indeed what it is. But as it hurtles roaring towards them and rotates for takeoff over the heads of the armored column, they recognize it as a threat.

Helmets snap round as the blue-and-white behemoth hurtles towards the Host, climbing into the air above them. Glaring bright lamps embedded at the roots of its wings cast an uncanny glare; metallic eggs clutched beneath its eerily paralyzed wings howl mournfully. But there is no panic in the file. Knights bearing portable air defense weapons turn in their saddles and raise their nightmares to eye level, bringing them to bear on the approaching target.

There is a flash of green light, far brighter than the rising sun. A tiny fraction of the carbon nuclei in the exposed non-metallic surfaces of the plane have been converted into silicon nuclei. The resultant ionization cascade dumps huge amounts of energy into bodily tissues and plastic or rubber. The composite radome forming the airliner's nose flares briefly and burns away: the heads of the captain and first officer explode simultaneously. Further aft, the backwash of the basilisk strike ignites the tires of the extended undercarriage, and a flare of flaming debris wreathes the central fuel tank and wings in a sheath of glowing plasma. The airliner wobbles above the heads of the Host, and for a few seconds it seems as if it may fly onward. But then the port wing dips slightly and, at low speed and with no corrective hand on the controls, the wing stalls. The airliner side-slips and noses down onto the outskirts of Otley.

Even at three kilometers' range, the impact of an airliner loaded with thirty tons of Jet-A makes a ground-shaking impact.

Airline travel is remarkably safe in the twenty-first century: TOM-3748 is the first passenger jet airliner to crash anywhere in the world this month. But it won't be the last or the largest to do so today.

The contrails of long-range airline traffic flash silver in the brightening predawn sky above the Yorkshire Dales.

The Dales lie roughly three hundred kilometers north and a hundred kilometers west of one corner of a sector containing the world's busiest air traffic. The London/Paris/Amsterdam triangle is occupied by three of the world's ten busiest airports, along with about a dozen smaller terminals. Transatlantic flights from Europe generally depart along a westerly heading, crossing the Bristol Channel or skirting the southern coast of Ireland. But there are other major international hubs to the south and east, and flights from these airports to destinations on the eastern seaboard of North America tend to fly northwest, directly across the British midlands.

Flight AZ-602 is an Alitalia Airbus 330 that took off from Rome's Fiumicino Airport two hours and ten minutes earlier, starting the 7,000-kilometer daily trek to New York. As it cruises over England at 33,000 feet, the cabin crew are serving lunch to the 234 passengers on board. It is half an hour since TOM-3748 sent a smoke-streaked fireball a hundred meters into the sky above Otley, and emergency services from Leeds Bradford Airport in Yeadon are still battling the blaze. A major incident has been declared in the Yorkshire town which lies eighty kilometers to the east of AZ-602's path, but reports on the ground are confused, with charred bodies and detonated cameras littering the high street. Two police cars are still burning in the center of town. There are no surviving witnesses, and the police superintendent who has been called in is baffled and angry as he tries to establish just what has happened in the early hours of Sunday morning, but the civil authorities do not yet suspect that the explosion of TOM-3748 is not an isolated incident.

Eighty kilometers away to the northeast, the Marne Barracks at Catterick—the British Army's largest base—is buzzing like a hornet's nest that's been kicked. Soldiers are hastily collecting their kit and prepping light armored vehicles for an unexpected excursion. The approaches to the base are on lockdown and, shockingly, a reconnaissance company with its Scimitar light tanks and a Striker missile carrier has deployed with live ammunition to cover the west of the base. But nobody at Army GHQ has yet realized that the nation's skies are under attack, much less notified the National Air Traffic Service or alerted the Royal Air Force's Quick Reaction Force.

On the heights above Malham, the Host's theater air defense crew watch the skies. It is a clear, bright day, with a frontal system moving in from the west, threatening rain by afternoon. It is dry, and the feather-edged contrail of AZ-602 is inching its way northwest across the dome of the sky.

We cannot know what the basilisk crew were thinking. (Subsequent events have rendered that question moot.) Certainly they could not possibly have mistaken the twin-engined Airbus for an enemy firewyrm, or indeed for any other variety of aerial predator from their devastated homeworld. On the other hand, Highest Liege of Airborne Strike had been most specific in her proposal, and with All-Highest's endorsement the *geasa* of obedience that bind all the subjects of the Morningstar Empire in thrall lend her operational orders the force of law.

The air defense crew do not immediately fire on AZ-602. But they painstakingly pull down the saurian necks of their living weapons and double-check the attachment points of their blinkers. They irrigate the monstrous eye clusters cautiously, from well back behind their carefully dulled shields; then the targeting crew installs the newly hatched brain leeches that will direct and aim the basilisks. The watchers use their mage-glass to survey the skies: and presently they identify a second, additional target matching Highest Liege's specifications.

American Airlines 759 is another Airbus 330, flying the 8,000-kilometer great circle from Athens to Philadelphia with 195 passengers and nine crew aboard. It has been airborne for nearly three and a quarter hours as it tracks northwest, thirty kilometers south of the Yorkshire Dales, a thousand feet higher than the Alitalia flight.

AZ-602 is already forty kilometers north of Malham Cove by this point, receding rapidly: it will be out of range of the heavy air defense basilisks within another five minutes. But with AA-759 coming into view from the south, there is plenty of time to line up the basilisks' heads on both flying machines, and release the blinkers that restrain their lethal gaze.

Heavy air defense basilisks are not like the close-range, observation-mediated weapons used elsewhere by the Host (and, it must be admitted, by the Laundry's defensive CCTV network). It is speculated that the large sauropod-like animals evolved their death-stare in an intensely hostile ecosystem, where the airborne apex predators are capable of flocking and stripping a twenty-ton land animal to the bone in minutes. Whatever their origin, their ancestors were acquired by the beast-masters of the Morningstar Empire and developed into a fearsome weapon. Their eye clusters aren't quite like anything else observed in nature, and the visual cortex that the eight retinas feed into is the size of an elephant's entire brain. Fortunately they're herbivorous grazers, and about as clever as a snail—unless something threatens them from above.

All basilisk processes require a carbon-based target and produce silicon nuclei and hard radiation as their output. (This is one of the reasons why the Host's soldiers wear silver-plated steel or wrought-iron armor, and part of the reason for the coming catastrophe.) It might be assumed that modern wide-bodied airliners, which for the most part are made of aluminum, would be resistant to a basilisk's gaze. But such assumptions are misleading.

Airbus 330s have plenty of non-metallic external surfaces. Like almost all airliners, they are painted in the airline's livery—using an oil-based paint. Alitalia's A330s wear the airline livery on their tail fin and fuselage, taking over 200 kilograms of paint. American's trademark polished silver birds use much less paint, but there is still on the order of 100 kilograms on the tail fin and the fuselage stripe.

In addition, there are numerous plastic and composite extrusions on the exterior of an airliner. Navigation light housings, antenna shields, and the nose assembly covering the weather radar, are all non-metallic. And the airliner has numerous windows, both portholes for the passengers and windshields for the flight crew.

To normal eyes, an airliner at cruising altitude is little more than a fly-speck. But the air defense basilisks' eyes are as sharp as an astronomical camera. They can resolve shapes hidden behind the glass of the cockpit windows, dimly blurred objects behind portholes, heads bent over their lap trays as the passengers eat. And when the basilisks open their eight dinner-plate-sized eyes and stare in terror at the alien sky, the shapes they see flare as bright as the noonday sun.

A series of explosions ripples through the port side of AZ-602 at seated head-level, spraying red-hot bone fragments through the cockpit and fuselage. There is a ten-meter gap in the line of death where the basilisk's line of sight is occulted by the wing, then the explosions resume. They are not small, and they are accompanied by the skin of the airliner briefly catching fire from the outside. The surviving passengers—those who do not have window seats—might have time to scream as the hull depressurizes. But the cracks propagate from shattered window to shattered window as the fuselage unzips and the roof opens up like a pod of peas, spilling passengers and banks of seats across the sky as the burning liner abruptly rolls into an inverted dive and falls apart at the seams.

The American Airlines plane is luckier.

The cockpit voice recorder tape, when it is replayed, reveals nothing at all out of the ordinary prior to the incident. Then, there is a short few seconds of dialog. Captain Adam Roberts, the pilot, has over 6000 hours logged in airliners of this type, since retiring from the US Air Force. He has his eyes up while First Officer Rachel Moore (700 hours on type) is head down over the instruments, confirming that they have updated their heading towards the next waypoint, just north of Liverpool. Captain Roberts has the aircraft in a turning bank, so that his side of the cockpit is in shadow. On playback we hear Captain Roberts exclaim, "Eyes up, there's some—someone in trouble, about thirty degrees—"

Then there is a sound that should never occur on the flight deck of an airliner.

Two seconds pass as the master caution siren sounds. Captain Roberts is heard to say, "Crap," then something inarticulate that the cockpit microphones don't pick up. There are no more words for eight seconds, then he shuts off the master caution alarm, continues the banking turn past the designated waypoint until AA-759 is heading almost due east, and begins to squawk 7700. There is increasing noise in the cabin during this time, and the depressurization warning sounds. Captain Roberts attends to his own oxygen mask, commences a rapid descent, deploys the cabin oxygen masks, and finally calls air traffic control: "American 759 Mayday Mayday Mayday. Request emergency divert to Echo Golf Golf Papa. Hull depressurized and copilot dead. We are under attack . . ."

The camera crews are waiting when AA-759 rolls to a stop on the runway at Liverpool's John Lennon Airport, with scorch marks on the tail fin and filthy black streaks along the fuselage. In the months to follow, AA-759 is going to go down in the books as the airliner that survived despite the odds—except for the unfortunate first officer, whose headless corpse is still strapped into her seat as the blood- and brain-spattered captain shakily pushes back his chair, orders the emergency slides deployed on the taxiway, and collapses. And, of course, the passengers with starboard window seats who receive a crippling dose of radiation from the basilisk stare's secondary activation isotopes. Forty of them are hospitalized and over the next six months eighteen of them will die. For Captain Roberts, it will be his last flight in the left seat: haunted by awareness that if he hadn't caused First Officer Moore to look up at exactly the wrong moment she would have lived, he takes early retirement seven months later.

But at least they survive to tell the tale, unlike the passengers and crew of AZ-602 and TOM-3748 and DL-415, a Boeing 767 with 231 passengers and crew aboard . . . and many of the residents of Leeds.

"Nasty little fuckers, likely to stab you in the kidneys as soon as look you in the eye, eh?" Harry says cheerfully as he walks away between two floor-to-ceiling shelving stacks full of ammunition.

"What would you know about that?" Brains calls after him. Pete trails along in his wake after exchanging a shrug with Pinky. They leave the loaded wooden pallet to fend for itself. It's not as if anyone is going to steal it while they aren't watching.

"Nothing, mate!" Harry calls cheerfully. "Just rumors. But you know there ain't no smoke without fire. And I've got just the thing for you."

"Yeah, well, if you put too much faith in rumors in this game you're going to wake up dead, like all the folks who thought H. P. Lovecraft was a tour guide, not a mad uncle in the attic."

"Where are we going, anyway?" Pete asks.

"Special Countermeasures Collection. I figure you've got all the guns you need on that pallet, but if you're dealing with pointy-eared dogfuckers with ritual magic you're going to be wanting some better protection, eh?"

Pinky catches Pete's eye. "Better protection sounds *good*," he says. "Better still, making this someone else's job . . ."

Ahead of them, Harry pulls a bunch of keys that resembles a dead octopus made of tarnished metal and rummages among its tentacles until he finds the right one to open a suspiciously solid-looking door. He swings it open with a grunt of effort. A light flickers on, illuminating the small, windowless room on the other side. It's lined from floor to ceiling with safe deposit boxes, and Harry moves methodically along the far wall, unlocking one box after another and pulling them out, so that their contents are accessible. "Help yerself, folks, just tell me which box number you're grabbing so I can keep a record." Harry steps aside and raises his clipboard expectantly.

"Unit 904. A dozen horseshoes. Probability weighting 0.14." Brains, who is reading from a list on his phone screen, shakes his head. "I don't think so." He shoves the drawer shut.

"Probability of what?" Pete is perplexed.

"Unit 906—" Brains drawls.

"There was this analysis project a few years ago," Pinky explains, *sotto voce*, "allocating probability of effectiveness to folkloric countermeasures. Very Bayesian, much uncertainty, wow. They fed the results to Forecasting Ops for a second opinion. Upshot: horseshoes and the fair folk don't match up, although they got our blood-sucking friends bang to rights with short-wavelength ultraviolet."

He turns to the next drawer. "This is *not* a four-leafed clover, but a laser projector that casts a Dho-Nha curve ten meters in diameter across a flat surface a hundred meters away. Close enough to a four-leafed clover to fool someone who doesn't know what they're looking at. Probability weighting 0.44, but we'll take it anyway. Needs a power supply." This time Brains pulls the drawer fully open and removes something that looks suspiciously like a disco light. "Here, catch." He passes it carefully to Pinky.

"Unit 908, grade six heavy-duty reflex wards, collar-mounted, times fifty. I'm taking the lot." He passes these to Pinky as well; Pinky, hands now full, turns and trots back the way they came in. "Okay, it's your turn, Vicar . . ."

Over the next thirty minutes they loot the Special Countermeasures Collection, transferring half its contents to the pallet of supplies. "There's no telling which of these items will work," Brains tells Pete while he checks the second row of drawers, "but if we don't try them we'll never find out."

"You're going full Munchkin on our anomaly," Pete guesses, feeling slightly smug at being able to deploy a term he picked up from his friend Bob Howard: "Is that right?"

"Insufficient data." Brains grimaces. "If we knew precisely what's coming our way we wouldn't have to guess. But quantity"—he hands Pete a shoebox full of mail gauntlets woven in a non-repeating Penrose tile design—"tends to have a quality all of its own. And this stuff isn't going to do us any good if we leave it down here."

An hour later, the van is parked in the underground car park under Quarry House and most of the contents of the pallet are on the second floor, via a goods elevator. Pete helps Brains move boxes and crates of munitions, esoteric and otherwise, into the empty office suite next to the conference room. The last he sees of Pinky, the tech ops guy is attacking the tow hitch cover on Ilsa the Kettenkrad with a socket set: a fat cylindrical post with a mounting bracket on top waits on the stained concrete beside the half-track.

It's four thirty when Pete returns to the conference room at Quarry House, bearing a handful of personal wards. "Brains sent these," he announces, passing them around the table. Jez Wilson takes one and nods: Lockhart merely twitches his mustache at it. "Class six. He seems to think we may need them. Is there any news?"

"Vik Choudhury says Ops can't raise anyone at West Yorkshire Met. They've clammed up tighter than an oyster's arse and there's word of a whole mess of fatal RTAs—traffic accidents—north and west of here. Police helicopter's tied up, too. Nobody knows what the hell is going on." Wilson stares at Pete. Her usual ironic detachment is completely missing, replaced by fear-driven intensity. "OCCULUS haven't reported back in half an hour. What kept you?"

"We just shifted nearly a ton and a half of weapons and ammo up from the special countermeasures repository." Pete pulls out a chair and flops into it. His arms and lower back ache, a reminder that he's a grown-up with responsibilities and a family rather than an overgrown schoolboy in search of an adventure story to call his own. The sense of responsibility is crushing: so is the nonspecific sense of onrushing doom. "Do we know anything else?"

"Sit." Lockhart points at a suspiciously new phone deskset which has materialized on the table in front of Pete's seat—so new, in fact, that it's still wearing its protective plastic caul. "If that rings, log it, screen it, and escalate as required."

"Is that what I'm here for?" Pete asks. "Because"—he yawns involuntarily—"this isn't what I'm trained for."

"You're here because you're a warm body and this is an emergency." Lockhart's expression is grim. "Hopefully this is just a full-dress cock-up and you can go home to your bed in a couple of hours. If not, you'll get a chance to exercise your professional skill set."

"What, checking ley lines for signs of drift?"

"No, Dr. Russell: comforting the bereaved."

This puts a damper on the conversation. Meanwhile, other organization staffers drift in and out: lights are coming on throughout this wing of the building as locally assigned employees filter in to their assigned readiness posts. Mrs. Knight from the Arndale office drops by, amiably businesslike. She could be dressed for an afternoon digging over her allotment, aside from the SA80 slung over her shoulder. Nicky Myers from that same office is busying herself along the corridor with a squad of residual human resources, leaning the blue-suited bodies against the wall beside the entrances to stairwells and offices that are in use, mumbling a continuous stream of instructions in Old Enochian (mostly to the effect that the RHRs should refrain from eating anyone wearing a staff ID badge: it needs repeating, for nothing damages one's attention span like being dead). Pete glimpses other people he half-recognizes through open doorways as the sound of ringing phones and muted conversation rises, along with the electronic whooshing inbox sounds of email applications.

Pete doesn't have to wait long before his own phone starts ringing. At first it's mostly local staff checking in—those who've received the alert email or text and who are confirming that they're expected in the office on a rest day and it's not just the mail server having a brain fart. (These Pete checks off against the personnel database and reassures that, yes, it is indeed a spot of bother and their assistance would be appreciated.) But the fourth call is different. It's Emma Gracie, the detective sergeant from the bunker site. "Dr. Russell, have you had any contact from the Territorial Army unit since they cordoned off the site?"

"Just a moment . . ." Pete blinks and looks around. Jez Wilson is busy keyboarding. "Any word from OCCULUS One?" he calls.

Jez glances up, then shakes her head brusquely. "No, nothing to report." He frowns. "They missed their last call a little over forty minutes ago."

"Right, right." Emma sounds distracted. "So you don't know anything about the lights in the sky or the big bang?"

"Big—" Pete freezes. If he was Mr. Howard, this is the point at which he would be emitting a stream of heartfelt profanity: but he isn't, so he bites his tongue for a second, offers up a momentary prayer for guidance in time of crisis, and reboots his brain. "—bang? From the bunker?" Across the table Jez Wilson has stopped typing and is staring at him.

"We finished initial crime scene logging and cordoned off the area an hour and a half ago," Sergeant Gracie recites grimly. "Captain Hastings requested a nearside lane closure on the southbound carriageway of the Otley Road so we took care of that, which is why none of my people were within two hundred meters of your site when the captain called me to say he was sending his men in to examine the site. This was thirty-six, thirty-seven minutes ago. Five minutes later there was a very loud noise—I hesitate to call it an explosion only because there was no light and no debris, but it was too big to be a flash-bang or similar. Immediately afterwards, shots were heard by the nearest officers to the site, who naturally took cover—it was full auto fire, on and off for almost a minute. Thereafter the site fell silent, but the greenish light intensified considerably. I'm unable to raise Captain Hastings on Airwave and he isn't answering his mobile number. Two ARU constables who went forward to scope out the scene haven't reported in either. What's going *on*?"

Jez Wilson is making grabbing gestures with her right hand, while Lockhart leans over the table and points at the speakerphone. "Let me put you on speaker," says Pete, pushing buttons frantically. "Where's your helicopter?"

"Police 42's unavailable: there are traffic accidents all over north Yorkshire tonight and our cameras are having a spot of bother." Her voice over the phone isn't shaky, but the over-controlled tension tells its own story. "Do you have any information you're withholding, Doctor?"

Lockhart hits the microphone switch on the speakerphone. "Sergeant, this is Colonel Lockhart. Can I confirm that you've lost contact with the OCCULUS unit and are reporting explosions and gunfire in the vicinity of the bunker?" He glances sideways at Jez, his mustache bristling, and she nods minutely.

"Yes, that's what I'm saying." Emma sounds distracted. "I've called the regional support desk but they say we're fully committed and it'll be at least half an hour before they can send backup—"

"You need to get everybody out of there *right now*," Lockhart interrupts her. "Close the Otley Road in both directions, from the intersection with the A6120 all the way out to Bramhope. I'd recommend a civilian evacuation of the whole of LS6 and LS17, but frankly there isn't time and there's nowhere to put everyone. Can you raise your helicopter directly? It's connected to that rash of RTAs."

"I can call them but I'm not sure they'll believe me, and I'm not sure *I* believe *you*. Let me repeat, Colonel, *what is going on?*"

"It's a major intrusion, Sergeant, and if it took out an OCCULUS team you and everyone else in the area are in immediate danger." Lockhart gets terse when he's on edge, Pete notes. "There is nothing you can do to help except to clear the area, keep bystanders out, and wait for Captain Hastings's men to surface or for us to get another team on-site—"

Sergeant Gracie suddenly says "Oh *shit*," very clearly. There is a crash of shattering glass, and a thud. Then the call drops.

Pinky, who has just entered, stands frozen in the doorway. "Was that what I think it was?"

Lockhart glares at him furiously. "Sitrep, then get out."

"What was that—" Pete begins, his words already in motion before he processes Lockhart's reaction.

"That was the last we'll hear from a very brave woman. Or a very stupid one. *Damn.*" Lockhart looks away from Pinky. "Report, blast it."

Pinky clears his throat. "I got Ilsa kitted out like you suggested," he says diffidently. "The Dillon Aero's mounted on top of the tow bar with a modified Humvee mount. Brains is finishing up the belt feed from the equipment carrier; we figure it can carry about two thousand rounds as long as we don't mind changing belts every five hundred rounds."

"And the shields?"

"They fit. I picked up four class-eight wards, and we hit the sixteenth-century collection at the Royal Armouries for three suits of munition plate. The cheap-ass kind: low-carbon steel with adjustable fittings, mass-produced for mercenaries rather than royal showpieces."

"Then get out of my—"

"What are you talking about?" Pete interrupts.

"We're going to see if we can get close enough to see what's going on. Maybe find out what happened to Alex and OCCULUS One," Pinky says matter-of-factly. "Me and Brains."

"Change of plan," announces Lockhart. "I want Brains here: if we lose camera coverage over Woodhouse Lane as well I'm going to need him to help man the monitor room when we fire up SCORPION STARE inside the Inner Loop. So you'll need someone else to drive the tank."

"Maybe we should wait for the army to get here? An hour either way probably isn't going to make much—"

"I can do it," Pete hears himself saying, from the other side of a cognitive event horizon: "I can drive and ride a bike if that's what you need." It feels like a dereliction of responsibility: he should be looking out for Sandy and baby Jess, not haring off on a half-track to fight monsters. But on the other hand, he has an uneasy feeling that if whatever's going on here isn't stopped *now*, before it's too late, whatever the price, Sandy and Jess won't have much of a future . . .

Lockhart turns to stare at him. "Are you volunteering?"

"Um, I"—Pete's life flickers past his eyes like a spool of burning celluloid—"guess so?"

"Stupid." Lockhart shakes his head. "But it's your own coffin to lie in. Just try not to do anything *unnecessarily brave*." He ends on a near snarl: "We've lost enough good people already today."

16: SCHWERPUNKT

It takes about a second to fall five meters. In that time Alex is aware of the black pool of water at the bottom of the stairwell rushing towards his feet, of the luciferine glow of eaters flooding through the close-fitting frame of the fire door, of Cassie's presence above him as she pounds down the steps three at a time towards a flock of ghastly mind-stealers she can't even sense—

He lands on his toes, a shock of cold dampness rising to his ankles as his fingers hook into claws and he leaps forward into the basement tunnel. It's an occult inferno illuminated by a glaucous glow from the walls and ceiling: the overhead lights are out. There is darkness beyond every doorway except for the far end of the corridor where a sickly emerald light pulses. There are eaters closing in on all sides, a shrieking rasp of excitement in the back of his head signaling their approach. It sounds like the chewing of chainsaw teeth on razor wire.

Eaters are among the simpler horrors that you can invoke with a targeted summoning grid and the right application of the fourth Turing theorem. Simple doesn't mean harmless: if they get their teeth into an unwarded nervous system they'll bed down like malware and take over its body. Luckily for Alex, PHANGs are immune to such hostile takeovers by virtue of already having reached an accommodation with their very own V-parasites. Unluckily for Alex, these eaters have already found host bodies, and as he hits the corridor the first revenant scrabbles into the corridor ahead of him and charges, beak gaping wide.

Alex's perception of the passage of time slows as the flightless bird—or feathered velociraptor: it's hard to tell—rushes towards him.

Details tell: the green-glowing eyes, the sickle-like claws, the mindless rage. He flinches involuntarily, hand tightening on the dagger Cassie gave him as the bird lashes out with a viciously curved blade on the end of a thickly muscled leg. The floor under his heels is slippery-slick and doesn't provide much traction, but he does his best and brings the knife up anyway. The bird screeches and begins to turn just in time to impale itself on the blade. It's as heavy as a big dog. Alex's breath whuffs out of him as it drags his arm down and twitches the knife out of his grip, dying gouts of arterial blood pulsing across his chest. And of course, that's the whole point of its suicidal leap: because there are two more behind it.

"Birds?" Alex asks plaintively as the ostrich-sized horrors bounce off the wall opposite the doorway they emerged from and turn on him with mad-eyed glares beneath rigid crests of crimson and electric blue. They're not true birds: they've got horny beaks fronting mouths sharp with needle-like teeth, ready to tear. They're flightless and as tall as a man, and although they've got arms—or wings—they're short and stubby, thickly feathered. Like the first, their eyes are green-glowing vortices, and their legs are tipped with three-clawed feet, the middle toes curling like vicious sickles. "You're kidding me—"

The first raptor is still thrashing and dying as Alex tries to pull his knife free. But it's wedged between ribs and he's out of time so he lets go and steps sideways, opens his mouth, and says the first thing that comes into his head. It's a macro in Old Enochian that he learned as part of his defensive training. There's no point in being able to summon up the eaters in the night if you can't boss them around fluently enough to avoid being eaten yourself, and as long as whoever called them also bound them to obey voice commands, then there's a chance that the ur-language will get their attention, much as two fingers hooked inside the nostrils will get the attention of an aggressive drunk. *"Obey me now! Stop! Halt! Obey me now!"*

They scream inarticulate avian shrieks of rage, but they go down on their feathered asses all the same, crashing to the floor as their legs fold up under them. Stubby tails thrash, feathers flaring. *Okay, not birds* or *dinosaurs, somewhere in-between.* He senses rather than sees

Cassie arrive at the bottom of the stairwell. He bends forward again, braces a foot on the twitching body by his feet and heaves the dagger blade out, then holds it up before the angry birds. *"Stay down. Don't attack. Don't move."* A memory percolates up from somewhere, something about the Romans using geese as avian guard dogs.

Cassie steps into the corridor behind him and crouches down, pointing her wand or mace or whatever it is at the birds—then says, very clearly, "Decoys." And everything goes to shit.

Bert the caretaker shuffles into the corridor from one of the side rooms. He is looking much the worse for wear. Last time Alex saw him his eyes weren't full of luminous green threads, twirling lazily in the twilight. Nor was his rib cage on display through the jagged slashes in his shirt, which wasn't black with crusted blood. Nor was he carrying a sword.

Alex locks eyes with the revenant and *pushes* with his will. His brain freezes and scrabbles as he hits the total absence of anything human. If Bert was still alive he'd be on the floor now, flooded out by the sheer impact of Alex's mind control power: but although Bert has left the building, his shambling body keeps on coming. It shuffles unsteadily forward as if unaccustomed to the weight of flesh. The guard-fowl are shrieking and struggling unsteadily back to their three-clawed feet, now that Alex has been successfully distracted by the arrival of a genuine take-no-prisoners zombie: and they're not the only attackers. All around him Alex can feel a press of invisible feeders bouncing about in frenzied hunger, losing all fine control as they discover they can't dig their mouthparts into his brain. *"Stop,"* he commands Bert, still in Old Enochian: *"Halt now, do not move."* But it doesn't work and Bert raises his sword, as slow and jerky as an automaton. One of the birds is up on one leg, holding the other sickle-claw raised almost to its sternum. *"Turn and attack,"* he tells it. *"Attack now!"*

Angry eater-possessed bird versus undead Crown Estate site security guard owned by an eater that seems more at home in a quadruped chassis than on two legs: Who will win? For a moment Alex doesn't expect anything to happen, but then the mutant cassowary spins and lashes out like a kickboxer. Then someone slams his head in a door and the corridor lights up like a set of Christmas tree illu-minations that have just shorted out a high-tension grid line.

His eyes are full of irregular purple blotches and his ears ring as Bert the caretaker's legs—no longer supporting a torso—topple over. None of the guard-birds or feathered raptors or whatever they are survive: instead, a pall of choking, oily smoke fills the corridor in front of him. He coughs as a wiry, surprisingly strong arm reaches around his shoulders. "Sweet idiot boy!" She shakes him gently. "You could have been hurt! That's *my* job!"

"Um." Alex straightens up, deliberately not thinking about Cassie's drastic approach to clearing the corridor. His phone has stopped buzzing, thaum sensor overloaded or burned out by her mace's dis-charge. He can still hear the eaters outside his skull yammering to get in—an unprotected human in this place would be zombified within seconds—but luckily neither he nor Cassie fit that description. "Let's just get to the ley line and go find your father. Do you think there are any more of these things in the way?"

"YesYes for sure!" She raises her voice when she's excited, and he winces as she gestures expansively with the mace, which is glowing like a radioactive cobalt source: *What is that, the elven equivalent of an assault rifle?* he speculates. "I can feel them yonder!" Cassie says. The tip of the mace twists in a tight circle, pointing at the second-to-last door along the passage like an amputee dowsing rod. "Let me go first—"

Some archaic sense of chivalry—or, more plausibly, the peculiar form of stupidity that overcomes young, heterosexually inclined males in the presence of a female they wish to impress—impels Alex forward along the corridor before Cassie has time to step up and play tank. Even as his feet carry him forward, Alex begins to doubt the wisdom of this course of action. He is a halfway-to-certified combat magician, long on theory and short on experience and reflexes, this deficiency partly compensated for by the whole blood-sucking fiend shtick which, he has to admit, has given him reflexes to die for along with the need for alarming nutritional supplements. Cassie, in con-trast, is the sort of thing you fire into unknown enemy territory and leave to fend for itself. She's *trained* for this job, Alex realizes, while he's just along because . . . because Cassie wants him along . . . because she wants him to . . .

That's when the other four incarnate eaters jump him.

The column of oily smoke is still rolling and churning in the pre-dawn sky above Otley when a phone rings in a small, beige-walled room at RAF Coningsby, fifteen kilometers north of Boston, Lincolnshire.

One side of the room is furnished with battered sofas, recliners, and a table with an electric kettle and tea-making facilities. Four men wait here, watching a DVD on the flat-screen TV or poking at one of the computers that sits on the table against the opposite side of the room, beneath a huge map of England and the surrounding over-water approaches. There are phones everywhere, but all eyes turn to the one that's ringing, because it's both red and ostentatiously positioned beneath the map.

One of the aircrew makes a grab for the phone, hitching up the back of his heavy rubberized overall as he leaves his chair. "Yes?" he says. Then he picks up a pen and hastily jots down some notes. "On it," he says; "I'll tell them." He looks over his shoulder. "Got a bad one," he says. "Airliner down off the end of the runway at Yeadon and there's something flaky about it."

"Well damn." His wingman kills the DVD and the others all stand up. "Let's get moving—" he starts to say, just as the Telebrief machine at the far side of the room begins to chatter and spits out a SCRAMBLE notice. He hits the red alarm button and runs outside as a siren begins to wail.

RAF Coningsby is one of just two Air Force bases in the UK that operate Eurofighter Typhoon fighters on Quick Reaction standby, twenty-four hours a day, seven days a week. As the home of 1 Air Combat Group it covers the entire southern half of the British Isles. The pilots jog out into the hangar, where two of the chunky delta-winged fighters are drawn up while their ground crew crawl over them, hastily closing out the preflight check. Two minutes later they're starting engines and accepting taxi instructions from the tower; five minutes after the SCRAMBLE order they're screaming northwest at four hundred knots, climbing towards 20,000 feet.

Behind them, Coningsby is preparing another two Typhoons—they can ramp up to twenty-four sorties within six hours, although only two squadrons are available and ready for intercept service over the entire country. Meanwhile, the Control and Reporting Centre at RAF Scampton comes online with new instructions.

There are two unidentified aircraft over West Yorkshire, not squawking but visible on primary radar, traveling east at low altitude. An E3-D Sentry from RAF Waddington will be on its way as soon as it can take off—unlike the QRA Typhoons, the big four-engined AWACS aircraft don't sit on the apron waiting for a scramble order twenty-four hours a day—but in the meantime, the CRC's Weapons Controllers are assigning them to intercept and identify.

The Q-force Typhoon FGR4s of Squadron 17 are scrambled to intercept—hopefully not to shoot at—any and all aircraft behaving oddly: from Russian Air Force Tu-95 long-range bombers over the North Sea, to airliners squawking an emergency transponder code or failing to respond to air traffic control instructions. Consequently, they carry a mix of two AMRAAM and four ASRAAM missiles, shells for the Mauser 27mm cannon, and spare fuel tanks. There's no call for bombs or beyond-visual-range missiles on this duty: opening fire on a target without positively confirming its identity is a wartime action, and apart from the regular Russian visitors nobody has directly threatened British skies for a very long time.

As Quebec-1 and Quebec-2 begin a banking turn to the west, skirting the edge of the controlled airspace around Leeds Bradford Airport, CRC's provisional identification of the two unknowns—heading east at roughly 120 knots, two thousand feet up—is that they are either helicopters or light planes. Their presence is suspicious because they're not responding to Air Traffic Control in any way, and they're minutes away from the site of an ongoing aviation emergency. Q-1 and Q-2 can see them clearly on their CAPTOR-M radar, using reflected energy from the airport's approach radar in active mode, but can't identify their type. Q-1 and Q-2 intend to close for a visual inspection and will try to hail the unidentified aircraft, then escort them to land at an airport with appropriate facilities—depending on what they turn out to be.

But all that is about to change: Q-1 and Q-2 are about to become the first RAF fighters to engage in air combat over England since 1945.

A door opens onto the rooftop of Quarry House beneath the stainless steel–clad spire. In the predawn light Colonel Lockhart's figure is a hunched silhouette, looking out across the low guard rail down onto the bus station and the gentle slope up towards Vicar Lane. "They're coming," he says quietly, fingering his bluetooth headset.

"Still nothing from OCCULUS One." Jez follows him, hands thrust deep in her pockets. Below him, the shuffling figures of a squad of Residual Human Resources are piling sandbags up on the edge of the roof and stacking ammunition boxes and spare barrels for a pair of M60 machine guns. "OCCULUS Two is inbound via the M1 and should be here in about half an hour. Catterick Garrison are throwing together a couple of recce squadrons, and they'll be double-timing it down the A1(M) as soon as they're ready. The Highways Agency is closing the northbound carriageway to facilitate, and Army HQ down south are waking up and kicking First Armoured Div and AAC for a squadron of Longbows, although the choppers are at least four hours away. Even if they close the motorway grid to civilian traffic, the first CB2s can't get here before late afternoon."

"Tanks." Lockhart closes his eyes for a moment. "I seem to remember a time when we kept Challengers at Catterick. None of this nonsense about centralizing everything in the home counties. Talk about keeping all the eggs in one basket . . ."

"Blame the 2010 defense review." Jez looks away. "We need to be prepared to hold out for at least twelve hours." They've already discussed—and discounted—any hope of help from the police and regular emergency services. The civil authorities will be too busy saving civilians. In any case, if Forecasting Ops are right about the scale of the threat barreling towards the center of Leeds the local Armed Response Units will be as much use as a wet rag in a nuclear firestorm. It's hard to be certain, though: the threat seems to be invisible, insofar as eyeballs or cameras that see it simply stop reporting. Maybe when Pinky and his forlorn hope make contact there'll be some more hard information, but until then all they've got is BBC News 24's and Sky News 24's rolling speculation on TV sets in one of the offices, plus the usual reliable fallbacks: Twitter and Facebook. The shocked voices of the TV newsreaders talking over the burning funeral pyres of airliners tell their own tale. The oppo have theater anti-airborne capability, which suggests something frightening about the scale of the attack; a squadron of helicopter gunships and a battalion of light armored vehicles certainly won't be enough to stop them. "I've got most of the machine guns set up under the car park top deck, and OCCULUS Two should arrive before contact, but we don't have enough people to defend the site against an effective assault force." She takes a deep breath. "I changed my mind and I think you're right about the cameras."

"Tell the Highways Agency to lock down all the approach roads on the north and west of the city first," Lockhart says curtly. "Set the signaling to red at the Armley Gyratory, down at Elland Road, and all around the outer ring road. Close down the inner ring road to stop anyone driving into the city center. A couple of hours of gridlock is a cheap price to pay if it keeps everyone off the roads." He pauses. "And get the bloody railways stopped. The last thing we need is a couple of intercity expresses dumping a thousand passengers in the middle of a battle."

The dawn light is beginning to cast a long shadow from the truncated tower at Bridgewater Place when Lockhart goes downstairs and returns to the makeshift operations room. If only they'd had another few months to get their feet under the table this might be a survivable situation, he thinks. The Laundry's migration plan includes provisions to turn the regional continuity of government center in the nuclear bunker under Quarry Hill into a properly hardened defensible location. But they're not ready yet. Expecting a skeleton staff to defend a barely prepared civilian office complex against a thuamaturgically equipped military force is madness and folly. Not for the first time, Lockhart wonders if it wouldn't make more sense to retreat down the motorway towards London. But that would leave a metropolitan complex—two major cities and outlying towns totaling over two million people—at the mercy of a hostile occupying force.

All the alternatives are unthinkable. And so, as he returns to his desk, Lockhart is already on his mobile phone to the Ops Center down south, requesting authorization for the first ever operational activation of the SCORPION STARE system.

The Host has been riding for three and a half hours as they count time—nearly four *urük* hours—following one or another of the broad, eerily flat stone roads that the *urük* use for their carts. For a while now the ugly fired-clay and stone hovels of the underpeople have been clustering densely alongside the road, although it is still possible to glimpse open fields through the gaps between them. The Host leaves a trail of darkened windows and stopped *urük*-carts in its wake, bodies tumbling where they fall: the primitives have no defenses against *mana*-powered weapons, and the cavalry have only drawn their knives to cut through tangles of wires and fences.

But their mounts have been running at an extended canter for too long, covering ground at a pace that would have been a full gallop for regular horses. Even though their steeds are supernaturally strong (this pace would have killed a horse within an hour) they need to pause occasionally to reject heat and drink water, especially when laden with armor and riders. Thus, shortly after the first and second battalions pass Otley, Third of Heavy Cavalry commands a brief respite. The riders dismount from their steeds and lead them down the embankment to a river that runs beside the road for a short while, covered by the force's air defense detachment and heavy weapon teams. Once the mounts are watered, their riders feed them a few kilos of meat, still raw and bleeding from the stasis cocoons. Then they take a few minutes to stretch their legs beneath the shelter of the defensive shield that the magi hold overhead.

"*Well, that was the easy part,*" Sixth of Second Battalion remarks to her adjutant as she extends first one leg then the other, watching the small cluster of knights around Third of Heavy, who is already back in the saddle. (His enthusiasm is unwise, she thinks: it does no good to be first on the battlefield if you arrive too sore to be fully effective.) *"Tell your troopers to stay close and keep their weapons in hand. We'll be in the thick of these slums before long and we can't count on the lack of resistance continuing."*

"Yes, my Liege." The adjutant glances round, taking in the field of riderless mounts slobbering and snarling over their fodder and the soldiers variously rubbing sore joints, stretching, and sitting down on the grass. *"I can't believe the foe hasn't noticed us. How can they be so passive?"*

"Oh, some of them noticed us all right!" Sixth glowers. *"I believe First Battalion only stopped collecting scalps when Third threatened to crucify the next idiot who broke formation."* Her frown subsides. *"Clearly All-Highest's plan was sound, and I suppose there'll be plenty of trophies to go round later. But remember Spies and Liars said that the enemy don't use mana much, not that they're defenseless."*

Adjutant of Second Battalion's ears flatten thoughtfully. *"Indeed? If they don't use mana what do their warriors use instead?"*

"Look to your sword," Sixth says sharply. *"That flying engine was no toy, was it? And from the fireball when it crashed, it had some sort of energetic power source. The fact that we couldn't sense it notwithstanding, we shouldn't underestimate them."*

"Undetectable high energy propulsion?" Her adjutant's expression is queasy. *"I will warn my vassals to keep their eyes open. If they can use it to project missiles or darts as well—"*

"Yes." Sixth pauses for a moment. *"Also, you have observed the lights along these roads, and the lightning-bearer wires?"* (The Host has lost more than two soldiers in the process of learning the hard way that steel armor and electricity distribution cables are best kept apart.) *"They don't use mana but there's clear evidence of organization here, a civilization of sorts. And the lightning-powered eyes on poles we keep having to burn out—who are the watchers, and what are they planning?"*

Adjutant of Second pulls out her mirror and peers into its glassy depths. She tucks a stray lock of sweat-dampened black hair back under her helmet (for when exposed to the gaze of basilisk weapons, even wet hair will burn), then frowns at what she sees. *"We pass them every two-fifths of a league along these ways. The blue ones, I mean. The small black eyes are irregular, and the yellow boxes seem to be random but are associated with symbol-bearing steel signs."* She slides her recording mirror back into its case, where it briefly illuminates the interior before it falls asleep.

"They serve different lieges," Sixth says slowly. *"And they're seen along the larger roads, not the smaller paths."* She smiles again, ears stirring under the fine metal weave of her mail coif. *"Once we are underway, instruct all unit commanders that they are to avoid dense concentration of lightning-powered eyes, if necessary detouring into side streets. They haven't struck at us yet, but . . ."*

Adjutant of Second's eyes go wide and her ears flatten. *"Oh yes,"* she breathes. *"I'll warn them at once!"* And with that, she scrambles into her saddle and nudges her mad-eyed steed into motion.

Highest Liege of Airborne Strike does not fly in the morning, for she is attached to All-Highest's staff, in overall command of the air defense and strike assets of the Host. The two active firewyrms that skim the hilltops due north of Bradford are commanded by First Wing of Airborne Strike and his wing-sister. They fly with bat-like wings fully extended, enclosed canopies covering the pilots strapped to their backs. Their flight-magi sit below them in mirror-finished cages, able to see the world around them without being burned to a crisp by the early morning light; behind and below the flight crews' howdahs numerous steel-jacketed packages are strapped to the dragons' side-harnesses.

To an observer with the right kind of eyes—eyes capable of looking straight at a pair of airborne strike wyrms without being struck blind—the dragons leave a faint exhaust trail of pale yellow-green vapor, exudate from their digestive tracts that drools from the incendiary glands located just behind their second set of circular jaws. It's only a few drops every few seconds, and most of it evaporates before it hits the ground, but where it settles the liquid burns away the morning dew and the pale fumes of combustion scorch the leaves and ground below.

· The two dragons are following an approximation of the Host's course, but moving considerably faster as they circle and turn south towards the vast *urük*-hive around the enemy palace. The pilots are tense, minds sunk deep within the sensoria of the brain leeches through which they control their mounts. They experience the world as firewyrms perceive it, while their magi maintain a perpetual watch for signs of hostile thaumaturgic emissions. But the *urük* don't use *mana* in combat, which is why the first warning of trouble the dragonriders get is when their mounts see the approaching sky-daggers directly with the light-sensitive scales coating their hides.

"*Contact,*" First Wing announces, a moment before Fourth Wing agrees. "*Targets approaching,*" followed by a bearing and distance loosely translatable as, "seven o'clock high and four hundred knots."

The dragons, being largely biological constructs (if somewhat heavily augmented by *mana*-powered weapons systems and counter-measures), are traveling at a relatively sedate hundred knots. The sky-daggers are closing the distance terrifyingly fast, and there's no way dragons can outrun them. It's more evidence of the *urük* penchant for inanimate not-magic witchery, if evidence were needed. Contact is inevitable within ten minutes: but the dragons have evolved in hostile skies where to be seen is to be eaten, and the Host's airborne combat doctrine has developed under similar circumstances, so they have certain advantages over their pursuers.

Meanwhile the crew of Quebec-1 and Quebec-2 have an unexpected problem.

"I'm looking for Contact One but I get nothing." Quebec-2's pilot says over the data link. "CAPTOR lock is firm but my head hurts when I try to eyeball them. Visual distortions."

"Roger that." Quebec-1 agrees. "My eyes are going funny, too. Countermeasures, go head-down."

"Confirm optical countermeasures," echoes the combat controller at Scampton. Eyeballs are a euphemism here: the fighter pilots each have a quarter of a million pounds of advanced electronic imaging equipment strapped to their heads. If they look at the floor of their cockpits they can see right through the airframe thanks to the high-resolution cameras plastered all over the aircraft and feeding their helmet-mounted displays. But where there's a sensor there's a jammer, and optical countermeasures are unwelcome but hardly unprecedented. Going head-down and closing on an unidentified target using instruments is something that fighter pilots hate; it means sacrificing situational awareness and ceding the initiative to whoever's in your blind spot. But on the other hand—

"Visual flicker goes away when I use instruments," Quebec-1 announces.

"PIRATE isn't locking in sector acquisition mode," says Quebec-2. The passive infrared tracker is the Typhoon's other main target acquisition sensor—a giant heat-sensitive eyeball mounted just ahead of the windscreen. Normally it can accept targeting information from the CAPTOR-E radar, but for some reason it can't pick up whatever the fighter's radar set is seeing. A metal airframe reflecting sunlight, or the heat of an engine exhaust, ought to show up like beacons. But Contacts One and Two are too dim to distinguish from ground clutter. Things have just gone from bad to worse.

For a couple of minutes the two pilots try to reset their faulty sensors. But it rapidly becomes clear that the multimillion-pound infra-red search and tracking systems on both aircraft are sulking identically. Radar can track the targets, but eyeballs—neither electronic nor human—can't look on. "It's a tightly focussed visual distortion," Quebec-1 tells Scampton. "Similar to what migraines are supposed to be like. Can't see the target with or without helmet cueing, just a moving knot in the landscape that hurts to look at. Closing to visual range may not help."

"Roger that," replies combat control. "Update on situation, we lost a civilian wide-body over the Pennines, adjacent to the ground track of Contacts One and Two. You are cleared for nose hot, engage at will if no-comply."

"Nose hot," confirms Quebec-1. "Select Fox-1."

At this point, the two dragons are thirty kilometers north of the oncoming fighters and their AIM-132 short-range homing missiles.

The Typhoons' Attack and Identification radar alone is enough to cue the missiles' on-board homing avionics. The missiles have their own infrared imagers, and as the AIS readies them for launch the thermal sensors chill down, ready to look at their targets. With weapons ready, Quebec-1 and Quebec-2 open their throttles wide and accelerate, closing to confirm before they launch that Contacts One and Two aren't an innocent air ambulance or a police helicopter that's forgotten its transponder.

This does not go unnoticed by the dragonriders.

"Sky-daggers turning in and incoming, seven o'clock high. Target one, shoot shoot shoot."

Firewyrms are living, albeit thaumically enhanced, organisms from a biosphere drastically different from the one we are used to. Their huge bat-like wings are supported by hollow, very light bones and support membranes as strong and light as spider silk. So as the sky-daggers stoop towards them on pillars of fire, the riders direct their steeds to do what comes naturally: to tuck in their wings and turn hard.

Jet fighters, for all that we think of them as maneuverable, are cumbersome in comparison to flying animals. A fourth-generation jet like an F-16 or a Typhoon can pull up to nine gees in a turn; the missiles they launch can briefly sprint at thirty to fifty gees before they burn out. But a peregrine falcon in a stoop—a mere bird—can pull around twenty gees. Dragons are bigger and slower than birds but have additional adaptations to help them survive in a sky full of terrifying predatory horrors: and they can keep fighting while their riders recover from *g*-induced loss of consciousness.

To the pilots of Quebec-1 and Quebec-2, the eye-watering knots in the sky that they are diving on (now at six hundred knots, holding back from supersonic cruise for the time being) suddenly change shape, narrowing and stretching. The CAPTOR-E radar switches mode frantically, trying to track them. Their ground speed drops abruptly to zero as they switch cleanly onto a reciprocal course and begin to rise, slamming on the brakes with impossible agility. To Quebec-1 it looks just like a cobra maneuver—a tactic pioneered by Soviet Su-27 pilots to break Doppler radar lock—and for a terrifying split-second he suspects the worst: that they've been suckered by hostile fighter aircraft—

"Fox-1 go," calls Quebec-2.

"Fox-1 go." Four flame-tipped streaks of smoke boil away from the fighters and drop down, slashing towards the intruders.

ASRAAM is a short-range air-to-air guided missile. It uses an inertial guidance system primed by the launch fighter's Attack and Identification System to aim towards the volume of air towards which the target is flying at the moment of launch. As it closes, the thermal optical imager in its head picks up the target and feeds course corrections to the guidance vanes that direct the airflow around the rocket's body. These missiles are not the stupid heat-seekers of the 1950s and 1960s, guided by a dumb heat sensor: otherwise fighters targeted by the missile could eject a bunch of flares and turn, pointing their hot engine exhaust away from the missile, confusing it. Instead, the twenty-first-century missiles carry an infrared video camera that feeds an onboard computer loaded with target recognition software.

A dragon—especially a dragon that is pulling in its wings to change direction, then actively *flapping*—looks absolutely nothing like any helicopter, fighter aircraft, airliner, zeppelin, or missile that has ever taken to the skies above England. Not only is it the wrong shape but it's cold, it doesn't reflect sunlight like metal, and the homing missile's guidance package can't make any kind of sense out of it. Also, the imaging elements are glitching like crazy, so that the picture the missiles are trying to interpret is little more than a field of random static.

Four missiles hurtle towards a volume of sky occupied only by a pair of rapidly diverging knots of noise. They slice on through the air trailing sonic booms behind them as they fail to lock onto their targets, until they self-destruct ten seconds after launch. A series of concussive thumps rattles windows across the northern suburbs of Leeds.

"Guns guns guns, target one," Quebec-1 announces calmly, and points his nose ahead of where the eye-watering hole in the sky ought to be as he sets up a deflection shot. His helmet is in sighting mode but keeps glitching and twitching as one or other of the optical sensors gives up on the target and freaks out. Above and behind him, Quebec-2 is drawing down on target two. They're still over open countryside, which is good (nobody wants to spray armor-piercing cannon shells across a city), but it means getting up close and personal with the target, which is writhing and turning as it hangs in the air like a demented bat—

"*Fire! Fire!*" orders First Wing, shivering with frustration as the onrushing dagger stubbornly refuses to twist aside and spiral into the ground. It's almost as if the damned *urük* sky-cart doesn't have a brain. For a couple of seconds First Wing was certain he was dead, that the flame-stabbing darts were going to turn towards him and slice the wings from his mount's body. But they slammed past his mount as if they hadn't even seen it. And now the dagger itself is wobbling in the air and turning towards him and his mage is silent, frozen in fear or concentration. "*Fire!*"

Finally one of the heavy bolts slung alongside his mount's body springs away from its clip and buzzes towards the enemy daggercraft on a surge of malevolent *mana*. "*Got it, my Lord,*" his mage gasps, her voice like living death. "*It's* not alive. *It's like an empty suit of flying armor—*"

First Wing screens it out, filing the information for later. He has other, more urgent problems. The onrushing daggercraft is spouting fire from its muzzle like a weird mechanical dragon, and he jinks hard and spreads his wings and claws, scrabbling at the air to throw himself aside from the spraying arc of white-hot pellets that hurtle towards him. He turns and climbs and, at the last possible moment before the daggercraft slashes past, he burps his mount.

The esoteric bioalchemy of firewyrms does not, regardless of garbled myths and tall tales, grant them the ability to breathe fire. Compared to the digestive hellbrew they carry in their five-lobed stomachs and use to incinerate their prey, fire would be an anticlimax. Few organisms can make any use out of elemental fluorine, but the dragons' ancestors were taken by the People from a place where biology followed a road less taken. They evolved—or, quite possibly, were designed by insane alchemists—to chew down on fluorinated minerals. Their leathery scales are permeated with polyfluorinated long chain waxes; as for their stomachs, it's anybody's guess how they contain their contents without liquifying their own organs. But if a firewyrm sprays digestive juices at you, you'll pay attention for as long as it takes your face to melt.

Quebec-1 takes his shot, discharges a twenty-round burst from his aircraft's Mauser BK-27, and races past the target, preparing to come about in a high-energy turn. As he does so the slow but impossibly maneuverable target pirouettes in mid-air and sprays a smoke-ring of misty liquid into his path. It shouldn't be possible for a liquid to propagate that far and that fast without dispersing, but evidently some exotic effect of turbulent fluid dynamics is at play. Either way, Quebec-1's engine intake ingests a good-sized gulp of the cloud.

Modern gas turbines are incredibly finely machined engines, made from exotic ultra-hard alloys and spinning at unbelievable speeds. They can take a lot of abuse, up to and including a frontal impact from a medium-sized bird. But they are definitely not designed to survive ingesting almost a liter of wyrmspit—a substance subsequently determined by defense establishment scientists to consist mostly of aerosolized chlorine trifluoride.

Chlorine trifluoride is about the most powerful oxidizing agent known to chemistry that is still stable at liquid-water temperatures. *Stable* is a euphemism: it ignites spontaneously on contact with sand, concrete, asbestos, water, paint, and fighter pilots. Both Quebec-1's engines suffer multiple uncontained blade failures and spray white-hot molten shrapnel through wings, fuel tanks, and the rocket motor of the unlaunched AMRAAM missile on Quebec-1's number 4 hardpoint. Which explodes, and in so doing detonates the missile's warhead, ripping what's left of the fighter into several pieces.

Quebec-2 is almost a second behind Quebec-1. Air-to-air gunnery is to some extent a statistical process: you throw a double-handful of fist-sized explosive shells at a volume of sky a couple of kilometers away and hope one of your devil's shotgun pellets intersects with your target. Quebec-2 takes his shot on the second target and instinctively pulls away in a high-gee turn just as Quebec-1 disintegrates.

Quebec-2 gets lucky. Fourth Wing is already turning his wyrm as a spreading burst of cannon shells expands towards him. His mage focusses furiously on his dazzlers and blinders, pouring *mana* into the circuits that should bamboozle and stun the vicious little attackers' minds, misdirecting them as they did the much bigger war-dart the daggercraft threw at him half a minute ago. But there's nothing there, no minds to confuse—it's almost as if the enemy is throwing insensate arrowheads at them across a gulf of leagues! Fourth Wing desperately tries to turn out of the path of the shells. But he's too late.

One of the thumb-fat rounds—a steel-sheathed shell surrounding a frangible tungsten core and a bursting charge—punches a hole in the crystal screen protecting Fourth Wing's mage, narrowly missing its occupant but shattering the canopy and exposing him to the early daylight before it tears into the body of the firewyrm and explodes. Exposed abruptly to daylight and a hundred-knot wind-blast, the magus and her V-parasites ignite like a roman candle. Fourth Wing swears and doubles up in his saddle as a pulse of agony cramps at his chest and left shoulder. It's referred pain from the brain leech, which vicariously relays his mount's senses for a fraction of a second before the leech, too, can take no more: it yanks its feeding proboscis from the base of the dragon's skull. The mortally wounded dragon coils in the air, draws in on itself around its lacerated stomach, and falls out of the sky. The last thing its rider sees is a spurt of greenish flame erupting from his magus's howdah, before a blast of sudden heat blots out his senses.

Backlit by sunrise, a parachute drifts towards the ground, its occupant dangling unconscious beneath it. The ejector seat detaches and drops towards the burning wreckage littering the fields below, its job done. In the distance, the surviving dragon and Typhoon turn and circle each other warily.

"All right, Lieutenant Cook, time to move out."

"Yes, sir." Lieutenant Jim Cook takes a deep breath, and looks at his platoon sergeant: "You heard the captain?"

"Sir." Sergeant Magnusson nods sharply, then gets on the troop voice circuit. "Okay, everyone, start your engines and sound off . . ."

It's six o'clock in the morning at Catterick Garrison in North Yorkshire, and a Sabre troop from C Squadron of the Royal Dragoon Guards—an armored cavalry regiment—is preparing to move out.

There's organized chaos on the ground as the soldiers prep their twelve Scimitar light tanks and grab every available Panther, truck, and Land Rover they can lay their hands on. They've scoured the barracks for every TomTom and Garmin satnav with up-to-date maps they can find. They weren't expecting action this day and the crews are mixed up, soldiers assigned to driving duty on the basis of their blood alcohol level rather than their regular post. Commanders, gunners, and drivers can swap seats as necessary once they're nearer the target. Cook is up front, riding ahead of the support troop in one of the Panthers, the better to be able to jump out and deal with delays while they're in convoy on the A1. The Highways Agency and the police should be holding the southbound carriageway of the road for them, but if one of the combat reconnaissance vehicles breaks down or sheds a track they're going to need an officer on hand and Captain Roberts is going to be too busy talking to everyone from the police to the Apache drivers from 3 Regiment (when they get here from the south coast) to have time for shouting at knuckleheads.

The call came in less than two hours ago: something insane is brewing up in Leeds and the Guards are needed on MACV—Military Aid to Civil Power—duty. Not for civil defense or assistance in the wake of a major incident, which would be comparatively welcome, but to deal with the kind of shit that they've just spent several years dealing with in Helmand. The stated mission is frankly bonkers, but Sergeant Magnusson has been too busy finding plausibly sober bodies to throw at vehicles and checking everyone's got the right set of frequencies dialed in and the right set of maps on board and Cook has been too busy quickly cramming on the terrain and the rules of engagement to worry about what the battalion staff have been smoking.

"Elves, Lieutenant." Major Moran shook his head, world-weary as if he was announcing another Taliban suicide attack in downtown Kabul. "Pointy-eared bastards with an allergy to cold iron. Get your laughing over and done with right now: I am reliably informed that this is *not* a joke, and not a case of contagious insanity either, unless the first lunatic in the asylum is the chair of the general staff. It's going to be all over the news by nine, and you can expect everyone to be distracted by families phoning in unless you get a tight grip. Tell them to set a voice mail message and send their texts before we move out, then it's deployment rules." Virtually no spot on the planet is without cellphone coverage these days: troops and their families can talk whenever they want. Which is fine, right up until Tommy Atkins's eight-year-old phones Daddy by mistake while Daddy is pinned down under fire next to a teammate who's bleeding out, or the local phone company engineers' families are taken hostage by hostiles who know precisely which calls they want diverting. Then it stops being fine and turns deeply, unpleasantly weird.

"Sir?" It's Cook's driver. "Ready when you are."

"Okay, drive on. Keep it slow until I tell you." Cook turns round in his chair, to watch as the queue of CVR(T)s fire up their engines from cold, blasting out clouds of blue diesel smoke.

The Scimitars are fast armored scout vehicles—light tanks suitable for battlefield reconnaissance in a war of maneuver. Just what you want when the enemy are riding around in Toyota pickups. They're able to engage infantry and other light units but it's not their job to go head-to-head with dug-in forces or artillery, let alone a real enemy with main battle tanks. Luckily that's been a thing of the past since the Iraq war, but nobody knows what's happening in Leeds right now except that maybe it involves cavalry, some sort of *Lord of the Rings* crap, and there's no sign of artillery. This is promising at first, but on the other hand, horses suggest mobile light troops who could pop up anywhere with who-knows-what: IEDs, guided antitank missiles, magic wands. Jim isn't sure what's going on, but from the way the armorers have been running around handing out live ammo by the crate—armor-piercing cannon shells included—he is willing to bet that it's so bad it's going to make the history books. The kind of civilian casualties that could result from a gunnery exchange in dense British suburbia don't bear thinking about. So he's particularly edgy as his driver boots the Panther command car south down the A6136, towards the motorway junction.

They make it onto the A1 in good order. The road is wide open and utterly empty, although the row of red and blue flashing lights astern tells its own tale. The northbound carriageway is logjammed with slow trucks as the police and Highways Agency try to clear a lane for contraflow running. Driving down the empty motorway at a hundred and ten kilometers per hour with a police escort is a surreal experience, but Jim is kept busy with radio traffic and intermittent data updates. At least the Scimitars are all keeping up, although a couple of the Land Rovers fall out: they get driven every day and stuff breaks more often when you throw squaddies at it on a regular basis. (The tanks and armored cars get fettled and stored under cover between exercises: nobody borrows them to go to the supermarket.)

Hammering down the motorway is thirsty business, so after less than an hour Jim gets on the radio. "Prepare to pull over, we're breaking at Junction 46, third exit, that's Junction 46, third exit, follow the signs for fuel." As expected there's a police car with lights waiting to escort them into the service area, where the bemused petrol station attendants come outside to gawp as if they've never seen a convoy of tanks queuing for diesel before.

There's controlled chaos at the pumps. Trooper McGarrett manages to scrape the Bowman aerial off the roof of Scimitar Three on the roof of the filling station, then backs up over the curb and crunches a bollard. Sergeant Stevens is running around making sure that the cars that run on unleaded don't get in the DERV queue and vice versa, while Jim dismounts with his radio op to stay well away from any fuel fumes. He's getting itchy twenty minutes later as the last of the Scimitars pull forward to the diesel pumps—at least they've all got Esso cards to pay with—when the major finally arrives, in the back of a traffic patrol Volvo. "What's the damage?" he asks Lieutenant Cook, tight-lipped.

"A bit over two thousand liters of DERV, five hundred of regular unleaded, and they're probably going to bill us for the pump McGarrett damaged . . ."

"Get your men back on the road as soon as they've locked their filler caps." Moran walks, stiff-legged, towards the petrol station office. Cook shakes his head and heads over to the Panther CLV. The armored car—an Italian/British equivalent to the MRAP—is kitted out with all the comms equipment he could ask for and a GPMG on the roof. It's also a much better bet for driving into a British city than a Scimitar, with its relatively restricted visibility. Even so, he feels a bit exposed without even a light tank's worth of armor.

Ten minutes later they're back on the road again, burning rubber south towards the junction with the A58 at Wetherby when the open channel lights up: "Incoming enemy aircraft!" From a reporting location less than twenty kilometers to the west.

"The fuck," Lieutenant Cook swears, and grabs at his own headset: "Eyes up, we have airborne incoming!" And he's just looking up to scan to the east, still waiting for confirmation, when the dragon soars over the treeline and sees the convoy.

PART 4

BLOOD OATHS

17: STATE OF SIEGE

Eaters: information patterns from another universe that are *real good* at taking over and subverting high-level adaptive neural networks with bodies, then using them to acquire touch-contact with *other* bodies containing neural networks. The information content of which can be quite handily nutritious to an eater because, well, that's what they live on. An eater without a body is relatively harmless as long as your brain is warded, or the eater is surrounded by a secure containment grid, or otherwise occupied by another eater. An eater *with* a body is a self-propelled viral infection with contagion by touch, zero incubation time, and a 100 percent lethal effect on the personality of anyone unfortunate enough to be tagged. With a couple of exceptions: being tagged by an eater is harmless if you're host to a different kind of high-level informational predator—the Eater of Souls, say, or the V-symbionts that cause PHANG syndrome, or whatever bizarre construct the elite of the empire inoculate their minds with.

Their touch still stings like a wasp, though, and an eater can do real damage if it's trying to tag you using the teeth of a great big German shepherd guard dog with luminous green-glowing worms in its eyes and an even worse attitude than usual.

Alex squeaks as the dog lunges out of the darkness and bites his left arm. The dagger in his right hand dangles uselessly as he flinches away. But the dog doesn't follow through. A real German shepherd would shove Alex off-balance, twisting and chewing and rending, tearing blood vessels and trying to get him on the ground where it will lunge for the throat. But instead of a canine mind the brain behind the dog's eyes is host to an eater, and the eater is frozen in something like shock, because it has just bitten into a juicy fruit and found itself gnawing on a lump of peach-painted wood. One touch of those teeth and Alex should be on his knees, identity bleeding into darkness. But instead Alex staggers, his arm burning, and the possessed dog does not push or snarl or bite, but staggers with him, and he unfreezes and nerves himself to swing the dagger, point-first, towards the doggy throat.

Alex stares into the undead dog's eyes for a moment that feels like a lifetime. The luminous green worms in the German shepherd's eye sockets spiral and twirl kaleidoscopically, speeding up as it tries to shove its will into his body. He has a momentary inkling of their meaning, a vast and chilly astonishment at his refusal to keel over and dissolve in the sea of the eater's appetite; then he shoves the dagger into its sternum. The sudden transfer of weight from his left to his right arm unbalances him as a gout of blood sprays across his hand and he begins to fall.

"Alex!" shouts Cassie, and the room lights up pinkish-white as she channels the force of her anger through her mace.

The next things Alex becomes aware of—in no particular order—are his ears ringing, his arm and ankles throbbing viciously, that his vision is occluded by huge purple blotches, his face seems to be on fire, and he has a splitting headache.

"Are you all right?" asks the bulky purple blob hovering anxiously overhead.

"Blooboob . . ." Alex spits. Dog blood, especially the blood of a dog that's had its mind chewed up and crapped out by an eater, tastes utterly disgusting, even before you add in the peculiar taboo against animal cruelty that haunts the British middle classes as they sit down to eat their Chicken Kiev—dogs are man's best friend, after all, and it is just *not done* to stab them to death and roll around in their blood, even when they've been possessed by undead alien foulness. "Not. Good. Help me. Up?"

Cassie grabs an arm and tries to lift him. Alex manages to catch his balance and staggers to his feet, blinking. His face is peeling and the smell of roast meat fills his nostrils. "What. Happened?"

"They didn't bring enough guard beasts so they harvested the nearby park for spares," Cassie reasons.

They find the occult diagram that anchors the ley line endpoint in the room at the end of the corridor that once housed the air filtration and conditioning plant for the bunker. Light the deep blue of Cerenkov radiation pours from the thaumic containment circle. "Whoa." Alex pauses. "Is that the—"

"YesYes . . ." Underlit by the grid, Cassie's frown turns her eye sockets into shadowy recesses as she crouches down to trace the script around the outer circle. It flickers and glitters, violet in the darkness. "Looks like they moved the dream road anchor through here. It's still entangled with the ley line." She rises, baring her teeth in a death's head grin. "This is the right route. Come on." She offers him her hand.

"Are you sure this is safe?" Alex asks ironically. He takes her fingers, feeling the sticky dampness of blood glue them together like a promise of violence.

"Of course not: my stepmother is trying to kill me. But I've met your"—she shudders delicately—"parents. Is it not proper that you should meet mine?"

"This is *so* not second date territory." Then he steps across the edge of the ward and the world unwraps itself around them, dropping them onto the ley line.

The National Air Traffic System is having a very bad morning.

Ripples begin to spread outwards within seconds of the first fireball over Otley as controllers divert aircraft inbound for Leeds Bradford Airport to other destinations—Manchester and East Midlands—and cancel flights that haven't yet departed. A full-scale investigation is going to shut the runway for at least a day. Phones begin ringing in bedrooms near Crawley, as the duty desk officer at the Civil Aviation Authority calls up crash investigators to set them in motion; but before they can ready a light plane to take them to the scene in Yorkshire, things go from bad to worse.

First comes the news of the disappearance of AZ-602 from radar screens over North Yorkshire. Then AA-759 issues its mayday call and diverts towards Liverpool, and finally the Air Force controllers at Scampton announce that there is a hostile incursion in British airspace. At which point the controllers in the NATS center in West Drayton put their doomsday scenario into operation: to shut down British airspace to all civilian flights and bring all airports to a complete ground stop.

It's happened twice before in as many decades: first on September 11, 2001, and again in April 2010 when the volcano Eyjafjallajökull erupted, spewing an ash cloud into the skies over Europe. NATS has a plan to handle such a shutdown. First, aircraft leaving British airspace are cleared to continue—but incoming flights are directed to airports on the continent, and new departures are cancelled. Luckily for everyone, it's the early hours of a Sunday morning, and Paris and Amsterdam can absorb the inbound intercontinental traffic. But the NATS shutdown propagates to EUROCONTROL, forcing most flights outbound from Western Europe to North America to make long diversions or cancel; and then the incoming red-eyes need to find new destinations, from Dublin and Shannon to Paris and Madrid.

Then Scampton notifies EUROCONTROL that the RAF have lost a fighter in air-to-air combat, and within an hour European airspace closes down from Ireland to Warsaw.

"Are you sure this is safe?" asks Pete, as Pinky tightens the buckle on the back of his cuirass and passes him the first gauntlet.

"*Fuck* no!" Pinky's head-shake jangles tunelessly, scraping metal on metal. "You really shouldn't be doing this, Vicar. Not your party at all. You've got a wife and kid to be thinking about."

"I'm thinking of them. I'm thinking." *Also a congregation who've probably forgotten I exist and a bishop who definitely hasn't,* Pete adds mentally. "What happens if we don't do this?"

"I don't know. Probably we don't die. I mean, maybe probably. Possibly maybe probably." Pinky passes him the other gauntlet. "Think you can see to drive in that thing?"

"Once I've got it adjusted." Pete finds the seventeenth-century helmet problematic, but not impossible. "I think I can make it work as long as I take things easy."

"Well then." There's a resounding clatter and clash from the back as Pinky climbs onto the rear bench seat. "Do you know the way to the bunker?"

"Yes. First I need to get us out of this car park and onto the Inner Loop, then—"

There is an echoing clash of metal on metal as Pete clambers over Ilsa's side and gets himself settled on the motorcycle-style saddle without impaling himself on any bits of armor. "Hey, this fits."

"It's cavalry armor: of course you can sit on a saddle!"

More importantly, Pete notes, they're both covered from head to foot with low-carbon steel. Ilsa's bucket-shaped body keeps his lower legs screened, and Pinky has some kind of chain mail horse blanket to wrap around his lower half. When Ops Control down south finally act on Lockhart's request to fire up the SCORPION STARE grid around the Inner Loop, they'll be able to move without bursting into flames: and if they're not the *only* thing that can move without halting and catching fire, the minigun mounted on the trailer hitch will come in handy.

"Dr. Russell." His bluetooth headset still works, despite the tin can blocking most of his field of vision. "Sitrep, please."

Pete turns the key in the ignition and Ilsa wheezes for a few seconds before rumbling to life. "Engine running, about to leave the garage. We should be there in about ten, fifteen minutes at this time of night."

"Good. Be aware that after you leave we will be activating the autonomous camera network around the Inner Loop. Any thaum field over twenty milli-Parsons will trigger an automatic basilisk reflex; your personal wards alone exceed that flux level, so you should delay your return until you have received direct clearance."

"We've got armor—"

"Armor or no armor," Lockhart insists, "you do *not* approach this site without permission. Firstly, we have passive defenses that might still target you, secondly, there are machine guns on the roof, and thirdly, the Army are on the way. Do you understand?"

"I totally don't want to get shot by mistake." Pete puts Ilsa into

CHARLES STROSS

first gear, releases the clutch, and steers towards the exit ramp. "Are you going to—"

"I'm transferring your call to an open speakerphone. Don't hang up, we'll keep it on mute until we need to talk to you; if you want anything, just shout."

Alex may be only half-trained in the basics of combat invocation, but he has been studying beyond his coursework. He has spent the past six months trying to broaden his understanding of the esoteric sciences, and Jez Wilson has seen fit to give him extensive background reading privileges in the research archives. So when he finds himself standing on a darkling plain that stretches to infinity in all directions, beneath a blazing fractal sigil that spans the void from horizon to horizon, he looks for the silvery path: and then he says, "Fuck me, we're standing on an unmasked affine spacelike brane and *we can breathe*?"

"I love it when you talk technical"—Cassie grips his elbow—"but don't stray from the path unless you want to wander forever."

Alex nods. The road is a ghostly trail of footprints, not a physical surface. Most ley line routes run along the surface of the real world, but this one dives through a different cosmos, thanks to the magi's meddling. The plain is so featureless that he can tell that if he strays too far to see the trail he might never be able to rediscover it. "Your people explored this continuum?"

"Some of it, a long time ago. There are more things here than ley lines. They discovered many treasures before they realized the unwisdom of opening gateways to other worlds. My ancestors tamed the dragons and the cavalry steeds. Took the ancestors of the lesser races as breeding stock," Cassie explains as she walks along the path. She sounds nonchalant, but Alex is learning to read the tension in her ears. "Be careful before you rush to judgment."

"But, but slaves—"

"Different species." She shrugs. "Are dogs people? Do cows vote? They are part of your *urük* civilization, whether you listen to their wishes or not. The master race does not ask for the consent of barbarians before it brings them the benefits of civilization." She stops, then turns and meets Alex's shocked gaze. Her face is as composed as a mask. Shaken, he wonders for a moment if her earlier displays of passion, hiding this total lack of affect, were feigned. But then she explains: "My father is the All-Highest. This is not merely his opinion, this is the truth of my People. It has always been that way among them. Power belongs to the strong in muscle or in mind, love is weakness and a source of shame. Your tongue has a word for it—psychopathy—and if you approach him expecting *urük*—human—values, he will kill you without a second thought."

"You said *them*."

Cassie's gaze flickers away, although her expression remains frozen. "I'm flawed," she admits. "Spying is one of the few vocations in which empathy is a useful trait that is open to a Person of noble blood. My mother protected me from the consequences of my weakness, saw me established in my calling—but she is dead." For a moment the shell cracks, revealing something like grief. But then Cassie composes her face again. "Remember this: when we arrive, any sign of vulnerability or compassion *will* be seen as weakness, on my part as much as on yours." She allows her cheek to twitch. "Pretend you have had Botox treatment, YesYes? And once we arrive, whatever happens, *show no affection*."

Alex swallows. His hunger is a silvery, burning ache, but contained: his power is awake inside his skin, leaving him feeling omnipotent, ready for anything. Ready, if he can, to help Cassie discharge her lethal curse, then rush her to safety. Ready to—

She's walking and he's following her. Her back is turned, as if to afford him room to do whatever it is that she is hoping for yet refusing to admit. Whatever she thinks he *should* be doing, if he were a sufficiently ruthless, cold, sociopathic manipulator to be a worthy match for a spy of the People. Alex mentally pinches himself, then pulls out his phone, falling behind as he stares at it. No signal. Well, *of course* Vodafone doesn't provide cell service in hyperspace, but that doesn't stop him from composing an email and queuing it to go out as soon as they reach the far end of the diverted ley line. Assuming she's right and it surfaces somewhere else in his own world, rather than in her father's headquarters underhill, it should update Lockhart and the DM on the situation. Next he composes a couple of text messages—their significance explained in the preliminary email—that will light the fuse on a deadly chain of events when he hits the send button. (Assuming, again, that he lives long enough to do so: and that the appropriate authorities receive them.) Finally, he starts the remote monitoring server on the phone and tells it to keep updating his location via GPS. It'll run the battery down sooner rather than later, but that can't be helped. This will all be over in a few hours and if they do what he suggests he'll have to get a new phone anyway. Assuming he survives.

They walk for what feels like hours beneath the bizarre fractal burning in the empty darkness that passes for a sky. They walk until Alex can feel the soles of his feet aching, until the sigil in the void seems to turn and spawns blazing streamers of dust that contains universes. They walk until a blazing blue circle appears in the distance, at the far end of the ley line through the continuum of the dream roads. Then Cassie stops and beckons him forward. "What," he says.

"*This.*" A moment later she's in his arms, shaking, clutching at him.

"What," he repeats. She silences him with a kiss. He hugs her and they mash their lips together, clumsy with desperation.

Finally she pulls back a little. "From now on, whatever you do, don't tell *anyone* your name—or mine. Names have power. I am known as Agent First of Spies and Liars, and I will live up to that: believe nothing I say once we cross the threshold until . . . well, until whatever happens, happens." She kisses him again. "Trust me, I'm a very *good* liar." Then she lets go and pushes him away, her face smoothing into a mask of haughty arrogance. "Remember, I have bound you as a vassal and you are compelled to obey me," she says. She turns to face the blue-glowing portal. "Follow me."

Together they step through the doorway to the Host's marshaling area.

* * *

By seven o'clock in the morning, the worst case of motorway gridlock ever recorded in the UK is rapidly engulfing London. Unusually, the cause is neither an accident nor a surfeit of rush-hour traffic: the police have simply closed the entire clockwise carriageway of the M25 between junction 7 and junction 23.

The proximate cause of the blockage is crawling north at barely seventy kilometers per hour: a convoy of thirty bellowing desert brown low-loaders bearing tarpaulin-shrouded payloads. Each low-loader—including its load—weighs close to a hundred tons. Many of the Army's heavy tanks have been sold off since the 2010 defense review, and most of the rest are stored in Germany against the ever-present threat of a Soviet invasion through Poland. But almost all the Challenger-2s in working order in the UK are now on the move, crawling from the complex of hangars in Hampshire where they're stored as fast as the mechanics can gas them up, arm them, and find transporters for the five-hundred-kilometer trip to Leeds.

The heavies don't travel unaccompanied. More low-loaders follow them, carrying recovery vehicles and spare engine packs; there's a steady trickle of regular trucks and Land Rovers playing catch-up, with as many spares as they can scour from the depot. Not that the tanks are ready to fight yet. Ammunition will arrive separately from one of the Defense Munition Centers in Warwickshire, converging as fast as the trucks can move it—again, with a huge police escort, because nothing gives the civil authorities indigestion like hundreds of tons of high explosives driving around the motorway grid in rush-hour traffic.

But it's going to be late afternoon before any of this stuff gets where it's needed, and by then the battle will probably be over.

It's eight o'clock in the morning on a Sunday, and the Right Honorable Jeremy Michaels is in a foul mood.

He's been booted and suited for three hours as he walks along the red tunnel to the door of the secure meeting room in the Cabinet Office building, where an extraordinary session of the combined Civil Contingencies Committee, Defense Committee, and a bunch of spooks from the Intelligence side of the table has been thrown together in a blinding hurry. Whitehall has been a self-kicking centipede orgy since four o'clock this morning, with phones ringing and secure email systems smoking since whatever it is that's kicking off kicked off in cloth-capshire or wherever it is up north, interrupting Jeremy's post-prandial beauty sleep. It shows no sign of dying down, and nobody seems to be able to tell him just what the purple throbbing fuck is going on. He's carpeted a couple of spads but whatever this is it's *not* a flying-under-the-radar exercise left running by one of the useless tossers who walked the plank during the last reshuffle. Losing airliners to some sort of terrorist attack is really bad PR and after the bollocking he's given them they should have a story ready for him to feed the inevitable press conference in a couple of hours—but what he's getting from the Home Office is that it's *not* terrorism, it's MOD territory—and what the blithering fuck is the Army up to in Leeds?

This, Jeremy has decided, is intolerable. And when he decides something is intolerable, he is in the habit of sharing the pain. So he's got the Chief of Defense Staff, the Minister for Outsourcing Arms Contracts—that would be, the Minister of Defense—Her Bitchiness the Home Secretary, and a chorus line of spooks out of their beds this morning. He is determined to get to the bottom of this clusterfuck, and God help them if they don't bend to it.

There's an empty seat waiting for the Prime Minister at the head of the table, and Jeremy takes his place without hesitation. It is his by right of birth, breeding, and the parliamentary equivalent of a quick knee to the balls behind the bike shed when none of the prefects were watching; and it's his job to chair this sesh and figure out what to do and who to blame for it.

Once seated he glances around, taking in his audience. On display are: a mixture of anticipation (Jessica Greene, the Home Secretary, is wearing her crocodile smirk, as if expecting a blood meal imminently), irritation (Nigel Irving, the Minister of Defense, has the red eyes and dog-breath of a habitual heavy Saturday-night binge-drinker), and lugubrious hang-dog guilt (a senior parliamentary secretary from the

Joint Intelligence Committee who apparently expects to be crucified). There are also some unfamiliar faces—a general, an RAF air marshal, and a couple of whey-faced spooks who look as if they'll burst into flames if exposed to daylight. In other words, the usual.

Jeremy opens the slim agenda on his blotter. The Cabinet Office staff, bless their socks, have at least sketched out a list of bullet points, and he scans it quickly in search of the usual suspects—Al Qaida, airliners, final demands—when—

"What on earth is this RED RABBIT thing?" he barks. "Is this some kind of joke?"

The Chief Cabinet Secretary, Adrian Redmayne, clears his throat. "I am afraid it isn't, Prime Minister," he says calmly. He slips in Jeremy's title as a placatory prophylactic: the PM can become quite *irritable* (to use the correct euphemism) when exposed to circumstances that threaten his authority. "It's an official contingency plan from the MOD's playbook. Although"—he glances at one of the bland-faced spooks—"I gather it's one of the Never-Happen scenarios we aren't routinely briefed on."

"Not briefed? *Why?*" The PM glares at the agenda, as if he expects it to confess that it's all just a good laugh between friends: but the paper remains stubbornly silent. He bottles his initial reaction, choleric and unquotable on TV before the watershed. "Who made that decision?"

"Let's find out." Redmayne smiles over the top of his half-moon reading glasses, like an executioner sizing up one of his customers for the drop. "Dr. Moore—do we have a Dr. Moore present? Representing, ah, Q-Division, SOE? Please could you give the PM a brief backgrounder on SOE, and what they have to do with an airliner crash in Yorkshire?"

Dr. Moore turns out to be one of the anonymous-looking spookside people. Subtype, female, early middle age, a bit plump, wearing a suit that Jeremy thinks his wife wouldn't be seen dead giving away to charity: cheap, very cheap (although it's not her fault she wasn't born into money).

Moore clears her throat and recites, tonelessly: "SOE, the Special Operations Executive, goes back a long way, historically: it was established by the Ministry of Economic Warfare in 1940 on the orders of Winston Churchill, as an espionage, sabotage, and reconnaissance agency in parallel to MI5. It was publicly dissolved in January 1946—but Q-Division remained in active operation and was transferred to the Ministry of Defense at the same time as GCHQ. The organization is tasked with detecting, evaluating, and responding to paranormal threats to the nation. As most aspects of the paranormal—magic, colloquially—are side effects of mathematical manipulation . . ." She stops. The PM is rolling his eyes. "Sir?"

Jeremy is ignoring the background noise. It seems more productive to examine his cabinet subordinates for their immediate reaction to this garbage. The Home Secretary appears to be doodling electric chairs on her blotter, eyes downcast to spare her neighbors the psychotic giggles: clearly her personal coach has been reminding her not to swallow baby mice in public again. Nigel has poured himself a water glass and is gazing at it as if trying to turn it into Absolut by sheer force of willpower. Redmayne is wearing a peculiarly glazed expression that Jeremy remembers from the headmaster's waiting room that time when the lower sixth were carpeted for hot-wiring Miss MacDonald's Mini Clubman and borrowing it for a panty raid on St. Ninian's—*oh. It's* that *serious.* Jeremy snaps back into focus, and latches onto the last word he remembers hearing: "Magic, you say?"

He's expecting bashful backsliding or at least a semblance of professional embarrassment, but Dr. Moore's expression hardens unexpectedly. She raises her hand above the desk. "Yes, sir. We anticipated this reaction: however, you are aware of the recent appearance of superpowers. I assure you that the two phenomena are connected. Allow me to demonstrate." She makes a very strange gesture, fingers twisting as if double-jointed, and quietly adds: "به نام پروردگار جهنم هفتم . . ."*

Jeremy misses the rest of the sentence because he's mesmerized by the green glow between Dr. Moore's fingers, and the way her hair writhes as if she's holding onto a Van de Graaff generator. "Very

---

* In the name of the Lord of the seventh hell . . .

pretty," he says dismissively, "but I can't go on *Newsnight* and do that, can I? And you still haven't explained what this has to do with the Yorkshire clusterfuck. Get to the point. What's *going on*?"

Dr. Moore's eyes blaze for a moment, as if she's about to mouth off—but then she bites back on whatever she was about to say and lowers her hand to the table. "Sir. Seventy-two hours ago our threat analysis division issued a storm warning—high probability of a high-powered incursion. These warnings are like earthquake warnings, rarely accurate and usually erring on the side of alarmism. But this time it appears to have been fully justified, and as of seven hours ago we became aware of what appears to be a level one incursion in progress—that is, an invasion by a Power from outside our universe. In response we immediately began mobilizing resources to contain the major incident, and the armed forces are responding in accordance with our prearranged contingency plans for a surprise attack on the nation." She looks pointedly at the Cabinet Secretary, who in turn is looking everywhere except at her: "I believe the MOD can give you more details of the conventional forces response posture and time to engagement, but the situation in Leeds is evolving rapidly—"

Jeremy dismisses her from his attention. "That's enough, now. Adrian, speak to me. Do we have any idea who is to blame for this? And is there a timetable for breaking this before the news cycle rolls in? What about social media?"

Adrian draws breath: "I took the liberty of announcing a 1 p.m. conference. That will kick the ball back just far enough to keep it out of the lunchtime programming, and with some careful spin we can ensure the newspapers don't get hold of the details before they have to go to press—"

The HomeSec looks up from her doodle. "Blame a supervillain," she says coldly. "That should plausibly muddy the waters. Start a bunch of rumors on Twitter, all of them obviously silly; it'll make it easier to control the direction once we provide a plausible narrative. If you like I can have my office put out a statement attributing it to asylum seeking supers from Syria, supporting the preferred immigration line. It'll take at least two cycles for the press to work out that it's a red herring and by then we can have a new story waiting in the wings."

Irving cracks: he raises his tumbler and chugs the contents convulsively, Adam's apple bobbing. Then he slams it down on the table. "You don't close motorways to make way for tanks just for a run-of-the-mill mad scientist!"

"But they won't know about that until later if we hit them with a DA-notice covering all military movements," Jeremy points out smugly. "It'll leak, but this will all be over by tomorrow, won't it?" he adds, trying to raise the morale of the various civil service nebbishes who don't rate a real seat at the table. He nods at Irving: "I want a full report on this Q-Division as soon as the dust settles. Obviously *someone* took their eye off the ball," he adds. "There will be a reckoning, I assure you. But not until the enemy at Broadcasting House lose interest. Smoke and mirrors, people, smoke and mirrors: we can't show them weakness." He leans forward. "Now, ah, General Stewart, can *you* tell me what's happening on the ground and in the air? Without any of this nonsense about magic."

18: SCORPION STARE

Alex has done some stupid things in his time, but following a self-confessed renegade from a culture of psychopaths into an armed camp full of dragons and battle magi is near the top of his list, second only to accepting a job developing new algorithms for an investment bank's high-frequency trading arm. (And look how well *that* turned out.) On the other hand: he has a working phone, a damsel in distress who needs rescuing, and he's doing it of his own free will. That's got to count for something, hasn't it?

One moment he's facing a swirling blue vortex of light. The next, he's stepping onto an uneven hard surface—stone, he thinks, but worn and natural rather than poured concrete—in darkness that smells of night and grass, with an edge of burning iron and sulfur that sets his nose on edge. Blood, too, fresh human blood has been spilled here recently. He salivates and his teeth throb in his gums as Cassie squeezes his fingers one last time, and lets go.

Figures step out of the darkness with raised maces. She answers in the grating, inhuman phonemes of an alien language, the *alfär* High Tongue: *"Halt! I come by order of All-Highest of this Host. I am Agent First of Spies and Liars and this one is mine."*

Alex forces himself to stillness. Her speech is hard to understand, the phrasing weirdly stilted and the accent abominable—but it's close enough to Old Enochian that he recognizes roughly two words in three. The four sentries, armed and armored like the two at the bunker, close in. One of them touches the tip of a mace to his back lightly: not pushing, just making its presence felt, as if it's a gun. He keeps his face motionless, suddenly grateful that he lacks the long and expressive ears of these people.

"*Welcome and hail, Agent First of Spies and Liars.*" A woman speaks, her hooded silhouette just visible against the shadows and starlight in front. There's some sort of rocky outcrop overhead, although open ground is visible beyond the greeter. "*Is your vassal entirely controlled? I smell the power of the magi—*"

"*He's entirely mine to control,*" Cassie replies sharply. "*A magus of the urük, bound and brought hither in accordance with the will of All-Highest.*"

She's not lying, Alex realizes, bewitched by the change in her speech and poise in this place. Cassie's posture is abruptly assertive and overbearing, her voice sharp, bearing an acrid tang of authority. She's very good at misdirection, he thinks proudly. The Civil Service has a term for this art: being economical with the truth. He begins to dare to hope.

His back pocket vibrates silently, as his emailed report departs on a pulse of radio waves. And now he is on a countdown. Assuming Lockhart agrees to his suggestion, assuming the clock in his phone hasn't gone too far adrift while they walked the dream road together, they have a handful of hours to make this work. And then there are the unspoken *ifs* it depends on. *If* Cassie keeps her side of their implicit agreement, the part she hinted at, unable even to speak it aloud (for treason never prospers among the People). *If* he can play his part. If either of them fails, they're probably both dead, or worse than dead, but at least Lockhart will know what's going on now, and can set events in train—

"*Hey, urük! Worthless human! You obey me, don't you?*" Cassie's words come as a shock but not a surprise. Alex nods slowly, trying to act dumb, then remembers: the People aren't familiar with the body language of other hominin subspecies.

"*I hear and, and obey, High Lady,*" he says haltingly in Enochian, not bothering to match her accent. (Best to sound barbarous: that's the next thing to stupid in a bigot's mind.)

"*Witness and observe! It is domesticated and obedient! It even talks! Hasten now and bring word to All-Highest that I come to report, as ordered!"* Cassie's whiplash expectation of obedience is unmistakable, part of her strident new personality.

"Yes, my lady. You: go." The woman who stands before them waves one of the guards off. She spins and runs away into the darkness, her armor (Alex is guessing here) muted, as if the sounds of metal surfaces clattering are muffled by distance. *"I celebrate your success. Please command your vassal to follow me: I will pen it with the—"*

"No." Cassie crooks her finger at Alex and he steps closer to her, slowly. The guard behind him follows, *mana*-saturated mace pushing at the small of his back. *"He is mine and I will not surrender him until I have presented him to All-Highest as commanded."* She bares her teeth in an expression that is anything but friendly: *"Lest happenstance deprive me of the evidence of the success of my mission."*

Alex is missing some of the nuances here, for the speech of the People is not only oddly accented but flowery and full of words that strain the limits of his vocabulary—the Laundry's analysts use Enochian as a tool, not an everyday tongue. But what he gets right now is the hissing disputation of two cats arguing over the fate of a captured mouse. He shudders and mentally rehearses the activation commands for two or three macros—brief memorized command sequences he can trigger at will if everything is about to go to hell.

"So Agent First has bound her first magus?" the woman says lightly. *"How novel!"* She has a tinkling chuckle. *"It's almost as if you're taking after your father at last!"*

"Are we waiting here forever?" Cassie demands.

The woman seems to come to a decision: *"No, follow me. Guards, attend."* She turns and strides into the night, Cassie following, Alex and his escort at the rear.

As they leave the shelter of the overhang Alex notices another group of armored figures heading towards the dream road at a jog: again, their armor is curiously muffled. They seem to coordinate without speech, he realizes, as if they've got radio headsets—or feel the invisible mental tugging of an intricate web of *geases* that prod them whenever they're needed. He feels acutely aware of his own ignorance, of the dangers it exposes him to: Who are they following? Cassie seems to know their greeter, and vice versa, but—

They're walking across the stone-strewn floor of a valley beneath a cliff that hangs above them like a frozen waterfall. The moon has set but the constellations are familiar. With merely human eyes Alex would be blind, but he can see well enough by starlight to know he's been here before. This particular valley is familiar from a long-ago school trip. Malham Cove is a unique rock formation, popular with generations of Yorkshire geography teachers seeking an educational day of hiking for their classes. The ground is strewn with treacherous velvet shadows, some of which move if he stares at them too hard. Then some of the shadows shimmer and pull apart, leaving them walking along an aisle between rows of tents made of something like ripstop nylon—*silk?* he wonders, then: *Don't be stupid.* There are more sentries, and there seems to be some silent recognition in play, some minutiae of gesture or microexpression opaque to him that nevertheless distinguishes friend from foe. Abruptly, they come to the entrance to one of the big pavilions, and this time there is light from a chilly sphere hanging from the central tentpole.

There's some sort of ground-sheet beneath their feet. A row of field tables stand against one wall and a map hangs like a tapestry behind them. At least, Alex assumes they're tables and a map. The tables are impossible, feathery metallic structures like cobwebs blown by a gallium-spinning spider. And the map seems to be made of parchment or hide of some kind, crudely stitched—but it shows a view which might as well be projected from Google Earth, in 3D. Colored triangles crawl across it, accompanied by strange ideograms similar to those he saw inscribed around the grid in the bunker. Two vampires— *no, magi,* he remembers—stand before the map. They wear plain-looking robes and cowls, and are by no means the most eye-catching individuals in the room: he wouldn't know what they were but for the chilly blast of power that rolls off them in waves, summoning a matching echo in his blood. They focus on the markers, and where they watch, the map springs into tighter focus. A column of red and yellow polygons floods through an eczematous patch of tiled roofs, spilling ever closer to the huge blotch at the right-hand side of the map. It can only be a city, he thinks, sickly conscious that he may be too late to help.

"*Ah, First of Spies! And what is this toy you have brought us?*"

A tall man wearing gothic, fluted armor plate that shimmers oddly in the were-light steps close to Cassie and her guide, smiling without showing his teeth.

"*Second of Field Artificers, this is the urük magus All-Highest bid me bring hither. He belongs to me. You may not have him.*"

Alex blinks, dull-eyed, and does his best to resemble a turtle. Second of Field Artificers is the first male of the People he's had a chance to get a close look at, and the sense of dread that already has his stomach in knots tightens further. They're not terribly tall, these *alfär*, and they are fine-boned. Only the incredibly prehensile ears mark them out as non-human. But something in Second of Field's expression frightens Alex almost as much as his one brush with a vampire elder, most of a year ago. There's a coldly reptilian lack of affect to the man. "*Too bad. My magi are tired and food is scarce. If he's bound I could use him.*"

"*Not until All-Highest has made his determination,*" says Cassie. "*My father would not have called for such a prize without a use in mind for it.*"

Alex tenses. Cassie and the Second of Field Artificers have shown no sign of noticing the woman who led them here leave. He's fairly sure she's some sort of officer, perhaps in charge of the guard detachment for this camp. Now there are only two sentries, although the one with the mace shows no sign of growing tired of holding it to the small of his back.

"*All-Highest is on his way,*" Second of Field Artificers says with assurance; "*I believe he has some business to attend to with Air Defense. In the meantime, put your plaything over there, away from my magi.*" Cassie waves Alex towards the farthest corner of the tent. "*Secure him, then come with me,*" adds the officer, and before Alex can move his escort takes a step backward and throws a handful of white powder in front of his feet.

Shit. Salt. Alex can feel his V-symbionts' anxiety as they demand to know how much, how many grains—then the sentry completes the job, upending a small pouch of salt in a circle around Alex's feet. Cold sweat prickles on his forehead and he's about to recite the word that starts the counter macro when he glances at Cassie. She minutely shakes her head. Ears motionless, she turns her back on him. Of course: body language among the *alfär* doesn't encompass such gross neck-twisting gestures. So it's a sign for him alone. He lets the circle of salt drag his eyes back down. Obviously it's too early to act. He's got to wait for the All-Highest to arrive first, to fill in the plan he and Cassie have danced around the edges of. To send the next queued message prematurely would be suicide.

Alex begins to count.

Leeds city center at half past five on a Sunday morning is about as desolate as it ever gets, night clubs long since closed and revelers snoring off their hangovers in their hotel rooms. There is some traffic, but word's gotten around from the police to the council cleaning trucks: stay the hell out of town, there's trouble on the wind. Pete turns his head to stare up York Street. Red, white, and blue lights are strobing in the near distance. As promised, the police are blocking all roads leading to Quarry House. They can't stop the incursion, but they can try to prevent oblivious civilians from driving into a firefight.

Although Leeds grew as a city during the nineteenth century, its streets can hardly be described as a grid layout—unless the grid was designed by a species of alien space squid who hadn't discovered Euclidean geometry. It was bombed by the Luftwaffe in the 1940s and subsequent attempts to rebuild it by pouring concrete and adding loops of motorway around the bomb sites didn't help. In an attempt to make the traffic flow, early in the twenty-first century the planners designated a bunch of city center streets as the Inner Loop around the pedestrianized zone, and configured them for one-way traffic, much like a white-line-enhanced circle of Dante's inferno. By day the three-kilometer stretch is full of passive-aggressive taxis and minicabs, but right now it's nearly empty—which is just as well.

Pete guns Ilsa across the intersection with The Headrow, towards the side of the Town Hall and the General Infirmary (beyond which he plans to fork off in the direction of Headingley) as his earpiece coughs. "Yes?"

"Dr. Russell? Lockhart here. How much fuel do you have?"

"Wait one." Pete has to crane his head forward to see the instruments. The petrol gauge on the antique half-track is more about wishful thinking than measurement. "I'm about three-quarters full. Why?"

"Change of plan, you may want to pull over."

"Hello?" For the first time, Pinky speaks up. Pete startles, but keeps control of the vehicle as he brakes and pulls in alongside the original frontage of Leeds General Infirmary.

"What's up?" Pete asks.

"We just got a fix on Alex's phone." Lockhart is worried. "Instead of Headingley he's in the middle of the Yorkshire Dales, about seventy kilometers northwest. He's definitely in contact, so instead of heading for the bunker we need you to get on the A65 out to Rawdon, then head for his current coordinates. You *do* have satnav, yes?"

"I think so." Pete raises his helmet visor and hunts around the dash. "Hey, Pinky—"

"I've got GPS on my watch, I'll give you turn-by-turn directions. If someone tells *me* where to go." Pinky sounds grumpy.

"You're not to use satnav!" Lockhart snaps. "You will follow the route as directed from this office. Which will be plotted to avoid contact with enemy outriders," he adds, slightly less oppressively. "We are losing camera coverage on the highways north and west, and that's where the incident reports are clustering. You don't want to go that way."

"Understood—" Pinky sounds a whole lot less grumpy all of a sudden.

"Is Alex all right?" Pete asks.

"He's texting and emailing updates, so for the time being we presume so, yes." Pete's stomach lurches. *Texting us updates* can cover a multitude of sins, including *captured by enemy* and *held at gunpoint*. "We want you to be prepared to extract or support him if necessary."

"Okay. Where are we going?" Pinky asks. Lockhart tells him, and

Pinky starts swearing. "It'll take us *hours* to get there and back again!"

Lockhart is unsympathetic: "There are reports of dragons: all flights are grounded. He's depending on you."

"Okay, we're on our way," says Pete. He's unsure whether to feel relieved (they're heading away from the onrushing incursion, taking a route that will give it a wide berth) or apprehensive about what they'll find at the far end.

"Drive on," Pinky tells him. "Then at the end of the street, hang a left and keep going up the Burley Road for as many miles as it takes." Pete lowers his visor and puts Ilsa back in gear again, then moves off with a grating and rumbling of tracks and chain mail.

Daylight finds a pall of smoke rising from burning buildings and crashed cars as the Host rumbles through the northwest suburbs of Leeds at a trot, the sun glinting off the heads of their lowered lances.

Entering an enemy's capital is one of the most dangerous tasks any land army can undertake. First there is the siege and the breaching of walls, tangible and otherwise. Then there is the grim prospect of advancing in the face of ambush at every corner, hostile warriors who know the ground intimately using each building for cover, of enemy magi dug in behind enchanted fortifications nullifying one's death spells and casting curses and glamours of their own—and that is before the final approach across the death ground surrounding the enemy sorcerer's keep, guarded by demons and the reanimated corpses of all those who have died earlier in the conflict, beneath skies patrolled by dragons and under the purview of basilisks, subject to attack by monstrous summonings. Normally it's a job for infantry with heavy support; cavalry have no place in such an assault, losing the advantage of maneuver that makes them so valuable on open ground.

But the Host's entry into the *urük* capital is not like that at all.

The *urük* are lazy and incompetent defenders, unable to contain the sprawl of their serfs' hovels within decent walls. Their roads meander across hill and dale without checkpoints or wards of any kind, much less stone ramparts sanctified with the blood of human sacrifices. While they are profligate with bottled lightning and eyeballs on sticks they seem to have very little idea of security, unless it is their way to build such ugly, sprawling, chaotic hives of laborers that intruders can't find their way through to the overseers.

Sixth of Second Battalion rides at the head of her fourth squadron, beside the standard. Two of the battalion's countermeasure magi and the unblind horrors they control follow close behind. In compliance with All-Highest's wishes, the First and Second Battalions have split up into four columns, running parallel across a front roughly half a kilometer wide. She rides with one of the inner columns, which keep to the broad *urük* highway they followed as far as the fringe of the city. The other three columns ride along backstreets and crash through fences and hedges between curiously pointless yards planted with animal fodder. They make no effort to remain unseen, but rely on their visual countermeasures. The *urük* seem to have no idea about prostrating themselves or avoiding the attention of their betters, and so the front of the column is marked by a chaotic shattering of windows and burning doorways as the savages gaze upon their new masters and spontaneously combust. They die in the hundreds, and the stench of roast flesh and burning wood rises up on every side, and *still* there is no sign of organized resistance. It's almost, Sixth of Second thinks queasily, as if they don't understand the concept of combined arms warfare.

The cavalry advances for an hour through endless masses of near-identical houses and drab store buildings, finally pausing beside the fount of *mana* spiraling out from the ley line anchor towards which they have been riding. Here, as their storage cells refill, the scouts report another large road ahead. And this is where they meet the first organized resistance.

This road is wide—by the markings the *urük* paint along such tracks, it seems to be built to accommodate six carts side by side—and there is an embankment planted with grass and trees to either side. According to the maps supplied by Airborne, this road circles the *urük* stronghold. It's the perfect place for an outer city wall: either one built of stone and patrolled by a garrison, or a shrike-fence of impaled living dead. But there is no wall. Nor are there any random *urük*-carts beetling along until their drivers see their death rise before them and expire. Instead, the way is blocked by a row of white-painted carts with flashing lights atop their lids, spanning the circular plaza where the two main roads meet. (This plaza contains only a circular bed of vegetation. It lacks a guard tower, gibbet, or crucifix-ion tree, or any other symbol of authority to remind the serfs who they belong to.)

Sixth orders a pause as the circle comes into view between the trees lining the boulevard leading into the city. "*Scout troop, clear the approach to that plaza. Second magus, provide cover.*"

The file of cavalry pounds forward, maces raised to scour the trees and buildings set back to either side of the road. Roofs shatter and crack, and trees go up like flares. But there is no more resistance than they have encountered so far, until the first four riders approach to within two hundred meters of the plaza. Then slingshots crackle into life, deafeningly loud and with a ridiculous tempo of fire: their wield-ers must be magically enhanced. Then a much louder roar heralds the arrival of some sort of crew-served projectile weapon. It lances to-wards the riders on a plume of flame and explodes.

Sixth of Second feels the sudden knife-sharp absence of two of her soldiers and the dulled-but-informative excruciation of two more as steel-jacketed pellets smash through armor and split skulls. "*Second Lance, wheel and flank left. Fourth Lance, flank right. First and Third, forward under cover. Fire at will.*"

There is a staccato banging as of giant slave lashes, then the flare and rumble of *urük*-carts torching off, the rock oil they carry in tanks boiling and exploding as the *mana*-charged impulse of a dozen cav-alry maces slam into them. There are screams, abruptly punctuated by the pop of deflagrating skulls. Sixth receives the all-clear from the lance leaders and approaches the roadblock. The wreckage of eight or nine white-and-red carts lies crumpled and burning, scattered across the intersection. Two more carts, these ones much larger and painted green, lie on their sides. The smoking corpses of the *urük* are sprawled behind these futile barricades, some of them in blue/black uniforms, others in the colors of dappled dirt. Charred, twisted limbs grasp strange angular contraptions: these must be *urük* bolt-throwers. "*Troop leaders, report,*" Sixth calls.

"*Scout: two dead, two down but serviceable. Bullet wounds—they're using steel.*"

Sixth twitches irritably. Iron is the oldest countermeasure; slaves are crucified merely for touching implements made of the metal. Bolt-throwers that can punch through armor at close range could be deadly, if the enemy has anything resembling defensive wards. The rocket weapon in contrast looks nasty but is ineffective against warded armor. To all appearances, the enemy have no battle magic whatsoever. Sixth begins to wonder if perhaps All-Highest's plan for the Host's diversionary advance might be excessively cautious, rather than the last-ditch gamble she believed they were engaged in. "*Magi first through fourth, chameleon cover. Magi five through eight, melt any eyes that see.*"

Magus sixth: "*What about the electric orbs?*"

Sixth: "*Those too.*" She waves at her adjutant, who raises the staff. The cavalry company forms up around her and the march resumes, crossing the Leeds ring road and the flaming wreckage of three police Armed Response Units and a platoon of Territorial Army soldiers. Smoke rises on the morning breeze as the Host burns a clear-cut half a kilometer wide on either side of their advance, firing a path through the thickening suburbs as they advance towards the witch queen's palace at the center of the *urük*-hive, now barely seven kilometers away.

Shortly after the Sixth Battalion crosses the ring road, decisions are made in the Quarry House control room that will subsequently be found wanting.

Gerald Lockhart, SSO8(L), Colonel (retired), Bronze Team Incident Controller (Headquarters North), has been on duty since 9 p.m. on Saturday night, after putting in a full day's work on other affairs during the preceding day. He was called in by the DM, in response to an urgent update on the previous week's assessment by Forecasting Operations. And he was OIC when the office received a notification of a Code Red incursion from trainee operations officer Alex Schwartz—me—shortly after midnight.

Over the following eight hours he coordinated with the West Yorkshire Metropolitan Police gold commander at Elland Road, the OCCULUS incident crew operating out of Wakefield, and the operations room established at Army GHQ in Andover. He has also briefed the Assistant Director of Operations at the New Annex in London, and (most recently) a very perturbed assistant to the Chief Secretary to the Cabinet Office in Whitehall. By dawn on Sunday he had been awake for over thirty hours, tracking a crisis of ever-expanding but indeterminate scope. A large body of operational research demonstrates that human beings suffer disproportionately from fatigue-induced errors of judgment after twelve hours of concentration at work; while Gerald Lockhart had long experience of pushing himself under crisis conditions, he was about to make a fatal mistake.

The garbled reports coming in to the incident room outlined a cone of silence approaching the city from the northwest. Outside the cone everything appeared normal, but within it, queries were not responded to in a timely manner, or at all. The Police gradually became less communicative and helpful as their assets were increasingly committed and their situational awareness degraded. Their emergency response telephone centers were overwhelmed by reports of road traffic accidents, house fires, and missing persons. The police helicopter was grounded, crew flying hours exceeded and an urgent maintenance interval overrun—it had been quartering the skies for hours, from one messy single-vehicle FATACC to another all night long, and the helicopter unit's ground controller reluctantly took the decision to withdraw it for urgent maintenance. Requests were submitted for helicopter support from other regions, but more aircraft would not arrive before mid-morning. At six thirty, purely on the basis of the spike in accidents, the police commander on duty put the major incident plan into operation, alerting regional hospitals and calling up off-duty personnel: but the expected influx of injuries hadn't materialized.

There were no survivors, and a steady trickle of police officers were going ominously dark, not answering their Airwave radios or mobile phones. Then news of the airliner accident near Otley arrived.

Lockhart and his ad-hoc team were confronted with a terrible dilemma. Forecasting Ops specified some sort of incursion targeting HQ North. Dr. Schwartz had gone missing after reporting an incursion out past the ring road. Lockhart had already mobilized all available personnel in Leeds, opened up the arsenal in the archive stacks of the Royal Armouries museum, and sent bodies to lock down the approaches to the office complex. Requests to the Police to send additional forces had been ignored: the Leeds Met were overstretched and all their civil emergency plans assumed that support would arrive from the Ministry of Defense, not flow in the opposite direction. However, an embryonic defensive plan was taking shape.

If Quarry House was really the target of whatever was coming, then Lockhart had a duty to defend the site. But with inadequate trained personnel on hand to mount a conventional defense of the site, Lockhart would have to activate the area defenses. Meanwhile, the Airwave receiver in the corner of the ops room was telling a terrifying story of escalation as successive police and emergency responders survived long enough to broadcast garbled partial reports.

At half past nine in the morning, Lockhart picked up the phone to the Regional Camera Control Center attached to the Police HQ at Elland Road. "This is Quarry House incident commander. I'm calling for MAGINOT BLUE STARS at this time." There was an exchange of authorizations, very formal: Lockhart (normally imperturbable) was seen to wipe his forehead with a tissue as he waited for acknowledgment. "Yes. Lima Sierra One to MAGINOT BLUE STARS, autonomous response at this time. Good. Activate it now." He puts the phone down and glances at Jez Wilson, who's watching: "So that's done."

MAGINOT BLUE STARS is the Q-Division-approved software that co-opts many of the roadside and urban infrastructure cameras in British cities, building an ad-hoc Basilisk network. Developed specifically to deal with outbreaks of eaters in built-up areas, the SCORPION STARE network performs realtime target recognition and transmutation. It is best deployed when the civilian population it is intended to protect are locked down in their homes, under curfew, and only alien monsters roam the streets.

Nine thirty on a Sunday morning in a city center is a good approximation for a lockdown situation. However, Colonel Lockhart had not performed a full risk assessment for the Inner Loop.

Mea culpa: this is partly my fault. Lockhart had just received my email explaining in detail the arrangement I have come to with Cassie, and my proposed course of action. Approving it is above his pay grade (not to mention mine): he forwards it to the Gold Committee at the New Annex for consideration. He also cced it to the officer commanding OCCULUS Two, still somewhere on the M1 south of Sheffield, on the sensible working assumption that he should be ready to act should the Gold Committee (representing the Auditors, Operational Oversight, and Mahogany Row) approve my request. For their part, the Gold Committee would eventually escalate the issue to the Cabinet Office, where it would be delayed, finally bubbling to the top of the agenda of the COBRA meeting at four o'clock in the afternoon.

(It's reasonable to assume that my report was a major distraction, and contributed significantly to his information overload.)

As part of the Leeds Regeneration Scheme, a number of high-density luxury apartment buildings had been built alongside the river over the past twenty years. There were also a number of budget hotels within a short distance of Leeds Railway Station. The student apartments on the north side of the city center were, thankfully, just outside the Inner Loop Lockdown Zone that Lockhart has requested, but the city center was not largely uninhabited early on a Sunday morning, contrary to Lockhart's expectation.

That in itself was not a critical error. SCORPION STARE uses a sophisticated neural network recognizer to identify and target proximate threats. Citizens unwittingly venturing out of their homes during curfew *should* be reasonably safe from the targeting algorithm—at least, reasonably safe compared to venturing outside in a city under siege by conventional forces, with rooftop snipers and random mortar fire to contend with.

But Lockhart failed to take account of a second factor: the Animation Festival and Anime Convention taking place on the Wharf, a couple of blocks from the Royal Armouries. Nine thirty was still early, but hundreds of convention-goers were even then eating breakfast in the Ibis and Radisson hotels nearby, and within half an hour hundreds of them would begin to converge on foot with the Riverside Plaza and the Exhibition Centre. This was the largest Anime Convention yet held as part of the annual Leeds International Animation Festival, and many cosplaying fans were present in character as their favorite heroes and heroines of superhero and fantasy fiction.

Pointy ears make the SCORPION STARE cameras track and focus intently. And the network responds to remote events: positive contacts nearby raise the weighting function by which a given node determines the probability that a target of interest may be another positive hit. As cameras in Headingley and out along Woodhouse Lane and the Armley Road repeatedly fail to lock onto elements of the Host (not to mention going up in puffs of smoke), the command and control system responds to defeat by lowering the recognition threshold. This is not a bug in the software, but an emergent hysteresis loop arising from the system repeatedly failing to recognize hostiles while under attack. While undergoing field tests in Whitby it persistently acquired a target lock on a certain Bride of Dracula, but as no targets were believed to be in the area this was discounted as a false positive, and the neural network was reweighted accordingly.

The SCORPION STARE system is adaptive by design. Unfortunately it was initialized with a set of training data that is lethally corrupted, reducing its ability to discriminate friend from foe. And it's about to go all Skynet in the middle of Leeds.

Third Wing of Airborne Strike has been having a frustrating morning.

She has been airborne over *Urükheim* for almost an hour on a sortie that commenced shortly after dawn. Initial reports were promising. Air Defense have confirmed that the *urük* sky-carts are unarmored and unprotected against the basilisk's death-stare. As her and her wingman's steeds climbed and turned east, putting the rising sun in her eyes, she saw the rising plume of smoke from the pyre of an unwary enemy flyer in the distance. The heavy brigade's path across the landscape is visible as a slashing line of trampled vegetation and burning buildings; where it travels along *urük* pavements her mount's sharp-eyed vision discerns wrecked carts by the dozen. There's nothing to do here; it will take her over half an hour to catch up with the Host, whose progress has been faster than anticipated.

But as Third Wing and Sixth Wing climb she feels a sharp stab of pain at her temples, and gasps. Images slam into her human mind: the dying vision of another rider. Alien daggercraft, giant arrowheads in shape, lance through the skies above *Urükheim* at impossible speed, throwing firebolts tipped with explosives at dragons. They're totally defenseless but terribly fast and they have fangs of their own, as Fourth Wing found out the hard way. Third Wing swears a horrible oath in the privacy of her own skull, then will-speaks her back-seater and the crew of her companion beast: *"Did you see that?"* she demands. *"Eyes open, eyes open, stay low."*

The two firewyrms descend, now skimming above the endless ribbon-curling roads of the *urük* countryside, barely higher than the curious poles festooned with ropes or cables that march alongside them.

"I see no daggers," says Sixth. *"How about our top cover?"*

"Too far to the rear once we close on target." Basilisks are a line-of-sight air defense weapon, and now Third Wing is swearing with even more reason: they are cumbersome and slow to move, and the sky above the enemy palace is beyond their extreme range. Wings Three and Six will be on their own if they encounter more daggercraft, and they're flying straight into the rising sun. It's not a good place to be, and Third spends the next half hour with a cold tension-sweat of focus trickling down her spine as the dragons race to catch up with the ground force ahead, whose mobile screen may yet afford them some degree of protection.

They are close to their goal when a new hail comes in: *"Salutations! Our forward columns have engaged enemy irregulars near a major road junction on the edge of the urük hive. We are taking light fire from elements arriving from the east. Our flank needs cover: Can you backtrack to their origin and stop them?"*

This is the sort of close support mission that Third Wing relishes, and she bares her teeth happily as she signals her assent. To Sixth Wing and their respective magi, she commands: *"Follow me!"* Then she turns due east, cutting across country towards a large turnpike she glimpsed in the distance before descending to treetop height.

Third Wing intends to circle around and come in from the north-west at low altitude, taking the *urük* resistance on the circular highway from behind and subjecting them to a gentle drizzle of wyrmspit and a brisk volley of death spells. Their reported lack of defenses works in her favor, and she'll be coming at them out of the sun: they'll die before they get an opportunity to aim their bolt-throwers at her receding tail.

What Third Wing has no way of knowing is that the distant highway she is approaching from the west as a waypoint for her approach is the A1(M): specifically the segment of that motorway between Wetherby and Leeds currently occupied by Lieutenant Cook's southbound Sabre squadron with its light tanks, armored cars, and Starstreak laser-guided air defense missiles.

Lieutenant Cook has just received the first threat warning over the air and announced, "Eyes up, we have airborne incoming!" when Third Wing soars over the treeline to the west of the motorway.

To human eyes, a firewyrm of the Host in full battle trim is immediately identifiable as a monstrous threat. If you can see it at all without throwing up or going blind, what you perceive is a rippling knot of curved air wrapped around a barrel-shaped horror with webbed wings articulated on a bony skeleton quite unlike a bat or pterosaur. An eyeless, tentacle-rimmed circular maw breathes straw-colored fumes (and if you are close enough to see *that*, your eyes will soon start to cloud over with chemical burns). Carbuncular metal capsules with mirrored portholes are strung along its spine and dangle to either flank. Its legs are vestigial, little more than paddles to assist its crawl across the purulent swamps of its homeworld. It's as unearthly as a nightmare out of an *Alien* franchise movie, and just as shocking to the eye.

A third of Cook's troops are looking in roughly the right direction when Third Wing comes into view. Of these, roughly half actually see what's in front of their eyes: the wyrm's anti-observation countermeasures are compromised by encountering such a dense clump of observers from a single direction. Gasps and involuntary screams instantly reduce the voice-cued radio channel to a sea of noise. Cook himself sees the outline of his own death bleeding through the sudden migrainaceous visual disturbance—and he's never had a migraine in his life—like something out of a florid fever-dream. He freezes for a second, then keys the override on the local voice channel: "Shoot! Shoot!"

Of the twenty-six men staring in the direction of the enemy, three faint, eleven are unable to process any visual information for the next five to fifteen minutes, six throw up, and two undergo immediate convulsions, in one case leading to a subarachnoid hemorrhage and death. The remaining five effectives hear Cook's order and light up the target. A second later the other effectives in the squadron recognize the threat and join in.

. . . Meanwhile, to the eyes of an *alfär* dragonrider, a Sabre squadron deploying in convoy along a motorway doesn't look much different from any other queue of *urük*-carts. So far, Third Wing has seen hundreds of the things, many of them crashed and broken at the side of roads. Perhaps if Third Wing was not approaching them from the west, squinting against the sun, Third Wing might have realized that a number of these carts are different—squat, windowless boxes of curiously uniform color, their wheels running on endless looped belts quite unlike any cart the wyrm crews have seen before. But tracked vehicles in general and tanks in particular are as alien to the Host's training as dragons are to a British Army armored cavalry unit's background. And even if Third Wing was in a position to identify the traffic ahead of her as hostile, she would be at a complete loss to spot the difference between a Scimitar light reconnaissance tank and the Stormer HVM at the back of the queue: a similar chassis capped by a battery of Starstreak laser-guided antiaircraft missiles instead of a turret-mounted cannon.

Two GPMGs and then a 30mm cannon roar to life almost simultaneously, elevating to track the dragon spiraling above the treetops. With less than two hundred meters' separation, Third Wing doesn't stand a chance: her eyes widen as the road in front of her flickers red and opens her mouth to cry out just as a burst of armor-piercing bullets rip through the canopy of her magi's palanquin. The sorcerer torches off immediately, burning like a magnesium flare; meanwhile, her mount gives voice to an ululating shriek of agony as it curls around its gut-shot abdomen and rolls into the coppice below, bleeding wyrmspit through wounds the size of fists.

When it hits the ground, it explodes.

Sixth Wing has barely any more warning. Flying in echelon three hundred meters behind Third Wing, he's shocked by the stab of pain from his flight-liege's mind. *"Contact ahead!"* he shouts at his magus, who is already releasing an angry hornet-swarm of death curses at the still-hidden enemy sheltering behind the trees. He desperately whips his mount into a writhing turn, begins to drop down to brush the treetops, and then he's out of time.

The HVM carrier's crew are both looking in the right direction when Lieutenant Cook's warning comes in, for their job is to provide close-range air cover for the convoy and the rumor of enemy airborne attackers have preceded the dragons. The commander is one of those incapacitated by first sight of Third Wing's monstrous steed, projectile vomiting around the interior of the fighting compartment. But his gunner is merely sickened, and he points his first missile straight at the middle of the whirlpool of nausea in the sky and hits the firing stud. There's no time to compute windage and no need for superelevation: he just aims the laser designator and fires.

Sixth Wing is barely five hundred meters away. That's just far enough for the missile's second stage to hit Mach 4 and burn out, then dispense the three laser-guided explosive darts it carries. Starstreak is a small missile, lacking the target identification and tracking features of the Typhoon's ASRAAM: this is a strength, not a weakness, when fighting the mind-warping magic of the *alfär*. Before the gunner has time to relax his trigger finger two of the darts punch into Sixth Wing's mount. And if the explosion of a dragon on ground impact was violent, the blast from the air burst sends trees flying like wooden shrapnel.

Meanwhile, half a dozen curses fizzle green and ground themselves out on the unfortunates trapped in the aluminum-hulled light tanks and their escort of armored cars. Sixth Wing's magus had no identification guide to the enemy, so his undirected spasm of fire lands at random. Where it strikes, men and women die. An escorting police car veers off the carriageway and crashes, the driver's headless torso still clutching the wheel. Two of the Panthers follow it, and a Scimitar suddenly skids and begins to turn in place on its tracks, a macabre fusillade of popcorn sounds reverberating from inside its hull as ammunition ignited by the burning corpses of its crew cooks off.

Lieutenant Cook draws a shuddering breath—trying not to throw up—and tenses. "What was *that*?" he demands, unable to bottle it in. He glances at Sergeant Magnusson, who is frozen in his seat, staring towards the fireballs rising behind the trees lining the motorway verge. He takes another breath, feeling the warmth on his cheeks. "Sitrep, Sergeant." Magnusson doesn't react. "*Sit—*"

As he pokes Magnusson's shoulder the sergeant slowly topples sideways.

"—rep." Jim stares for a moment. Then he keys his mike again. Unnaturally calm, he hears words coming from his mouth, as if from a distance: "Medic, Panther One, man down, man down. All vehicles, sitrep by numbers, report casualties . . ."

Nothing (8,224).
    Nothing (8,225).
    Nothi—
Alex has been alone in the circle of salt in the tent for ages. His knees are beginning to ache and he's shivering with tension and a creeping sense of dread. But he's got an ace up his sleeve. As soon as they left him alone he subvocalized a word of command and his counter macro was up and spinning in the edge of his vision. He keeps his gaze locked on the circle of salt, but its power to drag him in is broken. And so he is free to think.

He's had too long to come up with questions and not enough time to come up with answers to his liking. Questions like, *if they don't have a lock-up for prisoners, what does that say about how they look after them?* Or *how do I know she hasn't already been murdered by her stepmother?* And *why don't I send the first SMS alert now?*

To which final question he *does* have an answer. Some time ago he furtively glanced up to see if anyone was watching him, then palmed his phone and sent the text, then put the phone away and went back to counting. *HELD PRISONER NOT DEAD YET.* No: just biding his time and counting all the grains of salt in the world. *Nothing to see here, Nothing—*

His skin abruptly tries to crawl off his body as the tent flap opens, admitting a luminous flare of daylight. It stops short of his feet, and he shudders. It's a reminder that there's more than just a circle of salt to bind him here. He has a tube of thick latex-based face cream in his jacket pocket, but he's unsure whether as an englamoured prisoner he should possess enough agency to use it without instructions. Being burned by sunlight *might* be fatal: but revealing himself to be anything other than a helpless thrall would be an immediate death sentence, both for himself and for Cassie. So he tries not to show any sign of noticing the light of the daystar burning across the ground sheet close by his feet, glittering off the circle of white crystals.

A squad of soldiers enter the tent. The dull finish of their armor changes color as they come inside, darkening from patchwork green and brown camouflage to a flat slate gray; crystalline visors retract silently into metal helms as smoothly molded as any fighter pilot's. Some of them wear swords with curved blades, which Alex vaguely recognizes as resembling cavalry sabers. Most of them bear *mana* maces, and all of them have the characteristic fine bone structure and graceful movements of the People. For a moment Alex's perception of their attire oscillates rapidly from medieval knights to futuristic powered armor, then back again: *any sufficiently advanced magic is indistinguishable from technology,* he tells himself. Then he blinks as one of the six officers at the middle of the group—he's pretty sure they're officers, with an escort of guards—removes her helmet and shakes her sweat-dampened hair. The others follow suit, revealing a mix of men and women. Aside from the fine bone structure and elongated pinnae, they could be a bunch of cosplayers. But the staggeringly powerful sense of barely controlled violent magic surrounding them, the defensive wards inlaid like wiring diagrams from their greaves to their pauldrons, and the oxygen bottles slung over the officers' shoulders, make it clear what they are.

"This *is the prisoner?*" the woman asks contemptuously. Alex notices small details. The tension in her lips, the disturbing likeness of a dragon engraved on her helmet (if dragons had tentacles). "*It doesn't look like much.*"

Her adjutant reads glowing runes from the surface of a magic mirror. "*According to reports this one accounted for a pair of sentries, broke the containment ward on a peripheral site, and smashed six eaters with its bare hands.*"

"*Huh.*" Highest Liege narrows her eyes and stares speculatively at Alex. "*So appearances are deceptive as usual. Typical for this orderforsaken wilderness.*"

Alex has been stared at by predators before. A year ago he took tea with an elderly gentleman of saintly mien, inside a government warehouse full of the vampire elder's victims. And earlier, when he was a toddler, his parents once took him to visit a zoo: a tiger took exception to the babbling apes on the other side of the fence and loudly announced its desire to play with his bones. (He's been scared of cats ever since.) Something about the Liege of dragons reminds him of that tiger, young and febrile and full of rage against the universe that will not give her what she wants. If she had a tail it would be lashing restlessly from side to side. Alex tightens his mental grip on his macros but keeps his eyes on the salt. *Pretend to count.* He's ready to activate his defensive wards, but he can't do anything here. Not trapped by daylight in a tent with a tiger and her officers, in the middle of an enemy camp surrounded by soldiers armed with semiautomatic death spells.

"*My lady, All-Highest requires you at the staff briefing.*" This from the man with the magic mirror, which is now smoking slightly, as if dry ice is boiling from its surface.

"*Really?*" Her cheek quirks in something like a smile. "*Will the Liar be present?*"

"*A moment—yes, my lady.*"

"*Good.*" She addresses two of the guards, her voice modulating into the formal-imperative mode used for directing animals, zombies, and demons: "*You discovered a feral urük in the camp. Go: stand outside and see nothing until I call for you again.*"

The guards step outside. That leaves four guards and four officers—two of whom make Alex's skin crawl in a way he has learned to associate with the hostile gaze of other PHANGs. Out of the corner of his vision, he sees raised visors that reveal hairless faces, gender-indeterminate. He tenses, in the grip of a very uncomfortable premonition.

"*My lady?*" It's magic mirror man—the other non-PHANG, non-magi officer. He sounds wary.

"*The Chief Liar is under geasa to report to my husband and to bring him an urük magus,*" she points out. "*If she can't bring him an urük magus, tough. And she is currently too busy being debriefed by Second of Analysts to be bothered with trivial matters.*" A faint smile shows teeth: "*I believe your mount is scheduled for the next support mission. I will be outside while—*"

Alex clears his throat—there seems little to be gained by playing dumb at this point. "*Is this necessary?*" he asks, his diction halting, keeping his eyes focussed on the salt grains in front of his feet. The defensive ward is ready on his tongue, but to use it will precipitate the barely leashed violence he senses all around. And one against eight isn't just lousy odds, it's suicidal—especially when at least two of them are PHANGs.

"*It can speak!*" Highest Liege of Airborne Strike claps her hands together. Something like an expression of astonished delight spreads across her face. "*Marvelous!*" She steps close to Alex, staying outside the circle of salt, and inspects his face at close range. She has cat-breath: he forces himself not to recoil. "*I sense possibilities. Tell me, creature, did your captor take you by force? Did she bind you by your true name?*"

Alex begins to frame an answer, then remembers his supposed place: "*I*"—he peers at his feet—"*can't think—*"

Highest Liege gestures at her soldiers: *"You and you: hold this one. If it tries to escape, kill it. You, break the circle. I want to talk to it."*

Alex finds himself at the focus of two maces as a trooper bends down before him and scatters the white powder with a finger, opening a gap. The noise in his head subsides. *"What?"* he asks, shaking his head, feigning dizziness.

"You—prisoner." She jabs a finger at him. *"Do you want to slay the one who bound you and brought you here?"*

Alex nods, unable to believe his luck. *"Yes,"* he says. It's a lie, of course, but he is coming to understand that the People are catastrophically bad at detecting bare-faced lies, because lying to superiors is forbidden by the *geases* that bind them.

"Good." She claps her hands again. A speculative light comes into her eyes. *"If I can free you from her geas will you fight her for me?"*

What? Alex is gobsmacked by the offer. But there's no time to think: *"Of course,"* he says, trying hard to look as if he's struggling to overcome Agent First's nonexistent *geas, "but I can't fight her* now."

First Liege seems to believe him, for her tooth-baring smile broadens. *"I will give you the opportunity, and if you satisfy me I will allow you to swear to me as vassal instead. It is a position of privilege: you shall have the honor of being my First of Urük Slaves."* She taps him lightly on the forehead with her mace, sending a shock of power through him: *"By right of seniority, as Second-in-Line to All-Highest-Who-Holds-All-Bindings, I hereby release you from all obligations imposed by Third-in-Line to All-Highest. Now we will restore the circle and you will wait here until All-Highest and Third-in-Line, the First of Liars, arrive. Speak not of this conversation!"*

He's still shuddering with the reverberations of First Liege's resistible but painful compulsion when one of the troopers carefully pours more salt into the gap, closing the circle again. Then, five minutes later, the tent flap opens and he's out of time for thinking.

19: ASYLUM

A tall male, stockily built as the People go, his fluted armor so heavily inlaid with wards that it seems almost like a form-fitting circuit board, steps through the awning behind a pair of soldiers with drawn daggers and maces. Behind him follow four veiled and cowled magi, armor clicking under their daylight-proof robes, then a gaggle of adjutants and runners, all awaiting his command. His helmet is surmounted by a slim gold circlet, and the circlet in turn is set with a colorless stone. If it's a diamond, it's the size of the Koh-i-Noor. He turns eyes the pale blue of liquid oxygen on Alex, then glances at Highest Liege: *"Honorable Wife,"* he acknowledges as her staff go down on their knees around her in a muffled clatter of metal.

"Husband." This smile is toothless, the expression slightly surprised. *"I gather your daughter has returned?"*

"All may rise. Yes, she has." The tent awning opens again. Cassie enters between two guards. Alex can't help noticing that he and she are the only people present who aren't wearing full armor. Or armed to the teeth, for that matter. *"I am well satisfied with her accomplishments. Here is the living proof, is it not?"*

Cassie straightens up. She points at Alex: *"Father: as you commanded, I bring you the key to the enemy palace, bound by geas."*

Enochian tenses can be tricky, but Alex is paying attention: *bound* is ambiguous with respect to past and present. Another not-lie, another not-brick in the wall. He does his best to look sullen and frightened, steeling himself, and hoping that she knows what she's doing and that there's a way out of here that doesn't involve losing too much blood. He keeps his eyes on the ring of salt, wondering what Cassie's stepmother has in mind.

"*Agent First of Spies and Liars has indeed done very well for herself,*" Highest Liege says, her tone hesitantly approving. "*Perhaps too well.*"

Alex sees Cassie tense with the corner of one eye. "*What do you mean?*" she asks.

"*Let's see, shall we?*" Highest Liege addresses one of her bodyguards directly: "*It can't tell us anything while it's in that circle. Free it.*"

A gauntleted hand descends on Alex's shoulder and pushes him across the edge of the circle. He stumbles, reaching instinctively towards his phone pocket. "*Stop your hand!*" barks Highest Liege, and Alex realizes he can't feel his fingers: they're as numb as tent-pegs. A terror sweat floods the small of his back. Since his regular protective ward fried, he's been reliant on his phone with its OFCUT apps for protection to a far greater degree than is wise. But phone batteries die in the field (usually when you most need them) and a phone won't work as a phone *and* shield you from the raw power of an adept with an heir's access to the Morningstar Empire's most powerful binding.

Hours ago Alex made a judgment call to rely on his phone as a phone: it seemed like a good plan at the time. But now, with his hand numbed in obedience to the cold iron will that holds down the remnants of an occult empire that rose before the dawn of Rome, he's defenseless in the middle of a triangle of predators. The peril of his position finally sinks in.

Behind and to his right stands Cassie. With the true sight that his release from all her bindings and subtle snares gives him he can see her as she truly is—which is no surprise, for she revealed herself to him earlier: but it's still a shock to see her in company with her kind, for they are spread out across the opposite slope of the uncanny valley, and it has steep sides indeed. Some of them look almost normal, if etiolate otherkin wearing Spock-ears and steel armor can be described as normal. Cassie (in cloak and dagger drag) would be entirely unexceptional at any fancy dress party or convention masquerade. But her father and stepmother are something else. Seen through human eyes the People are subtly disquieting, inducing the quiet apprehension of sleek, well-fed carnivores contemplating their next meal. And that's before Alex looks at them with his inner eyes open.

Alex can *hear* the binding of the Morningstar Empire with the ears of his V-symbiont passengers, the chittering flock of febrile attention-points that clog up the back of his skull. They are perturbed. They leave his throat and sinuses feeling congested, as with incipient hay-fever or a clot-growing nosebleed, as they crowd forward in their eagerness to feel the strength of the massive *geas*. And *he* can see it too, with the spectral vision the symbionts lend him: a greenish aura that extends tendrils to every head in the pavilion, one vast, pulsing branch leading through a fabric wall, presumably leading in the direction of the All-Highest's army. It is centered on a fuzzy blob—the head of Cassie's father, who is a lean-faced older male version of his daughter's true form. Upon his brow the diamond brightens unbearably around a laser-stippled heart of light. His symbionts hunger for that light and fear it: it's food for their kind, but so intensely concentrated that it promises dissolution and disaster if they approach it, as moths to a blowtorch. It's all that remains of the willpower that sustained an empire, the last few drops of a mighty reservoir. Even so, it's pushing on him hard enough that his temples throb. That will be the force of Highest Liege's command, freeing him from obligations to Cassie—

(*Of course,* Alex realizes momentarily, *stepmom thinks Cassie bound me to both the imperial* geas *and to her own will, because that's what stepmom would do.* Whereas Cassie avoided binding Alex entirely, by asking him to accompany her willingly after dissolving her own earlier *geas.*)

Barely a second has elapsed. The phone in Alex's jacket pocket is buzzing like an angry swarm of bees: All-Highest is raising his hand. "*What is that?*" he demands.

"*It's a, a*"—there is no word for smartphone in Old Enochian—"*a far-speaker? An enchanted mirror—*"

Highest Liege glances sidelong at All-Highest, then at Cassie. "*Is this correct?*" (Not, Alex notes, *Is he telling the truth?*)

Cassie's ears lie flat in submission. "*I believe so. I have one, too: the urük use them freely.*"

Highest Liege snaps her fingers peremptorily: *"Show it to me,"* she demands. This is a breach of protocol but All-Highest permits it—either indulgently, or with a weather eye to the possibilities of subterfuge and assassination by his ambitious young spouse. Alex's fingers tingle painfully then are free to move again. He reaches into his pocket, pulls out the phone, and holds it towards her.

Highest Liege glares. *"What is this? I feel no mana."*

Cassie says tonelessly: *"Urük mechanisms do not use mana."*

All-Highest watches, face impassive, but Alex senses the blade of a guillotine rising inchwise towards the top of its guide rails.

"Make it work," says Highest Liege. Alex realizes the All-Highest's consort is pushing for something, but he's too rattled to be sure of exactly what. Waiting for him to scream and leap to bite out Cassie's throat? He looks at the phone, which buzzes in his grip like an angry hornet—the thaum field counter is still running—then swipes his passcode. *22% battery remaining.* Without hesitation or outward sign that this is anything but routine he taps into the messages app, retrieves the draft of the second text message, and hits SEND. A small indicator is visible at the top of the screen: *remote monitoring client active.* A dialog flashes up (*Allow access to location services, microphone?*) and he hits *yes* immediately. Then he taps the soft key for voice recognition.

"Dial Cassie," he says, very carefully trying not to think about what he's doing. About Lockhart and the ops room in Leeds, monitoring everything he says through the phone's microphone, tracking its location via GPS and internet. About the email he sent asking for what he gathers the Air Force calls a fire mission, zeroed in on the coordinates of his phone, wherever it happens to be at the time. About how likely he and Cassie are to be able to escape before—

The phone vibration intensifies briefly. *Incoming text.* He glances at the screen. It's from Pinky:

RESCUE ON THE WAY, RUN FOR ILSA WHEN YOU SEE US.

Cassie's phone begins to sing a song of sixpence, and she produces it from her belt pouch with a flourish, opens it up: "Hello?" she says, speaking English. Aside, to All-Highest, she observes: *"Urük mecha-nisms can only speak the urük tongues."* (Because of course that's how an *alfär* solution to the mobile phone problem would work, if they didn't already use direct brain-to-brain transmission of pain.)

"Lockhart needs to know that I am in a tent with the emperor commanding the invasion force. It's time for that drone strike. I'm going to make a run for it with Cassie a minute or two after we end this call."

"I hear you," Cassie replies, also in English. "Do you want me to keep faking commands or—"

"Enough," says All-Highest, and snaps his fingers. *"Can these con-trivances compel obedience or influence minds remotely?"*

"No," Cassie replies.

"Useless toys, then. Take them," All-Highest orders. To a guard: *"Secure the urük."*

Alex can't stop his arm extending. Highest Liege plucks his phone from his nerveless fingers, steel-sheathed fingertips scraping the screen. Cassie stares daggers at her stepmother, but hangs up and hands her phone over. Highest Liege gives All-Highest a look, then hands the clearly-not-cursed magic mirrors to one of All-Highest's bodyguards. Another guard pulls Alex back into the circle of salt and pushes his head down to stare at the scattered crystals, but not before Alex silently utters the command to restart his counter macro. He stares at his toes, feigning fascination while he eavesdrops.

All-Highest turns to his daughter. *"This urük magus. Can it get us inside the citadel?"*

"It works in the enemy citadel, Father: I met it outside the fastness but observed it entering and leaving freely."

"Good enough." The rumble of an adult male lion's voice, deep in his throat. A tonal shift follows, as All-Highest addresses another: *"Infantry Second, ready the strike column as ordered. Magus First, take your staff and join the column. Guards, attend me."*

Alex is weak-kneed from tension and blood-hunger: he itches to run, but forces himself to stillness and a semblance of passivity. *Not yet.* There is a muffled clatter of armor and the spider-legs-on-scalp crawling sensation of half a dozen magi and several officers leaving the tent, but he's still nowhere near alone—All-Highest goes nowhere without bodyguards, and the pricking in his thumbs (and the rattling buzz from his phone's thaum detector) tells him that some of them carry enchanted weapons of quite startling power.

"*Daughter.*" All-Highest's voice modulates again. Proud indulgence. "*You have exceeded my expectations of you, which were admittedly low. I thought you* weak: *I am no longer confident of this judgment. So there is that.*" Another tone shift, threatening: "*Honorable Wife. I was interested to hear of your special instructions to Agent Second of Spies and Liars.*" There is a muffled rattle throughout the tent, as of a dozen armored bodies shifting their balance in anticipation. "*I make no determination yet, but one of you may be weak, and one of you may be disloyal, and I am not sure which. It matters not: this urük will suffice to gain entry to the enemy's citadel, so I choose to indulge your mutual animosity.*"

"*Wait—*" First Liege pleads urgently, but All-Highest's voice rolls on, now in the thunderous cadence of the imperative command mode.

"*I leave this tent now, with my guards, to afford you dignity while you settle your differences. One of you will leave the tent with the urük magus bound to your will; the other will be dead. By surviving you will disprove the charge against you, be it of weakness or disloyalty.*" (*Fuck me,* Alex thinks dismally, *he's setting up a trial by combat?*) A pause. "*The urük magus* will *be rendered to me tractable and bound, or you will both die.*" (No, worse: *they're going to fight for control of me* . . .)

The clank and thud of All-Highest's retinue leaving the pavilion is joined by a more distant pounding outside, as of infantry marching in file. Alex concentrates, steeling himself for what he's terrified is coming. Then, without waiting for the inevitable, he triggers all his defensive macros at once.

Time slows: the air warms and thickens, syrupy, light shifts towards the red end of the spectrum and dims. The chittering of V-symbionts in the back of his head rises towards a deafening roar. Alex's stomach contracts painfully and his jaws clench, but he forces himself to stand with bowed head inside the circle of salt for a thousand subjective years.

Footsteps move, a sideways crab-shuffle within the tent. It's Highest Liege and Cassie—*no, Agent First,* Alex forces himself to remember—circling warily around him. *"You should be dead,"* Highest Liege says contemptuously. *"Weakling."* The word, in the People's dialect of Enochian, carries connotations of corruption and perversion, of wrongness and waste. *"Like your sister."*

Cassie moves sideways again, sliding towards Alex's left. *"Assassin,"* she says coolly. *"Liege-killer."* The word for *Liege* that she uses is gendered female, so she can't be referring to the All-Highest, but the compound noun *Liege-killer* is even stronger and more offensive than *weakling.*

Highest Liege hisses. *"Your mother was a weakling, too."* A jingle and creak of armor as she moves right, circling in front of Alex. Her hands move in small, tightly constrained gestures as Cassie steps behind Alex. *"The Host has no food for useless mouths in desperate times. You'll join her."*

She gestures with her left hand and the awning of the tent blows open, a morning breeze sighing in to shift the grains of salt across the rug, forming dizzying patterns before Alex's eyes that disappear as fast as his counter gets to them. Alex begins to mumble, keywords that trigger more macros in Old Enochian that he's spent the past hours of immobility memorizing. The hunger redoubles: his eaters are becoming impatient. *"Remember our conversation?"* Highest Liege tells Alex conversationally, smiling brightly as her right hand flashes out to make a gesture in the air, a deflection ward against Agent First's anticipated shot from behind cover. *"Now is the time. She's yours!"*

"Yes she is," says Alex, as he turns and jumps.

Pete's coccyx takes a pounding as he guns Ilsa up the long and winding road towards the North Yorkshire moors.

The drive takes the best part of two hours, even though there's virtually no traffic. Even the feral milk tankers that patrol the B roads to make collections at all hours are conspicuous by their absence. He's able to open up the engine and let it rip, within reason: Brains's refit with a modern four-banger seems to be stable, but he's terrified that if he goes over fifty kilometers per hour he could throw a track, and then they'll be completely stuffed. Once they pass Keighley he switches to the narrow and winding secondary roads, steering a wide course around Skipton on Lockhart's advice. It's a *really* weird way to be spending a Sunday morning: normally Pete would be in the vestry, drinking coffee and reminding himself of the running order of the day and the main talking points for his sermon. Not yet robed up to welcome the church-going public, but that's definitely on the Sunday morning agenda. Whereas this particular Sunday he's roaring along a country road between fields surrounded by dry stone walls, weighted down by layers of suffocatingly hot armor that's older than any of the churches in the parish he's nominally responsible for, while a mad scientist with a machine gun rides pillion.

Overhead he hears a distant droning. It's a prop-driven aircraft, breaking the stillness: it must be military, he realizes. Lockhart has passed on the news about something on the moors south of Ribblesdale murdering airliners; the invaders have even shot down a fighter jet. Indeed, that's part of Lockhart's updated instructions. "Your goal is to get Alex and this girlfriend of his out of there alive, but if you see a chance to fuck up the antiaircraft weapons, that'd be very helpful in nailing down this mess. You've got a minigun and a couple of thousand banishment rounds: see to it."

Easier said than done, he thinks grimly. Not for the first time Pete worries that he's made a horrible mistake, a life-altering and potentially fatal one. And he did it without even thinking to phone Sandy and talk it over first. When—if—he gets back from this, she's going to have every justification for hauling him over the coals in her usual quiet, thoughtful way. The trouble is, it's too late to back out now. *You volunteered to be a hero, don't be surprised when they send you to fight dragons.*

Nothing moves on the A65 when they hit it from the south and turn west. It's an eerie ghost road today. This sets Pete's hackles on edge. He drives across the bridge over the River Aire, which is far busier up close to its headwaters than the placid flow that passes through Leeds, and half a kilometer later they rattle through Coniston Cold and the GPS sends him veering off to the right on a narrow country lane winding up into the hills. Ilsa rattles and grumbles as the trail rises and he turns onto the lane running atop Kirkby Brow. Then they're descending again towards the valley, and Pete is so totally focussed on driving that when Pinky claps him on the shoulder to get his attention he nearly drives into the ditch to his left. He wrestles with the front forks and brakes, and Ilsa reluctantly grinds to a halt in the middle of the road.

"What?" he demands.

"Something's wrong." Pinky has to shout to make himself heard, but he holds up the display of his K-22 thaumometric analyzer. Pete flips his steel visor up to see better as Pinky scans the analyzer around in front of them. It goes wild when it points a fraction west of north, flux readings going off-scale; it drops off rapidly as he swings it clockwise, although there's still some signal even when it's due east. There's nothing to the west. "Ley line's to our east, west is dead, so what are we driving into?"

Pete squints up ahead, past the visitor's center and the car park, trying to see over the treeline. The Pennine Way footpath runs through the site, past a row of Portakabin toilets. It's early on a Sunday but there's nobody about, which is distinctly odd. "Let's take it easy. We've got to go off-road here anyway, the path's a dirt track from here on."

"Do that." Pinky hesitates. "If you see trouble, do an immediate U-turn and brake while I hose it down. If I hit you on the shoulder it means *drive*. Got it?"

Pete nods, gorget and helmet rattling. Another thought strikes him: "What about gates and stiles?"

"If you see a gate with nothing beyond it, park up and I'll open it and let you through. If you see a gate with hostiles beyond it, treat as trouble. If you see a gate and there are live hostiles *behind* us, remember you're driving a tank."

"Amen." Pete checks the fuel gauge (adequate, if it isn't lying through its teeth) and engine oil temperature (hot but not embarrassingly so), then guns the throttle. "Okay, here goes nothing."

The Pennine Way is one of Britain's best-known national trails, running for over four hundred kilometers along the Pennine hills, the backbone ridge of England. It follows field paths through the Yorkshire Dales National Park—in which Malham Cove and the famous limestone pavement are located—and due to erosion it's expressly closed to bicycles, never mind off-road motorbikes, sport utility vehicles, and half-tracks driven by vicars in armor. Luckily the near-total lack of traffic, not to mention hikers and ramblers, means there are no witnesses to Pete's desecration of a national treasure.

There seems to be some sort of camp or fairground—lots of tents, although it's hard to see clearly—nestling in the base of the cove, but the footpath diverts Pete away from the edge of the ridgeline. It's quite deeply eroded, so that at times Ilsa is surrounded by meter-high ramparts of packed dirt and grass. They bump along at a tooth-rattling twenty kilometers per hour as the ground rises below them. It's sweaty, hot work wrestling with a Kettenkrad in steel armor, but the eroded gully finally ends as the incline steepens, giving way to a flight of shallow steps carved into the hillside and held in place with wooden boards.

"Damn." Pete brakes to a halt and stares at them. It's a personal affront. How on earth do you take a half-track up a staircase? But then he realizes: the steps are shallow. A motorbike or a four wheel drive truck would have a hard time, but Ilsa is low and long and has tracks. Taking the rise at an angle would be asking for trouble, but this is nowhere near a thirty-degree slope. He half-turns and sees Pinky looking up at him. He raises his visor. "I'm going to drive up the slope," he calls. "It's convex near the top, so I'll turn round and reverse the last bit. Staying, uh, hull down."

"Are you sure you can make a safe turn up there without rolling over?" Pinky sounds dubious.

"Yes, I think so." Pete hopes he sounds more confident than he feels.

"Okay, then do it. Just keep your lid down and don't expose us to the skyline." Pinky holds up the thaumometric analyzer. "Whatever's beyond the crest is putting out a flux footprint the size of a necromantic summoning."

Pete slides Ilsa into first gear, low ratio, and crabs sideways across the grass, sliding slightly until the track cleats grip and begin to bite into the hillside. He twists the throttle grip carefully and eases up on the clutch until the front forks begin to rise alarmingly. The engine bellows beneath his seat as Ilsa begins to climb the slope. To his right there's a steep drop-off, angling towards the cliff edge; to his left, the steps. Ahead, the brow of the slope is a sudden horizon masking a view of empty sky. Once he's moving he doesn't dare stop or change direction. If the half-track begins to slide—or worse, rolls—he and Pinky will have to jump or be crushed.

The minute it takes to climb the rise feels like forever, and Pete has a subjective eternity in which to worry. He spends it angsting about what they'll find at the top, about what might be radiating that dangerous thaum flux, about whether it can hear them coming. But eventually the ground begins to level out. The steps are of uniform height, but now they're set further and further apart. When at last the ridgeline begins to creep close, Pete slows to a crawl and then, very carefully, locks the right track and slews Ilsa round until he's facing out across the cliff overlooking the hanging glacial valley. Finally, with the half-track leaning alarmingly to the right, he brakes the left track to a halt, selects reverse gear, and begins the opposite turn to bring Pinky's jumpseat round to face the crest of the rise.

"Stop." Pinky's hand on his shoulder. "Wait here, I'm going to take a look."

"What, on foot?" Pete is appalled. "But I thought you said we mustn't show ourselves—"

"Nope, not going to do that. Brought a selfie stick for my phone."

Ilsa bounces slightly as Pinky steps down, and Pete feels cold in spite of the sweaty padding and layers of steel. He changes gear just in case, although it seems unlikely they'd still be sitting here undisturbed if anyone had heard them coming. With Ilsa idling, he hears the droning from above again, like the world's largest mosquito circling lazily as it looks for blood.

Seconds pass, then Pinky materializes beside Ilsa's left track—now parallel to the steps—surprisingly quietly. He taps Pete. "There's something fucking bizarre over the ridgeline, all right." Pinky fumbles with a rectangular leather box, about fifteen centimeters square and four centimeters deep, sealed with a tarnished padlock. "I'm going to need you to be very, very calm and very clear about what we're going to do," he says, in the sort of voice normally used by doctors explaining to their patients that they've got cancer.

Yup, he thinks we're going to die now, Pete tells himself, trying the idea on for size: it's a bad fit, but they don't have time for dramatics, so he dismisses it. "What's over there?"

"About two to three hundred meters in front of you, on the other side of the ridgeline, there are a bunch of bad guys dug in—they've got slit trenches—around something I couldn't see properly. I burned out my phone camera trying to lock onto it," he adds conversationally. He unlatches the box and opens it, to reveal a mummified human hand, crudely amputated at the wrist: Pete cringes as he recognizes it. "I suspect it's some kind of basilisk gun. Or maybe a real basilisk. Two of them. They're big, about the size of trucks. I don't know if they're armored, but they're what Lockhart wants us to nail, for sure."

"Oh." Pete thinks for a moment. *Don't ask about the hand.* "How come they haven't heard us?"

"Maybe they have, but we're out of sight. Thing is, our usual toys won't work on this. For sure they'll have heavy defensive wards. *Luckily* we had the foresight to bring a giant can full of whoop-ass and they're criminally sloppy about posting sentries, maybe because they're on a high spot and anyone who gets a direct line of sight on them is dead meat. But if Lockhart's not yanking my chain, Alex is in the tents in the valley, right under their nose, and if they see us as we're riding back down there we're dead. So we've got to kill them first before we rescue the princess. Here's how we're going to do it . . ."

Sixth of Second Battalion rides close behind the front rank of skirmishers as her squadron pounds through the stony canyons of the *urük* hive, spreading death and chaos in all directions.

The sun is above the horizon by the time they clear the improvised obstacles from the peripheral highway and, passing a methodically arranged row of night soil ponds surrounded by woods, find themselves advancing along continuous built-up roads lined with the dense, ugly red-clay hovels of the enemy. Abandoned carts are strewn alongside every side street, providing far too much ground clutter for comfort. The main boulevard narrows rapidly, forming a chokepoint barely wide enough for four to ride abreast. Meanwhile the buildings rise to two, three, even four floors.

They encounter the first site of serious resistance three kilometers before they reach the enemy palace at the heart of the hive. A slab of poured-stone store houses on one side of the approach road buzzes with an ominous energy. It's competently warded, with an aggressive defensive posture that promises grief to any who try to breach it. The first two skirmishers to gallop towards it come under fire from bullet-throwers on the flat roofline. Sixth swears and calls them back, but one of their mounts is limping, roaring and snarling its fury at the steel-jacketed bullet embedded in its left haunch. (A mere horse would be screaming and convulsing, or dead, but the Host's mounts are made of sterner stuff, and it is already regenerating skin and muscle around the wound, forcing the fragment to the surface.) *"Enemy defenses ahead,"* Sixth calls to her field pyromancer: *"Reduce them."*

"As you command." The magus's enclosed palanquin moves forward, then the golems that carry it go to their knees, joints locking into position, as the sorcerer raises her periscope. *"Range eight hundred and fifty paces, bearing minus forty—that is the target? The warded building?"*

"Confirmed," snaps Sixth.

"Cover," the pyro calls laconically. It's a formality at this range. For a couple of beats nothing happens, then the air between the cavalry lance and the building begins to shimmer. Abandoned carts sink on their melting wheel-rims, then burst like so many fiery roses as their fuel tanks rupture. Pale, almost colorless flames erupt from the eaves of buildings opposite, and a decorative row of trees planted on the opposite side of the road go up like torches. The fortified building holds for a handful more beats, and Sixth of Second steels herself for counter-battery fire—but then the defensive ward around the Arndale Centre office quenches.

The blast wave is visible over ground as it hurtles towards the troops, hurling wrecked carts aside, shattering windows and scattering roofing tiles like flocks of startled starlings. Sixth braces herself in her cavalry saddle and her mount sways briefly as the hot wind pulses past her. The sound is beyond deafening, like having one's helmed head slammed in a closing door. When it passes, the target isn't there anymore: it has been replaced by a mound of burning rubble surrounded by the wreckage of *urük* hovels. The heat, even half a league away, is uncomfortable; close to the target, the road surface has melted into a shiny black puddle.

Sixth glances sideways at Adjutant of Second. *"We need a detour, I'm not waiting for that to cool down before we advance,"* she says. *"See to it."* Adjutant of Second salutes: ten minutes later the cavalry column re-forms and is moving again, bypassing the burning rubble of the Arndale Shopping Centre and smashing a path through suburban Headingley in the direction of Woodhouse Moor—the shortest route into the city center.

Meanwhile, three kilometers away in the aforementioned city center, college students Ami Goldsmith and Jan Baker are applying the finishing touches to their makeup before they head for the Animation Festival. They're sharing a cramped Travelodge room with a couple of friends who are crashing in sleeping bags. They've come up from Sheffield for a weekend of videos, cosplay, and partying: they're young, mostly broke, and so intent on making the best of their time that nobody complained when Jan's phone alarm woke them all at seven.

This morning is a big event: the main screen is due to show the first two episodes of Book Three of *Legend of Korra: Change* starting at ten—at least, that's the excited rumor that's been going round—and nobody wants to miss it. Ami's cosplaying Kya, and Jan—well, Jan's *much Galadriel, very pre-Raphaelite, wow*, as her ironically detached hipster friend Gilbert would say. Which is maybe why he's back in Sheffield polishing his unicycle this weekend.

"You ready yet?" Piglet demands intensely. She's bouncing up and down on her toes like an impatient ferret, all black-eyed manic intensity. "We'll be late!"

"No we won't," Jan assures her, smiling stiffly as she shakes out the dagged sleeves of her dress. "Ami? Got your tickets?"

"It's Kya!" she insists, reaching unconsciously for the leather belt-purse she found in a charity shop the week before last. "Yes."

"Well come on then!" Piglet is vibrating with energy. Eight thirty and she hasn't had any coffee—or breakfast, breakfast is extra and they've agreed to hit a Greggs or McDonald's after the showing for an early lunch, penny wise—and hunger makes her tetchy.

"Oh all right . . ."

They get as far as the lobby of the hotel before they realize something is wrong. The breakfast bar in the restaurant is closed, but it's full of people—out-of-town festival-goers and a couple of very hung-over stag-night parties, all talking at the tops of their lungs. The receptionist is out from behind the counter and flapping around before the front doors, which are shut. Outside the streets are deserted, but for a flicker of red and blue emergency lights.

"What's going on?" shouts Ami.

"I don't know!" Piglet heads directly for the lobby doors and is intercepted by Miss Front Desk, who is looking increasingly rumpled and desperate in spite of her company uniform. "What's going on?" she demands.

"You can't go out! The police say there's some sort of emergency outside and the whole city center is cordoned off. I'm on my own here! Day shift hasn't been able to get in, that's why the kitchen's closed." The woman is about their age and has been hung out to dry on her own, to keep a lid on roughly two hundred guests as they wake up on a Sunday morning and discover that breakfast, beer, and *Legend of Korra* are no longer options.

Ami comes up behind Piglet, who is looking nonplussed and increasingly irritated. "You can't go out," repeats Miss Front Desk, "it's not safe—"

Behind her back one of the stag-night parties makes a bid for freedom. Four lads in hoodies and jogging bottoms emblazoned with BATLEY NIGHT OUT duck around her back and shove the powered sliding doors open. Two of them stroll out into the drop-off area up front: "Hey, tha's talking bullshit!" one shouts back at Miss Front Desk, as she stands in the doorway calling them back.

"Stand aside, miss," says another lad—improbably polite, Ami realizes—then he pushes her aside and shoves through the door himself. "Wait up!" he calls to his mates as they head towards Briggate and the city center beyond.

"Come on," Jan murmurs to Ami, "they're right, this is bullshit. You can't lock everyone in a hotel with no food, ey? And Piglet's right, we don't want to miss—" They drift along in the flow of bodies emptying through the open front doors—

There is no traffic.

Ami twitches and grabs Jan's arm. "Something's *wrong*."

"What?" Jan seems bemused: or maybe she's just getting in character. She walks left, along the curving street that leads towards the dock and the conference center where the festival is being held.

"Where are the frigging *buses*?" Ami hisses.

"Buses?" Jan takes a step back. Piglet stops dead in the middle of the pavement.

"Ami, are you all right?" Piglet asks. Then she follows Ami's gaze in the direction of the bus station. "Uh." She starts to frown. There's a vibration in the ground like distant underground trains. Overhead, the sky is completely clear, a vacant blue bowl unblemished by the surgical tracery of jet contrails. She sees flashing blue lights in the distance, stationary, abandoned, nobody else in sight. No police, no firemen. No buses.

"They must be filming a movie or something," Piglet rationalizes. "They do that early in the morning on weekends, don't they? When nobody's about. They stop the traffic—"

Smoke rises in the distance. Somewhere out towards the edge of town a building is burning, but the breeze is carrying the smell and smoke away from them. The drumming underfoot isn't going away, it's getting more intense, as if they're trespassing on the tracks and an express train is hurtling towards them.

"I don't like this," Ami's voice catches in her throat. "Something is *wrong* and I am going back to bed until it's over." She starts to turn towards the hotel doors, now almost sixty meters behind them, and pauses.

A torrent of magic has crested the top of Vicar Lane and is flooding downhill on a thunder of hooves.

Nightmarish knots of light writhe and glow around the column of mounted knights in silvery armor, who sit astride giant chargers with mad-eyed blue stares and vicious spiral horns. They ride five abreast down the four-lane-wide high street, holding maces with green-glowing heads that spit sparks of lethal lightning.

Ami freezes. An idiot lyric from her granddad's CD collection repeats in her head: *Guided by the beauty of our weapons, guided by this birthmark on our skin—*

Around her people are screaming and falling, some of them writhing in tetanic spasms, others doubled-over and projectile vomiting. Ami is one of the few unaffected, blessed by an accident of heredity with some natural resistance to the Host's glamour. All she can see is the terrible beauty of the onrushing nemeses, and the instinctive apprehension that it would be a *really bad idea* to be standing here when they arrive, to be standing anywhere in sight while all around her are dying—

She grabs for Jan's hand. "Run!" she shouts. Jan is rooted to the spot, shuddering and gaping as if she's touched a live wire. Ami tugs and tugs: finally Jan stumbles and nearly falls, then begins to limp alongside her, dull-eyed and panting.

Ami looks over her shoulder, then forward at the hotel doorway, which is clear. Forty meters to go. The nearest riders are between a hundred and two hundred meters away, slowing and diffusing into the side streets as they face off towards the hill with the big government building and the Playhouse on it. At the top of the hill, smoke begins to pour from the roof of the Odeon, and to either side of the riders the shops lining the street erupt in pale flames. She can feel the heat on her face as she turns back towards the hotel. "Let *go*," Jan whines, tugging her hand free, "I'm going to be sick—"

Ami feels her friend's fingers slide through her grip. She hesitates for a moment, then cold terror grips her and she breaks into a run. The

CCTV camera under the awning over the hotel door is rotating towards the high street. She reaches the doorway and darts inside, then turns to shout encouragement to Jan: "It's only ten meters and there's a toilet in the lobby, silly—"

Galadriel flashes quicksilver-bright and explodes before her eyes: an echoing flicker like flashbulbs going off saturates the lobby with the terrible light of a hundred human candles, until a patchwork of retinal purple blocks her vision completely. All across the death ground around the foot of Quarry Hill bodies are bursting into flame: from the spearhead squadron led by Sixth of Second Battalion to hungover stag-night tourists and pointy-eared anime fans. SCORPION STARE's targeting neural network has given up discriminating friend from foe, and decided to kill them all and leave it to whatever gods machines have faith in to sort them out.

The world flashes black around Alex as he leaps at Cassie. Her expression is frozen in shock, gradually twisting into indignation—the obvious misinterpretation of his move—as he ploughs into her shoulder-first. He manages to curl an arm around her head as they fall and, falling, he mumbles his final trigger word. A ring on Cassie's left hand flares crimson with a laser-speckle of coherent light, building up a spike of energy. His blindsight tells him that behind them Highest Liege is raising a mace which is carrying a monstrous charge, an aviation canon to Cassie's handgun. The *alfär* are stupidly wasteful, throwing raw thaum currents at each other as if they don't understand the elegant mathematical underpinnings of magic: *How inelegant,* his inner detached observer thinks scornfully as the new macro he triggered begins to count up from zero.

"Get *off*—" Cassie begins to struggle. She's strong, but Alex is a PHANG and he's on top and he's not afraid to push back, locking his knee and elbow joints and using his weight to hold her down.

"Keep down," Alex hisses in English.

Behind them, First Liege chuckles. The skin in the small of his back tries to crawl right off his spine because he's heard that kind of laughter before, from Basil a moment before the lights came up, and all bets are off if First Liege wants Cassie dead more than she wants to add another PHANG to her string—

But the macro has now reached double digits and the voices in his head are beginning to react to a cacophony of incoming feeders and he knows it's working.

Cassie goes limp beneath him and he shoves his face against her neck and tries not to imagine what it would be like to bite his way through her sweet-smelling skin to the febrile, panic-juddery arterial pulse of blood. (Never mind what she says about high-caste People being immunized against V syndrome, he can imagine how it would feel, his lover's blood entering his soul, filling the hole in his heart: and he shudders with need.)

"*Get off her, Magus.*" First Liege uses the imperative-command case and Alex's limbs jerk spasmodically despite his best efforts to control them—

But the feeders are arriving, one by one, responding to the summoning wrapped in the counter macro that he just triggered. Calling a single eater is a trivial exercise, so minor that any CS undergraduate can master it in a couple of hours. (Surviving the summoning is a trickier matter.) Summoning up 65,535 of the fuckers is also trivial, if somewhat inadvisable: you just wrap your summon-an-eater macro in a loop counter, much like the loop you wrote earlier as a wrapper around the crowbar that unlatches your V-symbiotes' attention from a pile of spilled sugar granules, one by one. *It's called automation, suckers.* Surviving the attention of (2^{16}-1) eaters without first making sure you're safely inside a well-prepared summoning grid is *not* an intern-ready task, and protecting your girlfriend at the same time raises it to do-not-try-this-at-home levels of inadvisability, or maybe a thesis defense: but Alex is not sanguine about either of their chances of surviving a psychotic dragon queen's attentions. So he shoves his tongue against Cassie's neck, seeking the closest contact he can get short of blood-to-blood, and prays that three different leave-me-alone macros *and* the presence of a bunch of hungry territorial V-parasites will keep the eaters away from her and that he's got enough self-control not to lose his shit completely, because she's the most delicious thing he's ever smelled in his life, and, and, *focus*: friend *not* food, *focus*!

There's a fierce scream, cut off abruptly, and a flare of power behind him that feels like a giant oven door opening. The side of the tent in front of him disappears in blinding daylight. A deafening cicada chorus of mindless voices yelling *hunger* reverberates through his skull. Cassie tenses up, quivering with terror or fury or both. The edge of daylight burns closer and closer as the buzzing swarm of hunger descends. A couple of hoarse gasps come from First Liege's body as she resists, her will-to-power straining to hold back the tide of the eaters. There are a couple of percussive bangs and something hot bounces off Alex's back: it's probably a protective charm or ward cooking off.

In the corner of his vision, an hourglass full of salt grains trickles up, not down, as the eater-summoning macro counts its way through a busy loop that might take as long as ten seconds—Old Enochian running on neural wetware is *not* the fastest procedural language ever invented, and it's semantics make AppleScript look like a thing of elegance and beauty—but then the hourglass inverts. Jagged shards of glass scream in Alex's ears as the eaters are torn from their feast one by one and sent packing in reverse order of summoning.

"What's. Going. *On*," Cassie hisses angrily, but Alex doesn't dare break skin contact for long enough to tell her, not while there are more than 60,000 transient parasites passing through his focus, embodied in his mind's eye as desiccating white crystals. She bucks and heaves under him, pushing his head dangerously close to the line of daylight. "*What did you why hasn't she killed us wait what's this why do I feel so—*"

The eaters take longer to banish than to summon, but the last of them finally flicker out of his perception, buzzing and turgidly replete. Alex closes his eyes and forces himself to pull his tongue away from her throat. He's weak-kneed with hunger, or desire, or a questionable titer of both. The mindless keening of the V-parasites is deafening and his limbs feel like lead as he pushes himself off her. "Eaters," he gasps, rolling on his back and trying to sit up: "I had to keep skin contact to protect you."

What's left of First Liege lies in the shadows of the back half of the pavilion, black and withered as a slug that has died in a dish of salt: wisps of smoke rise from her curled limbs.

Cassie pushes herself to her feet, looking dazed and very angry. "If you ever do that to me again"—she bends over the body and deftly pulls the mace from a mummified claw—"I will—" She blinks, and bites back indignation. "WhatWhat?"

"I'm hungry." Alex takes a deep breath. Then another. "I need blood. Also cover. Then we need to run."

"Run?" In the sudden silence Cassie's eyes widen. "What did you do?"

"Your father took my phone." Alex looks her in the eye. She's lovely: *I could gobble her right up,* part of him thinks. "Do the People have GPS? Or drones?"

"No, but the air defense—" Cassie blinks and finds her feet abruptly fascinating. "Let's get you fed and clothed."

"Where is he?" Alex wraps his arms around his stomach, trying not to rock with the force of the hunger pangs.

"He'll be with the—" She stops and takes aim as two guards clatter around the back of the tent. *"Halt and obey the Heir of the All-Highest,"* she commands, in the same voice of authority that set Alex's hair on end when her father used it. The guards freeze. "Oh my," Cassie says in English for his benefit, her face slowly brightening into a luminous smile. "I could get used to this." She points at the guards. *"Step inside. Do not look at this magus—man. Remove your helmet."* The guards seem hesitant, stumbling as if drunk. *"I order you to disarm and kneel!"*

The words batter at Alex's ears like brass gongs, and he's not even the subject of their terrible imperative. The soldier Cassie pointed at slumps slightly, knees going out from under him. The other turns as if to run and Cassie begins to raise her mace, but before she points it at him he collapses like a puppet with its strings cut. Blood trickles from his nose and ears, but Alex can tell instantly that it's no good for him: V-parasites can't eat the dead.

He watches, woozy with hunger, as she pulls the kneeling soldier's helmet off and pushes his head down towards the ground sheet in front of his feet. "Eat, dammit," she snaps. Frustration rises in her voice: "Why are you standing there? What are you waiting for, why won't you feed?"

Alex watches himself as from a great distance while he shuffles over to the kneeling sacrifice and crouches close to the rushing, frightened pulse—

I can't do this, he thinks despairingly. The kneeling man is paralyzed like a mouse beneath a venomous snake. When you're dying your whole life is supposed to flash before your eyes, but Alex finds that in this situation he stands witness to someone else's life. Not a good life, perhaps, but not a life nearing its end in a hospice bed, riddled with cancer or dying of dementia: this is a healthy adult in his prime, with many years ahead, who kneels terrified before him with throat bared. *I'm not a murderer—*

"Alex," Cassie says, close to his ear, "if you won't do this, we're both going to die here. I can't carry you." There is a tiny quaver in her voice as she adds, "And I'm not leaving without you."

Shock rushes through him. Then disbelief. *She's bluffing. Isn't she?* Then embarrassment. *It's blackmail!* Then pragmatism: *He's an enemy soldier and if he wasn't under her* geas *he'd be trying to kill us both—*

"Just do it. Blame me. We can work it out later, YesYes? But I won't let you die here—"

Alex blanks. When he opens his eyes again, his mouth is full of warm wet love and he has a painfully sensitive erection: the V-parasites are crooning their satisfaction in his ears.

"Oh God," he says incoherently, and begins to weep over the body.

"Shut up," she says through gritted teeth. "Hold your arm out." She's sliding something over his right arm—a sleeve. "Left arm now." It's a padded leather jacket, tight in the shoulders. It laces together: she begins to tie him into it. "You keep invoking some God but I don't think he's listening right now," she adds in a quiet singsong under her breath.

"But I bit that man's throat out, like I'm fucking Dracula . . ."

"Shut up. Stand up. Put this on. That's right . . . if you were the kind of man who found it easy to do that kind of thing do you think

I'd bother with you?" Her question takes him by surprise, rattling his introspective daze.

"How long has it been since your father left?" he asks as she snaps the breastplate into place around him. (It has cunning quick-release fasteners, more like the clips on a bulletproof jacket than the buckles and straps on the museum pieces in the Armouries.)

"Three . . . no, four? Minutes. No more." Alex shuffles uneasily: his trousers feel warm and wet, and when he looks down there's a dark stain across his legs. Blood or urine, he can't tell. Cassie hands him a helmet. He pulls it on, feels an unfamiliar tight headband, and adjusts it so that it doesn't pinch his temples. "Quick!" she urges, then yanks the glass face-plate down, grabs his hand, and tugs him towards the open back of the tent.

"Wait, my eyes—" But then he's in daylight and his face *isn't* on fire and he can see clearly through the tinted visor. "What are we doing?"

"Act like you're a guard and I'll get us out of here as long as we can avoid my father. Where's your rescue party?"

"How should I—" Alex looks round. There's a murmurous rumble and clatter from beyond the tents clustered between the pavilion and the edge of the cove. He can't see the cause of the racket but from the snorting and snarling it sounds as if a cavalry troop is mounting up on Bengal tigers. He looks up, scanning the edge of the ridge above them, putting the picture together. Malham Tarn has been popular with school trips for decades, so much so that half the population of Yorkshire must have been here at one time or another, which means the walking path must be over there— "Wait, what's that?"

Something monstrous moves beyond the top of the cliff. Alex sees a neck like a tree trunk and the body of a giant elephant—no, it's a big-ass dinosaur, a sauropod, like a brontosaurus. He squints. There's something wrong with its head, an efflorescence of tentacles and iridescence—

He looks away in time. The warded visor saves him, but he's blinking rapidly and his eyes are stinging furiously as he draws breath to ask Cassie what they should do; which is why he hears, rather than sees, Pinky put his cunning plan into effect.

*   *   *

A droning roar like a storm god unzipping his chain of lightning reverberates from the clifftops.

Pete crouches down in Ilsa's legwell, his shoulders hunched, as hot brass cartridge cases bounce off the limestone slabs embedded in the reverse slope of the hillside. Strays from the rain of hot brass ping and clatter off his shoulders. He can't see what's going on—this is a good thing—and he's having difficulty even seeing the controls, which is perhaps less of a good thing. So he concentrates on keeping a tight grip on the mummified hand with the burning fingertips, tries *not* to think about where it came from or how its unfortunate owner met his end, or even why the Laundry's armorer came to have it in the special stores room at the National Firearms Center. *Obviously* the government would have maintained a stockpile of Hands of Glory, the amputated appendages of hanged felons, even though they ended capital punishment in 1965. It's all he can do to refrain from prayer. God probably doesn't want to know what he's doing here this morning, a borderline accomplice to evil in service to a greater cause. If you should find yourself on a slippery slope some questions are best left unasked, lest you find yourself already fallen from grace.

Pinky stands on the bench seat behind Pete, methodically directing a roaring torrent of gunfire over the rise. He beats the ground around the trenches with a heavy steel-jacketed rain, working the minigun by dead reckoning, for he can barely see the ends of the spinning barrels—the Hand of Glory is doing its job, and Ilsa has become a numinous vision of cobwebs on the breeze, functionally invisible. So are the things in the enemy dugouts, of course, and in this battle if you can be seen you will die: but iron and steel have a way of slicing through enchantments, especially when they're augmented with a banishment circuit embedded in the base of each and every round.

A jaw-rattlingly loud detonation sends an oily fireball rising over the crest of the hill. Pinky releases the firing switch. In the sudden ear-ringing silence, the echoes of the burst bounce back and forth between the hills. A monster bellows a plaintive soloist's refrain against a chorus of higher-pitched human screams.

Pinky thumps Pete on the shoulder. "Back up ten meters!" he shouts in Pete's ear.

"What? But that'll put us on the ridge!"

"Yes! I need to see what's back there. Let me finish this."

Pinky slides back down behind the gun. *This is a really bad idea,* Pete tells himself as he twists the throttle grip. Ilsa lurches and begins to slowly reverse up the ever-gentler hillside. Pete orients himself by looking sideways at the steps, guessing how far he's come, and he's still crawling backwards when Pinky hits the firing switch again, the rotary gun barrels spin up, and the jackhammer roar resumes bashing on his helmet earpieces.

The world lights up pink as the grass in a circle around Ilsa ignites, smoking and sparking and fizzing. Pete's skin prickles and he bursts into a cold sweat. *Basilisk!* He's wearing wrought iron armor and holding a Hand of Glory, but the vegetation around here is quite capable of burning and the secondary radiation is also potentially deadly. If it wasn't for the machine gun two meters behind his ears he could hear the grass flames hissing. He feels itchy and sick, squinting against the deadly light. *Don't look round.* He screws his eyes shut. The basilisk is there—

A huge explosion shakes the ground from the vicinity of the enemy and the pink glare vanishes. Pete blinks furiously, trying to clear the green and purple blotches from his vision. *I was looking away with my eyes shut,* he realizes. *How bright was that?* Pinky lets go of the trigger and the echoes subside. "Pinky?" He calls. "Pinky?"

"Dude." Pinky's voice is shaky and muffled by the ringing in Pete's ears. "I got them both."

"Both what?"

"Fucking big-ass sauropod dinosaurs with compound eyes and tentacles around their mouths. And minders in armor. Shot one, then the other reared up and began flailing around and looked at it and then it like, exploded." He pauses. "You'll have to get us out of here."

"Wait, what do you mean?"

"I mean I can't see anything. I'm only flash-blind. I hope." Pinky is matter-of-fact about his sudden loss of sight.

"Hell." Pete thinks for a moment. "What should I do?"

"We're still alive so they're all dead back there. Clearly, or we'd be dead, too, sitting around with our thumbs up our ass like this." Another pause. "Look for Alex and his chica down below. Pick them up and drive us out of here."

"Okay." Pete raises his visor. He feels shivery and his skin is prickling. The hilltop around them is scorched black and gray with ash, smoking and smelling of fireworks and ozone. He looks down at the hard-to-see tents in the floor of the valley. "How long have we got?"

Pinky doesn't answer immediately, but the silence is filled by the ringing in his ears and a new uncomfortably familiar sound, like a lawnmower buzzing in the distance. "Just move," says Pinky.

As the torrent of mounted cavalry floods down Vicar Lane, the flicker of hundreds of bodies exploding is joined by a crackling roar that drowns out the faint screams of the survivors.

In the control room inside Quarry House, Brains and Jez Wilson watch horrified for endless seconds as targeting stills flash up on the screens around them. "This is *wrong*!" Brains shouts, appalled. The mounted whirlpools of light seem almost immune to the carnage around them, but there are people on the pavement, people around the bus station, flickering statues that crack open with a violet flash and a sullen red glare as of molten lava. "Why isn't it locking on properly?"

"I don't care. Hit the kill switch." Jez's eyes are wide. "Shut it the fuck down on my authority, *right now*."

"But we'll—" Brains is already typing a series of commands. "Fuck, they're coming at us—"

There's a final eye-searing flash outside a nearby hotel and the sequence of camera stills freezes. "*Fuck*." Brains mouses over one of the images. "There's a cosplay convention in town? Who ordered *that*?"

"Later." Jez pushes back her seat and keys her headset. She updates an unseen observer on the situation, biting back her words, then turns to him: "All right, we're useless down here so it's all hands on deck upstairs." There's an SA80 rifle on her desk. "Do you know how to use one of these?"

Brains slumps, then stands up. "I could pull the trigger. Doubt I'd last long enough to need to know how to reload it."

"Huh." Wilson slings the rifle over her shoulder: "Follow me anyway, I'm sure we'll find something for you to do."

Outside the soundproofed basement control room there's a racket going on; it sounds like dueling road drills holding an argument with an industrial metal band. Metallic shrieks and groans joust with the intermittent hammering of the machine guns on the roof. Jez dashes up the emergency staircase, taking the steps two at a time; Brains, five years older and twenty kilos heavier, is panting by the time they arrive on the third floor at the makeshift ops center Lockhart established the night before.

They meet the man himself coming out of the door. "I'm taking this to the roof," he says flatly. He's found a ballistic vest somewhere, and is wearing it under his suit jacket in place of a waistcoat. "Are you warded?"

"Class eight," Brains manages. "What's going—"

"Too many civilians. Let's see if we can draw their fire."

Brains glances back and forth. Lockhart, he realizes suddenly, doesn't expect to live through this. Neither does Jez Wilson. They're both ex-Army and he has a numb feeling that they know more about this kind of situation than he does. "Can you manually run the perimeter cameras?" He realizes Wilson is talking to him. "Not in autonomous mode, I mean, manually designate targets for the basilisk guns? *Inside* Quarry House?"

"I could . . ." He trails off, horrified. "What?"

"I want you down in the camera control room behind a locked door," Lockhart rasps. "They're here to storm the building or reduce it to rubble. The wards are holding and we've got guns on the roof, but they'll get inside our perimeter sooner rather than later. I'll call you when that happens and then if you see anything or anyone on the ground floor you should assume hostile."

"What, on my own—" Brains stares until Lockhart gives a sharp jerk with his chin.

"Go on," Jez says, not unkindly. "This isn't your kind of fight."

They wait until Brains has scampered back into the emergency stairwell before Lockhart says, "Let's hope he remembers to lock the door and keep quiet."

"You think he'll make it?" They head up the corridor past an open office door.

Lockhart steps inside briefly and hands her an Airwave radio and headset, then picks up a box of preloaded magazines. "Maybe."

She snorts. "It's going to take a miracle."

They climb the last two floors to the roof at a more measured pace—there's no point arriving breathless—and step out into chaos.

Every body that can fight, warm or otherwise, is already committed. Lockhart has been coordinating from the control room downstairs, but under the guns of the enemy and with the nearest reinforcements still an hour away he can do more good upstairs. Not that one more person is going to hold things together for much longer. If they had an active sorcerer of their own, someone from Mahogany Row, it might make a difference: but aside from Alex Schwartz (who is tied up elsewhere) there are no ritual practitioners on-site in Leeds this weekend.

The defensive wards around Quarry Hill are under such intense attack that their surfaces are visible to the naked eye, a shimmering indigo soap bubble the size of a city block that flickers with an un-healthy, oily sheen. It rings like a bell whenever one of the marauding enemy sorcerers hits it with an inordinate and wasteful invocation. The two machine guns on the rooftop cupola beneath the spire, and the other pair on the car park roof, rap out irregular conversational bursts, unimpeded by the occult barrier.

"Keep your head down," Lockhart advises. "They've got some kind of kinetic weapon as well as all the thaumic lances, and the wards won't keep a well-aimed arrow out. They might want to take the building intact if Dr. Schwartz is correct but that doesn't mean they won't go for an easy target." He sounds disapproving. "Subtlety is *not* their—"

There is a loud *crack* and a section of sandbags in front of one of the GPMGs disappears. So does the upper half of the gun's loader. Blood sprays everywhere, briefly. *"That,"* Lockhart snarls, "is *too much.*"

Another Night Watchman shuffles forward to take his place. Face expressionless but for the glowing green eyes of the possessed, the undead guard begins to assemble a belt of ammunition—

"No!" shouts Lockhart, "Get down! Move! Not there, *there*!" Wilson grabs his arm to stop him darting forward in his frustrated urgency to see the zombie move the gun to a less exposed location.

She can see at a glance that the situation is dangerously close to irretrievable. The enemy cavalry—eye-wateringly painful to look at, even with a defensive ward—are too close to the periphery of the defensive bubble around the foot of the hill. The guns can't depress far enough to shoot down at them without the crews exposing themselves to whatever just made a hole in the roofline, and while the Night Watchmen are heedless of physical hazard (being dead) there aren't enough of them. Meanwhile the mounted soldiers are clustering around covered palanquins from which the bubbles of defensive wards are expanding, and more of the riders will be circling around behind the complex—

"Do you have any grenades?" Jez asks the nearest defender.

"Only RPGs, and not enough of them." Doris Knight points a thumb in the direction of a stack of boxes under the big satellite uplink dish. "But there's an AA-12. Harry thought it would come in useful, bless his heart. Can you use that?"

"I'll give it the old school try." Jez makes a beeline for the stockpile and finds the big automatic shotgun and an unopened satchel of ammunition. A relatively short-range weapon, it wasn't much use until now. "Can you spot for me?"

"There's a reinforced sniper's hide over on the west wing roof, I thought it would come in handy. But we've only got forty rounds."

Together they crouch down behind a clutter of cell tower aerials and prepare their kit. It's just a matter of time before the enemy try to storm the entrance: maybe the explosive shells will slow them down.

"What we need right now is a miracle," Jez mutters during a gap in the gunfire. She raises her weapon and carefully aims through the firing slot.

*   *   *

Cassie is right about one thing: getting out of the camp is easy enough, as long as they stay close to the tents and supply stockpiles and keep out of sight of the soldiers massing at the foot of the cliff itself. The tents are mostly empty, and the few serfs left behind to handle teardown and transport are dull-eyed and deferential. Cassie doesn't need to order them to pay no attention: to Alex's blood-stunned eyes she glows with Highest Liege's borrowed power, and they fall to their knees and prostrate themselves before her as automatically as if she's a living god.

Which is a good thing, because Alex isn't sure he can play the role of bodyguard effectively if push comes to shove. The armor chafes and fits poorly (it's a miracle it fits at all, because he's short and stocky compared to the *alfär* warriors), he has no more idea how to use the mace that goes with it than the terrifyingly technical-looking battle rifles on display in the Royal Armouries, and he's stuck somewhere between a post-binge bloat-out torpor and total exhaustion from overexertion. Given an hour to recover he'll feel better, and given a couple of hours of instruction and a couple of weeks of practice he might be able to make the mace glow blue and spit fireballs and lightning, but right now he feels like dead weight. Self-loathing dead weight at that. He's done his job, delivered the smartphone to its target: Cassie clearly doesn't *need* him at this point, not in any practical sense—

"Where are the sentries?" Cassie asks uncertainly as they pass the furthest tent and strike out across the gently sloping basin of the valley, into the trees paralleling the stone walls alongside the stream. "This is *wrong*. There *must* be sentries." There's a pile of oddly assorted statuary to one side, and a trampled trail that looks as if a small herd of elephants has stampeded down the valley floor towards Gordale Scar, but there's no sign of dugouts or a defensible line: just traditional dry stone walls, defending against cows. Nor are the expected sentries visible. "Father must have stripped almost every living body from—" She does a double-take. "But this means he must think he can take the enemy palace from within with only a squadron!

What is he *doing*? Did he think he could use you to—" Her eyes widen further. "He was going to steal your face and memories," she says faintly. "Take the fortress by stealth and lower the wards when his forces arrive. Of course. Which means—"

Some half-glimpsed movement and the distant mutter of a tractor engine prompts Alex to turn and look up at the heights leading to the crest. "Look," he says, turning and pointing.

Cassie's eyes go wide. "FuckFuck!" She grabs his arm and yanks him towards the pile of human-shaped ashy stones. "Get down! Hide!"

Alex stumbles and falls, bashing a knee painfully on a withered stone arm with fingers clenched around the shattered concrete semblance of a Garmin GPS. Things become chaotic for a time. He has impressions of a surreally bright pink-tinted light, speckled and shimmering, that drenches the ground on all sides. A buzzing roar of automatic gunfire starts up: it's very fast and weirdly familiar, and after a while he seems to hear the frequency of alternating mains current in it. It goes on forever, although forever can only be a few seconds, echoing and shimmering from the heights above them. Something bellows in agony, there's a brilliant flash of lightning, and a thunderclap explodes from the cliff above the cove; the pinkish radiance cuts off abruptly. More gunfire follows, then another blinding explosion, like a power substation going up.

"Whatever that was, it's distracted them." Alex kneels, then stands, bracing one arm against a thing of horror that was once a scout troop leader. He leans around the ossuary stack and glances at the ridge line above.

The force assembling at the base of the cliff for All-Highest's strike through the shadow road to the center of Leeds is breaking up: infantry head for the slopes up to the crest of the ridge, while mounted knights keep close to a core group who take shelter directly before the cave mouth at the base of the cliff. Meanwhile something is driving down the side of the hill, roughly paralleling the footpath. It takes Alex a moment to recognize what he's seeing: it's Ilsa, but there's a pile of stuff on the back bench seat and the driver appears to be wearing a suit of armor.

"Come on," he pants, tugging at Cassie's arm. "Our ride's here!"

"But we'll—" She stands, looks round at the cliff, then back at the hills. "Run!"

Alex doesn't stop to ask why. Cassie darts across the floor of the valley, keeping low and zigzagging between trees. He follows her, sticking close behind. There's a wall and a row of tents and stacks of emptied crates between them and the cavalry, but they're sure to be seen within seconds. He mumbles the trigger for his last field-expedient ward as he runs, hoping nobody tries to hit him with a death spell. *Now* he fuzzily remembers why Cassie is with him— All-Highest needs him alive in order to break through the perimeter defenses around Quarry House. Manic laughter bubbles up: he shielded her from the eaters he summoned with his body, now he's her human shield.

There are shouts a long way behind him. The tiny half-track churns up a spray of grass and dry mud as it slews downhill in a barely controlled rush. Whoever's driving is doing a good job of steering into the skid, but if he loses it they're going to roll over on the slope. The mound on the back resolves itself into another figure in armor wearing what looks like a chain mail rug. It's clinging for dear life to a multibarreled gun mounted on a post sticking up from the tow hitch.

A hundred meters until their paths converge. How fast can you run a hundred meters in armor? His suit only weighs about twenty kilos, but Alex is out of shape and it isn't properly fitted to him. He feels a rumbling as the ground shakes behind him. He's panting and Cassie is sagging, but his limbs feel weirdly light. The V-parasites are pulling their weight—*no, they're pulling* my *weight,* he thinks. There'll be a bloody price to pay later of course, and there's a distant buzzing sound in his ears, like a lawnmower the size of a freight train. Ilsa is nearly at the bottom now, and the driver brakes hard and slews around until the guy on the back is facing them—

"Pinky! Brains!" Alex shouts. "It's me!" He waves. Cassie waves. Then he's staring directly down the fascicular barrels of a most enormous-looking Gatling gun.

"Who's there?" shouts the gunner, his face completely obscured by the steel visor. He casts around, as if he can't see. The vibration in the ground is growing: Alex hears snarling and shouting from behind.

He does a double-take. "Is that you, Pinky?"

"Good guess." Pinky flips his visor up, then leans on the gun. Its barrel rises, pointing over Alex's head. His face is flushed and shiny with sweat, and there's something wrong with his eyes. After a moment Alex realizes they're bloodshot and his pupils are massively dilated. "You're going to have to work this thing."

Whoever's driving up front revs the engine and Ilsa growls. Cassie staggers, panting: Alex pulls her arm over his shoulder and staggers forward. "Move over," he tells Pinky. "This is Cassie." He clambers up on the middle of the bench seat and hauls Cassie up beside him. It's a tight squeeze and he ends up standing with one foot between each of Cassie's and Pinky's, hanging on to the back of the minigun and trying not to touch anything by accident.

"Are we all aboard?" the suit of armor up front says in Pete's mild tones: "Because I really think we ought to be moving . . ."

"GoGoGo!" screams Cassie. "Do something, Alex!" She wrestles a strip of ammunition over her lap like a seat belt, pulling more loops from the box behind them. As Pete shoves the half-track into gear and hits the gas Alex is thrown forward against the spade grips of the skyward-pointing gun, but he barely notices: he's too busy gaping at the sight of an armored cavalry squadron in full cry.

Eighty troopers in armor are galloping after them, lowering bright-tipped lances that converge to a point on his breastplate, which suddenly feels as flimsy as a sheet of kitchen foil. They ride armored steeds that at first glance resemble heavyset draft horses, but have blue-glowing eyes set narrow to either side of a fluted, spiraling horn, mouths that snarl to reveal the gaping fangs of a carnivore. A growing shriek of pure, animalistic rage rises from the mounts: the soldiers sit astride them in deathly silence. It's as if they're puppets dangling by strings of power from the furious will of All-Highest, emptied of volition and set atop the equoid mass like grotesque trophies as they give chase.

Ilsa lurches as Pete botches the shift up into second gear. Alex gasps and hugs the twin grips. There's some kind of box between

them with a green-glowing light and a red switch-cover, and a button
atop each handle. The nearest riders are leaping the dry stone walls;
as he watches, one ploughs right through the wall. It explodes in a
spray of stone chips. The unnatural mount keeps right on coming, as
oblivious as a tank. A vicious headache clamps the top of Alex's skull
in a circular vise, squeezing until it feels as if his head must explode.
Cassie screams in pain and flops backwards and Alex feels a sudden
spike of rage, his own anger adding to the conflagration as he squeezes
his thumbs on the firing buttons.

A juddering roar like the end of the world spews bright sparks
from the spinning barrels of the minigun. The ammo belt jumps and
lurches across Cassie's lap like an angry python. Ilsa rocks and bucks
beneath Alex's backside and he loses track of the barrel, letting go of
the firing switches as it veers skyward, still spewing a tinkling rain of
hot brass cartridge cases across Pinky. Pinky is shouting something
but Alex can't hear, because his ears are ringing as if he's just spent
three hours in the mosh pit of the very loudest industrial gig ever. *Better bring earplugs next time you come to a cavalry charge,* he observes. "What?" he shouts.

Pinky repeats himself, twice, with increasing vehemence. Alex
struggles to bring the gun barrels back down as he finally gets it: "Go
for the eyes, Boo!" The first riders are barely a hundred meters away
and closing the gap. Alex's head is rattling in his helmet like a pea in
a whistle. He compromises and points the gun in the general direction
of the riders' heads, then clamps down on the firing buttons again and
walks it left to right, then back again. The results are explosively,
bloodily messy. The horse-things keep going even when bullets punch
holes in their chest plates and tear great chunks out of their legs: it
takes a head shot to drop one. Cassie moans but hauls another intes-
tinal loop of ammunition out of the box on the back. Pinky is giggling, or screaming: it's hard to tell over the roaring jackhammer of
the gun.

We're not going to make it, Alex realizes numbly. *There are too
many of them.* The whirling barrel tips are glowing red and there's a
stench of hot metal and gun smoke. Horse-things are going down,
snapping and biting at their riders—he sees one snip an armored head

right off a body, as neatly as a guillotine—but there are more of them coming. Ilsa's too slow and the gun must be running low on ammunition and he has no idea how to reload it. *They want me alive, but the others are of no interest*—All-Highest has no use for Pete or Pinky, and as for what he'll do to Cassie if he catches her—

Alex desperately tries to recall his eater-summoning macro, but realizes the cavalry will all have protective wards. Then the belt of ammunition snaking across Cassie's lap lashes its tail at her—she cries out—and vanishes into the gun, leaving nothing behind. With the roar silenced, the world seems as calm as a snow-covered landscape.

"We're out of ammo! Can you do anything?" he shouts in Cassie's ear. She still has her mace gripped in both hands, but its tip is dull and her eyes have rolled up as if she's having a seizure. There's another lurch and Pete notches up another gear. Alex looks around desperately. They must be doing almost forty kilometers per hour, juddering and bouncing down the footpath. But the surviving knights are gaining ground. "Don't those things ever *stop coming*?" He doesn't realize he's given voice to the thought until he bites his tongue, painfully hard, and feels the weirdly acrid tang of vampire blood. "I can't hear myself think," he mumbles. He can't hear much at all. He can feel Ilsa's engine bellowing, feel the grinding of tracks on dry mud through his legs. The deafening clangor of nerve damage rings loud in his ears, and his own voice is curiously muffled. He can just about discern the sound of a lawnmower or light plane, rising to an angry hornet buzz: then the Reaper drone comes over the cliff.

Most drones are toys. But this is an MQ-9 Reaper, the real thing: a military aircraft the size of a small airliner, with cruciform wings, a pusher propeller, and ominous racks of Hellfire missiles under each wing. It's a dedicated ground attack aircraft, used in situations where the skies are too hostile for manned aircraft or helicopter gunships, and it's zeroing in on the emissions from Alex's phone—the phone All-Highest is carrying. The sky splits open and rockets lance overhead, converging on the rear of the column of pursuing cavalry. A smoky fireball rises, shattered fragments of armor and body parts flying as four antitank missiles tear into the clump of All-Highest's guard. The band of pain around Alex's forehead vanishes instantly, as

All-Highest's thaumic offensive ceases to batter against his ward. For a second it's silent, and then the thunderous noise of the explosions reaches them.

"What the fuck?" The cavalry are slowing their headlong charge, equoid steeds nipping at each other's flanks, riders shaking their heads as if dazed. Some are still following, but others turn and raise hands to point at the sky behind him. Alex leans back as the draconic shadow of the killer drone soars across the valley. "Was that—"

A hand grips his left shoulder as Cassie sits up. "Yes," she says hoarsely. He can still barely hear her.

"What?" he demands, looking around for something to throw at the closing riders, now barely twenty meters behind them.

"It's all right." Alex looks round sharply. Cassie's smile is luminous, her eyes glowing the precise same shade as the will-o'-the-wisp dancing in the head of her mace. "I can take things from here," she assures him as she raises her right hand in a stiff-armed salute to the charging cavalry troopers, and continues in the mode of imperative command: *"I rule you now! Yield to the new All-Highest!"*

Suddenly and without warning, the wards over Quarry House fade out.

"What." On the rooftop, Jez Wilson stares up at the sky. "The fuck!" She pulls out her phone and checks her OFCUT app. Blinks, exits the app, and restarts it.

"They've stopped zapping us." Doris Knight is peering at her own phone in disbelief.

"Huh. They had to run out of available energy sources sooner or later—"

"No," Doris says urgently, "they've also stopped throwing those darts around. What's going on?"

"I have *no* idea—" Jez pauses. Then she nips around the side of the barricade and looks over the edge before she drops and crawls rapidly backward. "You're right, though," she calls. Her ears are ringing, so she has to shout.

"What *now*?"

Jez looks round. Lockhart is standing in the middle of the roof, well back from the parapet, talking into his radio headset. He sees her and beckons. "I'm being summoned. Over here."

She finds Lockhart in the middle of a small knot of arriving warm bodies. His expression is vacant, as if all capacity for thought has fled. "Cease fire, cease fire," he calls, his voice flat. "Conserve ammo. Prepare to start up again on my word, but"—he takes a deep breath—"just hold everything."

He notices Jez standing there. "What happened?" she demands.

"Word from Forecasting Ops: if they stop shooting, we're to stop shooting, too." He takes another deep, panting gulp of acrid air that stinks of diesel fumes and smokeless powder. "They haven't been wrong so far, so . . ."

A sudden spike of hope as he meets her eyes: "Maybe Dr. Schwartz got us that miracle?"

"Witness."

Alex licks cracked, dry lips with a tongue that throbs in time to his pulse as he steps down from the Kettenkrad and walks towards Cassie.

She stands facing a half-circle of dismounted knights in armor, their occult weapons sheathed and their knees bent. Beyond them, other soldiers are silently safing their mounts with muzzles and hobbles. (Some are dealing with the injured chargers: it's a tense and bloody business, for damaged equoids don't simply scream piteously and wait to die like horses.)

"Witness: I am your liege," Cassie—All-Highest—repeats, striking a pose that bespeaks all the depths of self-confidence that Alex knows he lacks.

The blaze of light around her head almost dazzles Alex's V-parasites. He waits patiently, holding his hands behind his back to conceal their shaking. He's out in daylight when every instinct says he should take cover from the lethal burning radiance of the daystar. Furthermore, he's standing in front of a bunch of skin-crawling alien monsters in unicorn drag, surrounded by the amoral psychopathic warriors of a master race that conquered Europe from Galway to the Urals and built its palaces in the drained lowland basin of the Mediterranean back when his own ancestors were figuring out better ways to knap flint. He's about to do something very inadvisable, something that will attract the attention of very important people. Worst of all, Pete is pointing a smartphone on a selfie stick at him, not merely capturing Cassie's speech but streaming it live to a projection screen somewhere where those very important people will be watching him. The way today is going downhill he's going to end up on the TV news, and his mother will give him hell ever after because his trousers look as if he's wet himself.

"*We recognize the All-Highest we are sworn to obey,*" chorus the half-circle of officers (and a few thoroughly shrouded magi).

She half-turns and raises her left hand. She crooks an imperious finger towards Alex. "You may approach," Cassie says in English.

Alex shuffles warily forwards. He pauses just beyond arm's reach and looks at her. Making eye contact with the All-Highest is almost painful. There's Cassie in there, but there's also an ancient and puissant network of *geases*, a mass of compulsions and obligations that once encompassed tens of millions of minds: a web of command, the central node of the empire which now rests upon her brow.

"For the record, please identify yourself as we discussed, in English and in the High Tongue," she says in English, then repeats herself for her audience.

Alex licks his lips again. "I am Alex Schwartz, enrollment number 5078031, a sworn member of Q-Division, Special Operations Executive, an agency of the Ministry of Defense." The Laundry, by any other name. *Just please don't ask me what my grade is, because it's embarrassingly low.* Then he translates as best he can in Enochian, paraphrasing the words where necessary and laying claim to a new alias: "*Magus Seventh of Occult Defense.*"

"*Witness,*" All-Highest repeats to her grim-faced audience.

"*We witness.*"

She looks at him, and Alex forces himself to meet her eyes. Is it his imagination, or does she look nervous? "I unilaterally order the forces that have come under my command to cease military action immediately, and offer their surrender to you," she says evenly.

Alex swallows. "I accept your surrender."

The mask of All-Highest cracks, and Cassie peers at him again, frightened and apprehensive. "Is there anything else?" he reminds her, acutely aware that this is the biggest gamble of all.

"Yes," she says quietly, then, louder, to the watching eyes and camera: "*YesYes*. I hereby declare that I, and all my people, are refugees under the terms of the 1951 United Nations Convention Relating to the Status of Refugees. We cannot return to our home because we have a well-founded fear of being destroyed by the Dead Gods from beyond the ends of the universe that have returned to feed on this and other worlds. Accordingly"—she pauses, then looks past Alex, straight at the camera lens held in Pete's slightly shaky grip—"I claim asylum for all surviving members of my people in accordance with the terms of the Immigration, Asylum and Nationality Act of 2006. That is all."

Then she walks into his open arms and they stand there, together for a while.

ACKNOWLEDGMENTS

I want to thank first and foremost my usual crew of test readers for kicking the tires and spotting the obvious defects before they ran over my feet. And in particular I'd like to single out Nelson Cunnington for his sterling work on untangling the timeline of the last half of the novel, Squadron Leader Simon Bradshaw (retd) for his insights into the likely complications of dragon v. Typhoon engagements, Martin Sinclair for advice on Army maneuvers, and all the other ex-forces folks who pitched in on this one.

I'd like to apologize to the Leeds International Animation Festival for moving the date of their event by several months, citing dramatic license in my defense.

I'd also like to apologize to the folks working on the Barnton Quarry Restoration Project for appropriating the details of their ROTOR R4 bunker, folding, spindling, and mutilating it, and using it for the Leeds War Room Region 2 site. (Which wasn't part of the ROTOR air defense network, but dates to the same era . . .)

ABOUT THE AUTHOR

Charles Stross is a full-time science fiction writer and resident of Edinburgh, Scotland. The author of six Hugo-nominated novels and winner of the 2005 and 2010 Hugo Awards for best novella ("The Concrete Jungle" and "Palimpsest"), Stross's works have been translated into over twelve languages.

Like many writers, Stross has had a variety of careers, occupations and job-shaped catastrophes in the past, from pharmacist (he quit after the second police stake-out) to first code monkey on the team of a successful dot-com start-up (with brilliant timing he tried to change employer just as the bubble burst). Along the way he collected degrees in Pharmacy and Computer Science, making him the world's first officially qualified cyberpunk writer (just as cyberpunk died).

In 2013 he was Creative in Residence at the UK-wide Centre for Creativity, Regulation, Enterprise and Technology, researching the business models and regulation of industries such as music, film, TV, computer games and publishing.

Find out more about Charles Stross and other Orbit authors by registering for the free monthly newsletter at www.orbitbooks.net.